# OZ, WONDERLAND & OTHER PLACES

A Novel

**By Dale Patrick Smrekar**

Oz, Wonderland, and Other Places is a work of fiction. Names, characters, places, and incidents either are the product of the author's imagination or are used fictitiously. Any resemblance to actual persons, living or dead, events, or locales, is entirely coincidental.

Thanks to my consultant and editor, Keith Long, for his assistance in completing this book.

Nicer          World          Publications

ISBN -13:978-0999861707

ISBN – 10- 0999861700

For my

Artist Wife,

Nancy

# Alice

A few short days after entering the parallel universe of OZ and Wonderland, Alice {not that Alice} knelt before Wonderland's Queen of Hearts, extended her neck and offered the Queen her head. It made sense to her at the time for an ancient librarian had advised her to pursue this mission without regard to risks of death. Although foolhardy, it would likely achieve the objective of starting a war between OZ and Wonderland, even if it meant the loss of her head.

Who is this Alice you ask? She would seem at first glance to be classified as a human, one of us, but alas, she is not. Run an ancestry DNA test on her and the results would be confusing. She's not from around here. She may be humanoid true enough, but her ancestry's roots are not from our dimension. Alice is tall, five-feet eight inches, with dishwater blond hair. She is slim, athletic and pretty, but not remarkably so. Her speech carries the hint of an accent from undetermined origin. Age? Who knows. Age is not recorded where she comes from. "Now's" are the only thing that matters there. She seems to be in her late 20's, perhaps early 30's.

She is assertive, a risk taker and inquisitive. She has a strong need to prove herself and takes risks in doing so. She's a scientist in her universe, specializing in parallel universe and dimension travel. What is her religion? I would say spiritual defines her. Everyone believes whatever they want to believe where she comes from. There are no churches.

What about government? There is a primary leader, chosen from amongst a slate of scientist candidates, who must demonstrate empathy and concern for others. They serve for life unless or until replaced by a governing council. Almost everyone is considered a scientist of some sort. There are fewer than one million remaining in their space, thanks to dimension travel. Dimension travel carries a risk of germs, microscopic life forms, viruses, and disease.

It took a while for her dimension to establish

protections and implement decontamination practices. Some in her world ignored the protocols because they believed in their own genetic superiority. They ignored many warnings from the discredited scientists of that Now. It turns out you can't fix stupid in any dimension, although germs, viruses and disease can. Alice explains all of this later.

It was an unseasonably warm December afternoon when I was stopped in my car at a traffic light, bored and waiting for the light to change. I noted on the left side of the road a woman walking across the concrete road median below an overpass. This woman I would come to know as Alice. She wore a brightly colored blouse, with various shades of blue vertical stripes and she wore gray pants. She walked briskly and with purpose. Whatever her destination, it was not apparent to me. I could see no strip centers, businesses, or homes in sight. I saw no other cars around. It seemed quite odd.

I watched as she walked across the median and suddenly, in mere seconds, "poof,' she disappeared. As my light turned green, I hurriedly made a U-turn instead of continuing through the intersection. My curiosity was ablaze. I felt a compulsion to investigate what happened to her. Turning beneath the overpass, I looked for her in all directions; there was no more walking lady. I gave up after a few minutes and resumed my drive toward my destination. During the next few weeks I passed through the vicinity often, and each time I detoured to revisit that intersection. Still, no mystery woman.

One balmy February day she reappeared. This time her blouse had vertical stripes of gold, but she wore the same gray slacks. Once again, she vanished in broad daylight. No, my eyesight wasn't failing me, it really happened! In the following month I continued my visits to the same intersection, and on one occasion I even walked across the median platform in the opposite direction hoping to bump into her and find out who she was and where she came from: was she an alien or maybe a ghostly apparition?

After another month of these visits, there she was again. This time she approached me as I walked on the cement median. She strode at a very brisk pace. She wore a multihued yellow and brown vertical stripped blouse. We nearly collided with each other in the middle of the median. Exasperated she spoke up, "You have all this space and you walked directly into my path?"

Breathlessly I replied, "I want to talk to you before you disappear again."

"What do you mean disappear?" "Go poof," I replied.

"Poof? What do you mean, poof?"

"You suddenly disappeared from my sight, and more than once."

"What makes you think I disappeared?"

"I watched you several times at this intersection. One time you wore a blue stripped blouse, another time a gold stripped blouse."

"Are you stalking me? Are you from your government?" She stiffened and reached into her pocket then placed her other hand over a large metal compartment on her belt.

"No, no" I stammered. "I just saw you disappear last December, when I was sitting in my car at this intersection."

"December?" She replied, sounding quizzical.

"Yes, December is one of our twelve months. It has 31 days, and during that month we celebrate Christmas and then New Year's Eve on the last day of the year."

"Ah, you have a strange concept of time, sir."

"I am right then, you are not from here."

"We need to end this, I'm late." she said impatiently.

"Late for what?"

"Just late." She pulled her hand out of her pocket. It was empty.

"That's good, you're not going to vaporize me."

"Vaporize you." she laughed "I wish I could at this moment." She vigorously scratched the back of her head. "You have tiny bugs here, they are different from ours. They drive me crazy."

"And that's why you have to go?"

"No, they just itch. My people are lousy hosts for

them. They give us shots before we visit your dimension to limit them, and they eventually die. They drive us nuts in their final stage before death."

"Are you for real, is this what you really look like?"

She frowned, "You don't like how I look?" She smiled, "OK I am really an invertebrate with tentacles. I'm wearing a species suit, and I'm here because you make a good food source."

I recoiled and stumbled backward in retreat. My effort to retreat ceased with her laugh.

"Do you really think I'm going to eat you here, to be witnessed by many? What kind of monster would you believe me to be? I must leave now." She stood for a moment waiting, it seemed, for me to get out of her way. Sensing the moment was becoming uncomfortable, she continued, "Relax, those types of monsters exist in other places but I'm not one of them. I'm one of you, but from a parallel universe or dimension as we call it."

"Another dimension?" "Yes"

"Are you from the past or the future?"

"Impossible! We cannot travel to or from the past

or the future. The past is the past. It's gone, and we face the reality that the molecular structures creating memories, stories and happenings realign themselves.

"The past does not exist as a molecular reality, even a few moments ago. Neither can one visit the future, because it hasn't formed."

"The future's molecular form is constantly changing and at this moment you would be traveling to something that is not there. Something that would have changed drastically from the moment you decided to visit it, during your first steps toward it, and finally in the physical future where you would arrive as an undefined blob of quivering matter, since you too have changed from the moment of departure from the present to arrival in the future.

"If the past and the future don't exist, then time in the manner which your world perceives it doesn't exist. Only Now's exist. I come from the Now."

"You mean, time travel isn't possible?"

"Absolutely not. Time travel is impossible. Your universe still chases that fantasy. Just like traveling through space to search for intelligent life."

"There's no intelligent life out there?"

"Of course, there is. However, you can't get there from here. Space is distance and distance is insurmountable. There are no shortcuts within our versions of space. One could spend two or three lifetimes traveling to some far-off planet in their universe where there are many Now's, and you would arrive as dust. Subsequent generations, perhaps two or three, would have to be born on the craft to meet the travel demands of the mission. Who knows if those new generations would have the same intelligence, morals or ethics as the original crew? Chances are the mission would be a failure. Our studies have proven suspended animation is not a viable option; our bodies decay and we gravitational beings are not designed for weightless travel. You have to live in the Now!"

"How does dimension travel work?"

"Would you really like to know?"

"Of course."

"So, you want the long or short version."

"How many hours will it take?"

"Hours, what do you mean?"

"You know hours, minutes, second, measurements of time."

"We have Now's, past Now's and future Now's. We live in a world of Now's, a lot of Now's. More than are here in your dimension."

"How does that work?"

"Time is an artificial measurement. Intelligent life in other parallel universes and dimensions track what you call time in a variety of different ways." She added "air quotes" to the word "you" with her fingers. She said,

"We live in Now's."

"So how do you know when it's time to leave? You said you were late."

"In this case the bugs tell me. For this trip, I use them as my indicator that it's time to leave. But often I stay and just scratch until the last one dies. I guess in your dimension you could say I've been flea dipped," she said jokingly and smiled. "Other times I stay for a certain number of your sunsets and sunrises" she advised, scratching her hair again.

"How do you schedule meetings, or know when to go to work, end a work day, or eat?"

"It's complicated. Contact notices go out for meetings with our communication devices. They are like cell phones here in your dimension. Teams respond and show up as soon as possible. Otherwise we just show up when we want and leave when we want. We eat whenever we feel hungry. Everything organized is based on these contact notices. When we receive one, we decide whether to participate or not."

"It sounds like chaos. Are there bosses?"

"Do you mean leaders? Sure, we have organizer types, but there is no rigid authority within various work groups. The organizers coordinate teams and are recognized as leaders, I guess.

"There's no chaos as you describe it. Our dimension experienced a mass extinction many Now's ago, which seems to have cleaned up and eliminated many less desirable traits and personality disorders amongst us. Things seem smoother compared to past Now's. Do you have other questions that'll keep me here and extend this Now?"

"You speak English well."

"Yes, how else would I be able to visit your dimension?" she laughed. "Some of our early dimension travelers arrived with no language skills. Your world doesn't accept strangers who cannot speak your language. We were placed in facilities, beaten, and some were even killed. We learned to assimilate into your society through the various language skills necessary to fit in. You have different languages here in your dimension. We have only two in our dimension, but we have knowledge of many languages from the dimensions we visit. In many parts of our universe we have adopted your language, what you call English. It is far less complicated than our language."

"So, you've been visiting for years"

"We've been visiting not only your dimension but others as well for generations, or I should say, for many Now's. And while we are perhaps more advanced scientifically, we are pretty much like you. Of course, in other dimensions there are You's who are totally unlike us, with differing biological makeup. Fair to say, you would not want some of them visiting your dimension. I'm getting hungry. If you are going to keep me here, can we find a place to eat? Maybe a dark corner where I can feast?"

I recoiled a bit, not sure of her intentions.

"Good! You are a little wary and unsure if the invertebrate will come out. This is going to be so much fun" as she clapped her hands together. "You need to stop being afraid of me and have a sense of humor. After all you're the one who stopped me. If you want to learn more you must feed me."

"What shall I call you," I inquired.

"You can call me Alice, but I am known by other names in in other dimensions.

"Part of your cover?"

"I guess you could say that. Can we eat now?" she said impatiently.

Our ride to the restaurant was filled with questions and answers. We ordered chicken Caesar salads. She took her time and ordered a second entrée, chicken quesadillas.

"Love this food, I love chicken. We need to bring some chickens to our dimension," she declared as she again commenced scratching at her dishwater-blond hair. "Food is good here. I know of some dimensions where food is not an option. I experienced bacterial issues from your food at first, but I've since adapted quite well."

"So, is there intelligent life in other universes?"

"You don't think I represent intelligent life?"

"You know what I mean."

"Yes, we have mapped 41 parallel universes or dimensions. Your own quantum physics scientists recently confirmed this on their own. They call it the Many Interacting Worlds Theory. They've seen how minute matter reacts and it suggests parallel universes. But, they have been stymied by repulsion issues and many of their own false assumptions."

"Is it your role to assist them?

"No way, we don't want to help your dimension achieve parallel universe travel. Please know that we are monitoring your efforts, trying hard to keep you from this discovery."

"Why."

"Do you really have to ask? Your world has a history of violence. You function on carbon-based energy and are barely a generation or two away from ecological catastrophe. Many of your inhabitants dismiss science because it doesn't fit their personal agenda. Do you believe we can accept your world traveling through other worlds plundering and destroying for personal gain?"

"Hmm, maybe not. So, what have you discovered?"

"Each universe or dimension exists in its own biological space. Most of the basic laws of energy and matter are universal. We visit universes which intersect or touch. Some touch periodically while others rarely intersect. There are all kinds of differing biological arrangements as we call them. Some are quite strange, unlike anything you can imagine. This is sort of weird, but when you look up into the night sky from any dimension you are in, we all pretty much see the same view. I don't understand it, neither does anyone else. That's just the way it is."

"Are there any universes you can't visit?"

"Yes, there are some because they aren't presently intersecting. We can't get to them if there is no pathway. We never go to Dimensions 40 and 41, because they have experienced cataclysmic events that changed their worlds. Those universes are uninhabitable because of gases, chemicals and stuff like that. And then there's 35, 36, 38, and 39. They are deemed too dangerous to visit."

"Why?"

"Well the original dimension travelers to 35 and 36 only got halfway into the dimension and we found only particles for the effort. Something or someone munched them, leaving remnants of mangled bodies on our side of the dimension. Our explorers to 38 and 39 never returned. So far over 100 travelers have disappeared traveling into those two dimensions. Either they're in paradise, or we became the best food source they ever experienced."

"Any chance I might get to visit your dimension?"

"Sure, just bring a crate of young chickens. I'm sure

I can get you through the portal if I can promise a chicken in every pot for our dimension dwellers."

"Do you just walk through a time portal?"

"Not time! Stop thinking in terms of time. It's a dimension portal. I can walk through because of the visualization belt I wear. When a front shield is pushed aside, it allows me to access entrances to an array of parallel universes. Don't ask me to explain it, I'm not sure how it works myself. We can only pass from one dimension to another if the dimensions intersect, and then we must be careful to exit before they separate. Some dimensions like yours always intersect. Others are rare occurrences. If we get stuck in one of those rare occurrence dimensions we may never escape. Stuff happens!"

"You speak of many Now's, just how old are you? How many times have you visited this dimension?"

"We never keep track of age in our dimension."

"No birthdays?"

"Birthdays?" she gazed skyward. "I understand you celebrate the day you were born, as well as some other days such as various religious-oriented anniversaries. You have political holidays and apparently some business celebrations. You are not alone in these practices, but life is much simpler without the stress such events create."

"Age?"

"You are a persistent one. I think in your dimension that is considered an inappropriate question to ask a female, at least from what I have heard and read. OK, I'm what's considered in our dimension, youthful. In a few other dimensions of less advanced species, I would be labeled good breeding stock. But we don't keep track of birthdays anyway and Now's are never related to measuring what you call time."

"How long do you live in your dimension?"

"Until we die."

"That tells me a lot."

"Well we do die, like all biological forms, that is informative. We have a spirit or being we believe continues. No one has quite figured out that after-life stage. I guess you have to die to figure that one out."

"I've been there, it's all black."

"You died?" she inquired. "You look pretty well preserved," she said humorously.

"Yup, a heart attack a little over a year ago. Face planted into a cement driveway. Found myself drifting into blackness without form, in the deepest blackness you could imagine. Funny I didn't feel fear or discomfort, it seemed familiar. I had no remembrance of traveling there. No idea how long I was there, it could have been an eternity. I have no remembrance of returning.

"I just awoke to the current situation. Medical personnel were all around me trying to save my life. Some people call that black place 'the Void.' Don't know if that was Heaven, another molecular reality, or maybe it was a parallel universe. It made me believe some part of us is immortal."

"You are the first I have met to have experienced that existence," She noted.

"We believe we are immortal and there is some form of existence after this one. Perhaps you know more than I on this subject?"

Both of us paused a few moments to let our conversation sink in. I broke the silence, "Do you have doctors in your dimension?"

"We call them bio-hazard specialists. But they can end life also if that is the desire of the individual. We get sick, especially those of us who are dimension travelers. We pick up all kinds of germs, viruses, even parasites. Upon return we immediately strip ourselves of our clothing and immerse into a bath that neutralizes bio-hazards we pick up. We are then scanned for parasites and kept under observation for a few Now's. Still there are always new biological surprises that even our extensive cleansing doesn't eliminate. One of our recent dimension travelers came back impregnated."

"Oops, local talent?"

"Not in the dimension she went to. There are no known biological possibilities. That dimension is mostly a plant world."

"Then what was it?"

"We are still looking for an answer."

"Looking?"

"For the sake of dimension research, she decided to bring it to term. She felt the need to know what species are able to cross biological barriers. Was she just a host for some parasitic being? Or was it a biological impregnation?"

"I bet she could die if it is the wrong kind of offspring."

"Yes, but only if it is a parasitic type infestation. She's very brave. On the other hand, she could end up with a nine-pound ball of something that she'll have to raise. It's an interesting wait and see situation."

A couple who were following our conversation in the next booth looked quizzically at each other. Not sure why they were eavesdropping on us.

Noting their interest, Alice stated loudly, "It would be a good premise for a story, don't you think?" and pointed secretively in the direction of the couple to alert me to them.

We returned to our meals in silence and noted when the couple left. Watching the couple leave, I stated,

"I bet they're confused. So, what's the worst thing your dimension travelers have encountered?"

"Biological extermination," she said bluntly. "A number of Now's ago dimension leadership wrongly concluded that our cleansing regime upon return was not necessary. It had been going on for so long with no problems, we assumed to be immune. A leadership directive decided to forego the cleansing step for those returning from a couple of inter- dimensional trips.

"They brought back a virus. Millions died, including all our dimension leadership, which in retrospect turned out to be a blessing. We learned in our dimension that bad decisions can have the salutary effect of eliminating the stupid among us. I think you refer to that as Darwinism here. Unfortunately, a lot of good people died because of that leadership's stupidity. It took a while to reorganize our world and so many more died needlessly because of failures in food production, water purity and biological stresses. We employed robotics and automation to achieve what it took millions to accomplish before. That was before my existence. From what I understand your dimension has suffered from variations of that same leadership stupidity."

I noticed a dark Mercedes pulling up outside of the window we were seated next to. Three men and one woman all wearing dark suits got out. Suddenly, surprised and nervous, Alice blurted out, "We've got to go, they're suits"

"Suits? Lots of people wear suits here."

"No these are predatory suits. I've interacted with them before. There are people in your dimension who attempt to collect dimension travelers like me. I'll explain later," she curtly exclaimed.

I laid two twenties on the table, as she stood up and reached in her pocket, withdrawing her hand that now featured a glowing ring on her middle finger.

"Run out that side door, now" she ordered. "You don't want to be gathered by these people. Get in your car and be ready to go!"

Instead of the side door I stepped around her toward the front door where the suits were just coming in. In an instant I was propelling myself through their midst, throwing elbows and shoulders. Two of them went down not expecting my rush. I tripped another suit as the first two fell. The female suit raised a gun to my temple and calmly spoke, "Stop."

A bright green light exploded between us sending both of us sprawling. I stumbled through the door and fell. As I looked back the woman suit seemed to be knocked out cold or perhaps even dead. Her legs and arms were jutting out in all directions. Suddenly a hand grabbed me; it was Alice helping me up. "Get to the car; we have to get out of here."

The male suits struggled to get up from the floor. I heard shots ring out toward us. I felt the whiz of a bullet move past my head. They are trying to kill us, I thought. I glanced back at our pursuers, another flash of green light lit up the front steps of the doorway and the suits hit the ground. As we reached the car, I could see the female suit regaining consciousness and gathering herself to her feet. A bullet from her gun hit my open car door which shielded me from its deadly outcome. We fishtailed into traffic, almost causing an accident and sped down the roadway.

Three of the suits got into their car leaving one male suit still sprawled in the doorway. "What was that green light?"

She replied angrily, "What were you trying to do back there. They could have shot you. That was dumb!"

"I didn't think they would pull guns and shoot. Who sent those suits?"

"As near as I can figure, they're not from your government people. I mean those are interested in us too, but they don't play as rough."

"Our government knows about dimension travel?"

"Yes, and a few others in your dimension do as well. Those suits acquired one of our travelers a Now ago. Fortunately, they ditched their belt and protection devices before being apprehended, so the suits didn't get them. We've haven't heard from our guy since."

"How did you learn about that?"

"There was a second traveler with him. She wasn't spotted and returned to advise us of her partner's apprehension."

I looked in the rearview mirror and saw a dark car almost on our bumper. I turned down a street that became a school zone. Young children from the elementary school were crossing the street, just as I laid into the horn. They scattered like roaches, giving way to my car and the Mercedes following us. I made a sharp right-hand turn. The pursuing car couldn't keep up with me and ended up running up on the sidewalk, almost hitting some children who screamed and were frozen awaiting an impact that thankfully never came. The black car never slowed down as it fishtailed back onto the street. The rear window of my car shattered from the impact of a bullet.

"Shit!" I exclaimed to my companion, "do something."

"I can't, the ring device needs a recharge! It's useless." She reached into her waist band and pulled out a small packet, put her seat down and leaned back to toss it through the open rear window as the black car gained on us. The packet bounced onto their hood and exploded in a puff of purple smoke. Their vehicle partially spun, slowed for a few seconds, and then continued its pursuit.

"What was that?" I hollered.

"A gas packet. it's designed to work in a closed room and causes momentary respiration problems. Didn't think it would do much, but it did make a diversion."

I wrenched the steering wheel to the left, sending my car sliding into a turn, then another immediate left, expanding our lead on the Mercedes. "Are we close to where we met?"

"Yes, only about a minute more to the elevated highway. I'll take the first exit and we are there. I'm dropping you off and you can get out of here."

"You're coming with me. If they can take you alive they'll likely torture you. They think you are a dimension traveler, like me."

Looking in the rearview mirror again, I saw the black car was held up by crossing traffic. It fell further behind and soon was almost completely out of contact. I raced onto the elevated highway and then quickly exited. At the bottom of the exit, there was a tall homeless-looking man hitchhiking. He had a ragged shirt with patches sewn and his pants were frayed at the bottom. His clothing was soiled. But he seemed somehow to give off an appearance of an elegant man who walked straight and tall. Perhaps down on his luck I thought.

Alice yelled to me, "Stop and give your car to that homeless guy and tell him to take off!"

"But it's my car!" I replied.

"The car is all shot up and without a back window. A lot of questions are going to be asked by authorities. You won't need it; I am taking you to my dimension."

I pulled up and yelled to the homeless man, "Take my car, go where you want, but drive fast."

He replied, "Did you steal the car?"

"No sir, people are chasing me." I said as we got out with the engine still running car.

"No way," he said.

Alice took off her ring and said to him, "Here take my ring," handing it to him. "You'll get good money for it. Then drive fast and ditch the car as soon as you get where you want to go." I stuffed a wad of cash into his shirt pocket and admonished him, "Don't let the black car near you."

"Cops?"

"No!"

"Drug dealers?"

"No, just get in."

"Man, you two are crazy, but I'll take your car," he replied, and leaped athletically into the car. "Hey, the back window is gone," he said.

"Remember, don't let the black car near you."

He peeled off at a high rate of speed, and u-turned north up the other side road next to the elevated highway.

"We probably just got him killed you know," I whispered to Alice.

"Maybe," she replied.

After reaching the median platform, she unhooked her belt and extended it around my waist. "Don't trip and keep up with me, walk with me in unison." We took a few steps and the dark car came down the exit hurtling toward us. Shots rang out, suddenly we were enshrouded by a cloudy mist. Immediately, my familiar universe was gone.

# Another Universe    2

It seemed we walked in blackness together for eons, but Alice assured me it was not very long in time. "Dimension tunnels are actually quite narrow, although they have turns, which if you're not careful will cause you to end up somewhere you don't want to be. Sort of like a maze. You can get lost in the space between dimensions. So just keep walking straight.

She said, "You'll see a dim luminous area shortly. If the suits chasing us can get into the dimension tunnel I could likely lead them astray and leave them wandering the maze for many Now's, until they were no more."

Thankfully, the luminous light finally appeared ahead, then a noise from what seemed like a rush of air, as we stepped into a brightly lit, but empty room. Alice closed the shield and loosened the belt, allowing us to separate.

A haughty male voice spoke through what I am

sure were speakers in the room, "Alice? Just what is the meaning of this? You know we are not allowed to bring other dimensional beings into our world. It's been forbidden since the Great Plague. "

"I had no choice," Alice replied "

Alice, you should have left this one there."

I remained silent.

"No sir, the suits would have killed him."

"Ah yes, the suits are causing trouble again in Dimension Two, are they?"

"So, my world is Dimension Two? I wonder why we weren't number one," I humorously noted.

"Silence traveler!" the voice demanded through the speakers.

Alice whispered to me, "Just shut up and maybe he'll let you stay for a few Now's. Otherwise you're going to get sent back straight into the suits' hands. You can't always expect a lot of empathy here in our dimension."

"Who is this creature, the one who you have brought with you?"

"He's ah, ah., ah, I don't know his name."

"Oh great," the voice replied in a dry tone. "That's reassuring Alice, so very reassuring."

I spoke up to support Alice, "My name is Patrick."

The disembodied voice replied, "Well Patrick, maybe Alice can place the belt back around you and she can take you back into dimension two. You can die here or back in your own dimension. Your choice! Which option do you like? Hmm?"

"Neither, I'm staying for a bit."

"A bit? You mean a Now?"

"OK, I mean yes, a Now."

"Well, if you must."

"He likes to put on a show," she whispered to me.

"I got that Alice!"

"OK you two need to get naked right now; time to remove whatever nasties you brought back with you." I looked over at Alice and she was disrobing without hesitation.

"You heard the man, time to get naked. We're going for a bath in the tubes ahead of us. Or are you modest?"

"No, I'm not modest," I said defensively.

"Good! Nudity is a part of our dimension travel, it's no big deal. You'll be immersed in some liquid, then scanned for parasites and subject to a few inoculations. Your clothes will be cleaned and returned to you before you are sent back into your own universe. It will take a few Now's. Once you're cleaned up you can stay here for a short period of Now's. Then once we are sure the suits have dispersed, I will accompany you back to your dimension. We may decide to use an alternative return location. Our mathematicians will figure out our best options," as she removed the last of her clothing."

"Alice are you putting on a few pounds? Alice?" questioned the disembodied voice from above.

"I weigh the same as when I left"

"Boy! Now, he's a real specimen," said the voice.

"Weight issues, Patrick? Tsk, Tsk."

"Drumbolt," exclaimed Alice. "Enough of your

games. Just because you've traveled to more dimensions than anyone else doesn't give you a license to be rude. Have you looked at your own reflection lately?" replied Alice. "You couldn't ride one of our winged insects in your shape."

"You ride insects here?" I queried.

"Yes, sometimes we do. We have huge insects here thanks to the importation of a variety of large flowering plants we imported after first discovering dimension travel. Everyone was a collector and we sort of turned our ecological world upside down for a period of Now's. They took over and altered our temperature. We are now about 10 degrees warmer than we were in the early Now's. We even have a few huge lizards, specimens you refer to as dinosaurs."

"Dinosaurs, I gotta see them," I exclaimed.

"Oh, look what you brought back, Alice. A child! He's thrilled with our big lizards. Of course, show the little boy our lizards," Drumbolt cackled.

"Drumbolt, that's enough. Patrick, you can put your clothes in the compartment over there by the tube."

She pressed a button near the tube and I watched the doors open. "Here, step in and get cleaned up. Or you might get cooked up and become his lunch."

I hesitated.

She laughed as Drumbolt spoke, "I would not want to eat this thing you brought back, Alice"

"So, you would prefer a smelly can of worms from Dimension Thirty-Four perhaps?" She replied.

"No," replied Drumbolt, "I prefer my regular diet."

"Get in," she ordered. "You're safe; I'm just playing with you."

Everything was a whirl; water, fluids, chemical smells, then heat, then more fluids, then very cold water, followed by a warm sticky liquid. It hung on my body for what seemed like an eternity, then finally a wash and warm windy dry. I imagined this is what a dish feels like in a dishwasher. The door suddenly opened. Alice stepped out of her tube the same time as I did.

"Walk over to the scan devices and lie on the gurney," she ordered.

The whirl of machines started up and crisscrossed my body over and over. Once done we got up from the gurneys.

"Excellent," exclaimed Drumbolt. "Neither of you brought any nasties back with you. I am surprised considering this creature you call Patrick is not from around here. Now Patrick needs to get inoculated. You can get dressed, Alice, or not. It's your choice."

Alice began dressing as two male figures entered the room and escorted me to a hallway. "I'll see you shortly," she called out as I was led through the door.

About eleven inoculations later, after my measurements were taken, a blood vial drawn, and some X-rays, I was then given new clothes and directed to pass through a door.

A large white-haired man of immense proportions was prone upon a broad lounge in a gold and white robe, smoking a long-hosed Hookah type pipe, near a bank of holographic screens.

"Patrick!" he coughed. "Nice to see you made it through our little process. Umm, it's been many a Now since we've transported someone into our dimension. Our last traveler was a strange man. His hair was wiry. I think his name was hmm, Albert. Yes Albert! And something else! I can't recall his last name, but it started with, I believe you call the letter an E. Anyway, he was a bright creature. I hope we'll find you just as bright."

I replied, "I don't think you will, if the last name was Einstein." "Yes, Patrick, as a matter of fact, that was his last name."

Alice entered the room. "Well now, you see why Drumbolt will not be riding any insects."

"Alice, I'm disappointed," the large man said, pausing to take another puff from the pipe. "that you'd take that approach in front of our new visitor."

Alice walked over to give Drumbolt an extended hug, "You know I love you Drumbolt."

"And I love you too, Alice." His eyes glistening.

Alice turned to face me and seeing my obvious confusion, laughed. "Drumbolt is my mentor, my trusted advisor, and he keeps me out of trouble in my dimension."

"Alice, you know," taking yet another puff from the pipe, "I adored your mother."

"I know, my grandmother and your father were close friends."

Drumbolt added, "As were their parents and grandparents. Our family relationship has been strong for generations. Unfortunately, I'm the last of my family. So, it will not," taking another puff, "continue long. It ends with me because I was too busy exploring dimensions to find a mate and have offspring. The Drumbolt name ends with me," wiping a tear from his eye. "Alice, promise me there will be more Alices. Don't get caught up in the thrill of dimension travel."

"I'm still young Drumbolt, and yes someday there will be another Alice, that is my promise to you. And maybe she will find her own Drumbolt, or someone like you who adores her and helps her through her life."

"That would be nice. I hope I am still here to see your little Alice."

"Another Alice?" I questioned.

"Yes, I am from many generations of Alice's. In our

dimension first-born females are always named after her mother."

"As it is for first-born males named for their father," interrupted Drumbolt. Suddenly a buzzer sound was emitted by one of the monitors arrayed in front of Drumbolt.

Drumbolt said, "Well time for idle talk, reminiscing, and sweetness to end. Someone is coming through a tunnel back home. Not sure who this is. No entries are scheduled. That's odd."

Suddenly into the reception room burst a bedraggled dimension traveler with long, unkempt hair and several days of beard. He was wounded with a long thin spear sticking out of his shoulder. His shirt was stained with both dried and fresh blood. He was fighting with a winged creature. Something akin to a flying monkey had wrapped its tail around the traveler's neck and was biting him eagerly on the neck and scratching with his small claws. The newly arrived dimension traveler's arms were flailing, his hands searching for a grasp of the monkey-like creature.

"Argh," a scream let out, "Help me, get this hellion off me. Help!"

"What the hell" said Drumbolt. "It looks like, could it be Adam? He's been gone for many a Now. He was one of the hundred or so who traveled to dimension 38 or 39, but never returned. Not sure which dimension it was now. Ah yes, my monitor tells me it was 38 we sent him. He is the first to return from that dimension."

Adam managed to toss the flying monkey or whatever it was off him. It hissed and bared its teeth defensively in a corner.

"Need help?" Drumbolt's voice boomed over the speakers. "Adam is that you?" "Yes, get me some help here."

"So nice of you to return. And you brought a cuddly little friend with you. Nice, but that's against the rules, Adam."

"Drumbolt, you are a suffering old coot. I've been trapped out there for so many Now's. I am wounded, and you bark about rules." Pointing to the winged monkey,

"This is no friend, Drumbolt."

"A parade and welcoming committee will greet you when you get through the cleansing. For now, however, you better deal with the monkey, or whatever it is," interrupted Alice.

"Alice is that you? It's been a while. Come help me deal with the monkey. I'm about done. I have no energy. The damn thing scratched me all up. Its teeth at least are dull, but the claws are another matter. I got chased to the dimension portal by a flock of these damn things, and this one hitched a ride on my neck. It's been biting my neck and back the whole trip through the tunnel."

The creature suddenly launched in flight toward Adam. Unfortunately for the monkey, Adam flinched, and it flew into the spear protruding from Adam's shoulder. "Off," exclaimed Adam, as the monkey banged into the spear. "Crap, that hurt."

The monkey ended up sprawled on the floor. Still conscious, but its bell had been rung. Drumbolt added, "Well Adam, I see you've dealt with your little pet. There's no need for our help. Gather him up and prepare him to get cleaned up."

Adam retorted, "Hell, I'm not snuggling up to that thing."

I added my own observation. "Alice, you were right about not a lot of empathy in your dimension,"

Adam turned and asked, "Who's that guy?"

Drumbolt replied, "You're not the first to bring a visitor into our dimension today."

"Does he bite too?" asked Adam.

Drumbolt asked, "Well Alice? Does this thing you brought with you bite too, hmm?"

"No, he doesn't bite, at least he hasn't yet," she replied. But if I were Adam, I'd watch him closely when you get through your cleansing and body repair work. You might be a tasty menu item for those from other dimensions. Perhaps they can sense weakness."

Adam didn't pick up on the dig and inquired only as to me. "What is he?" asked Adam.

"One of us, he is just from another dimension," replied Alice.

The reception room door opened, and the first man through entered with a net.

"No, never mind," said Adam, as he waved the man away. He grabbed the monkey with his good arm by the scruff of the neck and started to accompany the men out of the reception room. The monkey struggled a bit but was disoriented and allowed Adam to transport it to the clean room.

"Looks like you've got a new friend Adam," said Alice.

"Maybe", replied Adam, "Let's see how it cleans up."

"Remember, we can't keep samples brought back from other dimensions Adam" announced Drumbolt.

Adam replied, "I didn't exactly bring him back. What shall I do, kill it?"

"No!" exclaimed Alice." I'd love to examine it. It's kind of cute with all those teeth and claws."

"It's all yours Alice," retorted Adam.

"Alice, you aren't going to be allowed to keep it here in our dimension," ordered Drumbolt.

"Sorry, I'm claiming it! Always wanted a flying monkey."

"But, you've never seen one before. How could you want one?" asked Drumbolt.

"I believe Frank Baum, who reportedly visited our dimension and traveled a bit to other dimensions, reported about them in his book the Wonderful Wizard of OZ. I remember reading his book when I was a child. And another traveler, a mister Carroll," said Alice.

I interrupted, "Lewis Carroll, the author of the Alice's Adventures in Wonderland book was here?"

"Yet another famous writer was CS Lewis," added Alice. "We have identified a number of travelers from your world. It was the rage before the era of our plague to bring interesting beings from other dimensions to interact with our leaders and dimension travelers. We especially loved good story tellers."

"Mr. Carroll knew my grandfather," Drumbolt interjected, "He was a lot like me."

"Yeah, you're all named Drumbolt," replied Alice. "That doesn't help Patrick here."

"My grandfather was a tad overweight."

"A tad overweight?" smirked Alice.

"Well, nicely proportioned if you must. He loved the pipe too," as he twirled a pipe between his fingers. "Grandfather was the inspiration for one of those characters, a caterpillar I believe."

"The caterpillar's name was Absolem," I blurted out. "This explains a lot. Or maybe it doesn't."

"I'd say, not so much," replied Drumbolt. "Nothing explains anything. It just is."

"Now that's quite a 'through the looking glass' statement," I replied, as I became immediately distracted from a squeal by Alice.

"I get a flying monkey!" exclaimed Alice.

"Patrick, since you arrived nothing has been as before. Alice, what have you started?" queried Drumbolt.

# Flying Monkey 3

Adam disappeared into the clean room. The first order of business was to have the spear removed from his shoulder and associated wound repairs. He was cleaned, scanned and inoculated. The flying monkey was muzzled, tied to a hook and cleaned in a separate tube. There was some commotion in the tube for a bit, but ultimate resignation. The monkey or whatever it was, sat stoically through all the fluid application and drying. As it was led out of the tube, he flapped his wings, attempting to fly, only to be pulled to the ground by a handler. It hissed and growled but remained submissive. A few moments later the monkey was secured to a gurney and scanned for parasites. A tube was forced down his throat and anti-parasitic medicine squeezed into his gut. More hissing. Oddly, he licked the muzzle. The fluid must have tasted good.

The flying monkey, if it could be considered a monkey, was perhaps 18 inches tall, and didn't weigh much. Its skin was like a reptilian leather, except it had fine hairs growing out in patches. One would swear it had the mange, but in fact it was a product of inbreeding from a colony of such creatures. Its eyes were very much like a cat's and it probably saw well in twilight conditions. Its tail was thick like a sloth's tail with a bit of hair at the rounded, boney bottom. The tail, in some situations was used as a weapon. It's most outstanding feature was a wide mouth, with thick monkey-like lips and jagged, but dullteeth.

While it might occasionally eat small animals and insects, its diet was primarily fruits and plants. It was not an animal that could inflict much damage with its bite, as the anatomy of its jaw lacked requisite muscle development. It could do more damage with its small claws than its teeth. Bottom line, it was not as fearsome or as scary as it looked. Drumbolt monitored the progress of both Adam and the monkey on his screens.

"They're cleaning up nicely I must say. The monkey is docile and Adam, well he seems a bit testy and irritable. He gives his attendants a really hard time. Even screaming at them. Maybe we shall keep the monkey and send Adam back to Dimension 38 where he came from."

A door to their room opened, and in rolled a robot with food, interrupting their conversation. A variety of fresh fruits, vegetables, some cheese, bread, crackers, and a small amount of meat on a large platter was served. It was placed on a table near Drumbolt and the three occupants of the room huddled around the platter, filling their individual plates.

I tried a sampling of the meat. "This one is a bit tart," I noted.

"Yes," Drumbolt agreed, "It's butterfly."

I dropped the meat immediately and spit out the contents of my mouth into a napkin.

"Butterfly is good, Patrick," Alice said assuredly. "They're huge, they breed constantly, and if we did not cull the species, they'd overrun our world. When they first arrived, an Avant Garde chef decided to carve one up and see what it tasted like. It's a meat we have enjoyed ever since for many a Now in our world."

"And the other meat?" I inquired.

"We have a variety of mammals here. There's a serving of lizard on your platter," she explained.

Drumbolt was busy stuffing his face with food, oblivious to the juices that dripped down his chin, and pieces of meat clinging to his lips. He was a messy eater and pretty much cleaned off the platter, during which time he ignored the rest of the conversation.

"You really go for it Drumbolt," I noted.

"I take enjoyment from my healthy appetite," he replied. The other meats weren't bad. In fact, the lizard was delicious! I stayed away from the butterfly however. Alice reached over to my plate and removed the last butterfly portion and dropped it on to her plate. "When you share a meal with Drumbolt, you have to grab the food quickly. There's never enough."

"Alice," admonished Drumbolt, as he took another bite of the meats.

"Well, it's true, Drumbolt!"

The meal was interrupted, by another door opening into the room. A freshly cleaned and repaired Adam emerged. He was six-foot-two, well built, perhaps a bit on the skinny side. His head was shaved, and he bore a slight scar down the left side of his face.

Alice stood up from her plate of food laughing and pointing at Adam. "You got the full head shave treatment! How rich! Must have had critters in your hair. Too funny! You were always the stylish snob some Now's ago, every hair was in place, a real pretty boy."

Adam fired back, "Just wait, one day you'll come back from some hell hole and have to get the full shave job too."

"For your information, that has already happened. But then again, I'm not hair obsessed like you are," she said, needling him. Walking over to Adam, she reached out to his injured shoulder and grabbed it roughly. Adam yelped. She smiled, and said matter-of- factly, "I guess you're going to be laid up for a while, pretty boy."

"Dammit Alice! No way. I am functional. I'm not going to be laid up, I'm just sore. You still act like a guy after all these Now's. Rough, tough, mean and totally unsympathetic, always trying to prove that you're just as tough as a guy."

"Well I am just as tough as guys. Hey, but I care for some people and some things. You're just not on my list.

And that crack about being a guy? Patrick, we went through the cleansing together, when I got undressed did you see a guy?"

"No, you're definitely not a guy," I replied.

Adam stiffened and joined in, "Are you sure you'd know. Maybe in your dimension the birds and bees are in test tubes."

Drumbolt spoke up, "OK, enough bickering. I see you have issues with each other." Puffing on his pipe once more he said, "We've got business to attend to. I've sent out a contact notice, everyone should be here shortly. Then we will debrief Adam and learn something constructive. Besides the fact that you like traveling with flying monkeys. Hmm?"

Adam started to speak, but Drumbolt hollered out, "Silence, then he shifted his weight on the lounger he was laying on and sighed, "We don't need to go through your story more than once. The stories all tend to sound the same when told more than once. I need a good story, it's been a while. And up until you showed up with your flying monkey, and Alice here bringing back this creature we call

54

Patrick, and relating something about suits chasing them, those were the only interesting things I've encountered in many a Now."

"You need to retire old man," replied Adam.

"Adam," Drumbolt retorted.

Another door to the room opened and in walked an attendant dragging a very submissive, muzzled flying monkey along behind him.

"What's the matter with it?" inquired Drumbold.

The attendant replied, "He doesn't like a leash. After I hooked it up, it just flopped on the ground."

Adam said, "Man, all I needed were a thousand leashes and I could have controlled all those  flying monkeys chasing me. That's good to know."

"Who gets it?" inquired the attendant.

"He's mine," spoke up Alice walking over to the prone flying monkey. "Aww, you don't like the leash do you little guy."

The monkey blinked through the ill-fitting muzzle, which was designed for some other creature. He turned his head upward to Alice but remained prone on the floor.

"Here," said Alice reaching into her pocket. "I rescued this sweet fruit from the clutches of Drumbolt over there." She placed a piece near the flying monkey's face. It sniffed at it and attempted to lick it through the muzzle. "Oh, you like fruit. Please remove the muzzle," she asked the attendant.

Drumbolt hollered out, "Alice, that thing will bite you for sure."

She ignored him and once again asked the attendant to remove the muzzle. The attendant did not respond. She sighed, "OK, then, I'll remove the muzzle." She reached down, unbuckled the various clasps and tossed the muzzle to the attendant. "I think you're done here," she stated to the attendant.

"No, stay," blurted out Adam. "She has no idea what she's getting into."

She placed the sweet fruit in front of the flying monkey's mouth and watched it bite into the morsel. Slowly it rolled up on its feet, grabbed the fruit into its hands and began devouring the fruit. She knelt and stroked its head and down its back. It raised its tail, just like a cat would in response to a stroke.

"He's cute," she said looking over at Drumbolt, who just rolled his eyes. She lifted its tail and looked underneath, "Well maybe it's a she." she announced. She took the leash from the handler and walked toward a chair. It followed eagerly, anticipating the next fruit. Once at her seat she took another fruit from her plate and handed it to the monkey, who took it from her hands, sat down and ate it.

Adam approached Alice. "Alice that thing will turn on you a soon as it's finished eating. The flying monkey turned toward the approaching Adam, flapping its wings, hissing and growling.

Adam retreated, "OK, don't say I didn't warn you."

Alice held more fruit in her hands and the monkey leaped up onto her lap. Everyone in the room paused, fearing the worst. It was face to face with Alice. "Pretty girl," Alice said, and then scratched it behind the ears. "Oh, you like this don't you? Now what will I call you little lady? That's it! Little Lady. Your name is Little Lady."

After finishing the fruit, the monkey turned around

and faced the others in the room and hissed. Alice stroked its head. "They're OK Little Lady. Just relax; you've had quite a day! No one will hurt you here. And you've already got the best of Adam, so he's no threat!" She smiled and stared in Adam's direction, continuing to rub Little Lady's head and shoulders. Adam just stared back at her, fuming at the continuing avalanche of insults from Alice. A bit later the monkey licked Alice's left hand, wrapped its wings around her own body and curled up into Alice's lap. Little Lady quickly fell asleep.

Drumbolt let out a whoosh sound, finally relaxing. "Alice, you have way too much faith in yourself sometimes. That thing might have bit off your face. Do you realize that?"

"No lectures please, Drumbolt!" replied Alice.

Adam interrupted, "We could have been picking pieces of Alice up all over this room."

Alice replied, "It chewed on you all the way through the tunnel and you were just fine Adam. Your assessment of danger is faulty, Adam"

The room stayed silent for a few moments as

everyone recovered from the stress of the moment. A door opened and in paraded ten people, both males and females. Drumbold's contact notice to respond for the appearance of Adam attracted an eager crowd. Little Lady's eyes opened and was suddenly airborne above Alice's head.

"What is the meaning of this, Drumbolt?" asked Yaeger, the tallest member of the committee. "This creature is not from our dimension and no travelers can be admitted." He glanced over at me.

"Not one, but two visitors, Drumbolt?"

Drumbolt replied, "I'm afraid so Yaeger. Yes, I know it's against policy. Alice brought him back," pointing at me. "She was in Dimension Two and pursued by suits. He, Patrick, was simply in the wrong place at the wrong time. If she left him there, then the suits kill him for sure. He seems an agreeable fellow. Not too bright. No Einstein, but probably the norm for his dimension. Which of course is not really saying much." Drumbolt haughtily puffed on his pipe once more.

"Thanks for the full-throated support," I said to

him.

The monkey was growing restless and began hovering above Alice's head. Alice reached up and pulled the monkey back to her lap. "Her name is Little Lady. Adam brought her back," she said.

"I did not!" forcefully replied Adam.

"It was attacking me as I was running into the tunnel. I tried to get it off me. It scratched the hell out of me. I've got bite marks on my neck. It just wouldn't let go."

"It sensed weakness!" stated Alice, getting another dig in.

"Please Alice, just shut up!" relied Adam.

"Well I see nothing has changed between you two," replied Yaeger. "For those of the committee who are unaware, Alice and Adam were sort of paired up at one time. Obviously, not the greatest pairing."

"Agreed," said Adam, as he glared over at Alice.

Drumbolt spoke up, "Committee members, Adam is the first to return from dimension 38. That is why I called you all here. The monkey, or whatever we call it, is a side show. The facts are Adam brought it back with him. It was unintended. Alice has now decided she needs a friend. It seems to me the monkey is more desirable to her than the creature she brought back, Patrick here," pointing in my direction.

Laughter rang out, as Drumbolt's dry wit lanced the potential criticisms for bringing multiple visitors to their dimension.

He continued, "Now I am not sure the monkey is completely safe, but for now it seems perfectly comfortable in Alice's company. So, that is not the subject of this meeting. Neither is Patrick. Adam should be our focus."

Lily, an assertive younger member of the committee spoke up. "Personally, I find the monkey the most interesting point of this meeting. I'd like more monkey time, but alas, Adam please share your report with us please, if you will."

Adam stood and walked to the center of the room as members of the committee took to chairs placed all over the room. Interestingly, Alice and Little Lady were both given a wide berth. Noting this, Alice spoke up, "What, no one wants to sit with me?"

Yaeger replied, "Alice it needs to go back. No telling what disease or virus it brings."

"But she's passed all screenings Yaeger. She's clean." Alice replied.

"Here I'll sit with you," said Lily. She was immediately joined by Gurgle, a dwarf member of the committee. Gurgle was a little barrel of a man, with a full head of thick hair that always appeared tangled and shaggy. He also sported a full beard and significant body hair. What he lacked in size, was made up for in the volumes of hair, high energy and storied fearlessness of his reputation. He was a lion of a man in a small package.

"It seems appropriate that I join the menagerie, or as some in Patrick's world would say, the circus," commented Gurgle.

Lily reached over and scratched Little Lady's head. Little Lady seemed to purr like a kitten. "Alice, this could be the next rage in our dimension. Flying monkeys for all," Lily proclaimed.

"Geeze," mumbled Yaeger.

Adam started his oral report, "I volunteered for a mission to dimension 38 seeking to find our people who have gone there and never returned. I got to the entrance, took a step into the world and was overcome by choking atmospheric gases but managed to stumble back into the tunnel. It may well be that Dimension 38 is uninhabitable, or at least a portion seems uninhabitable. There may well have been some cataclysmic event on Dimension 38 or maybe it just never developed properly.

"Or maybe it is a shield set up by natives to prevent dimension travelers?" questioned the elder Herack. Herack, like Drumbolt, had traveled to many dimensions, but age crept up on him, and he now walked bent over and had a pronounced limp from an injury he incurred from dimension travel. Even the most advanced of bio hazard skills could not put him back together.

Adam continued, "You could be correct Herack, or maybe it's a place we should never have visited in the first place. Like 40 and 41, maybe we should rule dimension 38 off limits as a visiting dimension."

"Where did you run into the monkeys, Adam," questioned Alice.

"On Dimension 37," replied Adam.

"Dimension 37?" quizzed Drumbolt. "You were never authorized to go to 37."

"Believe me I never intended to do so," said Adam. "I became disoriented from the gases and as I made my way back through the tunnel, I got disoriented, took the wrong turn, was lost, and finally after a Now or two passed, I found myself in Dimension 37."

"How did you know it was 37?" Inquired Yaeger.

"Well, little people, flying monkeys, a mad queen and witches, or at least a woman who posed as a witch. I've studied various reports on dimensions and this matched the descriptions of 37," he responded.

Georges, a short bulbous mathematician within the group spoke up, "There is a theory among our mathematicians that in addition to direct travel between dimensions, dimension tunnels may converge and lead a traveler to other dimensions. There are very rare recorded instances of travelers ending up in the wrong dimension or

64

universe as some call them. It hasn't happened in many a Now, and the initial claims of converging tunnels were dismissed as miscalculations which caused a few travelers sent into the wrong universe or dimension. Your experience Adam may again re-open this area for research. We know that our dimension and Dimension 2 have continuous intersecting dimensions. Which is why we have traveled so much to 2, and over the Now's, we allow a handful of their residents to come here. We permanently intersect with four worlds, the lizard world, the water world, the unusual world of elongated beings and the world quite like ours, dimension two. Perhaps 37 and 38 are permanently intersecting worlds. Your experience suggests they are. So, it's seems very possible to travel between 37 and 38."

Alice spoke up, "We lost many of our people on 38 and 39. My mother was lost on 38 along with others we all know of. Adam's experience makes me wonder if perhaps 37, 38, and perhaps 39 are continuously intersecting universes. Maybe some of our travelers ended up on 37 like Adam did and for some reason were unable to return."

"Yes, it would," agreed Drumbolt. "And now that we know such gases on Dimensions 40 and 41 may be present on 38 as well, we must take precautions," He puffed on his pipe. "We should consider sending out a properly equipped search party in the very near future. The idea of just traveling from dimension to dimension without breathing apparatuses to combat environment issues should now be reviewed. Is everyone in agreement?"

A chorus of Yes's rang throughout the room. "I want that mission," asserted Alice.

Drumbolt was a bit irritated replied, "Your mother disappeared there, Alice. I am not losing you also to Dimension 38. Others must go first."

"So, tell us about 37," Adam, said Yaeger. "What is it like now?"

"It's a strange place," replied Adam.

"Yes, it is," mumbled Gurgle. "I have been there. So, tell us what's happening on my favorite little dimension?"

Adam, responded, "So you've been there? That makes sense. There are a lot of your kind there: small, diminutive people. There are two distinct worlds. On one side you have an angry, vindictive queen who locks up strangers and demands to have her every whim realized. There are many magnificently dressed guards and an assortment of strange animals. There's almost a hallucinogenic quality about the place. You would swear the animals talk."

"Oh, but perhaps they do," interjected Gurgle.

"Maybe one who professes to enjoy the pipe and a variety of beverages such as yourself Gurgle might believe animals do talk. Perhaps the pipe and the drink makes you unable to discern reality from fantasy," interjected Drumbolt.

"I believe they do talk," countered Gurgle.

"Well none the less," continued Adam, "There are many tall buildings, behind which it is claimed are smaller buildings which disorient those who venture into them. It's easy to get lost in those buildings."

"Who says that?" questioned Yaeger.

"The Queen's men, and the little people. I never made it into the buildings, I just saw them from afar."

Adam replied and then continued his story. "On the other side of that world there are witches, or at least a woman who calls herself a witch, flying monkeys, hordes of them, and small people like Gurgle. Supposedly there are both good and bad witches, but I've only encountered the one and I'm not sure what kind of witch she is. Both sides spoke of their hatred for the other side."

Yaeger spoke up, "It was Dimension 37, to which the story telling visitors from Dimension 2 traveled after visiting our dimension. First it was Lewis Carroll, then quite a few Now's later a guy named Frank Baum. Mr. Baum called the witch's side OZ and Mr. Carroll called the other side Wonderland. It is said each only visited one side of Dimension 37 and then wrote about it when they returned to Dimension Two."

Adam continued, "The mad Queen captured me just after arriving on 37. She locked me in her castle for quite a few Now's. I escaped with the help of, well I don't know how to explain it. It was some animal form that appeared and just as quickly disappeared. I got out through a tunnel underneath the castle. I can't believe I am talking about castles and queens, how archaic. You

68

must think I've lost it."

"I could believe that," replied Gurgle.

Adam replied, "Do you agree, or do you just think I've lost it?"

"I mean I agree," Gurgle replied.

"A very strange universe," Drumbolt added, "We stopped going there because there was nothing to learn from their world. It seemed backwards!"

Gurgle added, "Well yes backwards, however my prospects with the ladies improved considerably on the witch side of 37. I visited there many, many times. There's probably some little Gurgles on 37." Laughter rang out.

"Hearing that, I'm not sure I'll be happy about it if you return to 37" said Lily wagging a finger at Gurgle. Alice, looked quizzically at Lily who was average height and about Alice's age. She had an hourglass figure, long reddish-brown hair, and when standing next to Gurgle she stood nearly a foot taller than him.

"So, it's you and Gurgle, huh?" asked Alice.

"Yeah, he's fun, and quite attentive." She replied,

causing Gurgle to blush. "I guess I'm too busy traveling to keep track of the social life here at home," added Alice.

Gurgle spoke up to get the meeting back on track, "Adam, please continue."

Adam said "Anyway, I made it to the other side, and found roads of gold bricks, thick thorny forests, and of course," pointing in Alice and Little Lady's direction, "flying monkeys. I was found almost immediately by the witch's men as the tunnel led from the Queen's castle to near the witches' castle. I was trapped in the witch's castle dungeon for a few Now's. I think there could be others in that dungeon, perhaps even some of our people. The palace guards are lazy and didn't mind their keys. When I escaped, the witch sent her flying monkeys after me. I hid in a town with the little people before returning here."

"Well Adam, you would stand out there among us little people," interrupted Gurgle.

"Leaving the little people's community, I returned to a meadow near the same dimension entrance where I arrived. I secured my belt and headed toward the entrance. A small spear thrown by someone sliced into my shoulder and broke off when I fell to the ground. I got to my feet and managed to stumble to the entrance when the flying monkeys caught me. I thought I was done for. Just then the Queen's men from the other side arrived and tried to capture me amongst all the flying monkeys. I had only a few moments to get to the entrance. Unfortunately, that one," pointing to Little Lady, "wouldn't let go. She had a death grip around my throat as I stumbled through the portal."

"It was so nice of you to bring her back to me Adam," replied Alice.

Yaeger spoke up, this time with a small smile, "Adam, I must say that bringing the flying monkey to Alice was not at all appropriate."

"Dammit everyone, do I have to repeat myself again? I didn't bring the damn monkey back for Alice." The room exploded with laughter.

"Thank you for your report Adam," offered Drumbolt. "Well, Adam stated there could be others on Dimension 37. What should we do?"

Wineborn, a gentleman prone to ostentatious

displays stood up from the back of the room. "A strong show of force is my thought. Send in a command unit with full offensive tools and equipment to bring these heathens to their knees."

Yaeger, spoke, "Wineborn, your solution to every problem seems to be a well-armed command unit."

Lily, after remaining quiet throughout the meeting spoke up, "Didn't we agree that we would avoid violence in other dimensions?"

"Yes, even when confronted with violence," replied Drumbolt. "It is our way, Wineborn, and has been for generations of Now's. We visit to observe and try to avoid interfering in their world. Of course, Gurgle here, has chosen to, well maybe confessed is a better word, to doing a bit more than interfering in their world."

"I want to invade Dimension 37 and bring our people out," said Wineborn

Adam spoke up once again, "I think there we may have people on 37, but, I can't be sure."

Yaeger added, "Wineborn, you're a bit too eager. I recommend we deny your request."

Alice started to stand, rousting Little Lady out of her semi slumber and she went into the air above Alice's head. "Why not me?" she asked. I can bring along others who have been on 37. Like Adam, who just returned, and of course Gurgle." Whispering to Lily and smiling, she said, "Lily, I promise to keep him out of the clutches of the ladies on 37." She continued addressing the assembled group "Equip me with a power ring, some minor defensive weapons. Don't forget, I'll have a flying monkey to guide me!"

Adam retorted, "Alice that monkey will take off just as soon as you get there and lead them all back here to find us."

"It's Little Lady, Adam! If there are thousands of flying monkeys as you indicate, Little Lady will want no part of the struggle for food among the hordes there." Little Lady seemed to respond by flying down near Alice's shoulder, wrapping her tail around her shoulders and resting her head on the top of Alice's head as she sniffed her hair. An air of apprehension rose but quickly subsided in the room. A squeaky little voice emitted from Little Lady, shocking the room. It was a language unfamiliar to those in the room. Little Lady's sounds repeated. "Then as clear as a bell it said, "Thank you, Alice."

"Oh my, you can talk Little Lady, you can talk!" Alice reached up and scratched Little Lady's head.

"Yes." Little Lady replied, then launched into her own strange language once more. She seemed content resting on Alice's head.

"Yep, I knew all along the animals on Dimension 37 talked," beamed Gurgle.

Drumbolt spoke up, "Well Alice, you and Little Lady, are full of surprises," as he continued measured draws on his pipe. "If you plan on going to go to 37, I suggest you take Gurgle and Adam, but only if you can make peace with Adam."

Adam spoke up, "Just try being a nice person for a change Alice!"

"Drumbolt, can I leave Adam there when we are done?" replied a clearly irritated Alice.

Yaeger spoke up, "Drumbolt is correct, this thing between the two of you has to stop, or you could endanger the mission to Dimension 37."

Gurgle spoke once more, "I'm not going to play baby sitter for these two on 37. There should be someone else along to manage the back and forth and help keep us on track. How about Slither? He's pretty no-shit about everything and has the right skills in dangerous situations."

Wineborn spoke up once again, "I stand to assert once more, a well-armed command unit will do the job. I'm still available."

"Maybe Dimension 39 is a better destination for you, Wineborn," Drumbolt replied. "Of course, finding a volunteer to serve with you after all the drama in the lizard dimension could be problematic. Any volunteers?" None were noted.

"Well Wineborn, it seems Dimension 39 is not on your itinerary either."

"Slither is not currently in the dimension," Alice suggested.

"He's scheduled to return soon," replied Drumbolt.

I spoke up, "I'd like to go."

Drumbolt replied, "No, Patrick, you are going back to your own dimension shortly"

"Can I still see the lizards and butterflies before I leave?" I replied.

"I will take him on a tour," offered Alice.

"That is fine," replied Drumbolt, "But he'll be leaving tomorrow afternoon."

"That's fair," I replied.

Drumbolt spoke up once more, "Time to bring this meeting to a close. Is it agreed by all that Alice leads the group composed of Adam, Gurgle and Slither to Dimension 37 to search for our people?"

There was an affirmative voice vote and the meeting slowly began breaking up and participants headed toward the door.

"So, we're a team," said Gurgle to Adam and Alice.

Lily felt left out and a bit unsettled about Gurgle heading to Dimension 37. She spoke up, "I'd still like to go. I have skills."

Alice looked to Drumbolt who said, "No Alice. Maybe if Alice's team is missing after some Now's, Lily, you can be available to form a rescue party and bring reserves in to Dimension 37. We'll see."

Adam reached over to scratch Little Lady's head and was greeted with her growls and hisses. "Well, I get the same reaction from the both of you!"

"Little Lady, let Adam scratch your head. You should get used to him because we are going to spend a lot of time together. "

Little Lady stretched out her body toward Adam and bowed her head. "She   understands"   said Drumbolt.

"That's remarkable. Now this has been an interesting day. Time to retire to my room." Drumbolt lifted his oversized body off the lounger and waddled off toward the door, pausing to caress Alice on the cheek with the palm of his hand as he passed. "You will be careful on 37."

"I will Drumbolt."

"OK, who's Slither?" I asked as Gurgle, Lily and Adam all followed Drumbolt out the door.

"He's a piece of work; let's just leave it at that. I have a feeling you'll meet him before tomorrow afternoon when you're scheduled to leave," replied Alice.

We all followed the others out the door as new monitor-watchers entered and sat at nearby chairs next to their monitors. An attendant stopped Alice. She motioned to me to walk ahead and talked for a moment with the attendant.

Alice quickly caught back up to me and said, "Up ahead, there's a room numbered 1014, that'll be your room, next to mine."

"Are you staying here overnight, Alice?"

"No, this is where I live. I dimension travel too much to have a real home."

"What about your new friend, Little Lady?"

"She'll stay with me in my room. I'll get an attendant to fix up a makeshift bed or something for her.

an escort to travel. OK? There'll be a platter of food in your room when you arrive. If you want something else, just ask the attendant standing outside your door."

"You really don't want me to leave the room."

"It's protocol. We have not had a dimension visitor for many Now's, and we want to keep your presence quiet until tomorrow."

Well when you take Little Lady out for our tour the secret will certainly be out!"

"It's being broadcast as we speak now, to let people know I'll have Little Lady with me when we tour our dimension."

"Umm, no mention of me?"

"Nope, you can pass as one of our dimension residents, so we're not letting the world know that we've got another visitor." "So, I'm to lay low tomorrow?"

"Yep, no squeals, no finger pointing, just act like you've been here before," were her words as I opened the door to room 1014.

An attractive lady attendant standing watch

outside my room greeted me.

Alice said, "This is Lucy, she is pretty hardcore and armed with ring devices, so I'd mind her and stay inside. You'll have everything you need inside; bathroom items, a very nice shower and a sauna room. Even a bit of bubbly or alcohol as you call it in your world. Just be ready in the morning, it'll be a long day and be prepared to travel back to your dimension."

# The Tour                    4

I awoke well rested wondering if this dimension's oxygen levels were higher than where I came from. I showered and dressed with clothing provided from the dimension. I felt ready for the day. They provided a short sleeve multi-colored striped shirt and pants to match.

Everything was tailored to fit, which provoked a question in my mind, how did they know my measurements? There was a knock on the door and in walked Alice with her flying monkey in tow, now relieved of its leash and hovering just behind her.

"I think Little Lady is more excited than you about this day," she said. "Has Little Lady said anything today?" I asked

"Only a little, mostly in her language, which I have not been able to figure out. I managed to understand that she's hungry. Come, let's have breakfast with Drumbolt." We walked down the hallway together as Little Lady veered off and began hovering above my head.

"I think she is more comfortable this morning. Stop for a second and raise your arm and see if she will land on it." I did as Alice asked and sure enough Little Lady lit upon my upper arm. Alice, reached over and fed Little Lady a nut for a reward. "I'm training her," she remarked. "I think she's more intelligent than we think. She has obvious language skills, more than just repeating things like she has heard parrots do."

"Not a parrot," Little Lady remarked. We both reacted with a mild look of surprise

"Way more intelligent, than I thought," replied Alice. "Maybe I have found a new friend."

"Yes, friend," the words came from Little Lady's mouth, and surprised us. "Yeah, friend, Little Lady," said Alice

Little Lady moved up a little on my shoulder, wrapped her tail around my neck and rested her head against my neck as we continued down the hallway.

In the monitoring room, we found Drumbolt stretched out on the lounger. He had a huge platter of food laid out in front of him. Seated around him were Adam, Lily, Gurgle and Yaeger. We announced our entry with a hearty, "Good morning."

When he saw Little Lady resting on my shoulders, Drumbolt asked Alice, "It seems your little friend changed sides."

"No, not at all Drumbolt, she's finally getting used to everyone." With that, Little Lady became airborne, flapping merrily, swooping up and down around the perimeter of the large room.

"I think she enjoys the exercise," observed Gurgle. Little Lady circled and hovered above Drumbolt.

"She wants to say hello Drumbolt," observed Alice.

"Hello," said Little Lady.

The concept that a flying monkey could talk took everyone some time to get used to. "Just how much does she talk, Alice?" inquired Drumbolt.

"Pretty much just a few words at a time. I believe she's learning our language. She mostly talks in her own language."

Immediately Little Lady started talking in her own language, as if to the entire group. It seemed she was showing off to everyone how proud she was of her own language. She found a tiny empty space on the lounger next to Drumbolt to land. She looked at the platter of food and back at the giant man. Drumbolt reached for the platter, grabbed a sweet fruit and offered it to Little Lady.

She responded, "Thank You."

"You're welcome," he replied. "This is really amazing Alice. I think I need to thank Adam for bringing her back with him."

"I didn't bring her back with me," Adam offered.

"Adam's flesh doesn't taste good," Little Lady replied.

The room burst into laughter. Feeling relaxed, they all turned their attention to the array of food. As usual, Drumbolt devoured food like no other. More platters were ordered.

In between mouthfuls of food, Drumbolt monitored the returns and departures of the day's dimension travelers.

"Busy day," he noted aloud. "Three have left, and two have now returned. Six more are scheduled to check in. Our cleaning section is going to be busy today. Slither is due to arrive later this afternoon. That should be fun," he said, thrusting a finger skyward to emphasize his point.

Gurgle spoke up brandishing an ear to ear grim. "Yeah, real fun. You are all in for an adventure."

Lily spoke up, "I don't care much for Slither."

"But you're not going along Lily, so Slither is not going to be an issue for you," replied Gurgle, rather bluntly. He paused for a moment and then announced, "Lily's not happy I'm going back to Dimension 37. She thinks the little ladies on 37 will be too enticing and I'll be back to my old ways"

Lily frowned in reaction to Gurgle's comment.

Little Lady looked toward Gurgle, pointed a finger in his direction, and commenced to talking once again, "Not type, too hairy."

The room exploded again in laughter. Gurgle was taken by surprise and responded, "Not you Little Lady, I am talking about the other little ladies in your dimension."

"Still too hairy." The room once again erupted.

Lily seemed a bit more relaxed after the reaction to Little Lady's surprising speech and added, "You don't know what you're missing Little Lady. All that hair, the attitude, oh there are so many, many things Gurgle offers," as she looked off into the distance.

"Lily, we're eating, stop, that's enough, no more please," interrupted Alice as another burst of laughter erupted again.

Adam was clearly in the mood to tease Alice, "Alice if you haven't tried it," pointing to Gurgle, "Maybe you're missing something. I'm sure the other little gentlemen in 37 will be more than happy to assist."

Alice responded, "I don't intend to go there."

After everyone finished their food, Little Lady made a final swing around the room, stopping to help finish what remained of the delicacies on their platters. She stopped to sample vegetables, some meats, cheeses and fruits. After she had her fill, she hopped up on Alice's lap and smiled. She was happy.

"Well, would you like to explore our world,

"Patrick? Are you ready?" asked Alice

"Yes!" I emphatically replied.

Alice attached a leash and collar around Little Lady. "Little Lady, I know you're not going to be happy about this; what you see may be a little overwhelming initially. I apologize in advance, but you're going to be the center of attention as we emerge outside. Know that our world is quite different than yours."

Little Lady, nodded, and appeared to understand.

The group left the monitoring room, leaving behind a very busy Drumbolt who was logging in yet another returnee.

"See you later Drumbolt," Alice hollered out as she went through the door. Drumbolt was engrossed in his work and didn't bother to look up. He simply waved a hand in her direction, without raising his head to see her depart.

They passed through a short hallway, an elevator, then another hallway before reaching a door to the outside. A crowd was gathered along the railing that extended 40 yards from the door.

Various robots could be seen moving about, attending to their duties as they were programmed. "Look at all those robots," I exclaimed, pointing in their direction.

"Yeah Patrick, so much for the idea of you keeping a low profile, huh?" replied Alice. "Our world is full of robots who had to assume duties the people no longer with us used to do. The plague, remember? We turned to Robotronics. There was no other way to sustain food production, keep our energy networks up, and provide essential services for our people. They are so efficient, we now use robots to do almost all the labor in our dimension. Few people work these days. It's optional, however. Everyone is guaranteed an income to assure a minimum quality lifestyle. If you are driven to achieve more, to have a higher standard of living, you may of course build your own business and provide services. Many, who don't have to work, nevertheless choose to, because it makes the Now's go faster. And yes, they receive income for their endeavors. They have nicer houses, better transportation, and so forth."

"Is dimension travel considered work to the people

in your dimension," I asked.

"Yep," replied Gurgle, "I do it for the thrill, the need to take chances, not the money"

"And the rest of you?" I inquired.

There was universal agreement. "Dimension travel is not for the faint of heart," replied Lily. "Dimension travelers die, get lost in other dimensions, are injured, and some disappear forever. But the thrill is worth it. Learning about other dimensions, seeing other life forms, investigating bio-hazard issues, it's a big 'wow.' I don't know anyone who does it just for the monetary reimbursement or better lifestyle."

"Most of us keep working until we're unable to do so," added Adam.

Yaeger added, "None of us lead normal lives, we are away for most of the time in other dimensions, having our adventures. Most of us choose to live in the travel facility rather than at home. We all have tons of money stashed away but rarely spend it. The few who have partners and live in the community have ensured their partners are well cared for and live elegant lives, which helps to make up for our absences. Regretfully, the lifestyle of dimension travelers usually results in a fractured home life. Partners and offspring are often strangers. Our partners sometimes are called upon to help nurse us through physical or mental injuries incurred during dimension travel. Some of us retire early because of these issues. We are required to take off one year out of every 4 years traveling, just to restore our mental health. Except of course for Alice. Drumbolt allows her to travel forever."

Alice responded, "I tried to take time off, but that lasted only a few Now's. I snuck back into the system and found myself living in the lizard dimension for an extended time before returning back here. The committee wasn't happy that I chose dimension travel for my time off, but I stood my ground."

"I remember, that was after our breakup," Adam volunteered.

"I needed closure and time away." stated Alice. "Look, are we going to stand here all day, reminiscing about passed history and what happened many Now's ago, or are we going out there?"

She rushed by the group, with Little Lady in tow on her leash. As she opened the door, applause greeted her. "The monkey! Show us the monkey." Oohs and awes emerged from the assembled crowd. Little Lady was somewhat taken aback and took shelter behind Alice's legs.

"They want to see you Little Lady. You're a big deal, they're excited."

"Not a monkey," stated Little Lady.

"Yeah, I know," replied Alice, "You're something else, but that's how you appear to them."

The group of dimension travelers caught up to Alice and the others. Sensing strength in numbers, Little Lady emerged from behind Alice's legs. Suddenly a huge colorful butterfly swooped down from above. It seemed as big as a small car and sported luminescent blue, yellow, and red colors. It drifted around in ever expanding circles above us, barely flapping its wings to stay aloft.

I let out a yelp and pointed up at it. Little Lady took to flight herself, hovering over Alice's head in a defensive manner and hissing upwards toward it. The crowd went wild and left Little Lady mightily confused as she hung close to Alice.

"It's OK; it's just a butterfly Little Lady. It's harmless. All it wants is a field of huge flowers. It likely was attracted to all the people out here wearing colorful clothing and it probably thought they were a field of flowers." The butterfly, having no appetite for people drifted off into the horizon.

Alice turned towards me, "You are really going to blow your cover Patrick. Stop over reacting. You are going to see a lot of strange stuff today. Act like you live here," she demanded.

"OK," I meekly replied. The skies in this place were filled with small billowy white clouds pushed along by a slight breeze. It was warm, maybe eighty or so degrees. There was little humidity. It would be described as a perfect day by dwellers in my home dimension.

Yaeger took the lead and walked toward the crowds. A ring of protective robots surrounded the party as they walked into the crowd.

"Let's take Patrick to the flower forest first, then he can see the lizards, and after that we'll take a tour of the city and have a late lunch. We won't have time for much more than that. He's scheduled to leave in a few Now's."

The trip to the flower forest was interesting. We were expressed to the site by transportation vehicles, something akin to a people mover. I couldn't discern what propulsion system they used. There were people on the tram but I refrained from talking to them, so I was trying to keep a low profile. As we traveled to the flower forest I noted a variety of butterflies gliding through the air. Everything was quite peaceful. Little Lady was of course the center of attention for all.

"May I pet him?" a young boy asked.

Alice said, "Its a she, her name is Little Lady,"

She asked Little Lady, "May the boy pet you on the head?"

Little Lady leaned over from her comfortable perch on Alice's lap and extended her head toward the boy. The boy exclaimed with glee, "Oh, so cool. You're beautiful."

Little Lady beamed and reacted with a broad smile.

Gurgle, who stood just a little taller than the boy, stood up and walked over to the gathering of interested observers starting to form around Alice and Little Lady. "Not too much excitement folks, Little Lady is new to our world and she could react negatively to too much attention."

Little Lady extended her wings and hovered above Gurgle. She descended onto his shoulders and wrapped her tail around his neck and rested her head upon his. Gurgle lifted his arm and scratched her head. "She's really nice, but she has not had much time getting used to our world, so please stay calm around her."

Little Lady once more took off into the air then landed on the floor near the gathering and walked among the people. She extended her hand to many and enjoyed being the center of attention.

"Nice," she said. Hearing a monkey talk caused many to step back with a reaction of shock and bewilderment.

"Yes, she talks some," said Alice. "Not a lot, she's still learning our language."

Little Lady then spoke up in her own language. "I have no clue what she's saying," Alice volunteered. "We're still trying to understand her language."

There was more conversation as the tram arrived at our stop: the flower forest. We disembarked from the people mover and stepped out onto an observation deck. Before us stood a huge forest of plants and colorful flowers stretching beyond the horizon. The plants were large, the flowers immense in size. Butterflies were gliding above the forest continuously, drifting from one flower to the next, then flittering aloft and spiraling overhead in search of new sources of nectar.

"They lay their eggs at the other end of the forest, far away from people," advised Yaeger. "Their caterpillars are huge and devour all they can. We manage the population by culling the caterpillars to assure they don't exceed their food supply. We ourselves harvest butterflies for food, which I understand Patrick here, doesn't care for."

"Who manages the butterfly populations?"

I inquired.

Adam spoke up, "Mostly robots and drones. It's very busy at the other end and designed so all we see are the beautiful side of the butterflies and flower forest. This is all an illusion to hide the slaughter and harvesting for food that goes on at the other end."

"Sounds like you don't approve, Adam."

"I don't. The butterflies and flowers create a false environmental existence. They should never have been imported to our dimension."

"Adam's a purist," remarked Alice.

"Indeed, I am," he replied. "And I don't relish the prospect that herds of flying monkeys will soon be omnipresent in our world."

"I think some more Little Ladies would be wonderful," replied Lily. "Not a lot, maybe 15 or 20."

"Pay no attention to Adam," admonished Alice to Little Lady.

"Not listening," replied Little Lady, as Alice reached down and unleashed her, inviting her to explore her new world. She took flight, hovering over one nearby beautifully large blue flower, sniffing the fragrance. "Nice," Little Lady remarked.

A large blue and gold butterfly appeared overhead. Little Lady flew up to meet it and maintained a slow flapping pace to keep her wings at a measured distance from the huge creature. She circled around the butterfly inspecting it as she flew. The butterfly seemed to ignore Little Lady as if she likely considered her just another strange looking butterfly like herself. Little Lady watched as it continued to periodically swoop down and extract nectar from the flowers. Little Lady and the butterfly were soon flying together hundreds of yards away. Little Lady happily danced in the air with joy, flying in tandem with her new-found friend.

Yaeger, expressing a sense of concern said, "Alice, I think your monkey is going over the hill. It may be difficult to get her back before your departure tomorrow for Dimension 37."

Alice replied, "She'll be back, she needs her space."

A few moments passed; still no Little Lady. Joy now

changed to concern for many in the group, but not for Alice. After a while, a small airborne figure appeared in the distance, hundreds of yards away. It was bumping into the tops of the flower forest. It seemed to have difficulty maintaining altitude. As the figure flew closer, it became clear that it was Little Lady. She was covered in blue pollen, restricting her ability to fly. She appeared exhausted, trying to maintain altitude.

Alice called out to her, "Come on Little Lady, you can do it."

Little Lady crashed again into the flower tops, then bounced back up into the air, grabbing at the pollen with her hands and managing to scrap some of it off before she eventually landed at the group's feet. Exhausted, she was huffing, puffing, and drenched in sweat from the ordeal. "Stuff attached to me," she said, noting the obvious.

Everyone smiled, including Little Lady. Alice helped clean her off, with the assistance of an attendant standing nearby, who provided clean towels with some sort of fluid that worked well cleansing the pollen off Little Lady. "No flowers," Little Lady said.

The group returned to the tram for their trip to see the lizards, which were next on their itinerary. The trip took several Now's, finally arriving in a barren area within the dimension. It was filled with swamps and green vegetation. There were dinosaurs visible. Once again Little Lady was the center of attention on the tram as passengers swarmed around her asking questions and trying to pet her. Their interest continued as they arrived at the lizard platform.

Adam, up to now only talked once on the trip to the lizards, and he was less than pleased. "We should have never taken her along; she's nothing but trouble."

Lily replied, "Adam, the people are curious and there's been no trouble. Maybe you don't like the competition for attention?"

Gurgle chimed in, "Adam, sometimes you are a wet dishrag! Everyone's having fun on this little excursion except you. And why? Because the thing that attacked you in the other dimension is now warmly accepted by other members of the team? Maybe is it just the Alice thing."

"Thank you Gurgle," replied Alice.

Adam chose not to reply, preferring to leave the group and walk toward a nearby building. "He's going off to sulk," stated Gurgle.

"Does he really have to go to Dimension 37?" wondered Lily, as the group let him toward the building.

"Unfortunately, yes," replied Alice. "He's the last one to return from 37 and knows more about their dungeons, hiding locations and various people there at this time. We'd be walking into the unknown without him. And yes, Gurgle, I know you've been there before, but it's been some Now's since your last visit and things have very likely changed."

"That is true," replied Gurgle.

Lily and Alice fell behind the pace and were separated from the main group. Lily asked, "How could you have had a relationship with Adam? He's so cold, distant and angry"

"He had some really bad dimension travel experiences. There was a stretch of three consecutive trips when others traveling with him failed to return. Many met horrible ends. He himself was injured on two of his trips. He became sullen, ceasing to care or able to get close to others. We argued all the time. He pushed me away. I was scheduled to take a year off from dimension travel and the thought of remaining around him in his state of mind was unfathomable. So, I took off to the lizard world."

"Wow, I always wondered what you were doing there and why you disobeyed command orders."

"I needed to clear my head. When I got back he was gone. He moved to another residence. Yesterday was the first time we have seen each other in many Now's. Since then I have heard he has regularly taken off on solo dimension travel trips, the most dangerous kind. Sometimes he came back injured. I fear he's on a suicide mission."

"And you're taking him along to 37?" asked Lily

"I have no choice. Look Lily, I know you really want to go along with Gurgle on this mission, but that's not going to happen!"

"I'm dealing with it," she replied.

They caught up with the rest of the group in the building and found them seated waiting for snacks. Adam stood up from the meal to make a statement. "I'm sorry, but I'm tired of us importing different kinds of things into our universe. I am also afraid we are heading into danger with a creature whose loyalties are questionable. We are being set up. The way this is currently organized, it is a suicide mission; many of you may not come back."

Alice replied, "Adam you seem to always be on suicide missions. Your recent trip to Dimension 38 which no one has ever come back from is a perfect example. This one presents risks, but no different than others you have been on."

"Yes, this one is different Alice, because you are involved in this dangerous trip. If we lose you on this mission, I'll have Drumbolt to deal with. You are his favorite and the rules have always been different for you."

"I resent that Adam," said Alice.

Yaeger entered the argument, "I'm going have to side with Adam on one fact. The rules are indeed different for you, Alice. You're admired for your courage, judgment and intelligence. And quite frankly for your ability to survive for quite a few Now's in the lizard dimension without getting eaten or taken hostage by the primitive beings in the lizard dimension."

"I don't want to be blamed if any of you don't come back," replied Adam.

"So, your concern is more about Drumbolt's reaction than our survival," noted Gurgle sarcastically, rubbing his beard and pointing to Adam. "Did I get that right?"

"I'm just tired of caring. When I care about people bad things happen. It's easier to focus on the task and not the people," said Adam sitting down to end the conversation and return to his food. A quiet moment overtook the group as they all finished their meals before them.

"Whew, now that was intense," I noted. Adam remained silent but reacted with a stony glare. Sarcastically, Lily announced "Well, this has been the best snack time ever. Let's go look at the lizards."

As the group exited the building they were again set

upon by throngs of people, eager to meet Little Lady. Recognizing their keen interest, Little Lady waded into the crowd and allowed them to pet and touch her.

At one point she declared, "fly," and took off hovering above the crowd just beyond their reach. The group followed the path into the lizard enclosure and listened as Yaeger began to tell the lizard history as they all walked among smaller lizards that were busy eating plant life nearby.

"Our dimension leaders decided once discovered we should have dinosaurs in our dimension. We harvested eggs from different variations of their species during our first few trips to their dimension. The meat eaters were found to be unsuitable for a very good reason: they were uncontrollable. Sometimes they killed plant eating dinosaurs just for sport. Eventually they turned on us and in one evening took to marauding through a nearby town, killing thousands of people. We basically had a war of us versus the dinosaurs. Fortunately, we won, or we could have gone extinct. We eliminated each meat eater variety and the larger plant eaters. Then, we culled the lizards down to five small plant eating species, the largest being the horned dinosaur or lizard you see over there."

"We call it a Triceratops in our dimension," I volunteered.

"You have them?" questioned Lily.

"Just fossil remains. They've been extinct for millions of years where I come from." I replied.

Everyone allowed my reference to time to slip by without correcting me. They probably thought since I wasn't going to be there much longer, there was no point going through the whole "time or Now's" tutorial.

The group meandered through the lizard area for most of the afternoon, stopping occasionally to pet or touch a lizard. Little Lady maintained a safe position on Alice's shoulders throughout the excursion which I took to suggest she was experiencing some discomfort being around these creatures. By the end of the tour, Little Lady fell asleep on Alice's shoulders, exhausted by her excursion into the depths of the flower forest. Adam remained distant not offering any opinions.

It was time to get back into the town. An express tram greeted us at the station, shortening the length of the trip back into town. Once we arrived we found the hustle and bustle of an active city. The difference seemed to be that most of the hustle and bustle was robot and drone generated. I saw only a few people in the streets. "Why so few people?" I asked.

Yaeger explained, "Most don't work, they shop on monitors and come into town for entertainment or dining. Little Lady was a big deal today, so more than usual made the trek into town just to see her. She's the new flavor of the month."

We entered a restaurant where the owner was on duty and thrilled to serve the day's celebrity. He was a large man with a mustache who obviously enjoys the food he prepares. "The monkey's OK?" questioned Gurgle. "

Yes of course," he replied.

"Are you serving Gurgle, or do we have to leave him outside?" questioned Adam in a humorous way.

The restaurant owner laughed at Adam's comment. "Oh, look Adam speaks!" observed Lily.

"And he's funny for a change," noted Alice.

The rest of our dinner was relaxing with abundant conversion and no tension. A well-rested Little Lady had her own highchair brought to the table and Alice saw that she got whatever she wanted. The restaurant owner even had his picture taken with Little Lady sitting on his shoulder.

I was preparing for my return home. We walked leisurely through the nearly deserted town, with only a small variety of robots racing here and there. I grew a little misty eyed on the walk back to the dimension travel facility. I wanted to stay longer and spend more time with these people. We entered the monitoring room and where we were greeted by Drumbolt, still reclining upon the lounger.

"Well, how was dinner? Wish I could have joined."

"There would have been no food if you had," replied Alice. "Probably so," he agreed. "Well Patrick, what do you think of our dimension?"

"I only wish I could stay longer," I replied.

"That won't be possible," noted Drumbolt. "We have you scheduled to depart very shortly. We, or should I say, they have a mission and that must move forward. I am sorry, I kind of enjoyed your visit"

"Can I come back?" I inquired.

"No, we didn't enjoy you that much," replied Drumbolt as the room burst out in laughter. "You will be accompanied back to your own dimension."

# Slither                5

I turned around to make eye contact at Alice expecting confirmation from her that she would be taking me back. Instead, she pointed to a darkened corner of the room where a low hanging grey cloud seemed to hang. A tall man emerged out of the cloud. It was the homeless man who took my car when I was in my own dimension. I saw he wore similar clothing to what he was w e a r i n g when we first met, a tattered shirt with patches, torn and frayed pants. He was still unshaven, he even had a pack of cigarettes from my world in his shirt pocket, although he wasn't smoking. He was tall and lanky, I imagined that if he held his arms straight out I could mistake him for a scarecrow.

"My name is Slither," he announced walking toward me to shake hands. He firmly grasped my wrist with his other hand. My hand went numb and felt useless. I recoiled from his grasp.

"Slither you are showing off again!" noted Gurgle.

"It's his way of demanding respect from you, Patrick. Among his tools is body manipulation. He can touch certain nerves and limit motion throughout your body. He can even render you unconscious. Quite a handy skill for survival."

"I've got other tricks." He announced

"And that's why I don't like you Slither," Lily added boldly.

"I'm not everyone's cup of tea, I think is the expression you use in your dimension. Correct Patrick?"

"Yes," I replied. Feelings were returning to my hand, I could feel it tingle. It seemed to be waking up from whatever he had done to it.

Slither turned to Alice, "Alice I have been briefed by Drumbolt. Gurgle, Adam and I will accompany you to Dimension 37 and look for missing members from our dimension. You will lead. And this must be the little flying monkey, Drumbolt told me about," reaching down to Alice's side to scratch Little Lady's head. "I understand you talk Little Lady?"

Little Lady said, "Yes." She was surprisingly at ease with Slither.

"So, we have queens, witches, flying monkeys, guards, soldiers, little people, and talking animals. Did I miss anything? I can't wait to meet your offspring Gurgle," he said in a comical aside.

Gurgle stammered as Lily turned and glared at him. "I'm not sure." He turned to assure Lily, "That was before us."

Lily sighed, "That type of comment is another reason why I don't care for you Slither," she replied. "You enjoy manipulating and toying with people. You like to play psychological games."

Gurgle glanced in Drumbolt's direction, "Sometimes you share too much Drumbolt."

I stammered, "Alice, you were in on everything. You knew Slither was waiting for us that late afternoon coming down off the elevated road. It was all by design?"

"Yes, at that point we had to get you out of there."

"And you placed yourself in danger," I exclaimed to Slither. "Did they catch up with you?"

"Oh yeah," Slither replied. "But that was fun for me. I deliberately slowed to the side of the road after the turn and waited for them to find me. They had no idea what to do when a tall dark man stepped out of your car. The black cloud cover that suddenly enveloped them was also unexpected. I never had to fire a shot. They just collapsed to the ground, vomited a lot, and then passed out. That black cloud stuff is nasty, but effective. I turned them over to one of our groups living in your dimension. The next morning, they woke up naked in the middle of a corn field about 1000 miles away. From the reports I got, a cop pulled up shortly after they woke up and they had a lot of explaining to do to the authorities. We also sprinkled some prescription pills around nearby, and they ended up arrested for possession."

Too funny, I wished I could have been there," I said. "And my car?"

"Good as new. The back window is repaired, bullet holes are patched, and it has a nice new paint job. One thing you don't know is ... shall I tell him Drumbolt?"

"Proceed," answered Drumbolt.

"We have many of our people in your dimension. When the plague struck us, some fled to your dimension to save themselves. It was in the early 1900's using your reference to time. They settled, raised families and merged into your population. Some of their offspring, because of superior intelligence and knowledge, became successful business leaders, scientists, and doctors. They are 'influencers' as you call them. Although some also became auto body repair people too." He snickered, "That is the reason why you will find your car just like brand new."

"I myself am of mixed dimensional heritage. My mother settled with a man from your dimension with dark complexion. I was raised in your dimension, but traveled frequently to home, as I call it, which I mean to say is this dimension. When I was a young man I decided to remain here and become a dimension traveler. My skills which Lily just mentioned have been acquired from my travels to other dimensions. Believe me, there are some strange dimensions out there. Everything you can imagine and more. My skills are very useful and have saved my life and the lives of many others on more than one occasion throughout the many Now's since my travels began. Yes, I like showing them off and sometimes I toy with people. It is what I do, no apologies from me. I am who I am. People can accept me or not, that is their choice."

"A no-shit attitude" interrupted Gurgle.

"Correct!" said Slither as he continued his discussion with me. "I myself, when returning to your dimension, the dimension of my birth, posed as a simple homeless man. It's a great cover. I'm middle aged and my family, who remained secretive and secluded because of my mother's origin, no longer walk in that dimension space. They have passed on to whatever there is beyond. I have relatives in your dimension, but I don't know them. I am in your dimension frequently, observing and interacting with your population. My main role today is simply relaying communications between our dimensions and taking care of those from our dimension who may encounter trouble in yours." He paused for a moment to allow me to absorb this unique description of his origins and his nature.

"So, we are not alone?" I finally asked after a few minutes of reflection.

"No Patrick, you are not alone!" Slither replied. "I travel to other dimensions and am called upon for missions such as this one. I bring everyone back, usually in one piece, unlike some," pointing to Adam. Adam did not respond. "By the way Patrick, here's your money back," as he threw a wad of money in my direction. "Thank you for trying to make a homeless guy's life easier, even if you did expose him to significant danger."

I conceded a short laugh.

"I am sorry Patrick, but it's time to say goodbye," interrupted Drumbolt.

Lily, Yaeger, Gurgle, and Adam all wished me well. Alice came over to hug me. Even Little Lady flew over, landed on my shoulders and wrapped her tail around my neck for a monkey hug. Surprisingly, even Drumbolt got up from the lounger and waddled over to shake my hand.

"Enjoy the trip back." he commented.

Slither pointed to the cleansing tube and ordered me to get naked. After entering the tube, I once again felt the cleansing cycle in the tube. I exited the process to find attendants who handed me new clothing very similar to those from my own dimension. Slither followed me through another tube and was given an identical outfit to the one he wore on the other side.

"I always wear the same thing anymore," he noted.

I received my own visualization belt and immediately placed it around my waist.

"Remember you're not keeping it," the attendant admonished me.

I waved goodbye to Drumbolt and received many warm goodbyes from the monitor room staff. On Slither's instructions I opened the case on the visualization belt and a dark misty tunnel appeared in front of me. Slither followed me straight into the mist. Our trip through the tunnel was uneventful, and soon we arrived on the cement platform where I first met Alice. It was late evening, almost dark.

"Your vehicle is over there. Here's your keys," as Slither tossed them in my direction. "By the way I wouldn't mention anything about where you've been. Nobody will believe you, and if you do anyway, then the suits will soon come a calling. Chances are I won't be around to save your ass this time. Take care, Patrick. Have a good life."

He took the belt from my hand, turned and disappeared into the mist.

I stood next to my car for about an hour looking up into the heavens and occasionally looking over to where the mist had been. I needed the time to process everything I experienced. Tears welled up into my eyes realizing I would never see Alice and the gang again. And I never have. If you thought this is my story, you are wrong. It's Alice's story. I only wanted to introduce you to the woman I met one afternoon, a few Now's ago. From here on out you will deal in Now's, parallel universes and the Many Interacting Worlds with Alice.

# Many Interacting Worlds 6

Slither returned immediately to his home universe, passing through the standard cleaning protocols before entering the control room. As he emerged, he announced "short and sweet," to Drumbolt, who as usual, was sitting by himself among the monitors. "Did you remember to bring Patrick's belt back?" asked Drumbolt.

"Yep, I left it with the attendants in the other room." He took a seat where he could reach the plates of food always within reaching distance of Drumbolt and started snacking. "Dimension travel always makes me hungry,"

Drumbolt turned his attention back to his reports and continued observing the monitors.

After a couple of minutes Slither reclined in his chair and looked toward Drumbolt. "Well old friend, I wonder how many times we have sat down together like this to catch up on life?"

"Not nearly enough, Slither."

"Life goes by quickly. There are too many Now's," Slither said reflectively as he watched Drumbolt nod in agreement.

"So, you're determined to send Alice on this mission?" Again, Drumbolt nodded affirmatively. "And you are depending on me to keep her safe."

Drumbolt sighed, "Yes, pretty much that's right." "She's like a daughter to you."

Drumbolt nodded in agreement. "I worry about Adam and her." Taking a draw from his pipe he continued, "Too much emotion and anger between them could interfere with their mission. They have gone through a lot. Adam's a good man, but he's had many unfortunate encounters in dimension travel. The losses are not his fault, but there's a bad karma that follows him."

"Bad karma can attach itself to people," replied Slither. "Sometimes it's power is greater than my own magic, or whatever my skills are called. I'll try to keep her safe, but I can't guarantee anything, none of us know how many Now's we have left."

"I want to live long enough" taking yet another puff on the pipe, "to see the next Alice."

Slither replied, "Well, sending her on this mission may threaten your hopes my friend."

"I know," replied Drumbolt, looking wistfully toward the ceiling. "I would lead this mission myself, but I am too old and fat."

"Fate has left you no other choice, Drumbolt. There is no one among the current dimension travelers with her survival skills. Not even me. She's a chosen one. She survives when many others don't and always without injury. Everyone gets injured dimension traveling except her, well perhaps and myself. She can walk through a field of carnivores in the lizard universe and they never touch her. She has lived with impunity for many Now's in the lizard universe. Me, I'm scared of that universe. I hate lizards!"

Drumbolt laughed, "You scared?"

Slither continued, "Now don't go blabbing that admission around. I depend on everyone being in awe of me. My mojo is important. It causes others to follow me without question. People around me believe they can do anything and they count on me to rescue them if they encounter danger. My missions are successful because the people with me believe they will succeed. I'm good, but sometimes I feel like I'm on borrowed time keeping others safe. It's going to go bad sometime."

"But not this time, OK?" s u g g e s t e d Drumbolt.

The monitor relief for Drumbolt, named Watson, walked through the door, and noted Slither was reclining in the chair.

"Slither," Watson said dryly. "Oh joy. I hope you are not sticking around to entertain me too."

"Everyone loves you, Slither." noted Drumbolt. "How do you maintain such popularity in our universe?"

"I'm just a nice guy," joked Slither, pulling a low-grade explosive cloud packet out of his pocket and whipping his arm in a manner as if he were threatening to throw it in Watson's direction.

Watson ducked and covered, holding out an arm with his hand outstretched toward Slither. "Please don't Slither." Watson pleaded from a crouched position.

"That would be a waste of a good bag. Stand up and get over here and relieve my friend. Drumbolt. We're going out for some bubbly."

Slither and Drumbolt headed out the door together for an evening of drinking on the town. The old friends shared many dimension travel memories. Drumbolt was his mentor in younger days. Their friendship ran deep.

Morning came quickly. Slither woke up stretched out on a bar table. As he awoke, he wiped his lips, rubbed his eyes and scratched his groin. He was hung-over. Searching around the room he located a snoring Drumbolt lying on the floor partially leaning against the wall. He walked over to Drumbolt bent down and nudged his head. A barely conscious Drumbolt swatted his hand away and turned away to allow his rotund body the opportunity to fully recline on the floor.

"Drumboooolt, oh Drumboooolt," called out Slither. "Morning is here, and we've got work to do."

Drumbolt, groaned, placed an arm over his head and groggily replied, "Morning is not at all here. Go away."

"It's time big guy," replied the now laughing

Slither.

The bar had been closed for some time. The pair were well-known and when the bar owner left he locked up the place, leaving the two inside with a note asking them to use the attached key to secure the place when they leave.

A groggy Drumbolt was not easy to get on to his feet. Slither tried unsuccessful two times, until Drumbolt finally became alert enough to help balance his large body and allow him to find his feet. They locked up the bar, put the key in the planter as requested in the note and walked with arms around each other's shoulders the two long blocks until they reached the gates of the dimension travel building. It was not an easy or an enjoyable walk. Their arrival coincided with the arrival of Yaeger and Georges, the short bulbous body mathematician.

Yaeger stood by the gate watching the two figures weaving and stumbling down the road to the building. It seemed to take them many Now's to reach the gate, but really, their two-block journey was completed relatively quickly. It was just highlighted with treacherous steps that threatened to spill Slither and Drumbolt upon the pavement numerous times.

While they were about 50 yards away from the gate, Yaeger yelled out to them, "I see you two have arrived fresh and ready for a hard day's work." Slither raised his hand to wave but had to bring it down quickly to keep Drumbolt from going splat on the pavement. The scene provoked a hearty laugh from Georges.

Yaeger commented, "The least you could have done was let me know you were going for some bubbly. I would have enjoyed a night's entertainment."

"Next time," called out Slither. "And you too Georges, next time, we promise."

Georges was unlikely to ever go because unlike many of the dimension travelers he had a family, and a partner who didn't approve of evening entertainments like Slither enjoyed.

Lily and Gurgle were next to arrive just in time to see Drumbolt stumble into the gate. He was able to remain erect only because he grabbed a railing at the last moment. Gurgle exclaimed, "Hey, how about me, I am supposed to get invited on the bubbly excursions too."

Lily rolled her eyes, as Slither replied, "Yes, we could have ended up playing throw the dwarf if you had been along, Gurgle."

"Another mark against you Slither," Lily called out.

Slither laughed. "Lily, face it, you really like me. You do. You protest far too much."

Gurgle noted dryly, "No Slither, truth be told, she really doesn't like you."

Slither was also still intoxicated, and in a swirl of his smoke grabbed Lily and hoisted her into the air and whirled her around. "Weeee," he cried out. Gurgle and the others laughed at Lily's predicament.

"Put me down," she cried out, arms and legs flailing around until a knee struck soft tissue belonging to Slither. "Ouch!" he exclaimed, receiving Lily's well-aimed thrust to his groin.

He let Lilly slide back to the ground to land on her feet. Slither received a push as she reached the ground propelling him into Drumbolt, who was still hanging precariously to the railing. Drumbolt and Slither both tumbled to the ground in a pile. A still groggy Drumbolt, exclaimed, "Lily, there was no call for you to do that."

Georges, Yaeger and Gurgle walked over to help Drumbolt managing to hoist him to his feet. Once there he dusted himself off. Slither remained on the ground nursing the pain to his groin. "Damn Lily, why did you have to do that to me? Maybe you should come along to 37."

"She's the reserve team," stated Drumbolt. "She, Yaeger and one other will go in if the first team is gone too long."

The announcement brought a smile to Lily's lips. She forgot their animosity and walked over to Slither and offered him a hand up. "No Lily, we've interacted too much already." He replied and gathered himself into a slightly bent, but upright position. Lily, having gotten the best of Slither, triumphantly led the group into the building.

The group entered a large planning room where Alice, Little Lady and Adam were waiting along with mathematicians, a few soft weapons experts, their attendants and several robots. Winebron, whose answer to every situation was a well-armed command team was not invited. Adam exclaimed upon observing Drumbolt and Slither entering into the room, "What in the universe did you guys run into? Especially you Slither. You look like a mess."

Gurgle gleefully responded, "Lily took him down at the gate."

"I thought Slither was on the team to protect us, and now Lily takes him down. Has he lost it or what Drumbolt?" replied Adam.

Drumbolt waved him off, not wanting to invest time in thinking up a snappy reply while still in his state of partial inebriation. Slither walked by Adam and took a seat and while passing Adam, he took the opportunity to reach out and give him a pinch near his spinal column. Adam crumpled on to the floor, having lost all feeling from the waist down.

"As you were saying Adam?" he asked.

"Slither!" Called out Alice, "You should have just let it go."

Drumbolt intervened, "No Alice, I think some proof

was needed that Slither is still Slither. Although I do admire the way Lily took him down. Slither got a bit too frisky and hoisted her up into the air. Lily appropriately countered with a very effective knee to his groin. "Never saw it coming," he said, while smiling with a broad grin.

Slither couldn't suppress his laugh and walked back over to help Adam into a chair. "It will go away shortly. It was a light manipulation. If it were full manipulation, you would not be going on the mission."

"And as for you, Lily, I may have met my equal." Lily beamed.

Little Lady, didn't quite understand everything going on so she took flight just after Slither dropped Adam. She stayed a safe distance away until Alice waved her to come back over to sit with her. "Let's concentrate on the mission." she admonished everyone. "No more horseplay, it confuses Little Lady." Little Lady returned to Alice's lap, gazing back and forth between Adam and Slither.

"I think she's looking forward to round two," commented Gurgle.

Georges began his presentation. "My team says Dimension 37 remains in the same position as it was for Adam. We have recalculated an entry directly into 37 instead of using a bypass route from Dimension 38. It should be an easy trip."

Gurgle spoke up, "It's an easy trip for sure, I've done it many times. I'm not sure how Adam ended up in Dimension 37 from Dimension 38. I usually ended up coming in in the mid-mark between the two communities of Wonderland and OZ. It's a wide-open field as I recall."

Adam confirmed that was the exact location he arrived at in Dimension 37, "That's the place."

Gurgle continued, "The only problem is we could have company when we arrive. It's a lot easier for a small single traveler than a large group. One person alone doesn't create attention, especially a little person."

Loco, one of the soft weapons experts spoke out next. "You'll have the soft weapon rings; the new ones are good for three or four discharges instead of two."

Alice spoke up next, "I could have used those in Dimension 2 when the suits chased us."

"Slither had one," he replied. "You should have stopped by and checked out the latest gear upgrades before your trip to Dimension 2."

"My fault then." she replied. "What else do you have Loco?"

"The standard issue bags, which you all have used before. And of course, you've got Slither's tricks, which he always keeps to himself. We do have a new electricity disabler, but apparently this universe doesn't use electricity. All they have are lanterns and torches..."

Gurgle interrupted, "No, OZ had electricity when I was there. Adam?"

"Yes, but only in the castle. Wonderland was only equipped with torches and lanterns."

Loco asked, "OK, do you want the electricity disabler?"

"It's not necessary," said Slither.

Adam agreed, "They have torches galore there. The electricity weapon is not helpful" "Well, we also have new

130

incendiary devices. They burn really hot and will ignite anything!"

"It sounds a little too lethal to me," replied Lily.

"Agreed," commented Drumbolt. "But I'd like it available for the backup team. What do you think Yaeger?"

"Maybe," replied Yaeger. "Look perhaps Loco should be a third team member for the backup team." He certainly knows the equipment."

"I'd like to go," replied Loco. "I've never been dimension traveling."

Loco was a young man who recently signed onto the weapons section. He was very intelligent, but an unworldly guy still trying to carve out a niche in some universe. He was a little intimidated by the talent and dimension travel celebrities assembled in the room. They were his heroes, and he didn't want to disappoint, yet he had an overabundance of testosterone which trumped his caution and reinforced his request to join the mission. He had potential.

"I'd just like to make sure that if a backup team is

needed to rescue our first team, we have all the top equipment. I don't want to lose anyone," stated Drumbolt. "Lily, Alice, Slither, Gurgle and Adam, do you have any objections to Loco joining the rescue team?" There were none.

However, Little Lady surprisingly spoke out, "Me?" pointing to herself.

Drumbolt raised his thick white-haired eyebrows for a moment, "You want in on this decision Little Lady?"Little Lady shook her head affirmatively and walked over to Loco, who stepped back a few steps as she approached him. He looked up at the others with a facial construct suggesting he wanted help. It was the first time he interacted with Little Lady.

Alice exclaimed, "Yes, let's allow her to make the decision!"

"It's a bit irregular if you ask me," replied Drumbolt.

Loco, stammered, "The, the monkey decides?" "I'm afraid so," said Gurgle. Little Lady sniffed around Loco's body, hovered near his face, then around to his back.

Loco turned his head to see what Little Lady was doing behind his back.

"A little nervous Loco?" called out Adam. "Get used to it. If you go with us, you'll see a lot of these creatures on 37, thousands in fact. See all these scrapes on my neck and head? That's where she chewed on me coming through the dimension portal."

"If you're trying to scare me Adam, you're succeeding," Loco replied. Little Lady having completed her inspection of Loco, returned to Alice's lap.

"Go," she said. And the decision was made.

"You are on the back up team," announced Drumbolt. The other weapons experts crowded around Loco offering him handshakes and pats on the back. After the short celebration it was back to planning.

Drumbolt offered a question to Adam, "What is your suggestion for the first objective on Dimension 37, since you've most recently been on 37? Damn, I miss my pipe. Can someone go get it from the monitor room?" No one offered, not even the attendants. "I guess that's a no then." He stated in resignation, looking down at the ground.

Adam, responded, "If we arrive at the field without being discovered, then we need to travel to the little people's village."

Lily humorously interrupted, "To see all of Gurgle's children, I guess." Laughter ensued.

Lily seemed to be no longer concerned about Gurgle's return visit to his old harem, or whatever one would call it.

"You're OK with it now, Lily?" Alice asked.

"I'll just take out his harem, when I get to 37." She replied.

A hush ensued among the assembled. There was a moment where everyone contemplated Lily's statement as an implied threat. Lily broke the silence with a smile, "Just kidding."

Slither commented, "If I were you Gurgle, I'd be a good boy on 37. Lily's quite deadly."

"You're not going to protect me on this one Slither?" Gurgle asked plaintively.

"Nope!" Slither said, "I don't have to bring

everyone back." There was a momentary look of surprise on every team member's face.

Drumbolt countered, "Slither, you must bring everyone back on this mission. What Lily does to Gurgle, after they return is her business." That brought laughter as everyone joined in the tension break in Drumbolt's reply.

Adam continued, "The little people hate the witch and her men who rule their side of the world. Their allies are whoever is against the witch and her men."

"That's what I found in my visits too," stated Gurgle. They don't care for the Queen or her men from the other side. Both have plundered their little community. Their village lay at the edge of OZ which has been claimed by both sides over many Now's."

"They supplied me clothing and supplies during my short stay there." added Adam. "I believe we can recruit them to assist us in our mission."

Little Lady spoke up once again, 'Scared, scared of me."

"That could be a problem Alice," noted Adam. "If

we bring Little Lady with us they may believe we represent the witch. She may have to stay outside the village, until they get to know us."

"OK," agreed Little Lady.

"I believe it's the witch who holds our travelers, but I recommend we travel to Wonderland after setting up camp in the little people's community. I fear the Queen more than the witches. She has many men while the witches rely on fewer men and their many monkeys." said Adam.

Little Lady interrupted, "Not monkey."

"OK," replied Adam, "You're not a monkey."

"Little Lady interjected, "They have men. Things like men, but not men, bottom." "Bottom?" questioned Adam. "You mean they are in the castle bottom?" Little Lady nodded affirmatively.

"Well that makes the mission a bit more exciting," stated Slither. "Men, who are not men, could be anything. Thanks, Little Lady!"

Little Lady replied by nodding in the affirmative.

"You will need diversions while you are there," stated Yaeger.

"We can play them against one another," suggested Drumbolt. "Start a war between them like Slither and I accomplished in Dimension 29, many Now's ago. We barely made it out of there alive."

Gurgle stroked his beard for a few minutes in the silence now engulfing the room while he contemplated what Drumbolt said. "I think it could be done easily," offered Gurgle. "We should drop an incendiary pack in the castle and when they see Little Lady, Wonderland will assume OZ has attacked and will immediately counter attack. We can get into the dungeon check for travelers and proceed to OZ. The two sides will be much more interested in counter attacking each other than us."

Drumbolt made an observation, "If we light them up then maybe we will need the new incendiary packs early on in the initial mission, instead of holding them back for the rescue group. There was universal nodding in agreement.

Drumbolt ordered, "Loco provide them with our

incendiary packs."

"Yes sir," he replied.

"I'm not crazy about starting a war," replied Gurgle. "The little people will be caught in the middle and risk being slaughtered."

"Maybe, they can evacuate as we initiate the diversion. Would they have anywhere to go?" asked Alice.

"They might hide in the thorny forest for a couple of days, but it'll be rough for them. It's an awful strange place. There are things there. You never see them, but you know they are watching," replied Gurgle.

"It's better than dying," observed Adam.

"Then the plan is to have the two sides do the killing?" questioned Lily.

"Yes, I guess you could put it that way," replied Alice. "They'll kill each other whether we are there or not. We just are speeding up the inevitable."

Adam spoke up again. "We can enter into the OZ dungeon, while they are busy with each other, check it out, rescue our travelers and get out. Should not be more than a few Now's."

"If I count more than 30-nightfalls during your travels, I will send in the rescue team," warned Drumbolt.

"Agreed," stated Slither. "Is everyone else OK with Adam's plan?"

Everyone agreed to end the strategy meeting. A meal followed in town for the entire mission team, but without Drumbolt, who was desperately needing some sleep and his pipe. It would be a pleasant meal for the team, as Drumbolt's famed gluttony wouldn't be a distraction. It was a leisurely banquet lasting much of the afternoon and evening. Talk of the mission was avoided leaving everyone in good spirits to enjoy each other's company. Adam and Alice sat next to each other and re-established communications that were absent for many Now's between the two former partners.

Little Lady fell asleep at the table on a full stomach and had to be carried back to Alice's room on Adam's shoulder. Alice hugged Adam and wished him a good night at the door. Down the hallway, a head peaked out from a doorway. It was Drumbolt, observing the affectionate hug between Alice and Adam. A tear trickled down Drumbolt's cheek, as he retired back into his room.

Little did anyone know that three of these dimension travelers would never return to dine in this dimension.

# Death and the Wisp 7

Morning dawned early for the mission team and their supporting members. At daybreak they assembled into the monitor room. Drumbolt, as expected, was seated on his lounger and being well rested and well fed, in good spirits.

"Welcome," he hollered out to Alice and Little Lady as they entered the room together. They were followed closely by Loco, Yaeger, Lily and Gurgle. A few moments later Adam greeted everyone. And finally, moments later, in strolled Slither, making a grand entrance in his usual attire. He brought with him a grey smoke cloud emitting showers of fiery sparkles, similar to a hand-held sparkler.

"It's gonna be a great day!" Slither announced. "We'll be surfing over a vast expanse today." Eyes rolled among those assembled. Too much showboat, too many tricks sometimes wore out his welcome.

"Well Slither is here," Drumbolt dryly noted.

"Anyone miss his entrance? We probably have it on tape. I can play it again on request," chuckling and taking another toke from his pipe.

"Sorry," he apologized; I just came up with the sparkler gizmo last night. Thought I'd try it out. What do you guys think?"

"Is it intended for children?" cracked Lily.

"I think it's pretty," offered Alice

"Well, that was not the response I was hoping for," as Slither looked toward the floor.

"Maybe sparks should be stronger, sort of fly out from the cloud, like arrows. It could be a great weapon to keep others at bay," commented weapons specialist Loco.

"Oh, I tried that Loco. The problem was the sparks flew out in all direction and dinged me a couple of times. It hurt like hell. I had to reduce the charge to protect myself."

"Interesting," replied Loco. "I can work on it some to see if I can improve it. Maybe it needs a shield for the user. I could see it would be a great tool for the rescue team."

"Nope" replied Slither, "All my stuff is my stuff. It's got to stay pure," as he pointed a finger into the sky reinforcing his point.

"Pure bull," added Lily. That provoked an exasperated sigh from Slither.

"Gee, and I thought we were friends after last evening. You didn't zing me once last night," as Slither imitated hurt feelings.

"We were off duty Slither. Today we're back on the job and someone has to keep you grounded for the task ahead," replied Lily. "If it makes you feel any better Slither, I'm actually developing a fondness for you. You love to be the center of attention, you crave it! But that's understandable after your story last night about being born in Dimension 2, then living a reclusive life because your mother was a traveler and you were afraid of being discovered.

"Not to mention your parents were of a different racial makeup, which is apparently upsetting to some on Dimension 2. Then you came to our dimension a as a young man with a dark complexion and tried to fit into this foreign culture which you didn't understand. Our dimension doesn't have anything but flesh colored members, so you always stood out. You probably felt like you didn't know where you belonged. Thus, you tried too hard to be one of us by showboating. It also explains your no shit attitude. You don't form bonds. You remain aloof, and sometimes say things without regard to how it will be received."

Drumbolt intervened in the discussion. "Nice analysis Lily, I think you pretty well figured Slither out. Although he and I have bonded some." Slither shrugged his shoulders and didn't offer any response. Lily's analysis was a little too close to home.

"I've realized despite all of that, I've gotten to like you Slither," continued Lily. "In spite of all the walls you built around yourself. After all, I might be the one who rescues you on 37. So, I should at least like you. Otherwise I'd just leave you to your unfortunate fate with some sub human creature."

"Don't you doubt she would Slither?" chimed in

Gurgle.

"OK everyone, let's get down to business here, the time for psychoanalysis is over folks." stated Yaeger. "You are going in one at a time. Adam is first, then Gurgle because these two know the lay of the land. Next is Slither and then Alice with Little Lady. We are spacing you a wee bit apart in case the first to arrive encounters trouble. We don't want to send subsequent travelers into harm's way if we can help it. We're planning a quiet entrance if possible."

Adam responded, "The field grass was a bit high when I left so it can provide a good cover we can use until everyone arrives."

"OK," said Drumbolt, "Any last questions or concerns." None were offered.

Sensing everyone was eager to undertake the mission, Drumbolt ordered the team to go over into the tubes and disrobe. The image of backsides from a bunch of naked bodies and a monkey was found to be too humorous for Drumbolt to resist. "Elbows, assholes and a monkey butt" he hollered out. "My life is now complete."

The rescue team, Loco, Lily and Yaeger were standing near Drumbolt and couldn't contain their snickers and giggles.

"Nice sendoff Dumbolt," replied Alice as she looked back at Drumbolt.

Each entered the cleansing tubes and after their washing machine experience, exited to the other side where attendants handed them their mission clothes. Alice was handed a mid-calf length, powder blue frilly dress.

"Umm, I'm not wearing that. Whose idea is this, yours, Drumbolt?" She knew he was watching on the monitor.

Gurgle spoke up, "All females wear dresses in Dimension 37. Most are fancy, except for the little people who always wear whatever they want. Still even for them most females in their community also wear dresses. You have to look like you belong."

"Belong to what?" Alice questioned. "It's powder blue, it's hideous, look at all these frilly sleeves. I can't fight or run in this. I suppose I have to wear high heels also?"

"No, except for fancy events women all wear flats." replied Gurgle. "I got to go to the OZ castle once. I never saw the witch though. Maybe she wasn't at the castle that evening. Some of the inhabitants of OZ were invited to provide entertainment for a formal event held by the witch's commander. The commander had the little people perform a bunch of gymnastics, then stage a dancing and singing ensemble for their entertainment. The night ended with a dwarf throwing contest as the commander's soldiers insisted on such an inappropriate exhibit of their strength. I wasn't chosen because I'm kind of large for a little person. They prefer the smallest little people, so they can throw them farther. There were several women in attendance all wearing heels for that event. But usually they wear flats."

Drumbolt interrupted Gurgle's long story that didn't seem to be going anywhere with a muffled laugh. "Personally, I'd put Alice in heels if I were going. It's be kind of fun to watch her run."

Slither volunteered, "I'd vote for heels also, and I am going, so I should have a vote."

Alice didn't respond to their digs, remaining composed and quiet. She took another look at the dress. She sighed and placed it over her head and let it slip down her body.

Adam was also dressed, and he walked over to Alice and whispered, "It looks beautiful on you, relax."

Everyone was now dressed, so Adam assembled the visualization belt on his waist, and placed a backpack filled with supplies, weapons, etc. over his shoulders.

Adam made a simple statement, "Wish me well," as he walked into the mist and disappeared into the emptiness of dimension travel. Gurgle would follow shortly after Adam who whisked through the portal tunnel and landed in the middle of the field he had previously landed in. All went as planned. It seemed different, however. A smell of decay filled his nostrils, and his eyes began to water. The foul stench of decay caused him to vomit. As he regained his composure, he wiped his mouth, covered his nose and looked around. As far as he could see were bloated and decaying bodies of hundreds, perhaps more than a thousand decaying flying monkeys.

There were all manner of flies, insects and carrion eaters from Dimension 37 feasting on the corpses. There were so many carcasses that the carrion eaters seemed overwhelmed with their grisly task. The field of tall grass was tramped down, indicating an epic battle involving many combatants had occurred there. He inadvertently nudged a decaying carcass with his boot, and instantly a swarm of flies and other insects erupted and enveloped him but just as quickly settled back down upon the dead monkey. The only remains were monkey. It seemed like a one-sided violent killing place.

"Geez," he exclaimed, "maybe it's too late to start a war because it's already over."

A few moments passed before Gurgle appeared. His response to the massive death array surrounding him was identical to Adam's. Gurgle regained his composure and wiped his mouth with his sleeve. Then he looked up at Adam.

"Did you start the war when you left or what?" Gurgle exclaimed. "We can't remain here."

"But we can't leave until everyone gets here. Ooh,

gross," replied Adam as a swarm of flies enveloped him and Gurgle when Gurgle carelessly stepped onto a monkey body near his feet.

They reached into their backpacks and grabbed some cloth to place over their faces to shield against the smell and curious flies. It seemed like an eternity before Slither arrived. As soon as he walked onto the field he slipped on an unseen monkey carcass.

"Shit!" he exclaimed as he was falling to the ground. Fortunately, he landed in almost the only patch of ground not covered in monkey. "This is bad,' he said, rising to his feet. Surprisingly, he was unaffected by the foul smell or swarm of insects. Brushing himself off he again muttered, "This is bad."

"What's bad about it besides the smell?" Gurgle inquired.

"Alice is coming here with Little Lady shortly. Little Lady will freak out," Slither replied. "I don't know if Little Lady is going to remain our friend or maybe she will turn into our foe after she sees this."

Gurgle spoke up once more, "Little Lady is coming

through on a leash with Alice, to keep her from getting lost in the tunnels. Alice should be able to control her."

Adam responded, "I'm not sure about that. You and I came through and spent the first moments puking our guts out. Slither came in, only to slip and fall. There is no way any of us would have even thought about controlling Little Lady if we arrived here with her. We need to be ready if things turn bad."

They waited and waited for Alice. Then suddenly she appeared with Little Lady seated on her shoulders. Predictably Little Lady freaked out. Her eyes bugged out and she screamed at the horrible sights and smells. She attempted to fly off. Alice seemed unaffected by the smells and visuals, so she held tight to Little Lady's leash. A very frightened Little Lady was now airborne but tethered by the leash. She moaned, cried out, and held her hands up to her face. She puked and then defecated in midair. Fortunately, her flight took her way up and away from the group below. Alice kept her long leash tight. It didn't help that her takeoff erupted in a cloud of flies and insects arising from the stench of death, all of which precipitated a variety of problems for the team.

Alice screamed out at Little Lady while trying to whisk away the bugs from around her face with her hand, "It's OK, Little Lady, it's OK. You're safe with us."

While she was trying to comfort Little Lady, two bugs flew into Alice's open mouth, forcing her to swab them out using her fingers.

Little Lady remained terrorized by the scene around her. Slither was ready with a weapon to use on her in case she attacked the group below her. She howled, moaned and cried for a long time. Adam yelled to her, "Little Lady, the Queen's men did this, remember? They attacked just as I was leaving. You were saved because you were fighting with me as I went through the time portal, remember?" She continued her howling and moans.

Slither commented, "If she keeps this up Alice she's going to attract a crowd. If you can't control her, I'll have to take her down."

Alice was frightened and pleaded with Little Lady, "Please come down. Please. Please come to me," as she stretched out her arms to her friend.

Slither raised his hand and positioned his ring to

take her out of the air. "Scared," Little Lady responded.

"I know Little Lady."

Adam and Gurgle urged her to return to Alice. Finally, the leash slackened as she hovered just above Alice before collapsing with sobs into Alice's outstretched arms.

"So many," cried Little Lady. "I hate Queen." Her body heaved from her uncontrollable sobbing." Alice stroked her head and back, all the while holding her close. "It'll be OK. We're a team. We have each other"

"Team," repeated Little Lady through her tears as Slither took his arm down and relaxed.

"Whew," said Adam. "We've got to get out of here before someone spreads the word we are here."

Suddenly a wisp of clouds swirled above their heads. Two golden eyes peered out from the sky. "Someone already knows you are here, Adam." The voice announced. A form slowly appeared out of thin air. "Hello Adam, nice to see you've returned."

Adam announced to the others, "This is the entity that rescued me from the Queen's dungeon in Wonderland."

"Yes I am. And you've brought others along this time I see. You weren't satisfied with the havoc you caused here the first time. You know this is your fault. Both sides converged to capture you and commenced this horrific battle laid out in front of you. This is now being referred to as the slaughter of the monkeys." Little Lady cried out again. "And I see a monkey survived."

"No, she came here with us," announced Alice. "And just who are you," the Wisp questioned? "I am Alice."

"Oh, another Alice in Wonderland. It didn't end all that well the first time, so you are coming back?"

"I'm not that Alice."

"I know that for sure, because I was there."

"You're the Cheshire cat," replied Alice.

"I am not a cat," said the Wisp indignantly. "Our world has almost no cats. In fact, it has almost no Wisps."

"What's a Wisp?" questioned Alice.

"A Wisp is me," it replied.

"I don't understand, what's a Wisp?" she asked a second time.

"Oh, I see you like repeating yourself. Well then, a Wisp is me! Does that help?" "No, and I don't like games" she replied once more. "This is getting us nowhere."

"Well ask a different question then. But why don't you ask it over there by that large tree on the ridge, away from all these dead monkeys surrounding us. That tree is called the tree of knowledge. It's where others in our world go to ask questions, for which they have no answers. We'll continue our conversation when we get there."

The group trudged through the field filled with corpses and carrion eaters. Periodically someone stepped in the wrong place and unleashed an eruption of swarming flies and insects. Little Lady buried her head on Alice's shoulder through their path of decaying flying monkeys.

Arriving at the tree of knowledge, they were encouraged by the Wisp to climb onto the low thick branches, some of which touched the ground. The Wisp said, "You have to be in the tree to get knowledge from the tree. There's a stream over there if any of you want to clean up a bit."

The team looked at each other and shrugged their shoulders. Adam, Slither and Gurgle accepted the invitation and went down to the stream to wash up then returned to join the others in the tree. Alice took Little Lady down for a quick dip to allow her to clean off after her entrance into the killing field. They were upwind from the carnage, so the air felt fresh and clean. Alice continued, "In Lewis Carrol's book he referred to you as the Cheshire Cat."

"Ah Mr. Carroll, I remember him!" The Wisp exclaimed.

"You were alive then?" questioned Alice. "That was many, many Now's ago."

"Yes, I was alive then. Finally, you asked me an easy question. I have been in existence for many, many winters. People and things have come and gone, yet I'm still here."

"Are there other Wisps?" asked Alice.

"Only one other," the Wisp replied. "You may meet him sometime. He is old and near his end. He's waiting to be reborn."

"Reborn as what?" asked Alice.

"A Wisp of course," replied the Wisp. "If he is a Wisp today, he will be reborn as a Wisp tomorrow."

"Is everything reborn in this world?" wondered Alice.

"You ask a lot of questions," said the Wisp "But the day is young, and I am not yet tired, so I will answer your questions. Most things in this world die, what happens to their souls I know not. But Wisps are reborn and there are two others who are reborn, but you do not need to know about that now. It's not important. I will tell you when and if I deem it important."

"OK," replied Alice "I will not ask about them now."

"Good, now on with my story. Mr. Carroll caused us a lot of trouble in Wonderland. He came here, left us, and then wrote a book. He returned with many copies of his book. I have heard the saying that sticks and stones may break your bones, but words never hurt you. Not true say I, as Mr. Carroll's words hurt a lot of people. He called me a cat for one. I am not a cat, I am a Wisp. I come and go as I please. I am sometimes the equalizer for good and bad here."

Gurgle spoke up, "I've been here many times, yet I have never seen you."

"Yes, I know Gurgle, but I have seen you among the little people many times. I know you have many children in their community." Laughter broke out!

"So, the rumors are true Gurgle." spoke Adam. "Lily will not be pleased," he chuckled.

"Where was I?" said the Wisp. "Oh yes, the book made the Queen especially very angry. She didn't like being pictured as heartless, cruel, and quite mad, even though she was all of those things. All Queens are mad, it's hereditary. Mr. Carroll wrote of buildings and doors both small and large that shrank and then grew big again. The Queen built many gigantic buildings at the edge of Wonderland to scare the witches of OZ. She thought if they believed we were a land of giants, they would be too afraid to attack. If they did and got through the huge

158

buildings, they would find miles and miles of walls of small buildings behind them, which they could not pass through.

"The Queen built the walls to protect Wonderland from witches who had magical spells that her guards could not defend against. She was very angry believing Mr. Carroll sought to reveal this secret in his book. He also spoke of drugs that Alice took to become large or small to pass through the rooms and buildings of her fortresses. The Queen did not like drugs and thought the book was written to tell OZ how to pass through her defenses. Mr. Carroll had to flee for his life from Wonderland and go back to wherever he came from. I guess he fled to where you came from, Alice. If you wish to go to Wonderland you will need to go through huge buildings to reach Wonderland."

"Go on," encouraged Slither.

"And who are you?" the Wisp questioned. "I am Slither. "

"Well you are quite tall and dark. Do you crawl on the ground?" the Wisp inquired.

"Sometimes he does," replied Gurgle.

"Sometimes?" questioned the Wisp glaring at

Gurgle. "I didn't ask you Gurgle." "Slither is from our universe. Well actually from two universes." responded Gurgle "Once again Gurgle, heed my words. I was not asking you the question!" said the Wisp. "This is a question for the one who calls himself Slither."

Slither replied sarcastically, "Oh great Wisp, I am Slither, it is a nickname given to me by my mother because I would always slither around on all fours before I learned to walk. My real name is Samuel."

"OK Samuel. Thank you for your answer." replied the Wisp, revealing a broad smile he intended for all to see.

The other team members whispered among themselves. "So, Slither's name is Samuel," stated Alice. "It's true, we have learned something in the tree of knowledge that we did not know before."

"It's still Slither to you guys," he replied.

"Anyway," the Wisp continued, "the Queen vented her anger on virtually everyone. And then a poor creature named Alice showed up on the scene one sunny afternoon. Mr. Carroll did not know Alice and she did not know of Mr. Carroll, or his book. She was just a visitor in the wrong place at the wrong time. The Queen was very unhappy that an Alice had arrived. Because of Mr. Carroll's book, the queen thought Alice was a spy from OZ and she had her executed. She cut off Alice's head in the palace courtyard for all to see. She also rounded up many rabbits and all the hatters she could find and did the same to them, for no reason, just because. Because can be all the reason necessary if you are a mad Queen. The Queen was quite mad. So, you see words can hurt you." The Wisp spun around in the air and once again faced the team.

"So, Alice is endangered being here?" questioned Adam.

"Yes Adam, Alice is indeed in danger of losing her head in Wonderland. Our dear mad Queen to this day does not allow anyone named Alice into Wonderland because of that book. Most people do not remember Mr. Carroll's book, but the Queen remembers it well. The Queen rewrote Mr. Carroll's book and made herself quite nice in it.

"She turned Alice into a drug dealer in the book to justify the Queen's execution of her. It made the Queen feel much better. For quite a while people were required to read the Queen's book, for those who could read. But today the Queen's book is forgotten. It was a terrible written book. The plot was that the Queen is good, which she is not, and Alice is bad, which that poor original Alice was certainly not. It is said few people read Mr. Carroll's book anymore, although I know there are copies left in Wonderland.

"Many, many winters have passed since Mr. Carroll's book was distributed in Wonderland. Most residents of Wonderland no longer know why Alice's are not allowed in Wonderland, but they are told to never name their young daughters Alice. The lineage of mad Queens continues to this day. It is the Queen who decides who can live in Wonderland. Everyone is in danger in Wonderland for the Queen is quite mad."

"So, there was no Alice in Wonderland?" replied Adam.

"Well there was once for a very short time, until she lost her head. It may be either good or bad news if there is an Alice again in Wonderland should this Alice go there," the Wisp replied. "But for now, she is in OZ."

"We need to get to the little people's community." stated Gurgle. "They will help us prepare for our trip to Wonderland."

"So, there will indeed be another Alice in Wonderland. Don't lose your head, dear!" said the Wisp, who turned his back and mysteriously disappeared.

# The Little People 8

Upon the Wisp's exit, the travelers were confused and very much unsettled. Little Lady was asleep in Alice's lap, so the decision was made to allow her and the others some rest before starting their journey to find the little people. After a short time two young little people approached the tree of knowledge, unaware the group was resting above.

Gurgle noted their arrival, leaned over from the branch above them and said, "Howdy friends." They jumped back, startled that someone was already in the tree. I'm Gurgle, you may have met me or perhaps heard of me. I'm from a few Now's ago."

"Dad!" one exclaimed.

"Oops" said a laughing Adam. The little people peered up into the tree. "How many of you are up there?" one inquired.

There are four of us, plus one flying monkey,"

replied Gurgle.

The pair leaped back from the tree and bandied their walking sticks about in a defensive manner.

"Shush, the flying monkey is asleep with Alice up there," Gurgle instructed, while pointing to the branch above him. "She's alright she came with us!" The one who called out to Gurgle as dad, climbed up into the tree and hugged Gurgle. "And who are you?" asked Gurgle.

"I am Ray." He was a tall, stocky, young dwarf and shared many of Gurgle's physical characteristics.

Slither commented, "He looks to be a chip off the old block. You ought to be proud Gurgle. My name's Slither, and that's Adam sitting there next to Alice. The flying monkey is called Little Lady." Little Lady stirred upon hearing her name and rose up slowly in Alice's lap. The little people pointed to her. "Be careful," one warned.

Alice laughed. "She's fine. Say hello to these nice little people, Little Lady," who sat up erect, and said, "Hello." The little people looked at each other, obviously surprised to hear a monkey speak to them. "You didn't know they can talk?" asked Alice.

The pair kept silent, obviously stunned. Then Ray stammered, "I, I never believed they could talk." His companion chimed in, "Neither did I. Also, we have never seen someone of Slither's skin color," he added. "Strange, we are learning so much from the tree of knowledge today."

"Adam remarked, "How about that, they don't even know that flying monkeys talk."

"I talk," said Little Lady.

"Little Lady," Adam asked, "do others like you talk?"

She nodded in the affirmative, then said, "Few can, but most cannot."

"Wow" said Ray. "I must tell our leaders about this. When they learn dad has come back, there will be a huge celebration tonight." He ran off back to the little people's community and called back to his fellow traveler, "Jacob, bring them all back to our town."

Jacob seemed disconcerted to have the responsibility to lead the group back to their community. He was quite leery of Little Lady; he flinched every time she moved. Alice rolled off the branch and landed next to young Jacob. Little Lady stayed back, hovering above. Jacob grasped his walking stick tightly as he feared Little Lady was approaching. Alice asked him to put his stick on the ground.

"You are making Little Lady nervous Jacob," Alice told him. Well, she's making me nervous." His fear prompted Alice to take the stick out of his hands.

"Now Little Lady come down and introduce yourself to Jacob." After hovering a while longer in the tree, she finally came down and leaned her head toward Jacob. "She wants you to rub her head Jacob."

Jacob tentatively stroked Little Lady's brow, which prompted a hug from her. While embracing Little Lady, Jacob looked up at Alice, "She's nice. We were taught to be frightened of them. Maybe we shouldn't be so frightened."

After a few minutes making friends with Little Lady, he took her hand and the two started down the trail toward the community. The team fell in behind. After experiencing the horrible deaths upon the return to her universe, Little Lady seemed relieved to have made a new friend. The trail meandered through a field surrounded by a small grove of trees, then suddenly a yellow brick road emerged heading in two directions, one toward the horizon and the other toward a town in the distance.

"So, Mr. Baum really did see a yellow brick road when he visited here," exclaimed Alice, who was skipping along and whirling about in her powder blue dress.

"Yes, this is the Land of OZ," said young Jacob who was the most prodigious reader in the community. He turned around and looked to those who were following. "I know you are not Dorothy, but this gentleman you travel with looks a lot like Scarecrow to me," he said, pointing directly at Slither. "And this one over here very much resembles the Cowardly Lion in the story," he observed, while pointing to the head of hair known as Gurgle. "I think this one could easily be the Tin Man," he said rather tentatively, while pointing at Adam who was bedecked in silver grey clothing. "I know I'm wrong. It's my overactive imagination."

"Was there a Dorothy?" Adam wondered aloud.

"I don't know" replied the little person by the name of Jacob. "It's only what I read. But here I do know we have witches and flying monkeys, and many were slaughtered in the field not far from our tree of knowledge only days ago. So, there must be some truth to his book."

"Slaughtered," commented Little Lady, looking up to Jacob with tears in her eyes. "Aw" Jacob said, noting her pain and reaching to hug her around her shoulders. They walked together for almost a mile as the gates of the community became visible. They saw a banner hung across the entrance but couldn't read the words. As they got closer they saw what it read: Welcome Home, Dad. Gurgle rubbed his face with his right hand, while twisting his beard and saying what all the travelers were thinking, "Lily better not see this."

"Gurgle, how many kids do you have," asked Slither.

"I think there are over a dozen," Jacob said, answering for Gurgle. He added, "He also has one or two grandchildren. You've been gone such a long time, Gurgle. You're considered our hero now; you could even be our mayor, or even king if you desired. Everyone wants their daughters to raise children by the Lion of Oz."

"The Lion of OZ?" questioned Adam. "How did a lion get that name?"

"By being so fearless," Jacob answered.

"How so?" replied Adam.

Gurgle, whispered, "I have no clue what he is talking about, Adam. No, their parents did not want me to impregnate their daughters. Neither did I for that matter."

"He's the stuff of legend," Jacob announced. The group dawdled behind Jacob and Little Lady, as they walked.

"Well perhaps the passage of Now's has changed everyone's perceptions" noted a chuckling Alice.

A befuddled Gurgle walked toward the welcoming throngs waiting for him. Some raced out to meet him. Many of the young men waiting to greet him did seem to mirror his stocky frame. Unfortunately, so did many of the young women. Soon the Lion of OZ's cubs surrounded him, eventually hoisting him and carrying him through the gates to their city.

Along the way his many children were introducing themselves to him. There were so many names, because of all the hoopla, that his memory was overloaded. He needed time alone with them to gain a proper introduction and induce some recollections. There was a roar from the crowds as he entered their community. The rest of the group followed along in his trail. The sight of a flying monkey being embraced by Jacob eased concerns from the little people about Little Lady. Gurgle was brought up to the podium where the mayor and important town's people were waiting.

"Welcome back, Lion of OZ," called out the mayor.

The mayor was tall by comparison, four-foot nine inches. He seemed to possess normal proportions which suggested his genes didn't come purely from little people. His daughter, Lizzie, rivaled his height at four-foot eight inches. It seemed likely that his size and perhaps his dominant personality had more to do with his election as mayor, than any political skills. Cheers rose up amid waving flags.

"We owe thanks for all the great things you have

accomplished, especially ridding our lands of those flying monkeys, or should I say those of the bad flying monkey variety, noting Little Lady's presence. You are safe here Little Lady," he quickly added. "Please tell everyone how you slaughtered those bad flying monkeys in the field, oh Lion of OZ!" the mayor implored.

Gurgle seemed totally confused. He looked around to his team for help. He had no clue what to say to the crowd. He didn't want to deny or accept their accolades.

Fortunately, Alice made her way through the throngs as Gurgle struggled with a response and said, "Ladies and gentlemen, the Lion of OZ never reveals his secrets."

Gurgle was visibly relieved and smiled broadly as he held up clasped hands above his head. The crowd roared. They needed no further explanation. Alice stepped away from the podium and gathered up Little Lady from Jacob's grasp, and hoisted her up on her shoulders. It was a tremendous homecoming scene for Gurgle. She whispered to Little Lady, "you know that Gurgle didn't really do any of that, right Little Lady?"

Little Lady replied, "Yes, I know."

As Gurgle ascended the podium it became more difficult for him to resist his new status. "Thank you everyone. Thank you for your warm welcome. The Lion of OZ has returned." The crowd went wild. "It's been so many years, but I am home now." As the crowd continued cheering, Gurgle looked over at the team, shrugged his shoulders and smiled. "I am a man of few words, and my team has traveled from far and they are very tired at this moment. Thank you for your warm welcome. I love you all." With that he stepped down from the podium and joined the rest of the team. The mayor heartily patted him on the back as he passed by and shook the hand of every traveler in the group.

After shaking Adam's hand, the mayor whispered, "Welcome back, Adam. It has only been a few days since you took shelter with us from the witch's men. I didn't think I would ever see you again."

"It wasn't my plan either," Adam responded.

"Thank you for finding Gurgle. He brought us much hope, when there was so little," said the mayor who gave him a final pat on the back and watched the travelers take their positions in a receiving line.

Slither stood next to Gurgle and whispered, "You said, I love you all, Gurgle. Truer words have never been spoken by you, based on all the children you have here."

Gurgle, as was his habit, rubbed his face with his right hand and whispered back, "I didn't know what else to say, Slither."

The townspeople passed through the reception line one by one as the travelers greeted each of them led by the Lion of OZ. Many brought young daughters. A colorfully dressed little woman introduced her daughter to Gurgle. "This is my beautiful daughter, Louise. She would love to have your child, isn't that true, Louise?" Her daughter nodded obediently in agreement.

The scene was repeated over again, all along the procession of well-wishers. Gurgle's dance card would have been full, if he had chosen to dance, so to speak. The team's hands were sore and red from all the handshaking. Little Lady gave up shaking hands and began patting the townspeople with a wing. Every so often she spoke a few words which thrilled the people in line. It became like a game for her, and she erupted in broad smiles throughout the length of the reception line.

The group was led to a private reception which the mayor and his senior staff organized in the hall. Food and bubbly were aplenty. It was there that Gurgle summoned up the courage to address the mayor. "I didn't do any of those great things while I was here. I enjoyed the company of your young women and helped your people at the palace show, but I am not the Lion of OZ, your-honor. You must have me confused with some other great warrior."

The mayor sternly looked at Gurgle and replied, "Yes, that is all true my good man, mostly the part about enjoying the company of our young women. Our community has no problems with what young people do together, and for some unfathomable reason you fathered many children. You are apparently very potent shall we say. But to rationalize the reality of your profligate behavior we created a little mythical story to the effect that you are a great warrior, the great Lion of OZ. We created so many stories and repeated them so often that after a while everyone believed them to be true. We decided to support the myth that we had created. So now we have the story of the Lion of OZ who has returned, and our town offers its daughters to you once again. Just be happy and accept it all, please."

"But I am not the Lion of Oz your honor," replied Gurgle. "I was a young man then, full of vim and vigor. I thought little about consequences. Now I am older and settled and have a loving partner who waits my return at home. Her name is Lily. She is aware of my past transgressions which have caused great strain in our relationship. She would not be pleased if she were here. I love her and want my days to end happily with her."

"And I wish you well then," replied the mayor. "Nevertheless, while you remain you will be known as the Lion of OZ, because these mythical stories of your exploits give our community hope. The die is cast. You are welcomed with open arms. Also, I must advise you that we have spread the story near and far that you are the one who slaughtered the monkeys on the field of death. The witch doesn't know how they really died. We hear there were horsemen, maybe from Wonderland, although that isn't certain. The witch will blame you for the slaughter when the story reaches her ears."

Gurgle was apprehensive and perplexed. He responded, "Why did you do that?"

"Well until you showed up, you were only one among many legends we created. We never expected to see you again. You were a convenient ghost we could resurrect to bolster our confidence. We hoped the stories we created about you would give the witch pause, and perhaps she would finally leave us alone."

Alice interrupted the mayor, "Once again we find that words do hurt people, your honor."

"Where did you hear that?" asked the mayor.

"From the Wisp," she replied. "We encountered him at the site of the field of death. Or should I say, he found us."

"We rarely see him anymore," replied the mayor. "There is so much bad in our world that he keeps busy equalizing it with good throughout the lands. Or at least that is his story. There are so many stories in OZ, we have trouble separating truth from fantasy."

"Don't we all" Alice replied.

The mayor continued, "It is both good and bad that the Wisp is watching over you. It's good because he can help you; but it's bad because you are in danger in the first place. It's very much a double-edged sword to have the Wisp following you."

"That's unsettling," replied Adam. "The Wisp has warned us that Alice will be in danger in Wonderland and now you say Gurgle will be in danger in OZ."

"And you may be as well," reminded Gurgle. "You escaped from the Queen and the witch's dungeon, so you are wanted by both sides."

"Ah, for a change it is nice that I am unwanted," observed Slither. Slither, always the one seeking attention, suddenly threw up a grey cloud about him that sparkled and evoked oohs and ah's from the assembled little people who rushed to ask Slither how he did that.

"Pretty," said Little Lady.

"I imagine if the witch learns you are still alive, you too shall be wanted Little Lady," the mayor observed.

"Well let's pretend that it's nice to be wanted after all. Let's enjoy the evening," said Slither standing amidst a gaggle of little people.

The festivities lasted long into the night and the group shuttled from party to party throughout the community of little people. Gurgle was able to spend time alone with many of his children and renew contact with their mothers. Most of them, but not all, were thrilled to have a child fathered by the Lion of OZ. The whole experience seemed to be all a whirl and the travelers' heads were spinning, legs grew tired, and eyelids so heavy they were barely able to remain open. So, the group finally retired to their sleeping quarters. The beds were so tiny the team realized they couldn't sleep in them. Only Gurgle relished the prospect of sleeping in these small quarters. Slither chose to fall asleep in a bed of hay he found at the last barn they visited. Surprisingly, an exhausted Little Lady found a place to sleep by his side. Adam and Alice retired together into a private room back in the great hall, where a series of small mattresses had been provided for them on thefloor.

Alice commented to Adam, "I wonder if Little Lady

will be OK spending the night with Slither in the barn."

"I don't think Little Lady is Slither's type," Adam responded, slightly amused. Alice giggled. Adam continued, "You know she's not a baby, she's an adult flying monkey. She is well able to take care of herself. I can attest to that."

"You're right." She replied, as they laid down side-by-side on the mattresses. "It's been many a Now's since we've spent a night together." she noted.

Yes, it has. I miss it. I miss you. I'm sorry for the many things I put you through," he confessed to her.

"Hush," she whispered, placing her index finger against his lips and followed with a passionate kiss. Dawn took a long time before entering their room.

# Planning for Wonderland 9

It was a late morning by the time most of the travelers awoke. Little Lady opened her eyes and found herself lying underneath Slither's arm. She silently slipped out from under his arm and examined the room looking for Alice, forgetting she and Alice separated at night's end. Slither was jostled by her movements and when he opened his eyes he found himself staring into Little Lady's eyes. He sat up slightly startled.

"What the..." he exclaimed realizing he just spent the night sleeping with a flying monkey.

Little Lady spoke up, "Not happy. No Alice?"

"Give me a few minutes and we'll find her," he said, reaching for his boots.

"Smell," Little Lady declared, pointing toward Slither.

"Well you're not exactly fresh either. Let's find somewhere to clean up." He remembered a trough outside the barn. Slither bent over and splashed water up on his bare upper body, while Little Lady dove right in, immersing herself in the trough of mildly stagnant water. A mild wind helped dry them. They then trudged off toward the great hall and met up with Gurgle a few steps outside the hall.

"Well three are accounted for," observed Gurgle. "I wonder where Alice and Adam are?"

"We don't know, but let's go inside and see who's here already. Maybe someone can lead us to a breakfast," said Slither. Once inside they found the hall empty. They explored the great hall and stumbled upon Adam and Alice's room. Opening the door, they found the two sleeping together, somewhat sprawled and intertwined amongst themselves under the covers. Slither, rather over dramatically cleared his throat loud enough to stir Alice who looked over in his direction.

"Oh, good morning you all, is it time to get up?"

She nudged Adam and got him to stir, though he was still unaware of their company in the room. He snuggled his face into her neck. Alice tapped him on the head, "We've got company, Adam." He looked up at the assembled group. "Damn, how about some privacy here guys." Slither and Gurgle giggled like school kids. Little Lady walked over to Alice and snuggled up against her.

"I think she's reclaiming her territory, Adam." said Slither.

Adam barked, "She {pointing to Alice} is mine, Little Lady. We can share, but it's a package deal, you have to take both of us."

Little Lady turned and flashed a huge grin back at Slither and Gurgle. She seemed pleased. "OK, give us some privacy everyone." said Alice.

The group hustled outside their room to await Alice and Adam's entrance into the hall. Their room had an antiquated shower facility, which basically amounted to an elevated cistern filled with room temperature water. Alice and Adam took advantage of it together before emerging back into the hall. The whole group stepped outside the hall onto the expansive raised front patio. The town had already assembled and was bustling with activity. "Well who do we see about breakfast?" asked Slither to anyone in hearing distance.

At that exact moment, three of Gurgle's children rounded the corner with the mayor in tow. "Ah you're up, wonderful," said the mayor. "They've prepared breakfast in a large building just down the street. Most of our homes are too small to entertain your team members." They all followed the mayor to the building. Once inside they helped themselves to a variety of beverages and a generous assortment of food and sweets. As they ate they were peppered with questions from others in the room who were joining them for breakfast.

"Where are you going? Why did you come here? How can we help you?" and so on and so forth.

Alice rose and addressed the little people. "We're here in search of fellow travelers like us who have been locked up in the dungeons of OZ and Wonderland. Adam, my friend here, escaped from those dungeons and believes there may be others like us held prisoner in the land of OZ. We are unsure if any are alive in Wonderland. We are here to ask you if you have you seen any other travelers like us?"

The mayor spoke up, "I can answer that Alice. Except for Adam here, you are the first travelers we have laid eyes on for quite some time. I think if any were here they would have stumbled upon us. Our town lights are bright at night and we are a pleasant, unintimidating bunch of people."

Ray, Gurgle's son and the first to find them at the tree of knowledge, also spoke up. "I may have seen someone a while ago while I was out for a walk. I do walk a lot and sometimes I stray into Wonderland. I never made it far though because of the defenses that have been built of huge buildings then small buildings along the border. They make it difficult to get around, but I have wandered about there." He laughed for a second, and then offered an observation, "Wandered about in Wonderland, how funny.'

"So, what did you see," asked Adam.

"I watched a man, at least I think it was a man, walking into the thorny forest here in OZ. I took notice because that's not a very nice place. I can't be sure if he made it out or not. Many are lost in there and the flying monkeys patrol the area from our skies. Of course, now that my dad, the Lion of OZ has killed so many flying monkeys, maybe it will be safer to transverse the thorny forest."

Gurgle buried his face into his hands. "This is too much," he whispered to the team.

"How can we help," inquired the mayor. "We need supplies and clothing," said Alice.

"Maybe even some hand weapons?" asked Adam.

"It's done," the mayor proclaimed. "Do you like blue? He offered as he pointed toward Alice. "Not especially," she replied.

"Our seamstresses will provide you a wide variety of colorful clothing," the mayor, replied proudly. "I'd like some dresses that blend well into the surroundings," she said. "If those dresses are too colorful I might be easily seen and maybe captured."

"Noted," the mayor said. He called out for Helen, and instantly an older little woman rushed over to Alice and without asking, began measuring her for new dresses. Alice graciously complied.

"Gurgle, you're easy. We've got lots of things that will fit you perfectly," the mayor observed with confidence. "Adam, what is your preference; do you want bright or muted colors?"

"Muted, if you don't mind sir." At that instant, another little woman appeared and raced up to Adam and began measuring.

"And Slither," the mayor inquired, "what would you like?"

"Just exactly like what you see," he replied. The mayor immediately said,

"Oh no, Slither, we can do much better than that patchwork of clothes you wore here."

"This is what I want," Slither replied.

"I enjoy lots of patches." The mayor acquiesced and said, "Of course, then if you insist. And make them colorful! I don't mind if people see me coming."

A pretty young little woman with a full head of red hair, a bit taller than most at 4-foot-8 inches and quite busty, rushed up to Slither and started taking his measurements. It was Lizzie, the mayor's daughter. She constantly looked up at Slither, smiling as she went about her work. Since Slither was so tall, she stood on a chair to reach his neck and arms. She gave him a pat down of sorts around his chest, and whispered "You are very fit. Most men here are not as fit, and none of course are as tall."

Lizzie smiled broadly as she moved only a few inches from his face while continuing all the while her work of taking down measurements. Her interest in Slither was evident to everyone in the building. Slither didn't mind the attention, but of course Slither loves all attention. As she left she whispered loud enough for others to hear, "My name is Lizzie. Maybe we will see each other before you leave." Slither cleared his throat, averting the collective stares from the group as she walked away. He remained a bit embarrassed from Lizzie's boldness.

As he sat back down, Gurgle confided, "I think that is the mayor's daughter." The mayor himself opined, "My guess is she is quite smitten by you Slither." Slither seemed at a loss for words. "He's a bit shy mayor," added Gurgle. The other team members chuckled.

Lizzie wasn't giving up and waved from a far table, motioning for him to join her. "I think he's too shy," the mayor told her.

In response, Slither stood up and walked over to her table and sat down across from Lizzie. It would be an interesting day of clothing selection, sizing, and a good bit of idle time for Slither and Lizzie. There were unexpected sparks between them.

Very little planning was accomplished the rest of that day, although Ray accompanied Gurgle on reconnaissance walks near the field of dead monkeys and quite close to the edge of Wonderland's tall buildings. Later that day they traveled back into OZ up to the edge of the thorny forest. Ray was helpful and knowledgeable. He had a sense of adventure and was a definite risk taker. He was almost as tall as Gurgle who theorized privately that Ray would one day make a good dimension traveler.

Gurgle was filled with pride as the day closed out with another meal in the great hall. Slither was absent from the meal. The mayor assured everyone Slither was well occupied.

In the morning, everyone but Slither assembled in the great hall as expected for breakfast. A parade of women carrying a variety of dresses for Alice and the others marched into the hall in a single-file line and spread their clothing among the many tables set up for them. The amount of clothing was staggering. They brought yellow, green, blue green, black, charcoal, gray, off white, navy blue, beige, light purple and on and on. Alice imagined she was shopping in a department store.

"Oh my, so many dresses," she said. "When did you have time to make them all?" A seamstress assured her, "Everyone who could, worked on them all night."

"Thank you," Alice replied, "they are so beautiful. They really are. But I only need three. One to wear when I leave, that will be the pine green one, and two others to carry in my backpack. Decisions, decisions, decisions."

The men, predictably didn't spend a lot of time choosing their outfits. Generally, the first three sets of clothes on top sufficed. One did select a powder blue felt hat for Little Lady with a strap to fit neatly under her chin. She was happy.

Slither marched in late to breakfast with Lizzie on his arm. He already had a change of clothing and two more sets stashed into his backpack. As requested, his shirt was covered in very colorful patches, and the pants he wore looked distressed, as he wished. Lizzie appeared quite proud of how he looked.

"Well, look who has finally arrived," Adam called out. "I don't think anyone can avoid spotting you in that shirt, Slither. I hope it doesn't get us all killed, because it will be impossible for you to hide in that garb."

"Ah watch and learn," he assured. Magically, the shirt turned into an olive green, then back again into its patchwork design as Lizzie pressed a small thin card in her hand.

"What the," said a puzzled Gurgle. "How did you do that?"

"Lizzie and I worked on it all night, well, for part of the night anyway," he said, smiling in Lizzie's direction "It's a trade secret how we did it, but some of it has to do with electrical charges, chemicals and metallurgy. I have said too much already."

The group settled down with the mayor and other leaders in attendance and set about further explaining their purpose in traveling there. Alice spoke first. "In order to check out both dungeons, we need a diversion, perhaps even a war."

"That may soon be happening anyway," added the mayor.

Adam spoke up "We plan to drop an incendiary device into the Wonderland castle and position Little Lady in the vicinity. We want them to believe Little Lady has set fire to the castle as an act of revenge for the monkey slaughter. Actually, Little Lady actually does want revenge."

Little Lady nodded in agreement.

"The attack will lead most of the Queen's men out of the castle in the direction of OZ."

Gurgle added, "There is a concern they may want to come through your community first on their route to the castle. We believe it is not be safe for you to remain."

"Where can we go?" asked the mayor.

Gurgle's son, Ray, spoke up, "We should hide in the thorny forest. The Queen's men avoid that forest whenever possible because it's a dangerous ambush site."

"Are you going along with the travelers, Ray?" the mayor asked. "No, I already took Gurgle yesterday out to the edge of Wonderland and right up to near the thorny forest. He knows very well how to get there. Instead, I want to help gather every one of our little people into the thorny forest. I am hoping the Wisp will show up to help us, although we haven't seen him anywhere so maybe we shouldn't depend on him." At that moment, a cloudy manifestation with golden eyes appeared and formed into a bulbous body hovering above everything.

"Someone spoke about me, did they?" The Wisp inquired. "I heard someone say you can't depend on me. Hmm."

The Wisp did a complete three-hundred-sixty-degree turn and stared directly toward everyone below him. The mayor waved a greeting back at him which provoked a similar response from the Wisp in his direction.

"You haven't graced our community in some time now," commented the mayor. "Oh, I've been here mayor, but I've chosen not to reveal myself."

The Wisp floated toward Lizzie, and inquired "How are you Lizzie?"

"I am fine Wisp." She replied and reached up to stroke the Wisp. The Wisp seemed pleased.

"What say you Alice? I see you still have your head. But of course, you haven't been to Wonderland yet."

"No, but I will assure you, I am not planning to lose my head in Wonderland," she curtly responded.

"Are you sure of that?" the Wisp asked.

"Yes," she said, placing her hands on her waist. "Now either join in to help us or you can go off and talk to someone else about losing their head."

"Well, I see, Alice." The Wisp made another complete turn and appeared to be upside down, now choosing to look directly into Little Lady's eyes. Little Lady tried to turn her head upside down and copy the Wisp's actions.

"I hear they have great plans for you Little Lady. Just remember do what you need to do with love and not hate." Little Lady looked over at Alice displaying a quizzical look on her face.

"I think the Wisp is saying you should act with good intentions and not with anger," explained Alice.

"Exactly," said the Wisp. "And yes, to the good little people I assure you that I will accompany you into the thorny forest. My brother, the other Wisp, lives there. But as he is much older than I, it isn't expected he will help us. He doesn't get around so well anymore." The Wisp paused for a second to rotate into a horizontal plane facing Alice. "Perhaps I will introduce you to my brother, Alice, when and if you visit the thorny forest. But keep in mind, all is not well there. There lurks an evil force infesting the thorny forest and even my brother can't rid the forest of its power. It may not be a pleasant journey, but I do hope to keep you all safe."

Alice replied, "With the Queen's men away, we will be able to get into their dungeon. We possess weapons you don't Wisp. We'll get in and out then leave immediately for OZ. We expect to avoid the great battles that are sure to envelope OZ. If the witch is drawn out and has only a few flying monkeys left she will be in for the fight of her life. We will enter her castle and search the dungeons for our people while the two sides are battling."

Adam spoke up, "I have observed that their dungeon guards are lazy and undisciplined. It was easy for me to escape and what's more, they were too fearful to offer resistance as I fled. OZ has placed their most incompetent men to guard the dungeons. It will be easy to enter and defeat these men."

"That's a nice plan Adam," replied the Wisp. "But it may not be the right plan. Beware the Witch may have other resources hidden deep within her castle." The room grew still with that new knowledge shared by the Wisp. And do not underestimate the Queen. For she has many, many men and vicious animals too"

"Yes, we know about what you refer to as the Witch's hidden resources," said Adam. "Little Lady has mentioned them. And I was carried by one of those mystery resources into their dungeon. It would be nice to know how many of them we may have to face Wisp. Do you know?"

The Wisp whirled around, hanging upside down and blinking his eyes.

"Enough," they have enough."

"Umm, a little clarity here is called for, oh misty one," said Slither somewhat sarcastically. "You are very impertinent Slither," the Wisp replied with a commanding presence.

"Yes, but 'enough' is not a good enough answer."

"I believe it is," countered the Wisp. "Indeed, I estimate there to be twenty, perhaps as many as thirty of these creatures. Whatever their number, I fear they have 'enough.'"

Well, interesting that we have narrowed that number down to no more than thirty," replied Slither.

"Yes," said the Wisp.

"Anything else you can add before you Wisp away?"

"Slither, Slither, Slither, are you never happy. I wonder if Lizzie managed to make you happy?" the Wisp questioned. "He's happy," answered Lizzie.

"Well OK then, Lizzie. I shall make my exit until the time comes to lead the little people into the forest. Good day." And with those words, the Wisp vanished as effortlessly as he appeared.

Adam summed up their mission, "If we succeed we will have rescued some of our people and can return home in victory. If the two sides destroy each other, there will finally be peace in this world. If we fail on the other hand, we will make it worse for your people. It's a gamble."

"I say it's a gamble worth taking," replied the mayor. "Get the word out to prepare full out to travel into the thorny forest in two days." Many of those in attendance rushed out to spread the word.

Supplies were loaded into backpacks and travelers were readied to exit through the gates into Wonderland.

# Exodus                    10

The exodus from the little people's community was like other huge social events in the town. People arrived all arrayed in their finest clothes and stood along the street from the great hall to the gate. Flags rustled in the wind, banners were unfurled, and of course, the mayor had to say a few words.

"All hail the Lion of OZ," he cried out. "Our hero has returned to bring peace to our land." The mayor went on for some time, offering much testimony as to the Lion of OZ's prowess. He relished in repeating all the tales of valor told for the many Now's since 'the Lion' had walked among them. Gurgle looked mostly at the ground, wringing his beard with his hand, and unable to hide his embarrassment from the mayor's adulation.

Slither appeared to be in excellent spirits after the night he shared with Lizzie. He mischievously gave an over the top show of rousing support for the mayor's many tales and accolades. After each tale of good deeds, he cried out, "All hail the Lion of OZ." Instantly, the crowd responded with great cheers.

"Oh please, no more," begged the modest little Gurgle. Slither replied with laughter, "This is your moment, seize it. I want to get on the road," he told Slither. This is too much."

Eventually Gurgle was called to the podium to say a few words and predictably Slither followed him up on the stage. Once at Gurgle's side at the podium Slither made a deep bow to the Lion of OZ and grabbed the microphone from the mayor. "It is with great honor that I and the other followers of the Lion of OZ join him in his quest. It is time for Alice and Adam to join me on stage. And let's not forget Little Lady" pointing into the sky up toward Little Lady, who was effortlessly floating above the assembled throngs to avoid being trampled.

Alice and Adam looked at each other with quizzical looks and Alice whispered, "When did we become followers of the Lion of OZ?"

Adam laughed and pushed Alice up on the stage next to Gurgle. Little Lady took a position hovering above

Alice and landed on her shoulders as Alice reached the podium, smiling and waving constantly to the crowd. Many of Gurgle's children rushed closer to the podium to be near him. His sons rushed onto the podium and gave him many hugs, his daughters kissed him on his cheek. It was a beautiful family scene. Even his two grandchildren were brought to the podium to allow Gurgle to hold each one high above his head to the cheers of the masses.

"Thank you," was all Gurgle could say.

Slither took over the microphone again, "The Lion of OZ is a man of few words, but a man of action and great deeds. All hail, our Lion of OZ."

The mayor led Gurgle off the platform to walk among the crowd. The townspeople swarmed around him. Lost in the scrum was Slither, who accompanied him into the crowds but was tossed from side to side in the surging mass of little people. Lizzie tightly grabbed his arm at the last moment, or Slither might have fallen to the ground and been trampled in the rush of over enthusiastic admirers of the Gurgle, their Lion of OZ.

For purposes of personal safety, Slither then

hoisted Lizzie into his arms and carried her away from the throngs engulfing Gurgle. After everyone said their goodbyes to Gurgle, a procession of little people led them to the gate. Slither passionately kissed Lizzie just beyond the gate, waved goodbye and then they were all off to prepare to make preparations for entering Wonderland.

"Man, I'm done, I could use a nap," exclaimed Slither barely 100 yards from the gate. "You were really over the top back there," noted Alice.

Even Little Lady commented, "Too much!" as she rested on Alice's shoulders. Gurgle remained quiet.

"So, what's our plan oh esteemed leader," Alice laughingly asked. Gurgle replied, "I'm never going to live this Lion of OZ thing down, am I?"

The group looked way too well dressed for combat as they walked down the trail toward their next destination, the tree of knowledge. Alice wore a pine green dress and black slippers, Slither was attired in a colorful patchwork shirt and distressed- looking blue pants. Adam had a form fitting blue and grey vertical stripped shirt and grey denim-like pants. Gurgle was dressed out in a tan animal skin, open V neck shirt and brown denim pants. Little Lady was adorned with the small powder blue cap and chin strap. They appeared as though they were going out to eat or to attend a theater performance. Instead, their goal was to take down a queen and only their backpacks suggested they might be carrying supplies and weapons for the dangerous task at hand.

When they arrived at the tree of knowledge, they climbed up into the tree to begin asking questions. Once ensconced on their chosen branches in the tree, and resting on comfortable perches, Alice started by asking Adam about his prior travels to dimension 37. "Adam, how many times did you visit the tree of knowledge when you were last here?" Everyone turned to listen to Adam.

"None," he replied. "When I arrived onto the field of grass I had no idea where I was. The tree of knowledge was merely a distant large tree off in the distance to me. It had no significance to me at the time. From the opposite direction I saw a procession of men on foot and horseback coming toward me in a disciplined, military formation. As they neared, I saw they were magnificently dressed in silk red and white clothing. Down the arms of the men on horses was a large bright red stripe that continued down their pants. On the right side of their chests they wore a large red heart emblem. The horses were also draped in a fabric with the same heart-shaped emblem. The footmen wore a white silk fabric, and their heart symbol was emblazoned across their chests.

"I waved to them as they approached and surrounded me. They asked a few questions, then unexpectedly tied my hands, blindfolded me and hoisted me up on a horse. They were professional and frequently checked on my comfort as they led me away. Their considerate manner made me believe I wasn't in danger. I don't know what path they traveled or if they went through tall buildings, but sometime later I was taken off my horse, my hands were untied, and they removed the blindfold. With my vision restored, I could see I was in a stable area outside a huge castle. The leader of the guards informed me I would be presented to the Queen.

"With that, they led me to into the castle and into a great hall. Along the way I saw animals strolling near the entrance and throughout the castle. The birds were pink, I believe they are called flamingos. A large white rabbit, some mice, and all sorts of different creatures traipsed across the floors. No one bothered them. Quite odd, I thought.

"At the end of the hall in a huge throne I beheld a red-headed woman. I took her to be the Queen. She was dressed in a magnificent red and white gown with vertical stripes along the bottom of her gown. The top was white silk without markings except for a heart emblem located in a small area on her wide shoulder strap. She was stunning with long beautiful red hair and a snowy white complexion; her dress was open at the top revealing an ample bosom."

"Sounds amazing," commented Slither.

"She was," replied Adam.

"And the women around you just blend into the background," announced Alice. "Plain women like us are not pretty enough to capture his attention," she said in an aside to Little Lady."

Little Lady responded, "We're pretty."

"The Queen was bat shit crazy," Adam volunteered. "She asked me who I was and what was my

205

purpose for trespassing into her kingdom. My answers didn't satisfy her. I asked for permission to approach hoping to charm her, but she was impervious to my charms and she rebuffed me with considerable disdain."

"Trying to sleep your way out of a sticky situation, huh?" observed Gurgle.

"Adam, you should have brought Gurgle along with you. He's irresistible on Dimension 37," noted an uncharacteristically sarcastic Alice.

"Sorry Alice, you asked me about my visit here." He replied. "The Queen inquired of me if I ever played chess. I told her I was unfamiliar with the game. She explained that it was a strategic board game and that my role was to be a piece in the next game, one of the pawns. She informed me that my survival depended on which player in the game won the match."

She stated "If your side is talented and you are brave you may be lucky enough to survive the first game. However, your time here is limited as all pawns eventually die. It is their role to sacrifice themselves for their King or Queen." She laughed, or should I say she cackled as she continued explaining my fate to me. "I'm going to enjoy watching you lose your head," she said to me. Then she observed, "Such a waste of a man, but all men die at some time and there are many others available to take your place. Enjoy my dungeon." She ordered her staff, "Feed him well for our purpose is for him to be a good pawn for my next game."

I was led off into the dungeon. Wonderland was something of an odd place because, except for the Queen, almost everyone was polite and appeared concerned for my comfort. After a few days passed, I was informed that I was selected for the next chess match. At that point, the Wisp appeared in the middle of the night in my cell.

Adam repeated the Wisp's words as he remembered them. "Things don't look good for you, my good man," he advised as his Wisp form settled onto a bed of straw in my cell. Adam said that his appearance startled him, and he remembered recoiling into the corner of his cell. "Relax," the Wisp advised, "I'm a friend here to help, unless you prefer to fight in the chess match and meet your inevitable doom. The choice is yours."

Adam recalled, "The Wisp wanted me to follow

him to freedom and I asked him how. The door was locked. He instructed me to try the door and to my astonishment it opened easily. I thought to myself maybe it was unlocked all along. I followed him down a dungeon path leading to a wooden door and beyond was my freedom. It was strange. The dungeon was always busy with guards pacing back and forth on some mission or another. But suddenly, with the Wisp's appearance, they all vanished. I wondered if the guards maybe were sleeping or in some other way occupied away from the dungeon.

"Anyway, I walked maybe two hundred yards in the moonlight, while the Wisp floated above. I came to a clearing with a large pile of boulders. He instructed me to push the largest of them aside and crawl into the natural cavern that lay behind it. I walked into the cavern being careful to follow red swaths of cloth which marked the path. The cavern was lit up by hundreds of small firefly type creatures who kept pace with me. When I arrived at the end of the tunnel I found the Wisp waiting and heard him say, 'now push aside the scrub brush and squeeze through that opening. When you reach the end, you will find yourself just outside the witch's castle in OZ. But don't go near that castle. Head instead toward a yellow brick road and stay clear from the castle while you make your way toward the little people's village. They will help you get to safety," he said.

"Unfortunately, when I emerged from out of the cavern, having successfully escaped from Wonderland, I was spotted from above by flying monkeys and the witch's men from Oz, who quickly tracked me down. These guys were not as nice as the Queen's men. They used the butts of their spears and drove me to the ground. Once driven into submission they tied me up and a large green, human-like creature hoisted me onto his shoulders and marched me into the castle. There I met the woman who calls herself a witch. She had long shiny black hair, a coal black gown and black jewelry.

"She was in a weird way attractive to me. I remember her skin seemed almost luminous, it was so white. She stood up from her chair and walked up to me, where she commenced accusing me of being a spy for Wonderland. She threatened to turn me into a toad or she mused, perhaps a dung beetle. As you know now, she didn't follow through on her threats. As I was being led out she stepped up next to me and when we approached the door, she did the strangest thing. She slid her hand down my arm in a caressing, sensuous manner, kissing the back of my arm, before taking a big bite of me from the back of my arm. She broke the skin from the force of her teeth. She instructed her men to return me back to the dungeon. The guards would not explain to me what just transpired.

"When I awoke the next morning, I had cold sweats and a fever. I couldn't eat for days and rested on a bed made up from strips of cloths. I believe my illness was some sort of a spell. After a few days, the fever subsided, but I was unable to summon any interest in leaving despite these harsh conditions. I was brought up to her main room daily to share mid-day meals with her, just the two of us alone in her private dining room. She was friendly and interested in asking many questions, occasionally replying to the questions I posed for her. During those mid-day meals, she frequently and affectionately stroked my arm as we talked but neither of us made any effort to go further. Time passed by slowly. I think she was just lonely and wanted to talk to someone. She seemed interested in my tales of dimension travels, even suggesting she would like to escape from her life as a witch in OZ.

"When in my cell, I occasionally heard painful howls from the floors below. There were several dungeon cells near mine and I thought a few contained other occupants, although I never saw or heard any of them. One day the spell seemed to completely wear off. I regained my motivation to leave. My guards were inattentive and appeared to be of low intelligence so escape seemed at first to be quite possible. I observed that sometimes they left the keys in the door. I decided that I could reach through a bar and grab them to secure my release any time I chose. There were other guards, but mostly they were asleep or intoxicated and they showed no concern with me. At an opportune moment, I took the key and released myself from the dungeon cell.

"In a dressing room on the floor above I found a guard's uniform which I put on over my clothes. I took a small bladed weapon nearby and placed it in a leather belt around my waist. I thought I appeared to look as if I belonged there, so I took a chance to walk boldly into the castle and toward the front door. No one paid me any attention. I looked like any of the guards on their way to an assigned task.

"I raced down the outside stairs of the castle and into a nearby forest line. Suddenly the skies came alive with flying monkeys. My absence was discovered and reported, with alerts sent out. I stayed under the tree line and managed to find my way to the little people's community. After hiding out for two days they helped me get back toward the field and the safety of the dimension portal.

"The path I took didn't go anywhere near this tree of knowledge. Along the way, I was discovered once again by the flying monkeys. I estimate I was only 500 yards from the universe intersection. As I ran, I was engulfed by hordes of flying monkeys. As things turned out, and it was ironic, I never would have escaped if it were not for the men from Wonderland. They were of course there to capture me and bring me back to my dreadful end as a pawn in the Queen's game. I heard one of those searching for me yell out, 'There he is,' and he pointed in my direction. But they soon found they had the flying monkeys to contend with who were vigorously attacking me. I continued attempting to throw the flying monkeys off me and regain my footing. They were all clawing at me.

"The men from Wonderland rode into this mass of flying monkeys and were then engulfed by yet a second wave of flying monkeys on the attack. The monkeys from Oz turned their attention from me to the men from Wonderland. Amazingly, the two sides were engulfed in a major battle and the participants were more interested in killing each other than me. I managed to walk out of this dimension with Little Lady, who was the last attacker hanging on to me."

Little Lady nodded in agreement then added, "The witch's orders: find you, or die trying."

"It seems I'm wanted everywhere in this dimension," Adam noted.

Alice leaned over to Adam on the large branch they shared, kissed him tenderly and then commented, "You are wanted in many dimensions, including mine." Slither and Gurgle hooted a bit in response to Alice's open show of affection.

Little Lady was embarrassed and covered her eyes.

"Well the tree of knowledge indeed has again

provided us much knowledge," commented Alice. "What else will be revealed here?"

They thought aloud, posing several more questions, "Will we survive?" "How many days will it take?" "Will we be discovered before we reach the castle?" And many others.

The Wisp's pair of eyes appeared, and he settled into a high branch on the tree of knowledge. "The tree of knowledge cannot answer those questions my friends. Those are questions of fate, and fate never reveals the future to anyone."

The Wisp blinked its eyes twice and addressed Alice. "Perhaps Alice should ask the question, should I finally open my heart to Adam completely? Gurgle, maybe you should ask, is it time to father children with your woman named Lily?"

He turned to Slither and said, 'May I suggest you should ask, where is home for me?' Finally, it was Adam's turn, "And Adam, you would do well to ask, what is worth sacrificing to keep Alice safe?'"

The Wisp rolled off his branch and drifted down toward Little Lady on Alice's shoulders, then turned upside down, "I am not sure what questions you should ask Little Lady for I cannot read you at all."

Then the Wisp righted himself and addressed the entire group. "The tree of knowledge provides answers only to the questions you can answer yourselves. Ask the right question and you can find the right answer from within."

"That was not what I expected to hear," said Alice.

The Wisp smiled, "Take the path through the huge buildings to Wonderland." Those were the final words of his lesson and he disappeared.

# An Odd Place 11

Everyone was quiet as the team walked toward a landscape of giant buildings. The trip was taking longer than expected, due to a detour they made to avoid the decayingflying monkeys. There were important questions to answer.

Gurgle commented, "It didn't seem this far when my son, Ray and I, were here yesterday. I swear the buildings seem at times to be receding."

"That's an optical illusion," Slither responded.

"Little Lady," Alice commanded, fly ahead and see how far we have to go."

Little Lady took flight and returned shortly. "Not far now," she announced.

Encouraged by Little Lady's report the group soon put the grassy plain they were traversing behind them as their feet struck a stretch of large cobblestone pavement, which made it difficult for them to walk.

"Are we sure we are on the right path?" questioned Gurgle. "I swear these cobblestones weren't here yesterday. Someone will break an ankle. "Strange, very strange," he murmured while twisting his beard with his hand, trying to come up with an explanation for the mysterious road that wasn't there yesterday.

"Maybe you took another path yesterday," suggested Alice.

"That could be." he said.

"Little Lady have you ever been this way before?" asked Alice. Little lady just shook her head no.

"There's only a couple of hundred yards left to those buildings from here." Noted Slither.

Suddenly, out of nowhere, three large ostriches appeared on their right. They were moving in a single-file line, grasping large feather brooms in their beaks. They were brushing the cobblestones clean. Another trio was spotted off in the distance and appeared to be doing the same thing as the first group. The travelers stopped, unsure of what to make of them.

"Sentries?" questioned Slither

"It looks more like the cleaning crew," replied Gurgle.

As the Ostriches approached the group, they suddenly stopped their sweeping activity and began staring at the group as if they considered them to be intruders. "Well, they know we are here," observed Alice. "Now what?"

Three of the birds in the nearest group dropped their brooms, hurrying toward the travelers, then as suddenly stopped and formed a circle amongst themselves, appearing to have a conversation. Heads were bobbing up and down. Every so often one head popped up and looked over toward the travelers. Then all three turned and looked fiercely at the intruders, spreading their wings, trying to appear as large and menacing as possible.

"Uh oh," said Slither, "It appears they have concluded we are not supposed to be here."

They emitted loud screeches. The group farthest away was still sweeping their cobblestones, but now stopped to watch the confrontation. The aggressive group of ostriches paused in their posturing to consider their next move, while at the same time the travelers were planning their defense. Suddenly, the ostriches charged toward the travelers, causing the travelers to scatter.

Slither hollered out, "I'm going to take these birds out."

Alice yelled out "No, not yet, Slither."

Three of the travelers, Alice, Gurgle and Adam, found themselves being chased by the giant birds and took the opportunity to race away in all directions across jagged, treacherous cobblestones that easily could have produced twisted and broken ankles. Little Lady took to the air. Slither stayed in his place, laughing, and enjoying the spectacle of his colleagues scurrying about on the rough cobblestones. Alice slipped and bounced onto some rough areas of the road, bruising her thigh and shins after failing to negotiate a sharp right turn trying to elude a charging bird. Her pursuer stopped short of trampling Alice who was lying flat on the ground. The ostrich bent down, pecking at her hair. "Are you OK?" hollered out Adam..

"No dammit, my leg is all bruised up." She replied.

Adam managed to elude his pursuer, successfully zigging and zagging out of the ostrich's reach while being chased. His pursuer eventually gave up the chase in favor of an easier target: Gurgle. Gurgle's limited endurance and the absence of any athletic talents were quite apparent.

Adam announced, "I'm taking it out before it attacks you," and he raised his ring toward the ostrich hovering over Alice.

"No, please Adam, wait," Alice implored.

From above Little Lady commented, "Stupid birds, stupid birds."

Adam brought his weapon down. Alice reached over toward the ostrich's leg to push it away. It pushed aggressively back and then did the strangest thing. It sat down calmly next to Alice. It paid no mind to Adam who ran up to check on Alice's injuries. While he was tending to Alice, the ostrich periodically reached over to lightly pull on Alice's hair. Adam's hair was way too short for the bird to grasp with its beak.

Meanwhile, the other two ostriches continued their pursuit of Gurgle. It didn't help that Gurgle's lion-like mane of hair blinded him at times while he was trying to outrun his pursuer.

"Run oh Lion of Oz," cried out Slither. Gurgle was predictably irritated by Slither's sarcastic admonition to run. Gurgle was tired and stopped on a dime to face his pursuer.

Almost too winded to speak, Gurgle cried out, "I give up!" He stood resolutely, bending slightly at the waist, holding his sides. His pursuers rammed into him and fell into a crumpled heap on top of the hapless Gurgle.

"Now that was a show," cried out Slither.

Little Lady glided slowly down to the ground and landed next to Alice. "Stupid birds, stupid birds," she repeated.

The farthest group of three ostriches were still watching from a short distance away. They now dropped the brooms from their beaks and lit off charging toward Slither. He was forced to duck, bobbing and weaving, until one of the new trio of birds collided with him and the two of them went down to the ground. The remaining pair now opted to charge him with the intention to pound him with their powerful legs, but they veered away at the last moment. Slowly turning from Slither, all three of the ostriches picked up their brooms and returned to sweeping the cobblestones, apparently satisfied with the message of discouragement they successfully delivered to the intruders into their space.

"Wow, that was an even better show," a now laughing Gurgle observed while still resting on the two ostrich's bodies. Every so often one of the ostriches would softly tug at his mane of hair or beard and Gurgle simply responded by patting them on their heads. He would remain in that reclined position for a few more Now's before rising to his feet, dusting himself off and shooing the ostriches on their way. All three ostriches would return to sweeping the cobblestones, no longer interested in the intruders among them.

Adam helped Alice to her feet. "I'm going to be sore for at least a day or two," she noted.

"Well that's Wonderland," noted Adam. "Everything is not what is seems, unless it is."

"Boy that was a mouthful of contradictions Adam,"

replied Slither. "Not sure what it means but it sure seems to fit this strange and magical place."

The group continued their journey toward the skyline of huge buildings and picked bits of feathers out of their hair and clothing as they went. Each of the buildings was about five stories high and looked as if they were constructed of brown stones. Everything was oversized including the front door. The door handles, the windows, even the flower boxes were giant sized. It was all very formidable, but not as challenging as the very large porcupine sitting directly in front of the door guarding the entrance. The group gazed to the left and right down the rows of houses looking for an easier path. Unfortunately, each of the other doors was also guarded by a large porcupine. Looking upward they noted the giant door handles were mounted two stories high. They were unreachable by anyone except a giant. At about normal waist height each door also had a very small door handle and brass key hole apparently for normal passage

The large porcupine in front of them stood up on its back legs as they approached and flared his quills as a warning. a warning. Around its neck was a small silver and leather collar, bearing the name, "Horace."

"Horace?" stated Alice.

The travelers approached the door of a nearby building on the left. They encountered another large porcupine which also rose up in an aggressive posture, like the first. It had the same silver collar with the name of Horace inscribed.

"Horace is a popular name here in Wonderland," theorized Adam.

"I'm betting the other porcupine-guards are all named Horace," Gurgle suggested.

"Makes perfect sense, aren't all porcupines named Horace?" asked Slither. "Stay away," advised Little Lady.

"Yes, we know to stay away Little Lady, but we have to figure out how to get by them so we can get to Wonderland," answered Alice.

"Horace?" called out Adam, "Can you understand me?" Horace the porcupine didn't respond.

"I should blast him with the ring." announced Slither. "That'll remove the obstruction from that door."

"No one is blasting anything Slither," ordered Alice. "The ostriches are not dangerous, and I doubt the porcupines are either. They only look menacing to you." "How many quills are you willing to take to find that out." countered Slither.

Alice separated from the group and walked back and forth in front of the door just a few feet from Horace. At one-point Little Lady attempted to pull her back from the doorway. "No, I'm fine Little Lady."

The porcupine stood his ground, with his eyes glued on Alice as she paced back and forth in front of it. When Alice tried to approach closer the porcupine flared out his quills.

"If you get quilled, Horace is a dead porcupine," declared Adam.

"Can we pass through the door?" she asked Horace, whose head surprisingly nodded in the affirmative as its quills relaxed and it stepped aside. "Thank you," replied Alice.

Horace sat quietly as the group of travelers approached him.

"We should knock" said Alice, "It could be someone's home. It's not polite just to enter someone's home without announcing yourself." Horace nodded its head in an affirmative manner.

"Everyone and everything is so friendly here in Wonderland," noted Adam, "except for the Queen."

Alice loudly knocked on the door but there was no response. She knocked again with no response. She turned to Horace, "Horace does anyone live here?" Horace shook his head from side to side.

"You just guard the entrance to Wonderland, right?" Horace nodded his head up and down. Alice reached for a secondary door knob which was positioned at waist height and tried turning it. It would not open. "Damn, it's locked," she said.

Adam, Gurgle and Slither each tried their luck with the door knob. Little Lady went over and sat over next to Horace where she watched intently. Slither suggested he jimmy the lock with the small tools he carried. After a while it was apparent he wasn't going to be successful. Giving up, he threw his tools on the ground and walked away huffing and puffing, running his hand through his hair. "Stupid lock!" he exclaimed.

Little Lady turned toward Horace and made a motion as if to open an imaginary lock with her paw. Horace nodded and then walked over to a planter nearby, where he grabbed a key and dramatically presented it to Little Lady. Little Lady walked over to Slither and presented him the key. The team broke out in laughter.

"As I said earlier, everyone is so nice here in Wonderland," noted Adam, "All you really need to do is be nice and ask, I guess."

Slither was slightly embarrassed as he opened the door and discovered a colorful hall filled with ornate lamps, paintings, and elegant furniture. It surprised the travelers. Everything was normal size; only the building was gigantic. The ceiling rose five stories above them.

"I could really get used to living here," commented Slither, as he walked into the hall and looked around. "It goes on forever," he noted.

Alice was still favoring her left leg from the injury she suffered after being chased by the ostrich. She gingerly walked into the hall, hand in hand with Adam.

"I could live here too," she said.

"We could live here," corrected Adam.

"Yes, that's what I meant," Alice agreed.

Gurgle entered through the door and commented, "I find it a bit too large for me. But Lily would like it."

Meanwhile Little Lady and Horace entered. Little Lady took flight and happily sailed around the room and up into the spacious cathedral ceiling above them all. She flew to the far end and back. "Smaller," she noted, pointing to the back of the room, and hovering above Alice and Adam.

Slither had captured one of the elegant sofas to lay upon and thoughtlessly put his feet up on an arm. Horace the porcupine walked over to the sofa and without warning swatted Slither's feet off the sofa with his front paws, knocking them to the ground. The manners-obsessed porcupine was seen shaking its head as he walked back through the open front door, pausing to close it behind him and looking back at Slither in disdain.

"Horace doesn't approve of your lack of etiquette," noted Alice. "You're lucky it was his paw and not a dozen of his quills."

They all wandered about the spacious room admiring the furnishings. "This is fit for a queen," Gurgle observed.

As they walked further into the gigantic room, they saw a full-length portrait of a beautiful redheaded female elegantly dressed in a white silk gown, emblazoned with a heart emblem on her shoulder. Adam exclaimed, "Behold, the Queen."

"That must be the mad Queen you've told us about," commented Slither. "Personally, I've found every beautiful woman a bit mad."

"It is more likely that it's you that drives them mad," laughed Alice, staring at the Queen's portrait.

"Hmm, that could be true," he agreed. "Do you think this is the Queen's private residence?"

Adam said, "I don't think it's her residence, she lives in her palace in Wonderland. This appears to be more like an ostentatious royal indulgence."

Gurgle called out to the others, "This room is strange, it appears to be getting smaller in size." The others, except for Alice, rushed over to him.

Alice remained fixated by the Queen's portrait. She stepped up to it, brushed a light coat of dust off a plaque on the frame. It stated, "In Memoriam to Our Queen."

"Guys, you better come back over here. This is not the Queen, at least not the current Queen." She called out.

The travelers walked briskly back to the portrait. "It sure looks like a Queen," said Adam.

"Well, the plaque says she's dead. So, either you met with a dead woman or she's was a dead ringer for the deceased Queen."

Gurgle replied, 'This is Wonderland, anything is possible, including Adam having conversations with a dead Queen."

"That would explain her being impervious to my charms," Adam said thoughtfully.

"Yes, my dear Adam, in your mind only a dead woman can resist your charms," Alice humorously replied.

Gurgle invited the travelers to join him as he moved farther back into the huge room. "See I told you it gets smaller. Look ahead. I know it's away off, but that door seems almost tiny, like my size." The travelers followed Gurgle toward the back of the room and eventually found themselves stooping down to keep from bumping their heads against the ceiling. The door Gurgle saw was astonishingly only three feet high.

"Well this explains Lewis Carroll's book," said Alice. "He no doubt traveled through this very room. That's how he came up with the idea of Alice getting smaller and then bigger. It's no wonder the Queen thought he was a spy who was telling everyone how to get past the defenses of Wonderland. This explains everything," she exclaimed.

"Or maybe it doesn't explain anything, Alice," said a Wispy figure with yellow eyes. "Nothing explains anything here in Wonderland, Alice."

"What are you doing here Wisp? We could have used you to help explain everything we have encountered so far in

Wonderland."

"Oh, you mean the ostriches and the ubiquitous Horace-named porcupines?" he asked.

"Yes, it would have been so much easier for you just to guide us into the Queen's palace," Alice said.

"But then you wouldn't learn anything Alice," the Wisp replied as he rotated 360 degrees vertically. "And pray tell, where's your flying monkey Alice?"

"Little Lady?" she exclaimed and looked about the huge interior, but Little Lady was gone. "Where is she?"

"She's gone Alice," informed the Wisp. "She'll be back if you need her, but for now she's involved in other business."

"What other business?"

"Things you will not need to know until a later time, Alice. I'll tell you when it's time" said the Wisp.

"Oh," responded Alice.

"It's a big mystery!" commented Slither.

Adam sought the Wisp's attention, "Is the Queen

dead or alive? This picture says in memoriam to the Queen and it looks just like her."

"Good question," responded the Wisp. "Does it matter?"

"Yes," replied Adam, it matters if we are dealing with a dead Queen or a live Queen. I mean if we were anywhere else I would never assume someone could be alive and dead at the same time. But, hey, this is Wonderland."

"Confusing, isn't it?' asked the Wisp. "That Queen is indeed dead Adam. At least the one represented in that portrait. The Queen you met, on the other hand, is very much alive, but she is the same person as the dead Queen."

"You mean she was cloned?" asked Slither.

The Wisp responded, "When one Queen dies another immediately forms, and continues with the same memory, the same experiences and the same appearance. She is a being like you, but not really you. She breathes, eats, has feelings, fears, can have offspring, lives and dies. She is never ending as long as her demise is not at the hands of her sister."

"There is another sister, then?" asked Alice.

"Yes," replied the Wisp. "There indeed is another. Remember, I told you we Wisps are reborn and there were others who are reborn continuously as well. But you apparently didn't remember what I told you" The Wisp seemed a bit irritated, and instantly dissolved into nothing and vanished.

"Where is my Little Lady?" pleaded Alice, once a again scouring the room looking for Little Lady.

"It sounds like the Wisp has assigned her to another mission.' said Gurgle, "He said she'll be back if you need her."

"We need her to come back and set fire to the Queen's castle," said Adam. "Otherwise, we will have problems."

A disembodied voice from a speaker interrupted their conversation, "Lights will be going out in 10, 9, 8, 7..." As the voice reached "one," all the lights went out.

"Oh crap," responded Alice. "Now what?"

Gurgle attempted to find the group in the dark but bumped into a table and heard something crash to the floor. "Damn," he exclaimed, "I can't see a thing."

A small light illuminated the group. Slither flicked on an old lighter and lit a candle he found on a mantle. "Lizzie gave me the lighter and candles before I left. She said I might need them. I wonder if she's traveled here before?" He lit two more candles and gave them to other members. Gurgle, being a resourceful man, found an oil lantern and lit the wick it with the candle. The lantern illuminated the room. They found some other oil lamps and soon the blackness was replaced with a comforting glow.

"So how do we get out of here?" questioned Alice?

Gurgle walked over to the small door to try the door knob, but nothing happened. It was locked. Alice picked up one of the oil lamps and accompanied Adam to the front of the room. That door was also locked. She knocked on the door and called out, "Horace can you let us out?'

She heard no answer. She knocked, again, harder;

still no Horace. They noted a silver tray on a tea cart placed near the door. It was filled with food and pitchers of various drinks. An attached note read, "You are safe for the night. No harm can come to you. Please enjoy the food and drink. I will see you in the morning, Horace."

"OK so the porcupine doesn't speak, but it writes," said Adam. "I thought the Queen was mad, now I'm thinking Wonderland has made us all mad."

"Well, Lewis Carroll wrote of talking rabbits, turtles, caterpillars, and all sorts of creatures, so maybe it's real, Adam," said Alice.

"Or it isn't real, and we are all going crazy," replied Adam.

"I hope Little Lady is all right," wondered Alice aloud. "She's with the Wisp, she will be fine, Alice," said Adam

"I miss her." replied Alice.

Adam replied, "Alice, you are going to have to learn to deal with the fact that Little Lady is not a pet, but a thinking, expressive creature. While she has befriended you, she has a life of her own to lead."

236

They pushed the tea cart over to where Slither and Gurgle were settling in for the night. "Food and drink, compliments of Horace," they announced.

Horace?" asked Slither.

"Yes Horace, or at least, that is what it says on the note." replied Alice. Everyone in the group enjoyed their meals by the light of the oil lamps and found a spot on the floor for the night. Sometime the next morning, lights flickered back on. They slowly stirred, wiping the sleep from their eyes and rose to their feet.

"Ok now what?" said Gurgle.

As if in response, a far door opened and in waddled Horace. "Horace so nice to see you!" welcomed Slither

Horace waddled over to Slither, handed him a key, and turned without waiting for a response, quickly waddling back to the door from which he entered.

Alice took the key from Slither walked up to the little door that had kept them locked in last night and placed the key into the keyhole. It turned, and they watched the door open to the outside. Getting out was a bit more difficult as each had to lie on their side and pull themselves through the tiny door. Gurgle who was smaller vertically was unfortunately wider across than the others, and his ample midsection got caught in the narrow door frame. After significant exertion, he popped through and onto the green grass on the other side.

They were greeted by the morning's light, white puffy clouds, a beautiful little grove of fruit trees, birds, butterflies, and rabbits hopping about; an idyllic scene. If this dimension was not ruled by a mad Queen, it would be paradise. Beyond the grove of trees was a deeply cut, rushing river, too wide to cross, but the bank was level enough to allow the travelers to climb down to the river. In a calm pool protected from the rushing water by a splinter of land, they took turns bathing and changing into fresh clothes. Alice changed into a dark blue dress with reddish brown sandals. Adam had a new grey shirt and similar colored pants. Gurgle chose yet another brown animal skin shirt and brown pants. Slither, predictably, continued wearing the same clothing he had on the day before.

"Slither change into something new, please," hollered out Adam. You are down wind and a bit rancid." Slither just laughed.

Across the river they saw rows and rows of small houses; they seemed to be a literal wall of houses, too small to enter with their sharply angled roofs which made climbing over their tops impossible. They formed an impenetrable barrier.

Slither looked over at Adam, "Just how did you travel to the Queen's castle?"

"I have no idea, but I'm sure the path is not through those houses. There's no reason to cross the river as the wall of houses appears impenetrable," replied Adam.

"Which way do we go?" questioned Gurgle.

"That way, or this way?" "Let's go south, or what I think is south," suggested Alice.

They placed their backpacks on and took a path southward. A massive herd of rabbits at one point blocked their progress, making the group wait for them to pass. Slither at one point reached in and grabbed one from the herd of rabbits. He held it high by its ears, "Rabbit anyone?" The herd stopped, with all the rabbits turning in his direction. Teeth were bared, and a few advanced toward him.

"Oops" he responded. "No harm, no foul; just kidding, guys." He said, gently returning the rabbit back to the ground. He turned to the others, "Well," shrugging his shoulders, "Do we want to do battle with a thousand rabbits? I don't think that would have turned out well. I mean we may not have won, right?" The others laughed nervously.

The thought of having their important mission cut short by a massive herd of rabbits was not something they would like to explain to Drumbolt.

"We have to remember, except for the Queen, these people and creatures are naturally friendly. When you grabbed that poor rabbit by its ears and threatened to have it for lunch, you offended the herd." responded Alice. "This is Wonderland and it's much different than what we are used to. These strange creatures seem bound by a code of decorum and etiquette. Not a single creature we have run into has approached us with ill intent. We must assume if we are approached they mean us no harm and we should act accordingly. As far as weapons, we must always have them ready, but we should not expect to use them."

As they walked beside the rushing river, Slither reviewed some of what they had learned to date. Slither said aloud to the group, "I am trying to get everything straight in my head. So far, we know the Wisp has been here at least from the time of Lewis Carroll, a lot of Now's in the past. And the Queen, according to the Wisp, is a continuous spirit who regenerates upon death. As does the Wisp and his successor Wisp. This would then give rise to the belief by some that we have immortal souls." Slither paused to reflect upon what he had just said.

"Go on," said Alice.

"None of us actually die. So where do we go when we die? And why does the Queen reemerge are questions we have no answers for at this moment. The Wisp also stated the Queen has a sister. Is she an immortal being who returned here? Are these just unique circumstances or are there others with continuous spirits in this dimension. Is this a dimension where the rules are different and perhaps the laws of life we as we know them do not apply to this world? We know of other worlds that have physical laws far different than ours. Is this one of those places where elephants go to die?" he questioned.

"Elephants?" replied Gurgle. "What are you talking about?"

"Elephants, Gurgle. In the dimension where I was born we have elephants. Large mammals with tusks who are grass eaters. Elephants are said to have some hidden place where they go to die before modern science made it clear they just die where they die. Where elephants go to die, became a saying where I am from that means a magical place sort of like an elephant heaven."

"OK, whatever," Gurgle replied.

Slither continued, "We know one thing, the Queen is mad. Two, we know that everyone including the animals are exceedingly polite. Perhaps they represent a balance for the evil that lives in the mad Queen. Maybe the Wisp has a hand in all of this."

He stopped talking to wait for input from the others, but when none was offered he continued. "What do we know about OZ? We know the Witch's men can be brutal. We know that the flying monkeys are not nice, except of course for Little Lady who is apparently off on some adventure with the Wisp. We know that the Witch is somewhat lonely, if Adam is correct in his assessment, and perhaps she would like to leave this dimension. We know the little people hate both the Witch and the Queen, as both have raided their village over the years. We also know that there is a war brewing between Wonderland and OZ because Wonderland slaughtered the flying monkeys. However, the Witch believes that Gurgle here slaughtered them because the little people have spread the story that the slaughter came at his hands. Who gets the blame is an unknown, but no matter, the truth will come out that Wonderland slaughtered the flying monkeys. There will be war. Is the mad Queen the main problem in this dimension? If so, how do we find her sister and does the sister wish her dead? I am wondering if setting the Queen's castle on fire is the correct action. I'm confused."

"So are we, Slither," answered Alice. "Everything is so idyllic here in Wonderland. I hate the idea that we could start a war that leads to destruction and may cause many of these wonderful creatures to perish. That does not seem an appropriate course of action."

"Then how do we find out if any of our fellow travelers are held in the Wonderland dungeon?" queried Adam. "That, after all, is our mission."

"Maybe we can just ask?" replied Alice.

Just ask?" countered Gurgle.

"Yes, just ask. We asked the porcupine and he granted our request and even fed us." Said Alice. "We just need to find the right person here in Wonderland to ask that question."

Adam questioned Alice, "OK and who might that right person be, and how do we stay out of the Queen's dungeon? Do we march up to the commander of her troops? That approach got me the dungeon and a date with death in the Queen's chess game."

"Damn, I got a fire pack and now I can't use it," interrupted Slither "Come on guys, I was looking forward to trying this little tool that Loco gave me."

"Why would you want to slaughter a lot of nice animals?" asked Alice. "Maybe I'll just call the rabbits back here and we'll stand back and watch you fight them off," she commented in a humorous manner.

"That would be fun," noted Gurgle.

"OK, maybe the fire packs are not the way to go here in Wonderland. But you may wish you had them, I'm just warning you," cautioned Slither.

"So, we need a new game plan," replied Adam. "We must find someone in Wonderland who knows the answer to the only question that remains. Are there travelers from our dimension here?""

"We're not sure, but our new game plan should be to get in and out with the answer and proceed to OZ." suggested Alice. We may need to start the war there and get into the Witch's castle once they ride off against Wonderland, so we can find our travelers, if indeed they do exist."

"That means the little people have been sent off into the briarwood forest for no reason," mentioned Gurgle. "They are expecting the men of Wonderland to attack OZ and that attack may never come."

"They are in danger either way," replied Adam. "At least, they will be safely out of harm's way in the thorny forest."

"Maybe," said Gurgle skeptically.

Slither, who was walking a few steps ahead of everybody, suddenly turned and faced the team. "I have a question guys," he stated, "Does anyone here have a feeling that we are no longer planning this mission?"

"How so?" replied Adam

"Well throughout this mission, the Wisp has shown up at key times, then shared critical information and hints of information he has which altered our plans. Anyone notice that? He seems to know our thoughts and anticipates our every move. Answer this. How is it that he mysteriously just shows up wherever we are facing difficult decisions? Don't forget the last time we saw him he dropped the bomb that the Queen doesn't die and now he's taken Little Lady away just as we are about to enter Wonderland, so we cannot use her to start a fire and implicate OZ in the setting of the fire as we were planning. The Wisp totally changes our plans at his every appearance.

"He instructs us to take the path through the

buildings. Why? Adam didn't go through the giant buildings. Why did we have to go through them? We can delude ourselves into believing we are planning this mission, but the Wisp is pulling all the levers. And whose side is he on? Ours, his, the Queen's, or the Witch's."

"Well I believe what the mayor says, that he balances out the good and evil here, so maybe he is on no one's side." theorized Alice.

"Or maybe everyone's side," added Adam. "I agree, it's confusing."

Slither added one more thought, "If we want to know whether there are travelers in either dungeon, I suggest we just ask the Wisp the next time he shows up. He seems to know all the answers."

"Problem is he already has said a couple of times, he tells us things only when it is important. So, he is unlikely to not answer that question until he feels the time is important," said Alice. Having settled nothing and arrived at no answers, the group continued along the river's path looking for some way to cross the river's swift current. It is a pleasant walk, lots of animals, birds, splashing fish and the ever-present sound of white water. The walk was long enough that the travelers took time to sit by the water and cool their feet in a crystal-clear pool. Small fish gently nibbled their feet while they tried to make sense of everything that has happened.

"They tickle," Alice giggled.

# The Teal Brothers

After the short pause in their journey the travelers were feeling refreshed and took up their mission again, rounding a corner and stopping at a clearing where they saw a bridge in the distance. As they drew nearer they could make out two large figures sitting on the edge of the bridge, their feet dangling over the side and apparently engrossed with something in their laps.

Slither said, "Just when we could use Little Lady to scout ahead and identify these two figures, she's gone. I recommend we get out our rings out for defensive purposes."

The group followed Slither's advice as they tentatively approached the bridge. A large young man saw them approaching and excitedly rose to his feet, pulling on the other man's shirt as he stood. "Look," he said to his companion, "Someone is coming."

"Just who would be traveling into Wonderland on

that path? There's nothing but the wall of houses up that way," said the other large young man.

Adam noted aloud to the others, "They appear to have swords in their belts, be careful."

The words were barely out of Adam's mouth when the two figures started frantically waving at them, jumping up and down to get their attention.

"They seem happy to see us," commented Alice as the team observed the pair running toward them from the bridge and waving with great enthusiasm. As the two got closer, the team could see something unusual about them. It was their color. Both individual's skin was teal colored.

"Who are you?" yelled one of the teal-complexioned pair. They were still a good 50 yards away. "You're going in the wrong direction to make it into Wonderland," yelled the other.

They were out of breath as they stopped about 10 feet in front of the travelers. Each of them carried a book. The one in the rear was unable to slow down in time and bumped into the first man, almost causing him to lose his balance.

"We're the Teal brothers," the first one said, still trying to catch his breath. He extended his hand to greet the travelers' hands. "Tell me, who are you?" Now that they were close, it was easy to see the Teal brothers were aptly named as their skin had a strong teal hue to it. It was obvious the two boys were twins, perhaps identical, except that the one in the rear had a tuft of blond hair at the front of his head while his brother was a grayish black haired young man. They were good size, standing about six-foot-four inches tall. It didn't look like they missed many meals. The one with a splash of blond hair was clearly exhausted from the short run and he was leaning over holding his sides and still trying to catch his breath.

He said, "My brother is a better athlete than I am," attempting to explain why his brother in front of him was still standing up straight and barely laboring to breathe.

"Give us a moment," the more fit brother asked. He admonished his brother, "Come on, suck it up. I can't have you gasping for air in front of strangers. They could be important visitors. I know mother would be unhappy to hear you huffing and puffing like you are. You are setting a bad example. "

The blond was getting his wind back. His brother said, "Sorry friends, he's badly out of shape. As I was saying we're the Teal brothers. I'm Smokey and he's Sunny."

"No, you're Sunny and I'm Smoky!" corrected the other twin. "That's not correct," stated the first.

"Yes, it is," He turned to Alice, "Ma'am which one of us has blond hair on the front of his head?"

"Why you do, of course."

"And what do you all see?" he asked each of the strangers, who all responded the same as Alice. "OK I'm Sunny and you're Smokey," he admitted to his brother. "My error, I forget sometimes."

"And I know who you are" said Sunny looking down at Alice dressed in a dark blue dress and reddish-brown sandals. He pointed at her holding the book he had been carrying up to the travelers. The title on the cover said, *The Wonderful Wizard of OZ*, by Frank Baum. "See you're in here," he exclaimed pointing to the book. "You're Dorothy and that man standing there is the Tin Man," pointing toward Adam. "I see you're the Scarecrow, aren't you?" questioning Slither. "You've got all those patches.

And I'd know you anywhere," looking at Gurgle, "You're the Lion. I knew this book was telling a real story. I knew it." With that, he jumped up and down and grabbed his twin's shoulders. "Smokey, mom is going to be so surprised when we bring Dorothy and her friends back home."

"Did you meet the Witch over there in OZ?" asked Smokey.

"We are big, big fans of yours." sputtered Sunny. "We share the same enemy. You're the enemy of OZ and we don't like them either. They're bad witches!"

"What's the other book you are holding?" Alice asked of Smokey.

"It's *Alice's Adventures in Wonderland*, penned by a man named Lewis Carroll," said Smokey. "Shh, please don't tell anyone, we're not supposed to be reading this book. It's forbidden. We found three or four copies in the great library far south of here. The Queen from a long time ago banned this book, *Alice's Adventures in Wonderland,* and wrote her own book about Wonderland. From that day on, everyone is only allowed to read the Queen's book."

"I like reading the Wizard of Oz because I like to see

the bad Witch get what she deserves. You get courage," said Sunny, pointing to Gurgle. "And you get a heart," talking to Adam. "And you, Mr. Scarecrow, you get a brain!"

Adam couldn't resist, "That's debatable about the Scarecrow having a brain."

Sunny looked over at Slither, "Gee, I sure hope you find that brain." Alice couldn't resist responding, "So do we all, so do we all." Alice whispered to Adam, "Should I set them straight, or should we let them continue to think I'm Dorothy?"

Gurgle overheard Alice's question to Adam and spoke up, "I'd tell them, Alice. They need to know, and we can't expect to continue the fiction about us forever anyway."

"OK," responded Alice. "Sunny and Smokey I need to come clean with you two. My name is not Dorothy, and these are not the Tin Man, or the Scarecrow or the Lion."

"But you all sure look like those folks from Mr. Carroll's book," Sunny replied, scratching the back of his head. "I could have sworn you were Dorothy."

"Ok then, who are you?" asked Smokey.

"My name is Alice."

Sunny and Smokey exchanged puzzled glances, "Oh my! That's not good" said Sunny.

"No, that's not good," responded Smokey. "That's a problem, I think. Now Alice, are you the real Alice?"

"I don't think she can be." said Sunny. "The Queen chopped her head off a long time ago because she snuck into Wonderland and spied on us. At least that's what it says in the book that the Queen wrote about Alice."

"No, I'm not that poor unfortunate Alice. I'm a different Alice, not at all like the one written about in Mr. Carroll's book there or even Alice in the Queen's book for that matter. You know Alice is a pretty common name."

"Not here it isn't," responded Smokey. "if the Queen finds someone named Alice, it's off with her head."

"Even if it is a child?" questioned Slither.

"Of course," Smokey was quick to reply. "The name Alice is strictly forbidden in Wonderland. Which is kind of sad, because you look like a very nice person. You seem polite. Isn't she polite Sunny?"

"Yeah, she sure is," Sunny agreed. "I think so too," replied Smokey. "Too bad she's got to lose her head."

"Yeah, it surely is Smokey. It's too bad."

Gurgle, spoke up, "How did your skin end up being a teal color?" he asked.

"Well, how did you end up being small," replied Sunny." "My parents were small," he replied.

"Well that makes sense, don't you think Smokey?

"Yup, I sure do, Sunny. Our parents weren't small, but, now that I think about it, we never met our father."

"But I don't think our dad was small, Smokey." "Hmm, I agree, probably not," replied Smokey. "So how did you become teal? asked Slither.

"How did you become a scarecrow?" Sunny wanted to know.

"Sunny, he's not the Scarecrow, and remember, Alice is not Dorothy," countered Smokey.

"Is anyone going to answer the question we all

want to know," expressed a now exasperated Alice.

"Oh yes, how did we become teal? Right," Sunny said. "There's a fruit tree or there was a fruit tree with teal colored fruit. Eating it changes your skin color. We weren't supposed to, but we ate some of that fruit. It was called a forbidden fruit. At least it was..."

"That tree don't exist anymore," interrupted Smokey.

"That's right Smokey; it's gone because mother cut the tree down after we turned teal in color. But you know Smokey," he said, holding his arm up to admire the color of his skin, "I've always liked this color on us."

"I have to agree," Smokey said. "No one else is our color, everyone else is beige or something close to that."

"But the scarecrow is a color I've never seen before on a person. He's black or chocolate, depending on the light," said Sunny. "That's a good color on you, Mr. Scarecrow."

"I'm not the Scarecrow," replied Slither. "My name is Slither."

"Not really," interrupted Adam. "It's Samuel according to what you told the Wisp."

"The Wisp?" replied Sunny, "You've met the Wisp? Oh, Smokey, Samuel has met the Wisp! How grand."

"How so?" asked Smokey.

"That proves she is Alice," said Sunny. "The Cheshire Cat which we know to be the Wisp, talked to Alice a number of times in the book."

Slither gave up on constantly correcting the Teal brothers, telling the others, "Let them babble on, I'm going down to the river to get a drink. "

"He's not very friendly," noted Smokey.

"No, he's certainly not polite either," responded Sunny. "Not polite at all. "

"So, what should we do now?" said Smokey. "If we bring Alice to the Queen it's off with her head," making a slashing motion with his right hand across his neck.

"Yeah, Alice will not look good without a head," responded Sunny.

"You talk a lot about losing their heads. Have you

ever seen the Queen chop off someone's head?" asked Adam.

"No, we are not old enough to watch," replied Sunny.

"We are now..." as he started counting his fingers and barefoot toes, "We are 19 winters as of today."

"No Sunny, we are 20. We just had a birthday, remember?" said Smokey. "Oh yeah, that's right, thanks Smokey."

Slither hollered up from the nearby bank, "Now you understand why I've gone over to the river bank!'

"Never mind Slither, or Samuel, as he will be known as from now on," replied Alice,

"He's an impolite person."

"You can say that for sure," said Sunny. "It's Slither, damn it!" responded Slither. Smokey and Sunny looked at Alice and shook their heads back and forth.

"So, what do we do now?" asked Alice. "If you take us into your castle, the Queen will behead us."

"True enough," replied Smokey. "First, we need to return these books to the library, especially *Alice's*

*Adventures in Wonderland.* Why don't we all walk together, and we'll try to figure out how to help you on our way to the library."

Their journey toward the library took most of the afternoon. The Teal brothers turned out to be a bit of comic relief. They never stopped talking and asking each other questions. They enjoyed ruffling Slither's feathers by calling him Samuel. Along the way they had to stop at different times as a herd of white rabbits, then hedgehogs, and finally an ocean of brilliant pink flamingos interrupted their path. The Teal brothers seemed like teal beacons in a sea of pink flamingos at one point on the trip. It was quite pretty.

"Is it migrating season around here?" Alice wondered.

"No, they are seeking shelter, replied Smokey. "I'm not sure how much you know about things here, but there is a war in the offing between Wonderland and OZ. The residents of Wonderland are retreating into the valley beyond the castle."

"There's never been a war between Wonderland

and OZ. Everyone is fearful," said Sunny.

"But then why were you and your brother relaxing on the bridge reading books and now you are on your way to the great library. You don't appear worried at all," Alice observed.

"Our mother is very powerful in Wonderland. We are confident she will protect us," said Smokey.

"And who is your mother?" Adam wondered.

"The Queen," they announced in unison. Everyone stopped in their tracks. "Your mother is the Queen?" asked Gurgle.

"I think we all heard that correctly," added Slither. "Their mother is the Queen, right?"

Yes, of course," they both replied in unison yet again.

"So, if you're sons of the Queen, why haven't you called her men to capture us? I mean we could be spies or people intent on threatening Wonderland," responded Alice.

"You know, she's right Sunny, she could be a spy.

All of them could be spies," said Smokey to Sunny.

"I guess that's true, but she's so polite and nice," offered Sunny.

Yes, I agree," said Smokey, stopping to gaze at Alice.

"But her name is Alice," observed Sunny. "We all know what mother does to women named Alice in Wonderland. "Well then she can't be Alice, Sunny," observed Smokey. We'll call you Dorothy," Smokey said to Alice.

"Do you think Samuel is a spy?" questioned Sunny

Smokey responded, "Let's ask Alice,"

Slither rolled his eyes toward Adam, and Adam just chuckled. "Alice, is Samuel a spy?" inquired Smokey. "I mean he's got two names."

"Yes, Smokey and Sunny, we are all spies," replied Alice.

Alice's honest response left the travelers confused and a little frightened. Smokey and Sunny looked at each other and reached for their swords. "Those weapons will not do you any good," announced Alice.

"Slither shoot toward that pile of wood over there." she commanded

A bright green flash exploded from the ring on his hand and the wooden pile was immediately transformed into a heap of smoldering wood. "Need another demonstration, boys?" asked Slither. They quickly replaced their swords into their sheaths.

"Are you going to kill us," said a frightened Sunny?

"I've never seen such magic," added a stuttering Smokey.

"It's not magic Smokey, they are modern weapons, far advanced from what you use in Wonderland," Alice calmly explained.

"You are from somewhere else?" said Smokey.

"Yes," Alice told them. "But we are not spies from OZ or the little people or anywhere else in this world. I'm going to level with you, Sunny and Smokey. We are looking for people like ourselves that your mother may possibly be holding in dungeons. She captured Adam here a while ago, but he escaped from her dungeons just before he was to be named a pawn in your mother's deadly chess game."

Smokey spoke up, "You do not want to ever be a pawn in mother's chess game. They never survive for long."

"No, they don't!" chimed in Sunny.

"You do look a little familiar now, Adam" said Smokey. "I might have seen you when mother held you in the dungeon."

"Is your mother holding people like us in her dungeon?"

They looked at each other quizzically, then Sunny said to Alice, "You're not going to hurt us if we can't answer?"

"We don't want to hurt you at all," responded Alice. "We like you two guys." "I don't know of anyone like these people in our dungeons, do you Smokey?"

"No, I honestly don't. You can take our word for it because we rarely go down there."

Sonny and Smokey let go a huge sigh of relief.

Sunny whispered to Smokey "I don't think they will kill us."

"Can we still go to the great library?" questioned Sunny, as he turned to the travelers. "Mother will be angry if she finds us reading the original *Alice's Adventures in Wonderland*."

"If you agree to help us, we will travel with you to the great library," responded Alice.

"See, she's so polite, isn't she?" said Sunny. Smokey nodded in agreement. With Sunny and Smokey leading the way they were off to the great library.

"The great library is also our home," noted Smokey running a bit ahead of the group. "Mother gifted it to us."

"We think of it as our own private castle," added Sunny, catching up to Smokey who was walking faster than he. "We spend most of our time there."

"It's what grown men do," noted Smokey. "It time for us to set up our own kingdom!"

They turned and walked on. Soon the Teal brothers were engrossed in another animated conversation, walking well ahead of the travelers.

The travelers stopped. "What was that all about?" questioned Slither. "You tell them we are spies, Alice. Have you got a death wish or something?"

Adam defended Alice, "Calm down Slither!"

"Yes, calm down. I mean if we walk into their castle, the first thing they'll do is introduce us as a bunch of spies they encountered along the road to Wonderland. After that, Alice is a sure bet to lose her head and we'll all become designated pawns fighting for our lives in the Queen's chess match. My task is to bring everyone back. At least that is what Drumbolt made me promise. You know how he feels about Alice. I can just imagine myself returning to him carrying Alice's head back to him."

He played a bit with the thought in a theatrical manner, "Drumbolt, I've brought Alice back.

Now she's a bit quiet, but in this state, she'll always be near you." Gurgle couldn't contain his giggles

Alice exploded, "Why does everyone think I'm going to lose my head around here? It's nonstop. Alice is going to lose her head; Alice is going to lose her head. I am not going to lose my head she stammered," stomping her feet in anger. "Slither, shut up, please."

Gurgle started to speak, "Ah," but Alice stopped him.

"Nothing from you either Gurgle. I'm in charge and we'll do it my way. Got it?"

Gurgle rolled his eyes and looked up in the sky while raising his palms skyward and mouthing the words, "Why me?"

"Look!" said Alice, indignantly. "Guys, Sunny and Smokey are the Queen's children. They are polite and harmless, if perhaps not very bright. But they are the Queen's sons," she said in a low voice. "We need to form a bond with them over the next few days or however long it takes to get into Wonderland. With Little Lady off on her own mission, we can no longer plan on starting a war using Slither's fire pack.

"The Teal brothers hold the key to getting in and out of Wonderland. It's up to us to explore all our options before we go starting a war. And I'm not sure if war is even necessary. I surely don't want the death of innocent creatures on my conscience. Wonderland is too beautiful a place. Remember our aim is to avoid interference on the world's we visit."

"It's your head," replied Slither "and all my smoke and mirrors stuff may not be able to protect you."

"I am tired of hearing about my head!" cried out Alice.

Her appeal caused Sunny and Smokey to hurry back to the group, "We'll help you keep your head Alice." Said Sunny.

"Please don't cry," said Smokey. "We don't handle sadness well."

Slither shook his head staring at the ground, and mumbling softly, "Idiots!"

Sunny and Smokey turned up the trail leading to the great library. Sunny whispered to Smokey "That Samuel is not a nice man, he just called us idiots."

Smokey shrugged his shoulders, "Maybe he's having a bad day. After all he's a visitor here and it's likely he is tired of walking. We'll continue being polite no matter what."

"If you say so." said Sunny.

There were no more words said among the team members as they walked along the road leading to the great library. As usual, Smokey and Sunny debated nearly every statement. If it wasn't for the fact they held the key the travelers' survival, it might have been considered funny.

# The Great Library 13

The travelers' path along the river had many twists and turns. They traveled through groves of bushes, stands of trees, and across small brooks which emptied into a rushing river. They overtook a large tortoise along the trail measuring close to four feet from head to tail and at least three feet across. The Teal brothers greeted the terrapin, calling it by name. "Todd, where are you off to so late in the day," they asked in unison.

"I am searching," Todd replied. The group of travelers were shocked because up until that moment they assumed only Little Lady could speak in their language.

"Searching for what?" inquired Smokey.

"I am searching out spies," it replied. "You see, the Queen ordered as many of us as possible to conduct a search to find strangers in our midst. It looks like you have found a whole bunch," it observed.

"You mean these people. Why that's Alice," said Sunny, who suddenly realized he called Alice by her name and not by her alias of Dorothy. Sunny cupped his hands over his mouth.

Smokey spoke up, "My brother meant to say her name is Dorothy, He's just been reading the book, *Alice in Wonderland,* and got confused. Pay no attention to him."

Slither raised his eyebrows admiringly as he glanced toward Adam. He was surprised the brothers could think on their feet so well. Smokey continued, "We've stumbled across very important visitors to Wonderland. This is Dorothy who killed the evil witch of OZ, and this is the Tin Man, and there is the Scarecrow and over here stands the Lion. Why don't you growl for him Lion?"

Gurgle looked at the others, shrugged his shoulders and obliged by softly growling. "You can do better than that," implored Sunny. Gurgle let out a loud roar. Todd the turtle was impressed, but since he couldn't read, he had no idea who Dorothy and the others could possibly be.

"Maybe it's our good fortune that you found them,

if they are who you say they are. Dorothy can help us kill the bad Witch of OZ. But I must tell you I am scared. Everyone has fled into the valley beyond the castle, because I am slow of foot, they may eliminate me first. I don't want to see the many creatures of Wonderland strewn lifeless about." A small tear dropped from an eye. "These are my friends and they are all I have left." he commented, as he continued wandering down the path.

"Are you just going to let him go off by himself?" Alice asked the Teal brothers. "If we can get him into the great library, maybe he'll be safe. He looked like he has just about given up."

"See," said Sunny, "Alice cares. She's so nice."

"Yeah, I agree that she is nice," replied Smokey. "Todd has been ordered by our mother to search for spies in Wonderland, so he has to obey her," noted Smokey.

"Agreed," replied Sunny, "Mother can get angry if anyone disobeys her; everyone needs to follow her orders, or we know what'll happen."

"Off with their heads," exclaimed Smokey making a slashing motion across his neck. Todd the tortoise was last seen lumbering off into the brush beyond.

"Do any other animals in Wonderland talk?" asked Adam.

"A few," answered Sunny.

"Not many, but some do," added Smokey. "Our tortoises do."

Gurgle whispered to Adam, "I knew it, Adam. This place is magical." Adam nodded in agreement. Finally, the travelers and the Teal brothers saw the great library in the distance.

"It's still a long way off," said Smokey. The skies which had become recently overcast started to drop their rain.

It's raining!" announced Smokey.

"No one melts here, right?" questioned Sunny.

"I'm good." said Slither.

The light rain persisted as they approached the great library. No one bothered to cover their heads, as the rain slowed to a light mist. There before them stood a medium sized castle. The castle walls were built with large cut stones and many of its windows were secured with bars. A series of wide steps in front greeted visitors. There were thirty steps creating a grand entrance. Along the edges of the steps were low walls, and every tenth step was adorned with pedestals. The first pedestals featured a pair of lion sculptures, the second had buffaloes, and finally at the top were a pair of sculptures of eagles in flight, prominently baring their claws. It was an artistically impressive grand entrance. Finally, the group found themselves in front of a pair of massive heavy wood grained doors with door handles made of heavy round metal rings dropping from the mouths of gargoyles.

As they reached the doors, Sunny commented, "It's nice to be home."

"Yeah it is," replied Smokey. "Hopefully the librarian is here, it is very late," as he glanced towards the rapidly setting sun."

Sunny, pulled the door handle down and pushed the door open. It moved with some difficulty accompanied by loud squeaks. A man from inside, spoke out, "I apologize for the sound of the door. I have not been able to get around to oiling its hinges. So sorry."

The travelers slipped past the massive doors and found themselves face to face with an ancient man somewhat stooped over and shuffling his feet as he walked up to them.

"My name is Clarity, I am the librarian and the keeper of the books." Clarity waved his arm toward the walls of books in the background. "I've survived 102 winters. Been the librarian since I was a young man."

"The library looks impressive, doesn't it." said Sunny. "You have an impressive store of books here," said Alice.

"And who are you?" enquired Clarity.

Alice looked at Smokey and began to open her mouth in response, but Smokey beat her to it, "Go on Dorothy, answer him," interrupted Smokey.

Alice paused to get the name correct, "I'm Dorothy or at least that is what Sunny and Smokey call me, Clarity. With me here are the Tin Man, the Scarecrow and the Lion."

"Ah, what a wonder. I am amazed to find these characters are real." responded Clarity to the Teal brothers. The *Wonderful Wizard of Oz is* my favorite book. There aren't a lot of books to choose a favorite book from here. There's just *The Wonderful Wizard of OZ* and the Queen's autobiography called, obviously, 'The Queen.' However, we have stashed away a few copies of Mr. Carroll's book, *Alice's Adventures in Wonderland,* but we keep them hush hush around Wonderland. They aren't supposed to exist."

"That's odd, you have thousands of books listed up there on the wall," Alice observed, "Surely there are many others to choose from?"

"Is it all right if I tell her Sunny?" asked Clarity the librarian.

"Of course, we both trust her," responded Smokey.

"The thousands of books you see reflect one author's work, it is our Queen's writing," he announced. "It's the same book, bound in thousands of distinct covers. Some bindings are blue, green, brown, gold embossed, there are lots of different editions, but make no mistake, they are all the same book. I don't recommend reading them. The Queen's book is a long, boring, biased, intolerant, and judgmental book, and did I mention it is not always truthful?"

"How so?" answered Gurgle.

"Well for one thing, she refers to you little people as 'the Rodents of Wonderland.' She accuses your villagers of crossing the border to raid food stocks in Wonderland. You are described as genetically lazy, and responsible for much of the crime in Wonderland. She accuses your people of bringing drugs into Wonderland. And that's just for starters. The Queen saves most of her venomous words for a girl named Alice. Everything is off her head, off with her head! Her books have two full pages of that same line repeated over and over. It's impossible to read such drivel."

"That Queen was not nice." commented Smokey.

"No, she isn't," agreed Sunny. "Alice however is a nice person and she should be allowed to keep her head."

Sunny threw his hands up around his mouth

realizing he had misspoke and maybe compromised Alice's identity."

Clarity noted his reaction and looked about for someone named Alice."

"There's someone else with you. Let's see, pointing to Adam, you are wearing a silver outfit. You are the Tin man. And you, Mr. Scarecrow are covered with patch-worn clothes. Here is the Lion, with animal skin from head to toe. And of course, we have Dorothy, so where is this Alice?"

"Well you screwed up Sunny, we might as well tell him the truth," insisted Smokey.

Sunny responded, "OK Smokey. Clarity, we haven't been truthful with you. And we are sorry. This girl's name is not Dorothy, it is in fact, Alice, and our traveling companions are not the Tin man, the Scarecrow or the Lion. This man's name is Adam," he said, as he walked over to Adam. "And this one," pointing to Slither, "is named, Slither, but he also goes by the name Samuel."

Slither helped clarify Sunny's remarks, "My name is just Slither, please."

"And this," Sunny said, draping a large meaty hand

on Gurgle's shoulders, "is Gurgle. These people are not from around here, or at least that is what they say."

"Sunny and Smokey, I am so disappointed in you." replied Clarity. "What have I told you about lying?"

"Sorry," they replied in unison.

Smokey continued, "We were just trying to protect our friends. If our mother finds out she is Alice, why you know what her fate will be. "Off with her head," interrupted Sunny.

"Look boys it's never right to lie for any reason. Too many people lie in this world. When I was a young man only bad people lied, but now it seems everyone lies."

He paused for a moment and then turned to Gurgle. "And you are not the Lion but Gurgle, correct?"

"Yes, that is true sir," he replied.

"Have others called you The Lion of OZ?"
"Yes," Gurgle answered.

"Other little people?" "Yes."

"Then you are from here?"
"No, I'm not from here."

"But you are little."

278

"There are little people like me in many other places."

"You are the only one who is called, The Lion of Oz? The questioning was becoming uncomfortable for Gurgle and the others became worried that perhaps Clarity was inclined to inform on them and report their presence. "You are the killer of flying monkeys." Clarity exclaimed.

"Yes, I have indeed been called that. But that story is made up by the little people in the village." Gurgle glanced toward his fellow travelers and mumbled, "Must I tell this story?" The others nodded in the affirmative.

Gurgle began, "The little people made the story up about the flying monkeys and many other stories about me because when I visited them frequently as a young man, I had a reputation for spending time with the young ladies of the community. A number of these girls eventually bore my offspring. It was not my intention I assure you. I was just having fun, or so I thought it was a kind of fun without concern for the consequences of my behavior.

The young ladies endured shame and were shunned because they had been impregnated by me. The mayor and leaders in the town wanted to protect them, and so they concocted a ruse, and created stories about me being a great warrior, the Lion of OZ. Instead of shunning them, the young ladies then were celebrated and elevated to much admired young ladies who had mothered a great warrior's children. It was a lie concocted to protect them. The little people have become so used to telling tall tales about me that when the monkeys were found slaughtered so horribly, they thought to credit me with the act, even though I was not even here when it happened."

Then Clarity spoke up, "Gurgle, you may not know this, but your problem has become very dire because of that lie. The Witches' commander was briefed on the story and shared it with the Witch who has now authorized bounty hunters and her own men to pursue and exact revenge upon you for the slaughter of the flying monkeys. Just yesterday, men from OZ stopped past here looking for the Lion of OZ. They were anticipating a huge reward of gemstones, gold and wealth promised them if they brought your body back to the Witch's commander of the guard. They offered 20% to anyone who helped in their capture of you. Now, truth be told, I don't trust them or their offer, for they are well known for making offers and then reneging upon them or just stealing what they want." Clarity paused for a moment before resuming, "Gurgle, you are the most wanted man in OZ."

Gurgle appeared shocked by the news. "All it not well," he responded." "No sir, it is most certainly not." agreed Clarity.

Smokey advised Gurgle, "I guess lying has consequences even when done to protect someone."

"Yes, that is the point I wanted you and Sunny to learn from this encounter," admonished Clarity. "There are consequences for lying. Now why don't you and Sunny get yourselves cleaned up, it's time for dinner." The rest of you can do likewise. You will be shown where to freshen up. The staff has prepared a feast for us in the dining room."

As Alice passed by Clarity, he reached out and touched her arm. "I would like you to come with me to the study. We must talk."

Adam overhead this and lingered behind, saying, "I

would like to join the conversation. You must understand we do not know you and haven't confirmed if you are friend or foe. I cannot leave Alice's side in such a situation." Clarity smiled and waved to them suggesting they follow him down the hall. "As you wish. You will find me a useful source of information in your travels."

Once entering the room, Clarity seated himself behind a desk containing a huge open book. He encouraged them to sit down in two large comfortable chairs. Adam, the skeptic, inspected the chairs offered him, pressing on the cushions and running his hand along the back and arms of the chair. Having satisfied himself it was safe, he sat down, while motioned Alice to do likewise.

Clarity smiled, "It is interesting you do not trust me, but you should, for we have a mutual friend."

"And who might that be?' countered Adam.

Clarity ignored Adam's question. "Alice," he began, "I have known you were not Dorothy from the beginning. Your traveling companions did resemble Scarecrow, the Tin Man and Lion, but I knew they were not, because *The*

*Wonderful Wizard of OZ* is only a story, a fantasy from the imagination of a story teller. Just like *Alice's Adventures in Wonderland,* the two are fictions, a grand escape for dreamers and escapism for those leading monotonous lives. Having been here 102 winters, I have seen much and even though the collection of books that you have seen is small, nevertheless there is great wisdom contained within them. Some wisdom is printed on paper, and some is written in the great book." He paused for a moment to let his words sink in for his guests. "We have a mutual friend." he repeated. When he announced, "That friend is the Wisp," Alice and Adam exchanged glances.

"The Wisp informed me of your visit, but in an unusual direction. He advised you would be entering our kingdom through the great wall of buildings. Now the great wall of buildings is not the way into Wonderland, it is a false front designed to intimidate those enemies residing in OZ. We have propagated that lie. Yes, lie if you wish to call it that, that there is only one way into Wonderland and that is through the great wall of buildings. Understand, the forces of OZ are great, perhaps greater than those of

Wonderland. We are not sure. Even the Wisp could not resolve that doubt. The Wisp wanted you to see the memorial to the Queens. Yes, that is what they really are, a series of buildings to celebrate each of the Queens who have ruled Wonderland. They are all the same Queen, of course. I believe you have been informed by the Wisp that this is so."

"Yes, that is true," said Alice.

"And you know when she dies, she springs forth again, with all her memories and experiences? Clarity questioned.

"So I was told." Said Alice.

"How many times has she died," asked Adam.

"Many," replied Clarity. "The great book before me contains all the relevant information about the Queen. It has been annotated by our librarians for generations. We are the true keepers of knowledge in this world."

"And who will keep those records when you are no longer among the people of Wonderland?" asked Alice.

"I initially hoped it would be either Sunny or

Smokey, but alas I am sad to say it, politely put, the pair are nice boys who care, they are brave and want to do the right thing, but seriously limited in their decision-making skills. In fact, sometimes I think Sunny is an idiot," he offered while chuckling. "Now, I do not intend to be mean or derogatory toward Sunny, but..." "We understand," replied Alice.

"I like them, I see their innocence and inquisitiveness, not to mention their continuous debates over menial subjects, and that brings an old man joy. It's like watching puppies play," laughed Clarity.

"Now back to your question about the Queen, Alice. She has died many, many times. If my memory serves me I believe she has died perhaps five times during my 102 winters. At 102 winters one is not always so sharp. Here let me search through the great book of knowledge."

Adam interrupted, "The Wisp called his resource of wisdom the tree of knowledge. And now we have a great book of knowledge?"

"Yes." replied Clarity. "We librarians keep notes on history. It is all in our book. Now, where was I? Oh yes, how many times has the Queen died. There's a special section devoted to our Queen's deaths. It notes a number before I made my presence in this universe known. Let's see here..."

Clarity flipped back pages and then went forward a few. "There's a lot covered in the book of knowledge and sometimes it's difficult to find. Ah here I am!" he exclaimed. "It is written she first died during my lifetime 100 winters ago because of a palace revolt. I was just a baby then, only interested in my next meal and when someone would change my dirty things. I obviously can't remember that far back. This is amusing if one can think of it that way. I have located a notation that the instigators of the revolt were not prepared to see her ever again after they viewed the Queen's body laying at their feet. A lot of people lost their heads that day it is told."

Alice interrupted "If we succeed in killing the Queen, is that what would happen?"

"Yes," replied Clarity.

"Almost worth doing just to see it," said Alice.

"Sort of like putting a coin an arcade machine to

watch chickens dance. You do it just to see it," added Adam.

"An arcade machine that creates dancing birds. Where would one find such a thing? And isn't it cruel for the birds?" questioned Clarity.

"On Dimension Two, they do things like that," offered Adam.

"Well where ever Dimension Two is, they do strange things." Clarity returned to the great book of knowledge, "Ahh, here it is, the Queen's second death. It is recorded she died by poisoning on this occasion. I was still a young boy, so I would not have noted much about it, especially since she basically reappears almost immediately after the death. It might not have even been known among the populace of Wonderland. There is no notation about anyone losing their head. A third occasion was recorded that she died by accident, tripping down the stairs in the castle, although some say she was likely pushed. Some servants lost their head on this occasion. I assume this was done to whoever accompanied her down the staircase at the time. This happened just after I became the librarian. The notation is in my handwriting, although it was so long ago, I do not remember writing it. "And there are more times since? You've been busy keeping track of her comings and goings," said Alice.

"I guess you could say that Alice, however I log everything that happens in Wonderland. The story of you, Alice and your travelers, is scheduled to be added soon, but for now I cannot enter any such notation for fear the Queen may march in here to gaze upon the great book of knowledge. I can't risk your visit being discovered and worse yet, that I administered you aid and comfort. I would surely lose my head, although at 102 winters no one would take notice." Clarity paused a moment and reflected on what he had just said, before continuing. "Would it surprise you to learn that I am looking forward to my demise Alice?"

"And why is that?" replied Alice.

"I have lived too long. Everyone I knew as a child, or as a young boy and even as a young man have now passed on to their great spirits. My mate of many years is also gone. They are all spirits or souls who have traveled somewhere else. It is what all of us ultimately do. The Queen's existence and reincarnation proves beyond a doubt that our souls are immortal, even when evil." Clarity chuckled, "I guess that old axiom, the good die young, but evil lives forever, may have originated here in Wonderland because our Queen cannot die." He paused once more, fanning the book through many pages, and bookmarking the Queen's death pages finding yet another kernel of knowledge to share with Alice and Adam. "It is written in the great book of knowledge that we must not fear death for our souls are everlasting."

Clarity then delivered a stern warning while wagging a finger toward Alice. "Pursue the objective without regard to death. Tell the truth as best you can. You are Alice, you must boldly announce that to all in Wonderland, truth is a weapon for them all."

Adam responded, "So you expect her to just march up to the Queen and announce she is Alice? Are you trying to get her killed? I am not going to let her be a sacrificial lamb led to the slaughter by your so-called book of knowledge. Just whose side are you on, buster?"

"I am on truth's side," he responded. "The truth will strike fear in the Queen's heart. It confuses her. It demonstrates the power harnessed in the truth. You will announce it to her in front of many. So many that the message will resonate throughout Wonderland"

"Then I will do it," announced Alice.

"I'm not allowing you to" exclaimed Adam.

"Not allowing me? It is my life Adam! I choose truth!" Adam rolled his eyes, fuming with anger, but said no more. "She is head strong," observed Clarity.

"What was the Queen's next death event?" Alice asked to return the focus of their conversation back on the Queen.

"She next died in childbirth while having Sunny and Smokey. But I plead with you, do not tell them. They do not know. In fact, they do not know their mother has died and was reincarnated."

"Who was their father," inquired Alice.

"It is said the Queen took many lovers and was like the praying mantis. It is assumed those she grows bored of end up as pawns in her chess game. "

"Whew," exclaimed Adam, "I was held in her dungeon and she met with me in the great hall, but apparently I was not of interest to her. Fortunate for me, for she is a beautiful woman and I might have succumbed to her beauty," Adam volunteered.

Alice responded in a friendly manner "Well it can be arranged once more, if you wish."

"No, I am fine," Adam stammered. "I am having enough trouble at this moment with women."

Alice responded once more now laughing, "My dear Adam, I'll be pleased to keep you safe and out of the clutches of the mad, but quite beautiful Queen."

Clarity resumed his review of the Queen's deaths. "Finally, she last died stepping into the path of horses which panicking during a parade of her palace guards. A canon went off unexpectedly, and the horses bolted while she was inspecting a line of men. Her windpipe got crushed, leaving her writhing in pain on the ground. Sonny and Smokey were there, but because she reappeared almost immediately, they never believed that she died.

They always thought she had only been slightly hurt. Many men, including the cannon charge man, lost their heads the next day. The Queen's soul cannot be extinguished, except if she is killed by her sister, who herself is immortal. "The Wisp told us that," said Adam. "At least, I thought he said that." "So, I am curious, who is her sister?" questioned Alice.

"That is a question I am unable to answer. It is beyond my knowledge. Supposedly the Wisp knows. But if he knew, I am sure he would have acted to level out good and evil in this world long before now. That is his role as I understand it."

"So, the Queen really beheads people," Adam inquired.

"I am afraid so Adam. I have witnessed many of her executions. It is a gruesome experience. Sometimes her orders are to carry out the death sentence by sword and other occasions by a mechanical blade that falls from the sky. The Queen is quite mad and rules by fear and is driven by a ruthless pleasure for causing despair and death. All Wonderland is afraid of her and no one dares question her orders, no matter how sick or perverted her wishes may be. For they know she is beautiful on the outside, but of immense ugliness on the inside."

He paused to take a drink from a glass on the desk then continued. "The Wisp directed you to my path. He could have simply shown you the path under the canopy of trees or through the tunnel from OZ to Wonderland, but..."

Adam interrupted, "I know of the tunnel between Wonderland and OZ. I took that escape into Wonderland. Unfortunately, I was spotted by a horde of flying monkeys and ended up in the OZ dungeon."

"Yes, I know Adam," continued Clarity. "Luck was not at your side in that moment. As I was saying, the Wisp deliberately sent you through the wall of houses to me. He wanted you to understand before you engage the enemy and make life and death decisions. Identifying those who are good and those who are bad is not always clear cut. He wants you to know that evil can be concentrated in a single person or many. There is much good in Wonderland, in our people and creatures. You must choose your actions wisely, so you don't kill those who are of a good nature here in Wonderland."

"Yes, I have learned much since traveling through Wonderland," said Alice. "I have learned that the Queen's sons are from goodness despite their heritage. I agree there is much good in Wonderland."

"Except for the Queen everyone is polite and caring," added Adam. "I thought it was so unusual that as a prisoner of Wonderland they treated me with such respect. People were concerned about my well-being and comfort. One of the dungeon guards even asked me one morning if I had gotten enough sleep because he saw me pacing the cell most of the night. He encouraged me to lie down and get more sleep, telling me he would inform his relief to allow me to rest. They fed me well and gave me time in the sunshine. When it was revealed that I had been selected to be a pawn in the queen's chess game, they seemed genuinely concerned. In fact, I believe they may have even left my cell unlocked the night that the Wisp guided me to safety from their dungeon."

"Yes, they did," replied Clarity. "In fact, that guard

who left your cell unlocked no longer walks among the living." Adam looked shocked.

Alice gasped.

"He gave his life for yours Adam." replied Clarity

"Why?" questioned Adam.

"Because," replied Clarity.

"But that's no answer," said Alice.

"Is there a better one?" stated Clarity. "Nobility comes in many forms. He left a wife and three children, yet he chose sacrifice. He sacrificed for a better Wonderland."

"How did he die?" asked Alice.

"In the Queen's chess game,' informed Clarity. "He was made a pawn and the Queen chose to play only his piece the first three moves to insure he would fight first. His first opponent was a great warrior, a man chosen for his brute force and violent nature. Somehow the prison guard emerged victorious. He suffered a significant, but not fatal wound. The dungeon guards were not known for combat skills and often were assigned to their dungeon roles because they were slow of mind or had substance abuse problems. He had been kept employed in the dungeons for 10 winters and lost whatever muscle tone he may have entered with. Still, amazingly, he survived. It infuriated the Queen and the crowds roared their admiration for him. That enraged the Queen who commanded everyone be silent or they would join him in the match.

"His next encounter was with a rook piece. The role of the rook piece was filled by a giant brown bear. The Queen's rooks in these chess matches are considered almost unbeatable. The guard having been thrown on his back and slightly mauled by the bear brought his sword upright between him and the bear and when the bear lunged downward to kill him, it impaled itself through the heart on the guard's sword. It collapsed onto the guard and for minutes everyone thought both had perished. Yet the guard eventually moved beneath the bear and with help from other pieces he regained his feet. The crowd roared once more, despite the Queen's admonitions. The guard was unsteady, and next set upon by a horseman knight. He fought valiantly, chopping at the horse's legs until he brought down the horseman. The fall killed the horseman. Now more unsteady from the loss of blood he fell to his knees as the crowd roared.

"The Queen rose from her throne and came down to the field. Everyone thought she would spare his life as a reward for his skills. Instead she unsheathed her hand sword and took his life herself, by slitting the throat of the brave guard. Boos rained down upon the field; whereupon palace guards were ordered to clear the arena. The guards followed orders but showed little heart executing her order. Ever since then we have had reports of sporadic disobedience and rampant vandalism. Many of the Queen's pictures are defaced. The guard who saved you is now a hero in Wonderland. He will be entered into the great book of knowledge at an appropriate time."

"Wow," exclaimed Alice.

"There is something else you need to know, and it may save your life. The Queen's chess game is not bound by the rules of the game of chess. Her rules are made up to meet her whims of the moment. She insists that when two pieces meet, they fight for the position of most leverage.

It does not matter if it be a pawn and a Queen or two pawns.

"Their fight settles the board position competition. The Queen is always undefeated, not because she is skilled but because she changes the rules to assure victory. She will boldly tell you that which is untrue without flinching. She refuses to apologize or admit an error when faced with a reality other than which she perceives. Her own hand maidens are most often her opponents. But they are as corrupt as the Queen herself and gleefully place their chess pieces in harm's way to curry favor with the Queen and allow her to always win."

"Eww," responded Alice. How could they sacrifice people and creatures without care?"

"They know nothing else Alice. They are selected as very young girls and raised in a world of violence. Do not turn your back on them. Alice, remember the way ahead will not be easy in Wonderland, but you can find allies among those of this world. You may not know how to identify them, but they can be revealed as needed. The Wisp does not wish you to burn the castle

down. You must

use the knowledge provided you to formulate the demise of those evil people in both Wonderland and OZ. But first you must understand who is evil and who is not. Alice, you have a role to play and it is not an easy one. Sometimes all you have to do is advance the right people into the right places like a chess master."

"That's as clear as mud Clarity. Can you be more specific?

"That is all the Wisp has told me." replied Clarity.

"How in the world do I ascertain who are the right people and their right places?" Clarity ignored her question.

"Are you hungry?" asked Clarity.

"Yes, very" said Alice.

"Then you must eat. I am sorry that I have not gotten to meet the flying monkey; I think you call her Little Lady. The Wisp told me much about her. I did not know they could talk, and apparently she is one of the good creatures from OZ."

"Yes, I found her to be so," said Alice, rising from her chair to leave the study.

"I miss her."

"She is with the Wisp and safe. She has an important role to play in OZ, a role that will possibly save many, and lead to the demise of many."

"Can you say more," asked Adam.

"Can I speak with more clarity?" said Clarity humorously laughing at his form of a pun. "I cannot, for it is information you do not need to know at this point and time."

"Boy how many times have I heard that," responded Adam.

"You will hear it many more times I am sure," as he patted Adam on the back and shuffled out of the study."

"You must remain here two days and let matters evolve for you. We have much to enjoy within the library and the grounds. If the many residents of Wonderland had not been so frightened from the impending war and fled into the valley beyond the Queen's castle, it would be even more pleasant. Wonderland is a beautiful world despite our Queen's existence."

Alice turned toward Adam who was a few feet behind her. "So, Slither is right, we are not in charge. We are not planning this mission. We are pawns in the ultimate game of chess."

"I'd like to think we are the king and queen in this game of chess," replied Adam.

Clarity added to their conversation. "Yes, you are both pawns, kings and queens; in fact, you may well assume all the roles of the pieces of the chess board before the game ends."

Adam and Alice entered the dining room and found Slither, Gurgle and the Teal brothers finishing their meals. Slither whispered to Alice as she sat down next to him, "Learn anything interesting?"

"Yes, we did. You have an uncanny ability to appraise a situation and come up with a correct conclusion, Slither." Slither leaned back in his chair, unable to contain his smile.

# Lily                                    14

After a few days passed on Dimension One, things remained about the same. Drumbolt seated himself at the monitors, per usual, greeting arrivals and saying goodbye to travelers. He was worried about Alice, and wondered how she and Adam were getting along, but he felt a sense of unease. He worried that starting a war among residents of other dimensions was not an easy mission, and it in fact violated their rules about impacting other dimensions. The rules were put in place because of spectacular failures of past attempts to affect changes in other dimensions. These efforts were always done with the best intensions, and with the idea to protect an innocent party, but the indigenous populations reacted badly to external interference, and perceived it as colonization.

These incursions led to much loss of life for both dimension travelers and residents of the targeted dimensions. Collateral damage is what it is called. Wars are never pretty and there are always unintended consequences from the best-intended actions. After just three days Drumbolt decided if he had the chance, he would pull the plug on the mission. Even if it meant leaving earlier travelers stranded in the dungeons of Wonderland or OZ. Something about it didn't feel right to him.

Meanwhile, Yaeger was on R & R {rest and relaxation} and tending to personal business while evaluating his own action plan for a trip to Dimension 37. He periodically stopped by for chats with Drumbolt, ostensibly to pass the time of day. As always, their conversations, returned to the current mission and their shared sense of regret for authorizing it.

After a discussion of culinary options for a planned evening in town together, Drumbolt brought the mission up once again to Yaeger. "My guts tell me we screwed up," as he took a toke on the pipe. "Sending Alice and the team to 37 has left me with a permanent, unshakable sense of dread."

Yaeger replied, "Alice is the best you could have sent; she is near bullet proof. She can go where no one else can. Imagine spending all that time in the lizard dimension and living to tell about it. I mean our rescue team, once we figured out she was there, saw her leisurely trot through a field of carnivores, daring them to chase her. Only one carnivore leapt at her; most acted like she was too much trouble to chase after. Go figure."

Drumbolt laughed, "I wish I had been there. I would have so loved to see that. Perhaps you are right and she's in a safe place in Dimension 37 and doesn't need my support to successfully accomplish her mission."

"I want to talk to you about Lily," Yaeger interjected. "She's taken an intense interest in our weapons section. Some days she's there all day and night. She's working on something with Loco and as near as I have been able to figure, it's very hush, hush."

"Well Yaeger, isn't everything hush, hush over there?"

"She is very much on edge without Gurgle. Her romantic involvement with Gurgle is causing her stress, I believe. What with his return to his harem so to speak."

"You seem to be suggesting that she might take off on her own to 37," said Drumbolt.

"Well we've got a history of that with Alice. She just goes where she wants, when she wants. Maybe Lily is another runner." Drumbolt smiled at the prospect. "You look pleased with that possibility," replied Yaeger.

"Well, you know, maybe we need another Alice in our world to worry about." Drumbolt responded.

"She'll go soon if she's going, is my guess. And you are going to let her go?" asked Yaeger.

"Who am I to stand between lovers?" he laughed. "I am not a believer in God, or prayers, mind you, but I do believe in fate, so maybe fate is my God. I am not sure if my strong sense of foreboding surrounding this mission is about professional planning or perhaps it is a private wonder lust impulse to join them. My position here prevents me from sharing the thrill of their mission because I am too old, too fat and incapable of engaging in strenuous activity. That may be coloring my concern for Alice and the others. I'd do anything to be there with them, Yaeger, anything."

"I know." He simply replied.

Just then Drumbolt's relief officer came through

the door and announced, "You're done old man."

"See what I mean, Yaeger? I'm old, fat, and incapable of being a dimension traveler any more. All I am good for is to be the butt of comments from a snot nose kid, no less. Someone I'd run rings around when I was younger."

His relief, realizing he had insulted Drumbolt, apologized to the old man, "I'm sorry sir, I mean no disrespect. I was just kidding around."

Drumbolt rose up from his reclining position on the lounger and patted the young officer on his shoulder as he passed by.

"No offense taken young man, you were just providing a truthful observation. I am old, fat, and clearly unable to qualify as a candidate for dimension traveling. This world will soon be in the hands of young men like you. I know our dimension travelers this evening are safe in your hands. Just do the right thing, young man."

He and Yaeger then walked out the door anticipating a feast in town.

A few Now's later, Lily entered the monitoring room

with Loco and the pair greeted the young officer who was Drumbolt's relief. She said, "I need to dimension travel this evening and transmit a new weapon for our team in 37," rolling up her sleeves and showing off a pair of silver metal forearm encumbrances suggesting a powerful, wicked weapon. What the relief officer couldn't see at that point was the full upper body shell constructed for the metal arm weapons containing energy sources, all of which snuggly fit against her upper body and were well hidden by her baggy blouse.

"I am sorry I have no such travel itinerary for travel to 37."

"But this is a special project, and you don't have authorization or clearance to deny my request." Loco nodded his head in support, "It's a special-weapons authorized project," he said in agreement with Lily.

"Very well," said the relief, "strip down and approach the tube for cleansing." "Is the weapon safe to go through cleansing?" he inquired of Loco.

Loco nodded his head in the affirmative and left with the comment, "I am going back to the lab."

"Very well," announced Drumbolt's relief, "then prepare for cleansing."

Upon seeing the full upper body weaponry after Lily was undressed, the young relief decided to contact Drumbolt, while she was entering the cleansing tube.

"It's my relief calling," Drumbolt informed Yaeger, as he spit a mouthful of food into a napkin in order to talk to him.

Drumbolt kept his relief officer on the phone while commenting to Yaeger with a twinkle in his eye, "Our runner is in the gates. And she's wearing a new, full upper body double arm weapons contraption. Loco has been busy!" He then focused back on the relief man, "Tell her I said," then he paused for a moment to summon up the right words, "Tell her to have a safe trip." He laughed as he put the communications device down.

"Sounds like she's loaded for bear with some confounding device from the inventory of our new weapons section."

Yaeger replied, "And you're OK with that?

"Yes, I just wish it had been me going. Lily can take

care of herself, don't worry."

Drumbolt picked up his communication device to contact Loco who stammered as he realized the jig was up and Drumbolt was on the line.

"Dru…Drumbolt, is that you?" he asked Drumbolt. "So late for you to be calling. I bet you need a new weapon."

"No," answered Drumbolt, "I need some insight into what new weapons you've sent Lily off with on Dimension 37."

"Di… Di…Dimension 37? She's gone to 37?"

"Now don't play dumb with me, Loco," Drumbolt told him. "I need the bottom line information about what this crazy new weapon is capable of."

"You're not going to fire me, are you?"

"If you had gone with her, yes, I probably would, that is assuming you returned from the carnage that might ensue. Lily doesn't need to be nursemaid for a rookie on a dangerous mission. Now, tell me, what did you equip her with young man?"

"Well, I liken it to a full body laser weapon. It's made of heavy strength metal framing that encompasses the entire upper body, and it contains a thin laser amplifier and energy pack carried on the back between its own metal framing. The metal framing has an impenetrable mesh between a row of skeleton bars. It repels arrows, spears, and primitive weaponry. If a sword strikes it, there cannot be any penetration of the metal framing or mesh. It may cause a dent and the wearer may possibly be affected by the blunt force impact, but the combat person can remain active.

"Then, down each arm I designed a special mesh that has wiring leads for the forearm weaponry, all controlled by a trigger alongside the wearer's index finger. That wiring is so flexible that it doesn't interfere with arm motion. The metal skeleton on both arms is reinforced and will survive sword strikes. Lily can raise her forearm and repel most weapon strikes. It has a great burn radius, invisible to the eye that will burn through almost everything quickly. If the combat wearer wants to burn through supports such as a bridge or tower, it can be readily done. The target heats up, and bam, it burns and rapidly melts."

"Hmm," replied Drumbolt. "set up a demonstration for me tomorrow."

"Sorry sir, but as it is, Lily has the only prototype. I haven't gone into production because it's so new. I can construct a new one, but it'll take a couple of days, sir."

"I assume that you actually have fired it?"

"Yes, Lily and I tested it yesterday. It's fully functional and ready for use."

"No glitches?" inquired Drumbolt.

"No glitches, I would never have released this weapon for her use if there were any glitches at all."

"Very well then," replied Drumbolt. "Lily gets to try it out on 37. Hopefully she won't decide to use it on Gurgle, or his harem," Drumbolt said laughing and ending their conversation.

When Lily emerged from the tubes she chose a plain pair of pants and a very loose- fitting blouse with baggy arms to cover her weapons. An attendant spoke up, "Lily, you need to wear a dress. It is what women in 37 all wear. You must fit in."

She replied, "Wearing this contraption, I have no interest in fitting in."

She placed the dimension visualization belt around her waist and proceeded to the entry point. The voice of Drumbolt's young relief officer came over the speaker system, "Drumbolt just called in to wish you a safe trip. He didn't mention this, but I'm betting he doesn't want you using it on Gurgle or his harem."

"Cute" she replied as she turned and walked into the tunnels and on to her mission in Dimension 37.

Lily arrived at the same field of death as the first team found. It was a few days since the battle there, so the carrion eaters had time to consume most of the monkey carcasses. The smell had mostly subsided, all that was remaining was decomposition goo. While exiting the large field of dead flying monkeys, she looked around for other types of remains, fearful that Gurgle and his fellow travelers could have met their demise too. Seeing none she concluded from the degree of decomposition these animals had died before the travelers set foot on the field.

Still she occasionally stumbled onto a pile of bones with some flesh remaining, the air became filled with flies and other insects, which promptly returned to their feeding and egg laying.

Trying to gain a perspective of her situation she looked to the left and saw in the far distance the tops of very tall buildings. To the right she saw a plume of smoke rising. Lily said aloud to herself, "Well I think Adam said they wanted to get into the dungeons in Oz first. These tall buildings are Wonderland, so they must have traveled the other direction to OZ where they believed our dimension travelers may be held. OZ is where I see smoke, so I'll go in that direction. I only hope my friends are there by now."

Lily set out from the field of death toward the east. She made her way toward a very large tree with huge low hanging branches that sometimes touched the ground. The stink of the field of death was thankfully gone. As she approached the large tree, suddenly a small winged creature took flight toward her. It was a flying monkey. Lily raised her right hand equipped with a ring and tracked it as it approached her. The flying monkey leisurely changed path and flew in large circles above her. "Little Lady, is that you?" she called out.

The flying monkey altered its path and flew lower near Lily. "Lily!" it exclaimed in a squeaky voice. Little Lady swooped down on Lily's shoulder and the two embraced, and Little Lady wrapped her wings around Lily's head.

"So good to see you, Little Lady. There are so many dead monkeys in the field back there." Little Lady nodded in the affirmative.

"Chased Adam there," she replied. "Where are the rest of the travelers, Alice and Gurgle and…?" Little Lady simply pointed toward Wonderland.

"Are they OK? Is Gurgle OK."

Little Lady shrugged and commented, "OK day ago."

"Then I wonder what the fire over there is?" pointing to the east right.

Again, Little Lady shrugged, shaking her head from side to side. Little Lady's limited vocabulary made it difficult for Lily to gather much information.

"I wish you could talk better," Lily said.

"Maybe I can be of help," said a disembodied voice

swirling above them from of a wisp of clouds. A pair of yellow eyes peered out form the wispy mist.

"And who are you?" questioned Lily.

"I am the Wisp. Come join me in the tree of knowledge so we can talk."

"What on earth is a Wisp?' she asked.

The Wisp didn't respond, but simply gliding over to the tree and occupied a low hanging branch. Lily found her own nearby branch and climbed up onto it. Little Lady simply flew down to a branch, so she could be near both the Wisp and Lily.

Once everyone was situated in the tree the Wisp answered her question, "I will now answer your question. I am the Wisp. Gee, I had this same conversation with Alice, and who are you?"

"Well I'm Lily, not Alice, so you'll have to explain it all over again."

"Or I won't" the Wisp replied. "I see you and Little Lady know each other."

"Yes, I know she came back into our world biting and

scratching Adam." replied Lily. "But she's nicer now and I like Little Lady."

Little Lady responded, "Like Lily."

"Well isn't that grand everyone likes everyone. How nice. Unfortunately, in this world hardly anyone likes anyone," opined the Wisp who swirled around horizontally 360 degrees and once again faced Lily.

"Aren't you the Cheshire Cat?"

The Wisp rotated one hundred and eighty degrees vertically, so its face was now level with Lily's, except that he was upside down.

"No, my dear Lily, you see Mr. Carroll decided I looked like a cat. Must be the eyes. I told Mr. Carroll, just like I told Alice and now you, I am not a cat, I am a Wisp."

"You knew Mr. Carroll? That means you must be quite old," replied Lily.

"Oh boy, here we go again. Yes, I was here when Mr. Carroll visited Wonderland. He wrote his book, which the Queen did not like because she thought it was written by a spy who was using the book to spread the message

317

that the Queen's huge houses were just a false front to make it appear giants lived in Wonderland. The Queen feared that OZ was much more powerful than Wonderland with their monkeys and guards. She thought Mr. Carroll's book would encourage OZ to launch an attack on Wonderland. Mr. Carroll had to flee Wonderland. Unfortunately, there was another Alice, a poor soul who accidently ventured into Wonderland and lost her head over that book."

The Wisp returned to a horizontal position.

"That's the short version of the story I told Alice. If you want the whole story, go ask Alice."

"Where is she?"

"Alice is safe with the others."

"And Gurgle, is he OK?"

"You are quite interested in Gurgle. You have not asked or mentioned Adam or Samuel," replied the Wisp.

"Who is Samuel?" she asked.

"He is the gentleman who is also known as Slither to some,"

"So, Slither's real name is Samuel. How rich is that," she said with a broad smile.

"Is Gurgle OK," she again inquired.

"Yes," replied the Wisp. "Ah you're the Lily he mentioned. You have come to visit his many children I presume?" he asked with a mischievous smile whereupon he rolled completely over to again face Lily.

"So how many children are there?"

"I would say about a dozen." The Wisp replied. "He was a very busy boy in his youth." Whereupon a glaze of anger darkened Lily's perspective. "If you are angry about this," noted the Wisp, "please know he is considered a hero in his little people's community. They call him The Lion of OZ. Do harm to him and you would acquire many enemies."

"I have no plans to harm Gurgle, Wisp. I love him. He is my man."

"A much shorter man," observed the Wisp.

"Is that a problem for you, oh Wisp," she added sarcastically.

"No, it's just an observation."

319

"Can you help me find Gurgle and the rest of our group," requested Lily.

"No because they will soon be quite busy, as will Little Lady. I am not sure why you have arrived here, but you are complicating my plans."

"And those plans are?" responded Lily.

"To achieve a balance between good and evil here," replied the Wisp.

Lily drew up her blouse sleeves revealing forearms covered by an intricate skeleton of metals, mesh and wiring.

"I believe this weapon may do a far better job balancing out good and evil here than any of your tricks, oh Wisp."

"And what do we have there?" replied the Wisp.

"I am armed with a high-powered laser weapon that burns, melts and explodes targets, which means I am the only real player here in your world."

Unless they disarm you through sheer numbers or a magical spell." responded the Wisp. "Remember nothing here is what it seems, and everything is what it is. Don't let your false pride and beliefs cloud decision making. You have entered a world, quite unlike what you know. This is a world where good and evil are quite transitory and sometimes not easily identified. A place where your friends can be your enemies and your enemies, your friends."

"So?" Lily responded.

"My point is that just like Little Lady who is good while her flying monkey brethren..."

Little Lady interrupted the Wisp, "Not a monkey."

"Yes, I know Little Lady." the Wisp replied. "But that is what everyone here in both Wonderland and OZ calls you and your kind. Sometimes perceptions, even those that are false become the truth, only because that is what people believe. As I was saying Little Lady is good while most of her kind are not."

"They are dead," observed Little Lady interrupting again.

"Yes, I know, and by the way Lily, your Gurgle is now a much-wanted man, because of lies spread by the little people of OZ, that he is the Lion of OZ and responsible for the deaths of the flying monkeys."

"What lie?" Lily once again questioned.

"The leaders of the little people made Gurgle into a hero to cover and protect the virtue of the many young women he impregnated during his visits to OZ. They fabricated many stories to embellish his standing to elevate those young women in the perceptions of the community. They told these lies so often, and yes Lily, they are lies, that when they learned about the slaughter of the flying monkeys they had to credit Gurgle with their destruction. Though Gurgle made it clear to me he was not even here at the time."

"That is correct," relied Lily. "Adam told us there was a huge fight between the Queen's men and the flying monkeys that allowed him to escape back to our universe. The slaughter was no doubt the Queen's work."

"Nevertheless, this embellished story has gotten back to the Witch and now Gurgle is a wanted man, which explains the plumes of smoke over yonder. They set fire to the little people's community. I was able to help some escape into the thorny forest. The rest are being held under difficult circumstances and some have even been tortured trying to get them to reveal where Gurgle is hiding. Unfortunately for them, though fortunately for Gurgle, they didn't know his location. Gurgle and his travelers left the community two days or so ago for Wonderland. The Witch's men just missed Gurgle, although the Witch's men are searching OZ and are now into the outskirts of Wonderland searching for him.

"Little Lady and I are on the way to OZ. Little Lady's mission is to reach the Witch and tell her the truth, that it was the Queen's men who slaughtered her flying monkeys. This will result in a reprieve for the little people and Gurgle, but will no doubt embroil this whole world in war. Many men and creatures of both good and bad character will surely perish."

Lily responded, "I am here to support my fellow travelers and assist them in their efforts to find and rescue our lost dimension travelers. It has been our intention to create a war between OZ and Wonderland to distract both sides while we search their dungeons for our people. They are destined to engage in war, and we are here to encourage that outcome. Our plans coincide, so count me in."

"Alas, it is not so simple as you seem to suggest Lily. As I started to say previously, good and evil are difficult to differentiate here in this world. Those from the outside who have not been here long are the least capable of knowing who their true enemies are. I on the other hand have been here for many Now's. You can rest assured I know the players. I have seen their intent. I understand their weaknesses and private ambitions for I am everywhere, and yet nowhere.

"My intention is to create a conflict that eliminates those of ill intent and low morals while minimizing deaths of those who are good. It is a planned culling of the various species, as some might call it. While it can never eliminate evil, perhaps it can restrict its growth. If you want in, then you must join as an ally and not as an independent operator. Agreed?"

"If Little Lady is an ally, then I too am an ally."
"Then you must carefully follow my directions."

"Yes, but my fellow travelers must not be sacrificed to

serve your private objectives."

"I cannot promise they will not sacrifice themselves for their own objectives, Lily."

"Some have to survive, Wisp. Especially Gurgle and Alice," said Lily.

"And Samuel and Adam are not priorities?" questioned the Wisp as he rotated once more and stared into  Lily's eyes.

"I did not say that they are not important, but it is true that to me some are more important."

"Well we all must live with priorities," replied the Wisp. "Very well, now let me think for a while about how to integrate you into our plans. You and Little Lady can have some time together while I ponder." With that the Wisp disappeared into a mist.

Lily looked over at Little Lady. "Does he always come and go like that?'

Little Lady nodded in the affirmative.

"I'm hungry," Lily said.

Little Lady replied, "Fly," as she lifted off the

ground and became airborne floating over to a nearby grove of trees. She quickly returned with some fruit.

Lily was quick to say, "Thank You," and she eagerly devoured the fruit.

"Tasty," responded Little Lady, who joined her in the snack.

A few Now's passed and then a wisp of clouds appears above their heads. The Wisp returned, displaying a wide smile and twinkling yellow cat-like eyes.

"Miss me?"

"No, not especially," responded Lily. "I have this question. You said good and evil are difficult to differentiate here in this world. How do I know which you are?'

"Excellent question Lily! You do not actually, but you must place your faith in someone. Therefore, I am here with your next task. Meet Molly."

From just out of view a white mare trotted up wearing just a bridle. She snorted loudly and stopped directly below the Wisp.

"Have you ever ridden a horse?

"Yes, in Dimension Two, I rode for entertainment, and pleasure. But I've never ridden bareback."

"Well this is a perfect time for a first in your life. I want you to ride Molly into town with Little Lady on your shoulders. Little Lady will deliver a message to the captain of the Witch's men that Gurgle is not who they should seek for retribution of the slaughter of the monkeys. Because she is a flying monkey, they will believe her."

"Is that all?" Lily replied.

"I know you are dying to try out your fancy weapon gadget here in this dimension, but it must remain hidden. There may come a time. But now is not it. I expect Little Lady to fly to the Witch's castle and deliver the message directly to the Witch. I can't be sure we can trust the Witch's men. They dislike little people because they refuse to bend to their will. If given the chance they will take the opportunity and destroy their community, if they have not already, and disperse the little people into other parts of this world."

"Will they go to Wonderland?" Lily responded

"No, the Queen there hates them as well, and blames them for everything bad that happens in Wonderland. She calls them rodents and claims they bring drugs into Wonderland. She says they are lazy and moochers. She keeps her subjects fearful of OZ and the little people by disseminating lies about them and maintaining a close control over her subjects. She will randomly choose a human or a poor innocent creature and accuse them of treason or collusion with OZ. If residents of Wonderland visit the little people without the Queen's permission, even by accident, they will stand trial. The trial is simply a show. The jury is composed of her handmaidens who are every bit as evil as the Queen. The verdict is always death, with a proclamation by the Queen's read by the jury: 'Off with their heads.' The innocent residents of Wonderland are dispatched at the time and place of the Queen's choosing. It's all quite sad."

The Wisp allowed a moment for Lily time to think about what he had just said.

"Ready now?" he asked.

"Yes, I guess" replied Lily. She dropped down off

her branch and walked over to Molly, extending a hand on her muzzle to allow the mare to smell her. She ran her hand up the side of Molly's face and down over her neck onto her back. Grabbing the bridle, she lifted herself with her arms and managed to swing her leg over Molly's back. It was not easy as Molly was a large mare. Molly snorted and turned toward the village of the little people. Little Lady was watching a safe distance away. She took flight and followed Lily and her mare, staying a few feet above them.

"Bye," the Wisp announced, as the three departed. When Lily looked around, the Wisp was gone.

"Little Lady I will need you to perch on my shoulders as we get closer to the village."

"Ok" replied Little Lady.

Molly broke into an easy cantor across the field of straw grasses toward the little people's community. Lily was a bit unsettled by Molly's bouncing gait. She clasped her legs tightly around Molly's body.

"Too tight," Molly responded. Molly's voice nearly caused Lily to lose her balance. She pulled up on the reins and bought her to a stop. She found herself blurting, "Oh hell, you mean you talk too. This is one weird place."

"Animals don't talk where you come from, Lily? Maybe we find it strange that creatures like you talk."

"Touché," acknowledged Lily.

"I am from Wonderland, and there are many animals who talk there. Not all but many. Some however you wish did not talk, because they make so little sense."

"One could say that about some humans," replied Lily. "So, explain why Little Lady who is from OZ talks."

"I don't know. I'm a horse! If you want to know that answer talk to the librarian at the great library, he may be able to tell you."

"Where is the great library?"

"It is built at the edge of Wonderland. But you probably will not make it there."

"And why not?"

"The Wisp says you probably will be unable to refrain from using your weapon system and end up swarmed by one side or the other. You will then be tried and likely lose your head."

"He does, does he? And how do you feel about me

Molly?" asked Lily.

"I feel like you are pulling too hard on the reins, and the bridle's bit hurts my mouth, if you must know. Otherwise you seem nice enough, but perhaps a little unprepared for what you will encounter in these lands of OZ and Wonderland. Now I have said enough. I really do not like talking all that much. I will resume my natural horse sounds and you can converse with the monkey."

"Not monkey," replied Little Lady indignantly.

"Yeah, yeah, I know, you're not a monkey! Then what are you? Because everyone calls you a monkey." Little lady shrugged her shoulders choosing not to say anything more.

Molly bucked slightly and took off in a moderate gallop in the direction of the burning villages ahead. "I see the Wisp has given us a temperamental mare, Little Lady." As they neared the village the extent of the damage became more apparent. The outlying homes and buildings were burnt out shells. Their approach gained the attention of the Witch's men who were forming a defensive perimeter for security. Lily brought Molly down from a gallop to a slow walk. She plodded along toward the sentries ahead. Lily waved a greeting. The men didn't respond but held their spears and swords in the direction of their approaching visitors. Little Lady took to flight, flapping her wings and flying in tight circles around Lily. The sight of the flying monkey caused the men to place their swords back into their sheaths and stand their spears upright.

One of the men walked toward them, "Halt, who are you and what is your business? Are you a member of the Witch's personal staff? We have not seen you before."

"Those are a lot of questions for someone who is simply bringing back one of the Queen's flying monkeys who I have nursed back to health after a large battle!" Lily's statement was a last-minute thought and seemed to ring true for the tall guard.

"Here turn it over to me so I can bring it to our commander."

"Pardon me," replied Lily. It is not an it, and she is a female, not a male, and her name is Little Lady."

Little Lady lowered herself onto Lily's shoulder and

looked at the guard. "I am Little Lady."

The guard was surprised that she could talk, and he stepped back. "What sort of sorcery is this? You must be a witch," pointing at Lily.

"I am not allowed to reveal the extent of my powers," she replied. "Just take me to your commander. I have a message to deliver to him."

The guard turned toward the center of town saying, "Follow me." "Well that worked well," Lily said under her breath

"Yes, very well," replied Molly. "Let's see how this plays out."

The guard led Lily into town. She observed considerable destruction on both sides of the street, and she could see no little people in sight. Not good, thought Lily. Finally, they reached the center of the town, where the mayor had once regaled the little people with the many tales of the Lion of OZ and wished Alice and the fellow travelers safe travels. Now it was swarming with the Witch's men. On the veranda of the great hall, Lily saw three or four little people held in shackles. They were bloodied and bruised and weaving back and forth on their feet from an apparently recent beating. The guard hurried over to the commander of the Witch's men.

"Another witch has shown up," said the guard. "She has given a flying monkey the ability to talk. I know not of her."

The commander looked over at Lily who was seated upon the mare and then at Little Lady. He seemed unsure what his next move should be. After a minute he thanked the guard and approached the Witch on horseback. The commander's name was Thaddeus. He was a large man standing six-foot-two and possessed of an immense ego. He had risen to his current level thanks to family wealth, rather than battlefield skills. He was a skilled orator who could appeal to the wants and needs of those around him and made many lavish promises which endeared him to his men. They would be happy to die for him. He was skilled at palace intrigue and even when facing failure, he was able to avoid repercussions for his actions by simply diverting the blame to others. In his mind, he felt destined to rule.

"My guard says you are a witch. Are you related to our leader, Cassiopeia?

"Aren't we all related to one another in one manner or another?" Lily replied. She skillfully deflected his question and the commander didn't seem to want to risk a variety of potential maladies or spells set upon himself or his men by pressing the point.

"My guard said you wanted to talk to me. What message do you bring?"

"The one you are seeking is not who caused the slaughter of the Witch's flying monkeys."

"And how do you know that?"

"Little Lady knows that. She was there," pointing to Little Lady. "Tell the commander who slaughtered the witch's flying monkeys."

Little lady responded with teeth barred and an angry look upon her face, "The Queen's men slaughtered us."

The commander stepped backwards as he had never heard a flying monkey talk. He looked around to the men assembled about the town center. Many gasped. It was obvious that these men had never ventured into Wonderland and knew nothing about the Wisp. That could prove to be useful information Lily thought to herself. She slid down from Molly and walked toward the commander and his men. They drew back slightly as she approached.

"Easy guys, I mean no harm to my fellow witch's brave men. I only seek justice and justice can be best served by ending the siege of these little people and returning to OZ to prepare for battle against the evil Queen."

The commander considered this course of action and consulted with his men.

Lily meanwhile ascended the steps of the great hall to get a closer look at the shackled little people. Three men and a woman stood in blood-soaked clothing with swollen eyes, missing teeth and evidence of broken fingers. She walked up to them and addressed a little man who had stepped forward as she approached.

"And you are?" she questioned. "I am the mayor, or at least I was the mayor. There's hardly anything left of our community."

Two more little people stepped forward; "I am a son of the Lion of OZ" stated one.

"As am I," said the other. A young woman stepped forward, "And I am the daughter of the Lion of OZ. We will die the sons and daughters of the great Lion of OZ. I heard them say you are a witch. I guess you have been sent here to dispatch us to the next life?"

"No, I arrived here to seek justice. The Lion of OZ did not slaughter the Witch's flying monkeys. The Queen's men did. I have nursed Little Lady back to health and now she is a witness to it all, and perhaps a lone survivor." The young woman stumbled and collapsed sobbing into Lily's arms.

"I try so hard to be brave, and they hurt me so badly. My fingers hurt. I will probably never be able to sew. They demanded to know where our father the Lion of OZ was. They kept hitting me. We told them again and again, we don't know. We told them he was here for two days and then left toward Wonderland. We did not know what purpose they in mind. We have not had any food or water today. Our clothing is soiled from the beatings. If you are here to kill us, please kill us now, I implore you!" Lily could not hold her any longer and the young woman sunk to the floor wailing in pain and suffering."

Lily was infuriated and flew down the stairs and stared into the face of the commander. "Time is up you worms! I shall dispatch all of you to feed upon only excrement and death the rest of your miserable existence," she yelled as she raised her hands in a sort of evil incantation.

All but the commander shrunk in response to her threats.

"I am sure we can come to an accommodation. And your name is?" "Lily."

"Well Lily, they will be released. Release them now," he ordered. His men rushed up to the shackled little people and took their encumbrances off their wrists.

"Feed them and provide them with clean clothing and a room to wash up in," Lily ordered. "If you have others release them as well, immediately, or face my wrath."

Soon the doors to the great hall opened and droves of little people ran out to embrace the mayor and children of the Lion of OZ. Among them was the mayor's daughter, Lizzie, who instead of rushing to her father's side strode up to Lily who was among the masses assembled at the top of the library steps.

"I am Lizzie, daughter of the mayor." she announced. "I don't know of you, but I could hear you speak from inside the library and I learned you are responsible for releasing my father and the children of the Lion of OZ. I thank you."

"Are you another child of The Lion of OZ," Lily asked.

"No, I am not," said Lizzie."

Lily let out a deep breath of air in relief. Noting her reaction Lizzie asked, "Does that please you?"

"No," said Lily preferring to cover a slip of emotions, "It means nothing to me, I am relieved I didn't have to turn these men into worms and sentence them to feed on excrement and suffer a slow death. It would have taken a great toll on my energy. I have traveled from afar and wish to only insure justice is served."

Lily returned to the commander, "The evening is ending soon, I will rest now, and Little Lady will set out for the Witch's castle and home. Little lady will deliver the news of the person responsible for the great slaughter of the flying monkeys. I suggest you and your men make your way back to the castle also."

"But as you said, it is late," replied the commander. "It is not wise to travel through the thorny forest at night. There is evil among those trees."

"Are you without sin?" She replied. "Evil should recognize you and let you pass for you will be among friends in that forest."

"Let us stay the night." The commander implored Lily.

Lily pondered his request, then responded, "You may stay the night, but you must sleep in the town's center. The main hall will be used to shelter the little people. You will share your food with them tonight. If you have medical staff, they will tend to the injured little people."

"It will be done as you say," replied the commander. He made his way toward his men. Being unsure as to the powers of Lily the witch, the commander chose compliance rather than defiance at that moment. Addressing his officers, he ordered them to bivouac in the town's center for the night while he tried to learn more about this so-called witch. Lily returned to fetch the bridle of Molly and led her to the only barn in town.

"You have handled things well," said Molly.

Little Lady, was hovering above during the negotiations, and now returned to rest upon Lily's shoulder. "Lily is witch?" Little Lady questioned.

"No, I am just an angry woman."

"An angry woman can be a terrible witch," replied Molly.

"You have a mission, Little Lady. Hover above me for a while, and then I will command you to rush to the Witch and give her the news."

"Little Lady followed the instructions and Lily in a very loud voice proclaimed to all within earshot, "Off to the witch you valiant flying monkey, fly off Little Lady."

Little Lady swooped around the town center putting on a show and disappeared off into the horizon as evening set down upon what was left of the little people's community.

# The Chiffon Sisters    15

Morning came to the community of little people. Those who had been abused by the Witch's men felt even worse as they awoke. For many, there was no amount of medicine that seemed to help.

The mayor's daughter, Lizzie, tended to the wounded throughout the night. She put new dressings on wounds and hugged those who hurt and were scared. She applied the herbal medications available to her but those had only a limited affect. She walked past the bivouacked guards, imploring them to provide food for her fellow little people. For a little person, Lizzie was tall, quite attractive and had acquired many skills for turning heads among men. She was not above flirtation when it came to achieving her goals. This was confirmed by her seduction of Slither a few nights before. Her pleasant, yet flirtatious manner insured many a stew pot was delivered to the town center for the little people.

Lily, meanwhile, discovered that her elaborate

laser weapon system which was comfortable during the day made sleeping nearly impossible. The metal skeleton structure dug into her skin and forced her to seek new comfortable sleeping positions amongst the pillows strewn about on the floor at night. She made a mental note to speak to Loco about this when she returned. Unfortunately, because of the presence of the Witch's men, Lily feared they might choose to test her and confirm if she were really a witch. She could ill afford to remove her defenses simply for a good night's sleep. Her life was worth more than a few hours of sleep.

Periodically during the night, she emerged from her sleeping room and restlessly roamed around the great hall, checking on the condition of the little people. If she couldn't sleep, she wanted to keep the Witch's men on their toes at night. She walked through their encampment at least three times during the night. She thought this might suggest that she was a witch who didn't need sleep and imply a terrorizing supernatural prospect for the bivouacked men.

During one walk she deliberately disturbed some of the slumbering men, to insure they knew she walked among them. That did provoke an inquiry from one of the commander's senior officers who asked her, "What is this, you do not sleep?"

"Why do you ask," she answered.

"Everyone must sleep."

She responded with a laugh, "Only those who are weak must sleep." She was enjoying her role pretending to be a witch.

A significantly inebriated lower level guard rose from his bedding, too far away to hear the conversation, and stumbled over to her, "Ah a woman of the night amongst us. I must thank our commander for his late-night gift."

He reached for Lily, grabbing her neck to draw her toward him for a kiss. His groin was vulnerable and just like she did to Slither, Lily lashed out with a well-placed knee that connected perfectly with the man and doubled him over. She followed with an upward movement that flung her metal encased forearm toward the guard's head, splitting his forehead open. The guard fell backwards onto the ground, a gush of blood flowing from his wound. Two men rushed to assist their fellow guard, who instantly lay unconscious on the ground.

Lily commanded, "Stop, let him bleed out. He is unworthy to serve the Witch of OZ."

The men retreated to their bedding in fear, with a certainty that the witch was going to cast a spell upon them in retaliation for the behavior of one of their fellow guards. She turned toward the commander's senior officer and offered an observation, "You do not have good control of your men. Tell me, what is your name?"

"Thorns, Thomas Thorns," replied the officer.

"Well Thomas, women must be treated with respect. Do you not agree?"

Yes, yes he nervously replied.

"Will I or any other woman have to endure that behavior again, while you remain here this night, or should I just expel you into the thorny forest now?"

"I will keep my men under control. I shall remain awake and ensure my men do as requested."

"Good!" replied Lily. Lizzie, was about 10 yards away and quietly observed the confrontation. She joined Lily and the two then exited the commander's encampment.

"I wish I could do that," she remarked to Lily

"Your name is Lizzie? I believe I heard you give that name."

"Yes, I am the mayor's daughter."

"How is he doing?"

"Better. They did not beat upon him as severely as they did the children of the Lion of OZ. He does not appear to have any broken bones, simply lacerations about his face and arms. His wounds will heal. My father and the other leaders of my community told a terrible lie that the Lion of OZ was the one who slaughtered the Witch's flying monkeys. Our community is now destroyed, and many people hurt for this lie which never had to be told."

"Truth is an elusive demon which requires honesty and strict adherence to principles. Vary from the truth and demon will exact a terrible price for many. It may not come immediately, but one must pay the price eventually," replied Lily.

"It is so," Lizzie agreed.

"I wish you a goodnight." said Lily, departing from

Lizzie.

Lily patrolled the town center throughout the night, and at first signs of dawn walked to the stables and placed a harness upon Molly. "We'll go for an early morning ride."

They galloped out of town past the awakening Witch's men. She did not care if they knew she was leaving, she needed time alone.

About a half mile out of town she came to a small stream, dismounted and stripped off her clothing to immerse herself in the refreshing waters.

"What is that upon your body," questioned Molly who noticed the metal skeleton surrounding her upper body. "Are you injured, do you need support."

"No Molly," I can't believe I am talking to a horse she thought. "It is a weapon system more powerful than anything ever seen in this universe."

"So, I am thinking you are a witch?"

"I guess so," replied Lily. She continued rinsing her clothes in the stream and hung them to dry on nearby plants. A wisp formed above her head as a pair of eyes peered down upon her.

"Good morning!" said the Wisp. "Sorry to come upon you at this time while you are not dressed."

"Go on," replied Lily. "We who travel the dimensions are often naked in front of others. It is of no concern to us."

"Very well. That is some contraption you wear," noted the Wisp. "I see you were wise enough to not deploy it yesterday."

"I heard that it was your opinion that I would use it and find myself headless at some time."

"There's still time Lily."

"You underestimate me, oh Wisp."

"Perhaps. I was impressed with your actions yesterday and through the night. You surprised me. The witch facade was genius, if I may say."

"You may say so," replied a now smiling Lily. "Compliment accepted! So, you watched me all day yesterday?"

"Yes, most of the day."

"You know curiosity kills cat"

"But I am not a cat!"

"Here kitty, kitty," she playfully replied.

The Wisp ignored her playful banter. "I bring you news. Not sure if it is good or bad news however."

"Go on,"

"You can expect visitors soon. How you handle them will determine your success in OZ."

"There are no clues, Oh Wisp? Are you going to let me walk into a trap without any knowledge? That seems unfair."

"But no one says life is fair, Lily."

"So, will you stop teasing me you old cat or do I have to take the ball of yarn away from you?"

"You are most impertinent!" replied The Wisp.

"Two can play at this game." replied Lily.

"OK Lily, you win." The Wisp swirled around horizontally and faced her, then he rolled over upside down and addressed her.

"I'm growing quite fond of you Lily. You have courage, a quick mind and are a risk taker. I shall try my best to see you keep your head."

"Thank you," she replied. "I will also try my best to keep my head. Now who is it that is coming?"

"You are going to like this; at least I believe you will. The Witch's two daughters will be arriving by carriage in the little people's village. Their names are Lemon and Lime Chiffon."

"They sound like deserts!"

"They look like deserts. You will understand what I mean when you meet them. They are only a little over 17 winter's old, identical twins I believe they are called. They are free of prejudices, hatred and sins, well most sins." They do have issues with pride, vanity, entitlements, and they are perhaps a bit slothful. Their most impressive trait is their interest in the welfare of others. They are neither cruel, rude, nor vengeful. Their Witch mother has done a good job raising them. They are two of my favorite people in this universe. But they have never met me."

"So, you're just a voyeur of young girls in real life?" replied Lily.

"Lily," exclaimed the Wisp. "I am unable to reveal myself to them because they don't yet have the maturity to keep my existence a secret. This would cause problems for them. They are good, and I am attracted to good. I seek a more peaceful universe and they may perhaps be part of the solution. One or both will succeed their mother in OZ. Our problem is they ride a dangerous and greedy beast. The Witch's guards are cruel and lack respect for others, and at times can be murderous. Their spells and incantations are an unequal match for the brute force and numbers of their mother's guards. There are also green men below the dungeon. These are men who are fearless and bred for violence."

"Then how has the Witch maintained her control of OZ?"

"Through the same skills you exhibited yesterday. She assumes a variety of personalities, advertises powers which she does not possess, and exhibits deflection skills. She possesses the ability to give people nebulous answers that confuse and leave them unsure and fearful. It is evident you and Cassiopeia, or the Witch as I have referred to her, are cut from the same cloth, you seem to share the same personality traits."

"I am not sure I wanted to hear that," Lily declared.

"You are alive today because of that. Now get dressed for you have visitors to greet." The Wisp then dissolved into nothingness.

Lily and Molly returned quickly to the little people's village. The Witch's guard was reorganizing their encampment and readying for their trip back to OZ. Lily dismounted and held Molly by the reins as she walked up to the guard's commander. "After the coming war between Wonderland and OZ I expect you to return here and help the people of this community rebuild." "That will be the Witch's decision," he replied.

"We'll see," said Lily.

Over the shoulder of the commander, Lily saw a golden carriage entering the little people's village. "Ah I see Lemon and Lime have arrived," she announced.

"You know them? the commander asked, stuttering.

"I know of them. Everyone has heard of Lemon and Lime Chiffon, the Witch's daughters."

Their carriage with guards pulled up to the commander's position. Out of the carriage stepped Lemon and Lime Chiffon. Lemon was bedecked in a bright yellow colored dress with short frilly white satin sleeves and a splash of ivory satin on a plunging neckline. Her hair was a startling blond color, her skin as white as white could be without being mistaken for an albino. Her eye liner was predictably yellow, and she wore a yellow flower above her left ear. She had matching yellow shoes and yellow socks. It was so blinding it seemed the sun was reflecting off them.

Next stepped out Lime who was wearing a bright lime green dress almost identical to Lemon's in design except for short green satin sleeves and a splash of green satin on her plunging neckline. As with Lemon, her hair was a bedazzling blond color, but with lime highlights. Her skin matched Lemon's strong white hue. Her eye liner was lime green and she wore a pale, green flower over her left ear. She had lime green shoes with matching socks.

Every guard and little person stopped what they were doing to watch the sisters disembark the carriage and walk to the town center. Lemon and Lime strode up to the commander. "And why?" questioned Lemon, "have you burnt this beautiful little community down? What possible reasoning could be behind this action." she demanded.

"We were searching for The Lion of OZ, the notorious killer of the Witch's flying monkeys."

"Have you not heard? A flying monkey has returned and announced that the Queen's men from Wonderland perpetrated the slaughter."

"Yes, we did hear that narrative late yesterday, but not until after we interrogated the villagers."

The mayor noted the Chiffon sisters' arrival and gingerly began his dissent down the steps of the great hall, helped along the way by his daughter Lizzie. "They tortured us," he cried out weakly.

Lemon and Lime looked toward the little person tottering down the stairs. Lime ordered the commander to follow them toward the stairs. "They tortured us," the mayor repeated. "We told them we didn't know where the Lion of OZ was. We only said that he was likely in route to Wonderland seeking out fellow travelers. We complied with all their requests, honestly. But it did not matter. They found the Lion of OZ's children {Gurgle's as he is also known} and beat them severely. They are up in the great hall recovering. They are in great pain."

Lemon and Lime looked back upon the commander with disgust. "If it were not for the witch Lily, who helped nurse the flying monkey back to health, there is no telling whether any of us would be alive this morning," continued the Mayor.

"Another witch?" they said in unison.

"Yes, I am," Lily announced, as she stepped forward and joined the assembled group upon the steps. "My name is Lily and I know you are Lemon and you are Lime. I love your clothes!"

"Why thank you," replied Lemon. "We are not familiar with other witches in OZ.

Where are you from?"

"Where I am from doesn't matter, nor when I may choose to return there. What is relevant is that I am here for justice and to set the record straight. The Queen's men slaughtered your mother's flying monkeys and they should be avenged.'

"You know our mother?" replied Lime.

"I know of your mother, she is a great Witch with much power. I do not believe she would approve of what has transpired here." "Nor do we," said Lime.

"Where are the injured?" inquired Lemon.

They walked up the stairs and into the great hall. Still laying on the ground were the Lion of OZ's three offspring devastated by their torture the previous day. They were suffering from the pain of broken fingers and a variety of painful bruises and lacerations. Lemon walked over to the young woman. "Close your eyes, I can make your pain go away."

She complied, and let Lemon lay hands upon the broken fingers, then in succession her bruises and lacerations. The young woman opened her eyes and smiled, then hugged Lemon. "Oh, thank you, thank you," she cried out and looked out upon her now healed fingers. "I will be able to sew again. It's a miracle."

Lime did the same for the two sons of the Lion of OZ. In a few moments all three were back on their feet. As the sisters left the hall, Lemon passed the mayor and similarly eased his pain and suffering.

The little people assembled in the hall watched and broke out in cheers. They ran up to thank Lemon and Lime. The sisters took time to greet and share hugs and handshakes with all the little people. Being about five-foot-eight, there were doing an awful lot of stooping and bowing down to reach the same level as the various little people. After a while they just shook hands as the effort to stoop wore on their leg muscles.

Once outside, the commander asked Lily so that the sisters could hear, "Why is it if you are such a powerful witch you could not have relieved their pain the night before?"

The question was unexpected and threw Lily for a moment. She stared at the commander but did not speak. Lime instead, spoke up, "Commander every witch has their own set of powers. Lemon and I can heal. Others can fly, but then some can turn others into different creatures.

358

There are witches who create mass destruction and others make flowers grow. Their powers vary."

"Well this witch," the commander said, pointing toward Lily, "killed one of my men last night. My man bled to death. She ordered us to not tend to his wounds, just let him bleed out. That is what she did. Your mother has one less guard today."

"Is that true?" asked Lime.

Lily answered in an assertive manner, "Yes that it true. He accosted me. He thought I was some lady of the night only because I was walking through the camp to confirm all was quiet."

"Well then, you just learned one of her powers, commander. She has the ultimate power to take a life. Hopefully you will not offend her as your man did last night. Otherwise Lemon and I would attend your funeral. And we would not like that would we Lemon?"

"That depends," replied Lemon, "I am reserving judgment."

"You are spoiled brats hiding behind your mother's powers. I'd turn both of you over my knee and give you the paddling you deserve. Maybe even leave you for my men's enjoyment. Neither of you frighten me. Perhaps now is the time for that paddling."

The commander suddenly moved aggressively toward the sisters, but his advance was curtailed by a green blast from Lily's ring, which sent him sprawling to the ground. It was so quick no one knew for sure if the blast came from Lily's hand or elsewhere. Some of the assembled guards who were eagerly surging forward a moment earlier with the cover of the commander's threat, now retreated in fear. The commander was still lying stunned upon the ground.

"Would you like to finish him off, or shall I?" Lily asked the sisters.

"Umm, mother would ask too many questions. Let him live," said Lemon. They left the commander sprawled out on the ground.

"He'll recover soon enough," advised Lily. "He'll live."

Lily, Lemon and Lime toured through the community and assessed damages done by the commander and his men. They noted burned-out houses and buildings, dead chickens, cows, horses and animals of all kinds. "They must bury this carnage before they leave," Lemon said to Lime.

"Of course, they will."

The sisters motioned to the guard accompanying them and ordered him to return to the town center and deliver their instructions to the men to clean up the dead carcasses.

"There's a quiet stream about a half mile away if you care to stretch your legs and get away from this smell and carnage," Lily offered to the sisters.

"We'd like that" they said in unison.

Lemon said to Lily, "We hardly ever get a chance to leave the castle, the carriage, or our staff. It's very boring being the Witch's daughters."

Lime added, "And we have no friends. No one wants to be friends with a witch."

"Well I guess we are all three witches," said Lily, "so to the stream we shall go."

Along the way Lemon showed off yet another skill.

As she walked into the field of grasses along the pathway they turned to see flowers sprouting out of thin air behind her.

"A trial of flowers is another of her skills," said Lime pride fully. "I wish I could do that. I haven't figured out how she does that yet."

"You can't?"

"No, we both can heal, but only she can make flowers grow." "And what can you do," interrupted Lily."

"I can become invisible, just watch." Lime swirled about and poof, she disappeared.

"Lemon called from across the field, "That's Lime showing off again," she said while laughing and running over to Lily side. "What can you do Lily?" "Just kill people, I guess." replied Lily.

Lime reappeared and said, "Oh, that's not a very nice skill."

"But one that is sometimes needed for survival," added Lemon. The sisters and Lily arrived at the streamside. Interestingly, Lemon never turned off her trail of flower powers and their entire path to the stream lay covered in flowers as they walked.

362

Lily brought up their mother, "I have never met your mother, I am somewhat younger, yet a bit older than you girls. We would normally never travel in the same circles."

"Girls, that's a nice term," giggled Lime. "No one ever calls us girls."

"It's nice, I like that word," said Lemon.

Lily laughed also, and then said. "Lemon if you don't turn off the flower spell us girls are going to soon be lost in a sea of flowers."

"Sorry, sometimes I leave it on all day without thinking, usually when I'm bored."

"And other times people start getting stung by bees and yell at you to turn it off," mentioned Lime. They giggled at that in unison. While there was an age difference between them, they still connected. "Mom loves us, but is pre-occupied with many things lately," lamented Lemon. "Yes, especially since her flying monkeys got wiped out," added Lime.

"Are they all gone?" inquired Lily.

"No there are some young, and a few too old and many of which were pregnant or injured at the time of the great battle. Mom only has about maybe 100 left. Before the battle, she had thousands." replied Lemon

"So Little Lady still has some of her kind alive?"

"Yes, but she is now the leader," said Lime. "Mom made her the leader last night before we left for the little people's community. She's very smart for a flying monkey."

"She talks too," interrupted Lemon. "That's unusual?" asked Lily.

"Well it's not common," replied Lemon. "Mom says she may be the first in over 100 winters."

"She's special? Asked Lily." "Very!" replied Lime.

"What else is happening?" Lily inquired.

"There's a power struggle between our mom and her guards. The commander and some of his senior staff want mom gone. If that happens, we are in trouble. You saw what almost happened back there in town," said Lemon.

"Mom has talked about marrying us off to a pair of the guard's senior staff members to keep us safe from harm should they overthrow her. The men she has chosen are much older," said Lemon.

"They are so gross!" said Lime.

'Look Lily," Lemon leveled with Lily, "All we can do is cast these minor spells and incantations, nothing like what you have."

"It is all mom taught us." added Lime.

"Why doesn't your mother just dispatch the guard leaders to the hereafter?" Lily wondered.

"Because she doesn't have many powers herself," replied Lemon.

Lime looked shocked as Lemon made that point. "Lemon, you should not have told Lily that. We hardly know her. We don't know if she is here to help us or overthrow our own mother."

Lily reached out and laid her hand upon Lime's hand, grasped it firmly and confided, "I'm on your side, OK. Remember the whole truth and justice thing."

Lemon, continued, "Our grandmother passed away before she could teach mom the book of incantations and spells. She only learned a few. Our grandmother was very powerful. Whether she was a good or bad witch is up for debate."

Lily interrupted, "Good and evil are often open to interpretation. Sometimes situations require differing responses. For instance, last night I killed a man. I could have encouraged his guard mates to help him and keep him from bleeding out, but I did not. Your guards are not good men, and sometimes one must be just as evil as their adversaries to prevail." The others paused for a few moments to reflect on Lily's words. "What else have you girls learned?"

"Other than healing, the flower trick, and the invisibility spell, not much I'm afraid. I've tried the invisibility spell," said Lemon. "It's not in me. I just can't get it right."

"We can't read the book of spells and incantation. Neither can our mother, Cassiopeia. There I've said it," said Lime. "We are no longer powerful and now with that knowledge you will overthrow us if you wish and take over."

"I don't want to take over girls. Since you have

shared your biggest secret with me, let me share my biggest secret with you. Then we will be on equal footing."

"Ok," said Lemon and Lime, once again in unison. "I am not a witch," announced Lily.

"But we saw you flash a bolt of light and knock the commander down. And last night you killed a man," noted Lemon.

"Yes, indeed I did those things, but the power bolt came from this ring. And my fighting skills, well the guy was drunk and sloppy; I kneed him and wacked him with my forearm, which opened a deep gash on his forehead. I hope you are ready for this." Lily stood up and took her blouse off revealing a metal skeleton surrounding her upper body and forearms.

"What in the world is that?" questioned Lime.

"It's my laser power pack. These holes on my forearm unit will emit a super- hot beam of invisible light that will set about anything on fire and melt most items. I may not be a witch, but I am the most powerful creature in this universe. "

"Wow, indeed you are," said Lemon. "I am not

from around here."

"Yeah, no kidding." said Lime. "So how do we get one of those?" "Consider that you have one. Me!" Lime and Lemon hugged Lily in joy.

"However, I am not alone here. There are four others with me in your universe. Or at least I hope they are still living. They are a woman named Alice, a man named Adam. A quite unusual man named Slither whose skin is black."

"Oh, that's interesting," said Lime.

"And finally, a little person named Gurgle, or the one you call The Lion of OZ. He is my man." Lemon and Lime looked at each other in a quizzical manner.

"Umm, he has a bunch of kids in the little people's community,' noted Lemon.

"Yes, I know, he was a popular man in his youth. It's something I am not happy about, but it was before I knew him.'

"He's also a lot shorter than you," noted Lime.

"Lily laughed, "Yes everyone reminds me of that. I

think that's so obvious. But he's very attentive, brave, and caring. I love him, warts and all."

"Aww," they both responded in unison. "That's sweet."

Lily continued, "We are here searching for fellow travelers. One of our group, the one called Adam, traveled here Now's earlier and was captured in Wonderland." "He's lucky he didn't lose his head," mentioned Lemon.

"He escaped by traveling through a secret tunnel from Wonderland to OZ." "Tunnel?" questioned Lime. "We know of no tunnel."

"He was captured just as he emerged from the tunnel. The monkeys spotted him. He ended up in your dungeon."

Lime interrupted, "That's not a nice place." "Anyway, I guess your mother met him."

"She did," affirmed Lime. "I remember seeing a man sitting with mom in her private reading room. We thought she was perhaps interested in him. She never brought anyone up to sit with her from the dungeons before. "

Lemon added, "He was a very handsome man. They looked good together. Mom is beautiful, she has long coal black hair, white skin like us, blue eyes and she's just about the most beautiful woman in this universe."

"I think she is," added Lime.

Lemon continued, "But the mystery man escaped one day and the last we heard they chased him near the tree of knowledge. I guess that is where the slaughter of the flying monkeys occurred."

"Yes, and now Adam is wanted throughout your universe," said Lily. "The Queen was angry because he escaped before she could use him as a pawn in her chess match. She wants to see him dead."

"Oh," exclaimed Lemon. "I've heard about her chess matches. We sent spies over there. Some have returned, but many have not."

"Mom was unhappy he left," responded Lime. "He was someone she no doubt liked to spend time with. She's lonely. She never wanted him dead. She wanted him to come back."

Lemon added, "If it weren't for us, her two

daughters, mom would have packed up and left OZ long ago. She hates all the scheming and backstabbing in OZ. She said once that she wished someone would just throw water on her, so she would melt."

"She would actually melt?" questioned Lily.

"No that's just from a book. Some guy wrote a book about OZ, there were good and bad witches, a cowardly lion, a tin man and a scarecrow." said Lemon.

"And a wizard," added Lime.

"Yes, but none of that happened here, it was just a dumb book. Our great grandmother who I believe was the witch at the time, hated that book, because Mr. Baum, I think his name was, wrote that a woman named Dorothy threw water on her which made her melt away. She was not the good witch in his book." explained Lemon.

"I heard they had a falling out back then," said Lime. "Mr. Baum came from somewhere else and they supposedly were friends for a while. Then they had a big fight and he snuck away then returned a while later with his book which upset our great grandmother. I think the book was his revenge for their big fight. She had the flying monkeys chase him away to where ever he came from. Or at least that is how the story goes."

"That's interesting," commented Lily. "Anyway, I am here searching for Gurgle. He and the others are in search of other travelers who may be in your mother's dungeon and we also needed to check out the Wonderland dungeon for ourselves."

"Boy, that'll be dangerous," said Lemon. "People generally don't come back from the Queen's dungeon."

"Are you girls aware of anybody in your dungeons who is not from around here?"

"No," said Lemon, "but then again mother doesn't allow us to go down there because of the large green men and because the guards are dangerous according to her."

"Look, if you come with us, we can all go together into the dungeons and look for them," said Lime. "Mom will not mind, especially since she is fearful of an attempted overthrow. You could be really valuable tous."

"Great!" replied Lily "We are a team."

The three clasped hands together and shouted, "Team," in unison. The trip back was joyous, and their new-found friendship blossomed. On the walk back to town, they saw the dead animals were gone and could see mounds in the distance where the animals had been dragged for burial. As they approached the town they noted the recovery had begun. The little people were no longer afraid of the guards, thanks to Lily's intimidation. The Witch's guards had packed up and were waiting for the young witch's return before setting off for OZ. The commander was recovering from the blast and stretched himself out in a wagon. He was alert, but considerably disoriented.

Lily walked up to the wagon ignoring the witch's men and motioned the little people to come close to her. She spoke to the mayor and the assembled people. "Residents of this village, you have a unique opportunity afforded to you. The Witch's commander is in need of continued care. Would you like to have the commander remain in your community and recover here? Perhaps you will show him some true hospitality."

An elderly little person jeered and spit in the

commander's direction. "I'd like to show him my cane collection. I will beat him for weeks!"

The crowd laughed.

"Well that wasn't the hospitality I was speaking of," Lily said. She walked over to the commander, "Do you want to stay?" The commander said nothing but shook his head from side to side.

"Well he declined, that's too bad. I think he would have enjoyed the cane collection." The crowd laughed again. The witch's men remained silent, most with their heads bowed. They preferred to just stand there, quite intimidated by Lily. No one wanted to risk an interaction with the witch they knew as Lily. Lily turned toward Lemon and Lime saying, "I must say goodbye to Molly the mare. I will only be gone a short time."

The sisters nodded and watched Lily walked over to the barn where Molly was being kept. As she walked into the barn she glimpsed a figure in the shadows. It was Lizzie. She walked into the light as Lily stepped toward Molly.

"And what do you want Lizzie?" questioned Lily.

"I was visiting Molly. When you came in I shrank back into the shadows, fearful that you may be one of the soldiers."

Lily responded, "I'm leaving Molly behind. I am traveling to the Witch's castle with her daughters, Lemon and Lime. They need my help. That means you can have more time with her."

Suddenly a wisp of a cloud formed atop a railing in the barn and a wispy form that Lily recognized immediately as Wisp, emerged with the yellow cat's eyes now peering at them.

"Good morning ladies. I see you have met the sisters. Lily, do you like them?"

"Very much, thank you." replied Lily "They are, as you said, very good!"

"Yes, they are, as is Lizzie here." "Thank you," replied Lizzie.

"Lizzie, you as well must bid goodbye to Molly, for you can't remain here. I need you to travel with Lily and the sisters to the castle. Along the way you can call for your fellow townspeople who are hiding in the great thorny forest. You must tell them to return to their homes and start rebuilding. They are being kept safe by the older Wisp who protects them from an evil infesting the great forest. But I warn you not to dawdle in the forest, as the older Wisp is weak and not far from death."

"Oh, that's not good," replied Lily.

"It is the way of life," replied a resigned Wisp. "However, a Wisp never dies. At least that is what I understand. He will be reborn, but it'll be some time before he can provide protection for others."

"You do not act surprised," Lily observed to Lizzie.

"I am aware of Wisp life spans," she said without further comment.

"Oh," replied Lily. Lily continued, "Then you want Lizzie to return with her people back to the village?"

"No Lily will go on to the witch's castle with you."

"Have you been to the witch's castle before Lizzie?"

Lizzie replied, "Never, but the Wisp wants me to go. So, I will trust the Wisp." "Does everyone just always obey the Wisp around here?"

"No, not everyone, but the smart ones do." said Lizzie.

"Then come with me."

The Wisp commented, "My work is done here!" and spun around and was gone. Lily and Lizzie walked back out to the carriage, where Lemon and Lime awaited.

"Girls!" Lily announced.

Lemon and Lime squealed at being called girls again. "We do like that term," observed Lemon.

"We will have one more with us on our travel back to the castle, her name is Lizzie."

"Hi Lizzie," said Lime. Lizzie returned the greeting.

"Good, we have another friend to travel with!" said Lemon. "This will be fun."

After a few minutes to pack, the golden covered carriage took off down the yellow brick road toward the castle, leaving behind the guards who were organizing their return to the castle and tending to a still woozy commander.

They traveled a few miles and entered the dreaded thorny forest. It was stark blackness full of tall, slender thorn covered trees with branches growing out in all directions. There were small immature thorny vines sprouting black berry looking fruit which were poisonous. They grew in any space that found sparse sunlight slithering into the forest. The nearly black leaves of the thorn trees formed at the top branches, which created a canopy over the forest. Almost no sunlight found its way onto the floor of the thorny forest.

Crawling along the ground could be seen all forms of insects such as centipedes, spiders, roach-like bugs and other insects that fed on dead vegetation or each other. It was a trail other travelers used only if frightened or running for their life. This is the kind of place that thirty little people had chosen to flee to. Gurgle's son Ray and other children of the Lion of OZ were among them. Finding them would likely prove difficult in such terrain. About a mile into the great thorny forest their carriage came upon the remains of a human.

"This was not here on the way out to the little people's village." said Lemon. "Or maybe we just were not paying attention," countered Lime.

Lemon stuck her head out the carriage window and yelled to the driver,

"Stop! Did you see that body back there on the side of the road?"

"Yes, of course I saw the body, but I won't stop for such things in the thorny forest. It could be a trap."

The driver hollered down at Lemon as he continued on, "One minds our own business in the thorny forest."

"Well that settles that!" observed Lizzie.

Suddenly the carriage slowed, and the driver was heard, hollering "Whoa there."

Lily glanced toward the front of the carriage where a large tree had fallen across the yellow brick road. Lemon looked out the window on the other side.

"I wish our guards were with us now. That's too heavy to move out of the way," commented Lemon.

The driver yelled down to the girls, "Ladies, stay inside. Don't venture out of the carriage. We may be in for trouble."

Suddenly the carriage was surrounded by little people and a large dark wispy cloud came to rest upon the tree.

It was the older Wisp. He opened his eyes and smiled displaying a mouthful of large white teeth. "We have captured someone." The old Wisp said.

"It's Lizzie," said one of the little people, "and those two are the Witch's daughters along with one other."

"Great let's take the Witch's two daughters hostage. We will ransom them for the release of our village." said another.

"Now I see why the Wisp requested me to come along," opined Lizzie as she exited the carriage.

"Seriously, do you guys want to get wiped out?" she asked, stepping down upon the ground. "Don't you realize what these people can do? I am not a hostage. I am traveling with them to the castle. These people are on our side. Well, I don't know about the driver."

The driver nervously spoke up, "I'm definitely on your side. My allegiance is to the Witch's daughters." He cowered in the carriage's foot space area and begged, "Please, don't hurt me," holding his hands up in front of his face."

"Driver too then," said Lizzie.

"This is witch Lily," said Lizzie pointing to Lily as she exited the carriage. "She turned back the Witch's men with the help of Lemon and Lime Chiffon, the Witch's own daughters. They healed my father and three of the Lion of OZ's offspring. They were beaten badly, and the town partially burnt to the ground. Any of you who are the remaining offspring of the Lion of OZ should be grateful that you fled from our village."

Ray, the Lion of OZ's son, stepped forward and barked a command, "Remove the barrier, I command it." The old Wisp looked at Ray, "You will give an old Wisp the time to remove himself I hope." The Wisp slowly rose from the tree and turned three hundred and sixty degrees before floating off to the side of the road.

"Where on earth were you hiding?" questioned Lizzie. "There is no place to hide, there's only thorns along the road."

"We cut sections out of the trees and carved out hiding places well back in the forest. It's not pleasant, and during the night creatures crawl all over you and bite. The Wisp has done his best to keep us safe, but he can't control the creatures on the forest floor. Any area not covered by your clothing invites all manner of creature bites."

"You can leave now and return to the village," announced Lily. "It is probably safe now. But wait until the Witch's guard has passed before traveling back down the yellow brick road. I do have a request, is it possible you can block the guard's path back to the castle? We need a bit more time to look for our travelers at the castle before they return."

Ray spoke up, "There are barriers ahead we will use to block their path. We can also remove this log, wait for them to pass and at the right moment, drop it in their path trapping them for some time in the forest." He joined his fellow little people and set about laying the traps. "We can leave the forest as soon as we have laid the traps," he announced.

The older Wisp smiled as he drifted along the side of the road. In a very deep voice he said, "So you're Lily, looking in her direction. My Wisp brother has told me much about you. He mentioned there were other travelers here. A woman and three men who are all brave and good people. If I were up to the task, although I know I am not, finding myself in the sunset of life and about to flame out, I would relish the fight ahead. But alas, I am an old Wisp who in these last moments has chosen to hide in the shadows of life and burn out dimly."

"Yes" replied Lily, "but even in your final days, you are providing a secure hiding place for those in need."

"I am indeed," the older Wisp replied. He then disappeared in front of their eyes, his cloud drifting back into the thorny forest. Everyone continued in the carriage and a few miles down the road, exited the forest.

In the distance the outline of a great castle rose into the sky. Its emerald green roof's tile work shimmered in the setting sun. Lizzie commented, "Oh my gosh, the emerald city!"

Lemon replied, "That's what Mr. Baum called it in our grandmother's time according to his book. The only thing that's more of an emerald color is my sister Lime." Lime giggled at the reference to her color palette.

"It's beautiful," replied Lizzie. "Just like what I expect a castle to look like."

They approached the gates and heard commands to open the gates. Two very large wooden doors slowly creaked open and the carriage slipped safely inside. Back in the forest, the little people that remained set their traps and as the Witch's guards passed, logs fell from all directions confining the guards to a narrow part of the yellow brick highway. As dusk approached, the guards were still attempting to clear the roads and pass onward toward the castle.

# Cassiopeia 16

Upon seeing the carriage return, the Witch's handmaidens ran down the steps of the castle to roll out a bright yellow carpet for the occupants to dismount upon. Lemon's toes touched down first, "Ah, there's no place like home." she announced as a tiny dog ran up to greet her. "Toto!" she called out.

Lime looked at Lizzie and Lily and commented, "She has read The Wonderful Wizard of Oz, and named her little dog Toto, go figure." Everyone laughed. After disembarking the carriage, Lime grabbed Lily's hand and tugged her in the direction of the castle. "Let's go meet my mom!"

"Come on Lizzie," Lemon said holding her little dog, "Hurry, it's almost dinner time and mom has a lot of questions to ask us. They all raced up the steps through the large castle doors and into the large foyer. Water basins are positioned just inside the door for washing up and handmaidens are stationed with towels to dry off. Lemon and Lime were excited to have their visitors to show off.

"There are dressing rooms to the left and right, and a variety of clothes in each for you to choose from," said one of the handmaidens. Noting that Lizzie was nearly a foot shorter than the others, a handmaiden waved her over to another dressing room. "We have small dresses for you in here. Choose what you like."

Lily's choices were mostly short sleeves, which would be a problem as they would reveal her forearm equipment for the world to see. No telling if members of the guard would be present. If so, they would recognize she was simply armed with a weapon and not a witch after all. She told a handmaiden she changed her mind and wanted long, billowy sleeves on her dress. A new selection of dresses was presented to her. This time she chose a black, long sleeve dress which fit perfectly.

Now properly dressed for dinner, Lemon was wearing her lemon colored dress, Lime in a lime dress, Lily in her black dress and Lizzie wore a blue dress. Lily allowed her brownish blond hair to fall naturally on her shoulders. Lizzie's long red hair was pulled back into a bun in a very formal manner. Lemon and Lime led Lily and Lizzie upstairs and into their mother's formal dining room.

Cassiopeia waited for them at the door. She wore as usual, a beautiful black gown, with plunging neckline. Her long black hair was leisurely tied back to hang down her back. Her skin was white as could be and her soft blue eyes had a penetrating glance.

"And who are your guests, Lemon?"

"This is Lily," Lemon announced, pointing toward Lily. "She's sort of a witch, well, I guess she is a witch, I guess."

"Oh, OK?" Cassiopeia laughed. "I didn't know there were sorts of witches."

"And this is Lizzie; she's from the little people's village. Except, she isn't quite so little."

"I think I can see that Lemon, but thanks for pointing it out," again laughing in response to Lemon's introduction." I am Cassiopeia," she announced to Lily and Lizzie, "the Grand Witch of OZ." Cassiopeia warmly hugged both daughters. I haven't had dinner visitors here in quite a while," she told Lizzie and Lily. "Come let's talk. Wine anyone?" They all nodded affirmatively, and glasses were filled. "Remember Lemon and Lime, one glass each only."

In an aside, the Grand Witch said to Lizzie and Lily, "A winter ago my girls snuck some extra drinks and didn't feel quite so good. In fact, Lime here used her invisibility power and got herself lost. It took her quite a bit of time to find her way back here."

"That was really scary too," Lime said.

Lily spoke up, "How is Little Lady?"

"Who is that?" questioned Cassiopeia.

"She's the flying monkey who was returned to you. That is what we have named her?"

"We?"

"Ok mom, we need to tell you something," said Lemon. "Lily isn't from around here. She's from another universe, just like that guy Adam you kept here for a while before he escaped. She's on our side and wants to help us."

"So do I," interrupted Lizzie.

"Lily has great powers, amazing powers. Far greater than ours, mom," said Lime. "She killed one of your guards who accosted her, she knocked the commander of your guards on his back with a blast of some kind."

Cassiopeia then addressed Lily's question about Little Lady. "The flying monkey, or Little Lady, as you call her, is in excellent condition. Thank you for asking about her. She will join us tomorrow. She's had a long day. Now about those powers Lily?"

"Let me come clean Cassiopeia, as I have with your daughters. I am from another universe. There are in fact five of us here currently in your domain. Adam, the man you held in your dungeon and spent time with has returned here. Alice, is the leader of the mission. A man named Slither who has dark skin, and a little person named Gurgle, whom you may know as the Lion of OZ."

"She's his mate," added Lemon, pointing to Lily. "You mean Lizzie is his mate?"

"No Lily."

"I'm confused." replied Cassiopeia

Lily spoke up again, "I love Gurgle, he is my man. And yes, before you say it, I'm a lot taller than him. But it works, does it ever!"

The Chiffon sisters giggled and blushed at her comments. Even Cassiopeia was a bit flushed. Sorry it's been a while, she laughed. "Lemon and Lime, behave yourself, you'll get there someday, hopefully not immediately."

"OK in the interest of full disclosure," Lizzie added, "I've been with Slither. It happened just before he left for Wonderland. Now that was nice!" The girls giggled again, and both Lily and Cassiopeia laughed.

"Is he your man?" asked Lemon.

"No, he is more of a dalliance for me. I don't presently need a man in my life. I am still young and not ready to settle."

"So, you just spent the night with him?" questioned Lime.

Cassiopeia interrupted, "I think this is on the verge

of getting too adult for you two girls."

Lime commented to Lemon, "Mom actually called us girls! First time!"

"OK, time for the big reveal," said Lily as she stood up, pulling the top of her dress down around her waist. "This is an upper body laser unit with forearm weaponry. These holes in the front of the forearms emit a colorless beam of light that burns through anything, blows up things and melts things. Besides that, I have this ring on my hand which emits a green light charge that knocks down or even kills its target. The metal framing is impenetrable from most attacks and the forearm guards are also used as weapons. That is how I killed one of your guards, by striking him on his forehead which opened a large wound and caused him to bleed out. Well not entirely. I told your guards that they were not to help him, so he died of massive bleeding. I am not sure they might have saved him, but I didn't care. He accosted me and intended to do me great harm. These are all modern weapons from our universe and quite frankly, I am the greatest power in your universe today."

"Are the others similarly equipped? Cassiopeia asked.

"No, they only have power rings, and Slither has a few tricks such as a smoke cover, sparklers, a fire bag, and quite likely other resources. No one ever knows for sure the arsenal he is carrying"

Lizzie spoke up once more. "Slither is dressed like a scarecrow. He has all these patches on his clothing. He had me sew them onto his clothes for him, in between the other more fun, intimate things we were doing."

"Fun things?" questioned Lime.

"Lizzie," Cassiopeia called out, "I see I'm going have to watch what you say around the girls. Too much information!"

"Hey, mom called us girls again" said Lemon.

"Sorry, I keep forgetting they are so young," replied Lizzie. "As I was saying the patches are sewn on in a certain manner, so he can place his tricks as he calls them in the patchwork."

"Ah," said Lily, "So the secret is out; he stores his tricks in the patches. Good to know. Cassiopeia, I have come here to keep you and your daughters safe. It is the Wisp's request."

Cassiopeia's eyebrows arched up, "You know of the Wisp?"

"Yes, the younger Wisp is who requested we watch over you and your daughters," replied Lily.

"We met a Wisp." said Lemon and Lime in unison.

It's been years since I have seen a Wisp," Cassiopeia said. I can't explain who or what they are. I know there are two. They are nebulous and everlasting according to legend. Where did you meet a Wisp?"

"In the thorny forest," said Lemon.

"Just today?" asked Cassiopeia

"Yes, he is a very old Wisp who hides in the thorny forest. He watched over the little people who fled from your guards."

Lizzie added, "I met the younger Wisp when Lily and I were talking in the barn in my village just before we left to travel here."

"That means both Wisps are about?" asked Cassiopeia.

"Well one is dying, mom, the one in the thorny

forest. But he didn't seem bothered by it," added Lemon.

"That's because Wisps never die, they are resurrected."

"Do we get resurrected?" asked Lime.

"It is believed, at least in our world, that we never die. We do not come back like the Wisps and from what I have heard the Queen of Wonderland," noted Cassiopeia.

"She never dies?" asked Lemon.

"That is what I hear." replied Cassiopeia.

"But she is said to be evil and cruel. That is not fair," said Lime.

"Life is not fair my girls."

"Mom," Lemon said, "Your guards are very cruel, they brutally beat some of the little people and burned down much of their village. They threatened to throw us to the men to do whatever. If Lily had not shown up I fear they would have killed many little people, and I don't know what would have happened to us"

Lizzie spoke up, "Yes they are quite brutal. They tortured the mayor and any of the children of the Lion of OZ they could lay their hands on. I believe they would have killed all of us little people."

"One of your guards told me they were going to lock us in the great hall and set it on fire. I don't know if that was an empty threat or not, because he also told me he would save me if I accompanied him to the barn and did some things with him. That would have been a mistake because there are numerous weapons I could use in a barn. Unlike others, I am not afraid to die and would have fought him to the end."

"I am sorry," Cassiopeia said, looking down at the table. "Unfortunately, I no longer am able to control them. They no longer fear my power. They realize I have but a few silly spells left as resources. I can bite someone and cause them to lose all will.

That's a strange spell, she chuckled, but useless. It doesn't last very long, and I am required to bite them again to be effective. Indeed, I must break their skin every six days. I can make it rain indoors, which doesn't impress or scare anyone. I can also do the flower thing that Lemon does. And all of us are healers, which is a wonderful gift."

"It is," replied Lizzie.

"Girls, from now on you have to stay in the castle, near me. Things are no longer safe for traveling."

Aww mom," they said in unison.

Enough pre-dinner wine was consumed by Cassiopeia, Lily and Lizzie that a nice buzz permeated the occupants of the room. Social defenses relaxed, and the women dropped all formality amongst themselves. Laughter filled the room. Then it was dinnertime. Wonderful hot hors d'oeuvres were served, followed by a delicious salad and a fish entre with a variety of vegetables. The women shared relationship war stories and commiserated about their love lives or lack thereof.

Lemon and Lime had never seen their mother in this light. The gaiety lasted well into the night. At one point they were near an open window and her guards' entry into the castle could be observed.

"We had a little trick up our sleeves in the thorny forest," announced Lily. The little people fled there, and they felled large trees throughout the forest making the guards' march through the forest quite time consuming."

"I really like you Lily! Thank you for making their

lives miserable. I cannot tell you how fearful and difficult the commander has made mine," replied Cassiopeia

"Hopefully I will continue to make his life a living hell!" laughed Lily. "And help you regain control of your kingdom."

The arriving commander regained his footing and waited for everyone to dismount. He assembled his troops in formation and dismissed them. He intended to enter the castle and announce his arrival to the Witch. However, he was rebuffed by the witch's attendants. "She is not taking visitors tonight, commander." Rebuffed, he stormed back to his living quarters to await the dawn. Things would be different tomorrow.

Late into the night after Lemon and Lime were in bed, the three women retired to the Witch's study. Before them was a large book of sorcery written in a strange language.

"Here is my problem," related Cassiopeia pointing to the book. "My mother died before she could teach me the language in her book of sorcery. Therefore, my witch training was very limited. I survived not because of my powers but my abilities to assume a variety of personalities, I appeared to possess powers which I really did not possess at all. I also employed deflection skills. I could display the ability to give people nebulous answers that confuse and leave one unsure and fearful."

"Those are the same traits the Wisp said I have." replied Lily.

"Well, fortunately for us, they have kept us both alive and well. But I am afraid that I have played all the cards I possess. The guards are getting bolder with every passing day."

She opened the book, paged through it and sighed. "I wish I could understand what it says."

Lily flipped a few pages herself. She saw old engravings of pastoral scenes, but the language was unintelligible. "What a beautiful book," she said.

Lizzie looked down upon the book as she turned the pages. Lizzie placed her index finger on a page and smiled broadly. "Now I know why the Wisp wanted me to come with you, Lily. I know this language."

What, that's impossible" Cassiopeia exclaimed. "How can that be? Are you a Witch?"

"No questions about how I know this language, please. And no, I am not a witch. It's a very old language and someone in my past read books written in this language and taught me the language as well. However, I can't remember exactly how to pronounce the words, but I know their meaning."

"This here is an incantation that turns men into animals. I would think that could be very useful for you Cassiopeia." Lizzie paged through more chapters, naming each spell or incantation she encountered as she flipped through the pages. "Now my problem is I am not a witch. I think there must be some other magic required as part of the training."

"There is. However, I am somewhat unsure whether I know what that magic might be. I am sure however that I can certainly guide everyone through some of the training. I could even perhaps teach a spell or two to you Lily."

"Maybe you should concentrate the training on Lizzie," said Lily, "I just prefer to just use my weapons. But

I would love to watch the training."

Cassiopeia replied, "Oh I wish you would. It'll be so much fun. I can't wait to tell Lemon and Lime." Cassiopeia started to cry. "I was afraid I would be unable to protect my girls. Thank you so much for coming here, Lizzie." A group hug ensued and later everyone retired to their rooms. The group outlasted the castle staff who already retired to their rooms or fell asleep in nearby chairs.

The next morning the commander made his presence known by swinging open the doors to the breakfast being attended by all the participants of the previous night's dinner. Cassiopeia rose from her chair in an angry manner, "Just what is the purpose of this commander? You shall not barge into my breakfast and disturb my guests."

"I shall do as I please, because I am the commander of the castle guards," replied the commander. He pointed toward Lily, "This woman killed one of our men two nights ago, and you dare to have breakfast with her? I demand you turn her over to me now. The people of OZ need to see that justice is served! And while here, I also will take custody of the little person at your table. The little people are hiding the one they call the Lion of OZ, he is the one who killed your flying monkeys."

"Umm commander?" replied Cassiopeia, "We all know it was the Queen's men who killed my monkeys. They attacked in the field near the tree of knowledge and unfortunately my flying monkeys were no match for their men. If you wish to fight a war I suggest you prepare for battle against Wonderland."

"Your flying monkeys are useless; they have been bred into passive, harmless creatures who serve no purpose. I slaughtered the remaining monkeys early this morning."

"What," Cassiopeia screamed. "They are all dead?" Lily rose from her chair as did Lizzie.

Lily warned, "Commander if you value your life you will exit this room immediately, lest you cease to exist. Yesterday was just a sample of my powers. Today I will gladly kill you."

The commander exited while keeping his back to the door, and eyeing Lily. As he left, he announced, "Cassiopeia, your reign ends today. You have no powers that I need to concern myself with, nor do your daughters, who I may soon throw to my men for their enjoyment."

Lily raised her arm to point it in the direction of the commander. Her weapon lay hidden by the billowy sleeves on her dress. Cassiopeia shouted, "Lily don't! We will all die." Lily dropped her arm to her side.

"Then you will turn your guests over to me?" asked the commander.

"No, I will certainly not!"

"Then you will not live to see the night skies," replied the commander as he left the room.

The prior frivolity and happiness of the breakfast was shattered by news of the monkeys' demise. "Poor Little Lady," said Lily. "Alice is going to be so angry. I cannot believe he could do that."

Lizzie spoke up, "I can, and I do believe they intended to slaughter my people yesterday. Your commander is evil, perhaps as evil as the Queen of Wonderland" Lizzie responded, "I don't believe the Wisp could allow this."

Suddenly in the air above the dining room table a wisp of cloud formed and settled upon the dining room table. A pair of yellow eyes blinked and stared at the assembled group.

A staff member having not seen the Wisp's entrance came up and attempted to shoo the Wisp off the table.

"The table is no place for cats," she said. The Wisp whirled around and grasped her hand in his mouth and bit down with enough force to make the servant yelp. The servant retreated holding her hand to her chest.

"I am not a cat for your information and if you grab me again I will relieve you of that grabby hand." After learning of the deaths of the monkeys, the room was a bit morbid, although soon a giggle or two was heard.

The Wisp whirled back around and faced the group. "Hello Cassiopeia, I can't remember how long it has been since we have been together, but I believe you were a young girl at the time."

"Correct," stated Cassiopeia. "It was shortly after my mother's death when you visited."

"I was trying to console you, but I think all I did was scare you."

"Yes, and I wanted you to come back, but you never did."

"That is only because you did not ask me to come back. Hello Lemon and Lime. I have been monitoring you for many years. You have good hearts, perhaps a bit vain, but kind. No one of course, is perfect, my young ones."

"We met another Wisp in the forest." said Lemon.

"Yes, he is quite old and ready for his resurrection, which will not be long Wisps do not die but come back to this place exactly as we were before. Most creatures' souls go elsewhere to the void, or some other experience. Some call that heaven. But we Wisps return here. As far as I know forever, and ever, with complete knowledge of our previous lives still intact. For instance, I remember your grandmother, Cassiopeia. A very powerful witch, but unfortunately she was somewhat egotistical and jealous."

"I have heard the stories," replied Cassiopeia.

"I must warn you that the Queen of Wonderland also does not die, and neither can her sister according to legend. You need to know this as a war may be approaching. It does not serve anyone to kill her for she will immediately return. She will be the greatest challenge of all time if you choose her for an adversary."

"Where is her sister?" asked Lime.

She has disappeared many, eons ago. Perhaps the Queen herself killed her." "I thought you said they cannot die?" questioned Lime.

"They cannot, except by the hand of their sister. It appears our universe is destined to always have the evil Queen amongst us."

"So why do we fight?" questioned Lizzie. "Is it not hopeless?"

"We fight because there is always hope my dear Lizzie. Perhaps Lily's weapons hold the clues we seek. I do not know. Yes, sadly even the Wisp does not know everything. But we will not speak of hopelessness."

"And why not?" asked Lily, "The flying monkeys are dead, including Little Lady."

"Well that's another part of the reason why I am

visiting you. Yes, the flying monkeys have been slaughtered. However Little Lady lives! I sent her on her way back to Alice, late last night. She has no doubt joined Alice by now."

Lily smiled. "That's wonderful and yet quite sad. She is now the last of her kind."

"Yes, but she is alive," said the Wisp as he whirled around. "And now you have to work hard to stay alive yourselves. The commander is plotting your demise Cassiopeia, in fact everyone's end of days. I have provided you the ability to read your sorcery book through Lizzie, but you don't have the time to practice. They are plotting your overthrow as we speak. Troops are assembling to rush your position. You have until tonight and no more."

"I will turn my weapons upon them!" announced Lily.

"There will be too many," the Wisp responded. "You will be overwhelmed.

Cassiopeia must deliver word to the commander that you have agreed to abdicate."

"But it is our castle," implored Lime.

"It's just a cold lonely castle honey," replied Cassiopeia." I have not been happy here for years. It is my fault for allowing this to happen. I sat brooding in my chambers for so long, so bored and lethargic."

"There are other places to go girls. Places where I am permitted the time to teach you the craft of sorcery, if Lizzie will come along and help us," looking over toward Lizzie.

"Of course, I will Cassiopeia. There is much to learn, and I want to learn the skills too."

"But where shall we go?"

"To the great library for starts," suggested the Wisp.

"But isn't that the path to war?" asked Cassiopeia.

"It will be," said the Wisp, "Some of you will have roles to play in the Great War between Wonderland and OZ." Lizzie and Lily glanced at each other. "I can say no more. Deliver your resignation to the commander and begin preparations to leave. Oh, by the way, I forgot, there are spies from Wonderland among your guards. Your commander is being set up. The commander is full of self-pride and adulation and unable to realize it. It is time to make my exit." And then the Wisp dissolved.

Lizzie addressed the group, "Anyone else here feel like we are all pawns in his game?" Many nodded yes.

Cassiopeia dispatched a staff member to request the commander return to her quarters and then had her staff pack some clothes in a small trunk and hide the sorcery book within them. The commander quickly strolled into the quarters, leaving two guards at the door. Things went unexpectedly bad. "Well Cassiopeia, have you reconsidered. Are you ready to turn over your two guests to me? I might even allow you to leave with your daughters," he said with an evil grin looking over towards Lemon and Lime.

The commander approached the two sisters. Slowly he inspected them placing his hands on their shoulders and running his hands down their arms. Lemon and Lime lurched back from his touch.

"They are very beautiful," looking over to Cassiopeia with a broad smile. "But they wear a tad too much makeup." He sighed and continued, "Oh well, that can be fixed. But the yellow and green outfits have to go."

He started to grab Lemon by the waist, but she stumbled backwards out of his reach. Lily raised her arm to engage her weapon. The commander looked at her and wagged a finger in her direction. "My men shall be upon you very quickly, witch Lily," pointing to the assembled dozen men at the door

He whirled around to face Cassiopeia and pointed at Lizzie and Lily, "I'll tell you what; give me these two and I'll let you leave in your carriage. He paused for a minute and then pointed to Lemon and Lime. "I would also like you to leave your daughters behind too."

Cassiopeia remained outwardly calm, but internally she was frightened. "I wish to abdicate and give up OZ to you commander. On condition that you will let my daughters, Lily and Lizzie, and my handmaidens leave with me in peace."

"That's not much of a deal Cassiopeia. Last week I would have made that deal, but times have changed. I already have OZ, it's not yours to give to me." He strolled over and placed his face just a few inches away from her,

"You have heard my terms." Cassiopeia paused for what seemed like forever and sighed with resignation, "What do you want now commander?"

"Is it wrong to want it all and everyone?" He emitted a hearty laugh. "You are toying with me commander."

You have heard my demands. Everyone stays with me except you, who I will allow to leave. You have a few moments to think it over. If the answer is yes, you will be allowed to leave and save yourself. If your answer is no, you will all die."

"And many of you will die commander," warned Lily.

"I have many men and some men who are not men. I care not if they survive, only that they follow orders." The commander then bid his leave.

"I am sorry." Cassiopeia said to her daughters. "I am afraid my inactions have caused all of this."

"I am sorry I did not kill him back in the little people's village when I had the chance," Lily said. "It is not your fault Cassiopeia, it is mine."

Lizzie addressed Cassiopeia, "You may give me up to him. I do not fear death."

Lemon then spoke, "Mom, things will be what they will be. Remember, you had previously considered marrying us off to two older guards to protect us, this will be nothing more than that. The important thing is you will live for another day."

"What if the deal is not really a deal but a delaying tactic," offered Lily.

"What do you mean?" questioned Cassiopeia

"It is obvious he wants you to give up everything and all of us, in exchange for your right to leave in your carriage. We must tell him there is an illness within the witch's quarters and it would not be wise for him to interact with us. In fact, I can cause myself to throw up when he arrives."

"I will too!" said Lemon. "If you stick a feather down your throat it causes you to gag and sometimes throw up." Lemon ran off to retrieve some feathers.

"This diversion gives us time to plan an escape."
"But you might not escape," replied Cassiopeia.

"If that is our fate, so be it," added Lizzie. "We cannot control fate." With that their plan was hatched and readied for the commander's entrance. A short few Now's later the commander knocked on their door and entered. "Well, do we have a deal?'

"Yes," announced Cassiopeia. "I will leave OZ by carriage now, and my daughters will remain, as will Lizzie and Lily."

"A good decision," crowed the commander. At that moment Lemon threw up, followed by Lily. For the rest in the room, vomiting stimulated reflex actions as each vomited in turn as they viewed the volumes of foods and liquids spewed upon the floor. The commander retreated to avoid contamination, but it was too late, as Lime spewed a stream of vomit upon his pants legs and shoes.

"I will depart now, before I come down with this plague or whatever it is. My girls have been throwing up all morning and now Lily and Lizzie have joined them," announced Cassiopeia, as Lizzie joined the group hurling the contents of her stomach upon the floor. The commander gave Cassiopeia a wide berth through the door as his medicine would not control such a plague. Cassiopeia, according to plan was the only one not vomiting in the study. A staff member followed with her trunk containing her clothes and the sorcery book. "I would not have your men go into the room for a day or two. I am not sure what these ladies have in the way of disease."

The commander seemed rattled and he quickly agreed, accompanying her down to the courtyard. As her carriage rolled up, Cassiopeia left without any further words as her driver implored the horses to move swiftly.

The commander's pant leg was now drenched in vomit. He told one of his senior officers, "She's on the run, as I expected her to. She is trying to save herself. Tomorrow send guards out and see if you can find and kill her! We have no need for a witch in OZ."

The witch's private quarters were a mess. Staff came running in and out with buckets and towels. The four cleaned up and changed into clean clothes.

"I am so sorry." Lemon kept saying to the staff.

"OK," said Lily, "We've got maybe tonight only to get ourselves out of the castle. I recall that Adam escaped from Wonderland through a tunnel to OZ. We have to find that tunnel for it can lead us away from here."

"I know there are exits to the outside world down in the dungeon. The commander's guards will not see us exiting," said Lime.

"We must wait until dark and make our way down there. Lemon and Lime, you will lead the way." replied Lily. None of the guards dared come up to the Witch's quarters that evening. All was quiet. Shortly after dark, Lemon led the group down a rear set of stairs normally only used by Cassiopeia.

"There are many hidden stairs and some secret rooms here, said Lime. "My sister and I used them to hide from each other, and we found many places. Each held a small torch as they descended into the castle, as the pathways were not well lit like the rest of the castle. At one point they reached a dead end. Lemon pushed a stone in the wall and a door to another room opened. This one was full of very old books.

414

"I believe this is a sorcerer's room. I am not sure even mom knows about this one." After a few more twists and turns, Lemon announced to the group, "Behind this door is the dungeon. Careful we do not know where the guards might be"

They pushed open a door and entered a well-lit hallway. There were large padlocked doors on either side. The dungeon was silent. Suddenly a guard rounded the corner. Surprised to see them he blurted out, "Lemon, Lime, does your mother know you are down here?"

It was apparent he didn't know what had transpired up in the castle. The sisters were not surprised since the dungeon is always the last to know. "Lily and Lizzie wanted to see the dungeon," was the best story Lemon could think of as an excuse. "They are guests of my mother. Lily is a witch with great powers and is curious about the design of our dungeon. She is building a great castle far away from here."

Sensing a chance to curry favor with the witch and maybe get out of dungeon duty the guard started a tour, "Well each hallway has eight doors one either side. We have four hallways so there are, let's see 8 and 8 are 16 and 4 is.... "

"64" replied Lime.

"Yes, that's correct, Lime. You're smart. I wish I was that smart. I hate being down here in the dungeon."

Lily inquired, "Are there people in the dungeon at present."

"No, we haven't had any one for a little bit of time, not since that guy Adam came here. There are the men who are not men down here, but they are on the next floor down. They are not held in cells. they live in large open rooms behind large gates. They are quite dangerous."

"How did Adam get here?" asked Lily.

"The monkeys spotted him, and our guards were able to capture him. He may have come through a tunnel on the grounds. We know there are many caverns underneath the castle. A few are connected   to somewhere and a few are not."

"So, there are no tunnels that lead from the

dungeon?" asked Lizzie.

"There is indeed a door that leads to the outside, but nothing that goes underground from inside. The caverns and underground tunnels are all outside the castle. I can show you if you wish. I will also show you the tunnel from where I believe the man named Adam entered OZ."

The group looked at each other. His offer was too good to be true. Lemon implored the guard to show them the tunnel to the outside. He complied and led them through a door, down a short tunnel which ended outdoors under some trees. Once outside Lizzie suggested they extinguish their torches for fear of being sighted.

"Why are you dousing your torches," asked the guard.

"We want our eyes to adjust to the dark so we can see better," replied Lizzie. "Besides witch Lily can make the night like day, so we will not need torches."

"Oh, I would like to see that!" replied the guard.

"Someday perhaps you will," replied Lily. "Maybe I will ask Cassiopeia if I may take you with me back to my lands."

"I would like that. The commander only gives me dungeon duty. Would I be able to see the sun if I went with you?"

"Of course, you would!"

The guard now had hope for a better future and noted, "The cavern where I believe Adam entered OZ is behind those boulders," the guard said. "I can't fit into the opening, I'm too fat, but you girls should be able to get in there and look around."

"Thank you so much," said Lemon. "You may leave now. I will tell my mother about this and she'll see what she can do to get you out of the dungeon."

"Thank you so much Lemon. I really want to get out in the sun again and feel the fresh air. As it is I must sneak out during the day. I love the sun." Happily, the guard walked back into the tunnel and into the dungeons.

"This will not go well for the guard when they find out we escaped with his help." said Lemon.

"Hopefully he won't confess that information," replied Lizzie.

"He doesn't appear very smart," noted Lime. "He's probably too dumb to think about the consequences."

"That will be a shame, he was so helpful," replied Lemon.

They walked around a pile of boulders and noted a small opening that seemingly led to nowhere. The always resourceful Lizzie pulled a lighter from her pocket, flicked the spark and it lit. "It's another of Frank Baum's gifts to our community. I also gave a lighter to Slither."

They relit their torches, and then squeezed through the opening into darkness below. The footing at times was treacherous and both Lemon and Lime took tumbles. Having young, flexible bodies. neither suffered anything more than a mild bruise which would heal quickly. They noted red strips of cloth strung along the pathway attached to a very old rope.

"I think we are to stay within the strips of cloth," suggested Lily. "I will take the lead as I have the weapons. Lizzie, please take up the rear and keep Lemon and Lime between us."

A few steps into the cavernous tunnel it became evident the attraction of their torches invited a swarm of small creatures that looked like fireflies. They lit up the tunnel. The tiny lighted creatures kept pace and seemed to guide the group as they moved deeper into the tunnel.

"I am not sure I need the torch anymore," suggested Lizzie."

Not only did the little fireflies swarm in the air, but the group of sojourners accumulated massive numbers of them from head to toe. Lemon and Lime giggled, "This is so amazing!" said Lime

"Be careful not to scratch yourself or rub up against a rock or something. We could kill our little friends," admonished Lily.

The little fireflies seemed to anticipate movements of their hosts and if one of the group traveled too close to a boulder or to one another, the creatures shifted to a safer position on their hosts' bodies. They were like moving lights on their bodies.

After walking a good distance, they came to a fork

in the tunnel. "Which way do we go?" said Lily. "The little fireflies answered Lily by choosing a tunnel for them.

"Hopefully they know we are traveling to the great library and not Wonderland," commented Lizzie. "I don't want to end up in Wonderland, the Queen hates us little people. I would surely lose my head."

A good distance down the path they came to another fork. This time the firefly-type creatures did not choose either path but rested on the surrounding stones.

Suddenly a wisp of cloud formed and settled on a nearby rock. The Wisp's yellow eyes peered out once again at Lily.

"Lily," announced the Wisp, "This is not the path I would have chosen."

"No kidding," was Lily's response. "But it is a pretty walk thanks to the fire flies."

"Is that what they are called?" asked Lemon.

"Yes," replied the Wisp. "You have reached another fork in the road and this one leads to the great library if you choose well."

Lily responded, "You are going to make a game of this oh Wisp. How cruel."

Lily looked down at nearby rock which the fire flies descended upon. On the rock was engraved the words, "The Great Library" and an arrow pointing clearly to the right. "Well obviously oh Wisp, the fire flies are not your friends. They just lit up a directional sign here on the rock," countered Lily.

"No, I guess they do not appreciate a conundrum. It would have been a good lesson in logic as I would have supplied clues for your travels."

"We have no time for games, Wisp," was Lily's retort.

"Then you need to know that the librarian, Clarity, awaits your entrance into the great library. Cassiopeia is making good time and will be there shortly. Unfortunately, your fellow travelers have already set out for Wonderland. You have just missed them."

"Do they know I am here?"

"No, I did not think to tell them."

"Or more likely that information was not in your grand scheme, oh Wisp."

"Anything else?"

"Perhaps, but it is not important at this point." And the Wisp spun around and disappeared again.

"Does he always do that?" asked Lime.

"Yes," answered Lily. The way to the great library started on level ground then about 100 yards down the trail a set of stairs led them up to a door.

Clarity stood stooped on the other side of the door, "Welcome to the great library. I am Clarity, librarian here. I have made some space for we await the Grand Witch Cassiopeia. You must tell me all about the happenings in OZ. The Wisp says you are to remain here under my care until the proper moment. So please make yourself at home. I promise to be a good host." Soon Cassiopeia joined them at the great library.

# The Queen of Hearts    17

Preparations in Wonderland for the coming conflict were proceeding nicely. The espionage campaign yielded great dividends. The Queen's spies were positioned everywhere in OZ and their manipulation of events was a great success. The Queen, known in her world as the Queen of Hearts, awaited the return of the man known as Thomas Thorns. He was the senior guard Lily encountered when she killed the inebriated guard two nights earlier.

The Queen of hearts wore an elegant gown featuring a heart on the upper righthand strap. It was a white silk flowing floor length gown. She wore silver slippers, and her red hair fell across her shoulders. A small white flower was clipped on the right side to her hair. As Adam mentioned, she was quite stunning; beautiful, but deadly.

The door to the Queen's throne room opened and in walked Thomas Thorns. He was a moderately tall man of six feet, with bulging biceps, black hair and a strong dimpled chin. He was admired in OZ for his warrior prowess and courage.

"My Queen," he announced. "I have great news! The witch of OZ has abdicated her throne. Thaddeus, her commander, has proclaimed himself King of OZ. The witch, Cassiopeia, has fled to parts unknown leaving her daughters behind with a lesser witch named Lily, who hails from some other land. By now the witch Lily is dead and daughters Lemon and Lime have no doubt been thrown to the fancy of the guards or perhaps some other appropriately ignoble fate."

"Wonderful!" replied the Queen, clasping her hands together in joy. "I knew if you revealed to the commander that Cassiopeia has no real powers, he would topple her immediately. And what of this new witch, Lily? I do not know of her."

"She killed one of my men and almost killed the commander. She had a mysterious power of green light which managed to knock the commander senseless. Fortunately, he has recovered. The witch Lily, accompanied by a little person, surrendered in the witch's quarters because of sheer numbers against her."

Did you advise the commander to kill her too?"

"Yes, and I bring more good news. This morning the King of OZ slaughtered the remaining flying monkeys. There are none remaining in OZ."

"Marvelous! And what will be done with the little people's village?"

"The King, following my recommendation, will soon be rounding the little people up to use in the front lines as shields for our fighting forces. I convinced him that your fighters would be unwilling to attack if their orders were to slaughter innocent people. He of course took credit for all of this as his idea in the strategy meetings with his senior staff members. I found the new King of OZ very easy to manipulate. He seeks the credit for everything and gladly steals other ideas."

"And that is why I have you. You will be sure to kill those lazy little people criminals who do nothing but steal, deal drugs and undermine Wonderland."

"Of course, I will your majesty, the very moment

you grant me the commander title we agreed upon, great Queen."

"I will do that momentarily. My current commander is on his way here now. He is far too sensitive to go to war. I need a hardened commander who is unafraid to do what is necessary to win."

"Your majesty, I have convinced the new King of OZ to keep the green men who are not men in reserve. He knows they are hard to control and was relieved not to have to use them. His senior staff prefers to shed the blood of the green men, who are not real men, and questioned the refusal to deploy them when the King first announced it. But he has effectively convinced them that he alone has great ideas, so they agreed to hold the green men in reserve."

"You and your fellow spies have done well. I know of every detail of their war plans including their use of the men who are not men. He will never understand what hit him and thanks to you, we will be one step ahead of him. A bag of gemstones will be waiting in your quarters."

"Thank you, my Queen" he replied.

"And how do you explain your absence Thomas?"

"The witch Lily killed one of my men two nights ago. I took possession of his body to hold for the right moment. I tied it to a tree and set it on fire just before I left. Since he was about my same build I left a note stating this killing of Thomas Thorns was in response to beatings the previous day in the village of the little people. I signed it as one of the little people. They thought it is my dead body and will seek revenge while they round them up."

"Very good, my commander."

"Here now, come and place this sword about your waist; my current commander is nearly here. I will toy with him for a while and when you see me touch the flower in my hair you shall run him through and thus become my new commander." At that moment, the Queen's current commander entered the room.

"I would like to introduce Thomas Thorns to you commander. He was our primary spy in OZ and brings good news. The Witch has abdicated her castle, the flying monkeys are slaughtered and the Witch's daughters along with two visitors have at this point joined the monkeys in the hereafter. It is a beautiful day in Wonderland!"

"That it is," agreed the commander.

"Thomas here devised a bit of subterfuge by instructing the new King of OZ to deploy the little people as shields in a first wave attack because we are known for never attacking innocent people. The King believes that. They are probably rounding up the little people as we speak. The King of OZ also believes it was the little people who killed Thomas, owing to a ruse where he burnt the body of one of his men and let the little people take the blame. The little people will be caught off guard when we ride through and slaughter them. Or should I send a column of bears to tear them apart in front of the people Of OZ? What say you commander?"

"You are proposing the slaughter of innocents in battle, your majesty?"

"Yes, justice is long delayed. They are bad people. They steal, bring drugs and a variety of other criminal activity to Wonderland. Thomas suggested we use a wall of Wonderland creatures to drive into their forces to disorient them, before our horsemen ride in for the slaughter. "

"My Queen, I do not think the men of Wonderland would fight that way. Sending innocent creatures to their sure death is immoral. And I do not relish the prospect of slaughtering little people."

"Too bad for you, commander." The Queen at that moment reached up and adjusted the flower in her hair.

Thomas approached the commander from behind and ran him through with the sword the Queen provided. The commander perished quickly as the blade was driven up inside his chest cavity between his ribs severing his heart in two. He fell to the ground without emitting any noise.

The Queen announced, "My new commander," with great pride. "Come, you shall dine with me today and perhaps much more." The Queen's staff was dispatched to remove the former commander's body and go to the commander's house to remove his wife and children from the premises. His family was never seen again in Wonderland.

Morning came quickly for the new commander

who spent much of the night entertaining the Queen of Hearts. He dressed in the finest of the Queen's guard uniforms and accompanied the Queen down to the courtyard for the announcement. The senior command was all in attendance, not knowing why they were called to assembly. The Queen was wearing a beautiful red and white stripped silk gown with her heart emblem affixed to a shoulder strap. She walked to the edge of the stairway.

"My loyal guards, on this great day we prepare to claim our victory over OZ. Thanks to Thomas Thorns here, your new commander!" The Queen was interrupted by outcries and rumblings from the assembled leaders. It was a shock, as would be the news of the disappearance of his wife and children later in the day. The new commander barked out an order, "Attention! Men act like the warriors that you are!" That silenced the men.

"As I was saying, I have chosen this brave man to be my new commander. Your former commander had divided loyalties and was untrustworthy. There are even some stories that he was communicating with our enemy, OZ. Those stories are being posted throughout the town as I speak. I encourage you to read them. Now a word from your new commander."

"Loyal guards of the Queen of Hearts, a great victory will come to Wonderland. Upon the instructions of the Queen," glancing back upon her, "I have been involved in a clandestine effort to not only change the leadership of OZ, but to lead them astray in their war efforts. Their remaining flying monkeys were slaughtered by their own men. You need not fear flying monkeys ever again." A roar interrupted his speech.

"I bring you more great news, the witch of OZ, Cassiopeia, has abdicated her throne and fled OZ. She will soon be hunted down by her own men from OZ and eliminated. Also, I am proud to announce her daughters are likely to have suffered the same fate as the flying monkeys. There will be no more witches in OZ! OZ will soon be ours!"

A hearty cheer arose from the assembled men. "Go now and prepare for a great victory," he commanded. The Queen and Thomas retired back into the castle and enjoyed a breakfast together. The Queen was quite pleased with her new toy.

"That went well Thomas, my dear commander. You have much to do now to prepare Wonderland for war."

"Yes, I shall begin right after breakfast and work long into the night to organize our efforts."

"Please don't work too late my Thomas, I shall desire your company once again tonight." That pleased the commander.

# To Wonderland 18

Just a few Now's before the droves of people fleeing OZ arrived, Clarity knocked on the door to Adam and Alice's room. They were once again a couple. Adam and Alice dressed and promptly joined Clarity in the downstairs dining room. "It is time for your departure," he announced. Slither and Gurgle were already in attendance and had begun to break bread.

"Ah, the couple has awakened from their long slumber, like tired dogs after a night of barking at the moon," announced Slither, who was still wearing his patchwork clothing.

Adam replied, "Your humor at such an early hour is unappreciated Slither. I see you still wear those old unclean clothes. Alice, we need to find seats upwind from Slither to enjoy this morning's breakfast."

"I smell fine," replied Slither.

Gurgle entered the fray, "I have nose plugs, so

Slither never bothers me."

"Your nose plugs look like thick unruly nose hairs," countered Slither.

"An evolutionary adaptation when one spends too much time with you," replied Gurgle. Laughter ensued as Alice and Adam were seating themselves for breakfast.

"And where are Smokey and Sunny," questioned Alice.

"They are always late risers," replied Clarity. "I will go roust them again." Clarity shuffled off to the Teal brother's room. He knocked on their door. "Masters, you will miss breakfast if you do not get ready now. Don't forget, you are leaving for Wonderland today to introduce these friends to your mother."

Smokey opened the door and peaked out at Clarity. "Just a minute Clarity, Sunny's got his, well... he's got his privates caught in the pants' zipper. It happens from time to time."

Clarity grimaced, "Does he need help?" Just then a scream came from the room. " I think not at this point," said Smokey. "Hopefully damage is marginal. We'll be down shortly," as he closed the door.

"Are you OK, Sunny?" questioned Smokey.

"I think so. No blood this time, but it hurts." "It always hurts," replied Sunny. "So why do you keep doing it?"

"I can't see down there, my waist is too large."

"My waist is just as big as yours, so why doesn't that happen to me?" "You're smarter than me, Smokey."

"Yes, of course you are correct. I am smarter. Are you ready for breakfast?"

"Yes, I'm hungry."

"You're always hungry." On the way downstairs, the Teal brothers debated who was hungrier and who ate the most. It was another unfinished debate. The Teal brothers entered the room.

"Sorry we're late. Sunny zipped up his private parts and it took a while to get them unzipped." said Smokey

"Eww," replied Alice as she put her food laden fork down. "Too much information Smokey."

"I agree Alice," said Sunny.

"That was too much information." "But they asked why we were late," countered Smokey

Slither was fed up with the back and forth banter and decided to enter the fray. "Gentlemen, stuff happens, but we are in mixed company. It was more information than was needed."

"So you've zippered your privates too?" asked Sunny.

Slither rolled his eyes as Alice began giggling. "Oh Slither, do tell us about how it happens?" Alice asked.

Gurgle volunteered, "Done it myself once."

"Please tell us all about it Gurgle," laughed Alice. "Is this a common thing among men?" she continued. "And my dear Adam, how many times have you done it? I've never noticed the scars." Adam remained silent.

Sunny volunteered, "I can show you what it looks like?" Which was met with are sounding "NO!" by the entire room.

Clarity sensing a need to change the subject

announced, "I have a special serving that arrived early this morning." Two staff members brought out a large covered serving dish and placed it on the table to the left of Alice. Clarity shuffled over to the center of attention.

"This is quite a delicacy in our world."

When he lifted the cover, a smiling Little Lady emerged. "Little Lady." Alice screamed out. "I've missed you so much."

Little Lady replied, "Miss Alice." They hugged and hugged. Alice planted a big kiss on Little Lady's cheek, who returned the favor.

"OK," Slither hollered out, "Enough monkey love, some of us are eating."

Little lady replied, "Not a monkey! Slither not nice."

"No, he's not," agreed Alice. "But we are stuck with him."

Little Lady replied with a smile, "Stuck with Slither." Little lady seated herself on a chair where a plate of fresh fruits were laid out before her." "Hungry." she replied. After a few minutes she pointed at Smokey and Sunny. "Blue!"

"Not blue, but teal, Little Lady. These are the Teal brothers. They are the Queen's son's" interjected Alice.

"The Queen's sons?" said Little Lady, now baring her teeth.

"They're with us, and they are good," replied Adam.

"OK," replied Little Lady as she returned to eating the fruit.

"A flying monkey!" noted Smokey. "I've only seen them in the skies. My mother said her men slaughtered all the monkeys."

"Not monkey!" replied Little Lady. "Some survived."

Sunny could not resist his curiosity so he got up to inspect Little Lady, who promptly hissed and growled when he reached down to look at her stubby ended tail. "No touch!" said Little Lady. Sunny touched anyway. In an instant she whirled around, faced him and took flight and hovered face to face with him.

"Don't touch!"

Sunny looked over to Smokey, "I guess it's fair to say she doesn't want me to touch her."

"Yeah, that's pretty obvious Sunny."

"I've never touched a flying monkey, Smokey." "Not monkey," Little Lady interrupted.

"I don't think you should touch her Sunny," said Smokey. Little lady gained altitude and hovered behind Sunny, whereupon she smacked him on the back of the head with her small fist.

It didn't hurt Sunny, but it caused him to turn around. In the time it took to turn around Little Lady was already maneuvering behind him once again and smacked the back of his head once more.

"She's too fast for you Sunny," commented Smokey between mouthfuls of food.

"Alice and the others were laughing. The positioning and smacking between the two of them lasted a while. Little Lady smiled broadly, as she continued to pummel Sunny. Finally she stopped while hovering face to face with Sunny once again.

"All I wanted to do was touch you Little Lady," implored Sunny. "Can't I Please touch you?"

"Yes, you may now," said Little Lady, "But ask next time." Sunny reached over tentatively and touched her head.

"Feels nice Smokey, I don't know why we're supposed to be afraid of flying monkeys. They don't hit hard and all they seem to do is fly around."

"I agree," said Smokey. "I think they'd be fun to have around. Maybe we can have some at the great library?"

"We have enough animals at the great library!" said Clarity

"I'm hungry." said a distracted Sunny, who left Little Lady in mid-air and returned to his seat. "Smokey almost ate everything while I was playing with Little Lady,"

"Staff will bring more," replied Clarity, shaking his head from side to side. Little Lady finished her breakfast of fruits and remembered she had important news to share.

"Lily here."

"What!" exclaimed Gurgle. "Lily is here on Dimension 37?"

"Yes," replied Little Lady.

"Where?" questioned Alice, "Were others with her?"

"No" replied Little Lady. "Just Lily. At tree with Wisp. To little people's village. It burnt, little people injured. Witch's men," she hissed. "Is Lily OK?" asked Gurgle.

"Yes," when I left, she OK. She a witch, men think. She sent me to OZ witch. Tell her Queen's men slaughter us."

"Anything more?" asked Alice.

"She with witch at OZ, but never saw her. Wisp sent me here, in night. Witch good."

"Yes, Lily is good," replied Adam.

"No other witch is good."

Everyone pondered her statement for a second.

Slither questioned Little Lady, "Is Lizzie OK?"

"OK. Lizzie and Lily talk."

They all looked to Adam for advice as he was the only one who had met the Witch.

"Well," asked Slither. "Is she good?"

"She could be. We spent time talking and eating together. As I said before, I thought she was lonely. Other than the spell she cast with her bite, she didn't seem violent, angry or prone to inflicting harm on others. So perhaps yes, but like everyone she has her own self-interests, whatever those are. As we all know, one can be both good and evil and do terrible things to protect those interests."

"Time together?" questioned Alice.

"Just talk," said Adam. "She never asked or seemed to be interested in anything but conversation. She asked me a tremendous number of questions."

"Maybe you were being interrogated for information to gather information to use against us," observed Gurgle.

"Perhaps, but the problem was her bite caused me to not only have no interest in escaping, but it also made me very compliant. I probably would have done anything she requested, if you wish to know the truth. I was not capable of exercising free will. Not until a few days had passed and the bite started to wear off."

"What did you tell her?" Slither inquired.

"I told her I was from a parallel universe among the many universes out there. I said I wanted her to set me free, so I could return. I talked quite a bit about the different universes I visited and our home universe. She wished she could travel to other places.

"She in turn told me she had two young daughters but was unsatisfied with life. I got the sense all was not well in OZ, but she never said any more about her problems. She talked about her daughters, although I never met them. Based on their limited development here in this dimension I do not believe she could use any of the information I revealed against us." Adam paused for a moment then continued.

"Besides her staff, she doesn't appear to have

much communication with her palace guard or their commander. I received rather rough treatment from her guard. There was always the end of a pole or butt of a sword to contend with. Without the attention she paid to me I may not have survived OZ. Most of the guards seemed intimidated by her, although the commander seemed more irritated than intimidated by her. There was bad blood between them."

Clarity added, "The Witch is not known for cruelty, or evil. She just exists."

Little Lady spoke once more, "Wisp told me to fly here and help friends. I know nothing more of OZ."

Smokey stated, "Mother says the Witch is quite evil. But she also says that of the little people. Gurgle, I do not find you evil at all."

"Me neither," commented Sunny. "Everyone here seems very nice. Well except for maybe Slither. Don't you agree Smokey?"

"Yes, I do." Slither remained silent.

Gurgle stopped eating and was concerned about the news that Lily was in this universe. He stared into his plate without any eye contact or communications.

Alice spoke first, "We have to believe she's fine. At least that is what Little Lady has said."

"Fine." added Little Lady.

"She's come alone, and it's my fault," Gurgle responded. "I should travel to OZ now."

"And do what?" replied Adam. "If you leave we are one person short and in a two-person team with one person missing, you can't really accomplish much."

Alice added, "I'm sorry Gurgle, your mission is here. Lily chose to risk her life coming here. Maybe it'll work out."

Slither added, "She took me apart the other morning. I think she can probably handle herself."

"You were hung-over Slither," replied Gurgle.

"No one's ever put me on my ass without a weapon, drunk or sober, Gurgle. Lily's dangerous, if you ask me."

"Well I'd rather be somewhere else."

"Great, one of us is somewhere else!" replied Alice.

"I'll stay, but if anything has happened to her, there's going to be a lot of death in OZ."

"I think most of us will join you," said Slither.

"Thanks." said Gurgle as he patted Slither on the shoulder.

Breakfast generated an extended debate between Sunny and Smokey regarding the qualities of evil possessed by Slither until finally Gurgle had enough and shouted out to Smokey and Sunny, "Shut up you two."

Everyone retired to their rooms to pack for the trip to the Queen of Heart's castle

Alice and her fellow travelers, along with Smokey and Sunny, assembled in the courtyard for their trip to Wonderland. Alice was now in a beige full-length dress with a multicolored blouse. Adam was clothed in a clean all grey pants and shirt set, Gurgle as usual, had on an animal skin shirt and rope tied pants. Slither remained in his days old patchwork pants and shirt fashion statement. The Teal brothers wore matching baggy overhauls with checkered red shirts and of course bare feet. They were farmland retro outfits.

The group selected three wagons as transportation with large oxen leading each. The oxen, like a number of other animals in Wonderland could talk. They were solemn creatures resigned to their tasks as work animals. They sighed as their wagons were fully loaded. The ox leading Smokey and Sunny's wagon looked over to Clarity.

"They weigh quite a bit. Could you not split them up to even out our load?" Clarity did not respond. Getting into a debate with an ox was not a productive way to spend Now's.

Meanwhile, Little Lady fluttered around the wagons before they left. "I wish I had wings" said the forward ox, carrying Adam and Alice.

"No doubt we'd still be pulling wagons," said the

resigned ox pulling Gurgle and Slither's wagon. "Besides, our wings would have to be so gigantic to even get our own bodies off the ground. That's an unrealistic thought."

"If pigs could fly," observed the ox carrying Smokey and Sunny.

"But pigs can't fly," said Alice's ox.

"It's just a saying," replied a third ox.

"Time to shut up and work," said Gurgle and Slither's ox.

"Good to see they wish to work," hollered out Slither. "For a while there I thought we'd just debate the day away. It's bad enough that Smokey and Sunny are constantly debating."

Slither's ox called out to the others, "One of my riders is very unpleasant, and his name is Slither."

That provoked a response from Sunny, "Yes, we agree with you ox."

Alice and Adam laughed. It was a quiet first leg of the journey. Gurgle was especially quiet. They traveled south to a bridge barely capable of allowing the width of one wagon. The bridges they passed previously were foot bridges. As they arrived at the bridge their path was blocked by a huge herd of rabbits stretching as far as the eye could see. Near that bridge was a large, older white rabbit who bore red heart shaped spots on its cheeks. One ear was bent to the front. Its eyes appeared shadowy with black circles around them. It seemed likely he hadn't slept in quite sometime.

"Hurry," the white rabbit admonished the mass of rabbits. "The end comes soon." He then screamed out in a loud voice, "We all are going die! Death and destruction! The end is near! Do not dawdle, make haste! Do not linger by the river! The prophecies foretold have confirmed this grave day! Hurry!"

"My, is he rattled," commented Smokey to Sunny.

"Quite," replied Sunny.

"Let's get out and talk to him. The hearts indicate he is one of mother's subjects." Smokey and Sunny departed their wagon and walked up to the hysterical rabbit.

"Oh my, it's the Queen's sons," noted the rabbit.

Hearing this, the surging mass of rabbits stopped dead in their tracks. "No don't stop," implored the large white rabbit. "You are all going to die!"

"They are not going to die," commented Smokey.

"Oh great!" interjected Slither to his fellow travelers. "We will sit here for hours while the Teal brothers debate with a crazy rabbit. Will someone please do something."

Smokey looked back at Slither, "We are doing something, Slither. You are not helping."

"He certainly isn't." responded Sunny.

"You haven't slept in a while have you, white rabbit?" asked Smokey. "War's approaching" the white rabbit screamed.

"Yes, it may." said Smokey. "OZ and Wonderland are destined to fight I believe. At least that is what my mother, the Queen of Hearts says."

"And you stand there and do nothing?" the rabbit screamed, "Nothing!"

"Look over there across the bridge white rabbit,"

suggested Smokey. As soon as the white rabbit turned its head, Smokey walloped him up beside the head with his large meaty hand, knocking him unconscious. He then turned and addressed the herd of rabbits.

"The white rabbit was acting like a lunatic. I had to do something. Give us a minute to pass and then follow our lead toward the castle."

Smokey picked up the rabbit by its ears and walked back with Sunny to his wagon. He threw the unconscious rabbit into the hay filled bed of the wagon and climbed up on the seat. In an aside to Gurgle, Slither said, "Wow, I didn't see that coming." Gurgle nodded his head in agreement.

"Nice job!" complimented Slither. "You should consider that option more often. You'll have fewer arguments and always win the debates."

"Smokey doesn't like to fight," responded Sunny.

Slither shrugged and waited for the rabbits to clear. Then they moved slowly forward, as the oxen of Wonderland were never known for their speed.

Meanwhile Alice commented to Adam. "This is all

so crazy. This dimension! I always thought stories about talking animals in *Alice's Adventures in Wonderland* was just that, a story for children. I never imagined they would really talk. I mean Little Lady sort of converses, but she has trouble with the language. These animals are fully conversant."

Little Lady said nothing for she was fast asleep, curled up comfortably in the hay in the back of wagon. "The rules are different in every parallel universe. Nothing makes sense; until it does," replied Adam.

"That's so Wonderland of you to say."

Adam chuckled. "We never know what we're going to find. I've seen some strange stuff. We've both seen strange stuff. But I agree this place is mind bending. Part of it is normal human activity but then there is the strange. Can you imagine if Lewis Carroll tried to convince the people back on his universe that Wonderland was real? He couldn't be able to! No one would take him seriously. He would have ended up confined among a bunch of crazy people or dead. I've heard some early inventors or scientists in his universe were executed for their beliefs,"

Added Adam.

"So, do the people of our universe know about the talking animals?

"I'm not sure, maybe many Now's ago, but that information has been lost long ago with so many other discoveries being made over the Now's."

"So, are we going to report it when we get back?" asked Alice

"You mean 'if' we get back. We've got a long road to go. We haven't even been to OZ yet. And Clarity has convinced you to just go up to the Queen and tell her you're Alice from another universe. It'll be like lighting a match in a room full of powder. We'll be in her dungeon so fast, you'll lose your head in the blink of an eye."

"Look we are playing the Wisp's game and so far, he's been pretty good at calling the shots. Both he and Clarity have said to tell the truth. They know the place and we don't. Well most of us don't, maybe you do,"

Adam interrupted, "I haven't got a clue about this place, just operating on instinct."

"They know, or at least I hope they know."

A small wispy cloud formed at the rear of the wagon bed, followed by a pair of yellow eyes and a familiar large toothy smile.

"The Wisp sometimes knows but sometimes he does not," was spoken by the Wisp to Alice and Adam which caused them to stop the wagon. They looked around. Little Lady was disturbed by the sudden halt and awoke a bit startled to see the Wisp's yellow eyes and teeth facing her.

"Hey everyone," hollered out Adam, "we've got a visitor. Say hello to the Wisp." Everyone stopped their wagon and hurried back to Adam and Alice's wagon.

"Go on," implored Alice.

"Gurgle, I will put your mind at ease. Lily is fine. She is at the great library with Lizzie, Cassiopeia, Lemon and Lime."

"Who are those other people?" asked Alice.

"Adam, you know Cassiopeia as the Witch of OZ.

Lemon and Lime are her two daughters. They are known as Lemon and Lime Chiffon. They are well. Cassiopeia has abdicated her throne in OZ and was given safe passage out. Then the new King of OZ ordered his men to track her down and kill her. The King will kill her for sure when he finds her."

"But she's a powerful witch?" replied Adam.

"No Adam, she is not. She knows only a little bit about sorcery. Her mother died before she could teach her the most potent incantations and spells. She has a few: the bite, some healing abilities, and perhaps a couple of rare and mundane abilities. She is unable to teach her girls much either. However, they have natural abilities. But alas, like her mother their abilities are not threatening. The commander, after some time observing her and with the advice of a leader named Thorns, figured out she was a paper tiger and pounced. Cassiopeia had to leave Lily, Lizzie, Lemon and Lime behind. I call them the four 'L's.' She had to either agree to leave them behind or all of them would die immediately. The commander said he was going to kill Lily and probably Lizzie and give Lemon and Lime to his men."

"Eww," said Alice.

"They escaped OZ through a tunnel; the same one you came out of from OZ, Adam."

"Can I see Lily, now?" asked Gurgle. "Maybe we should go back and get them."

"No, you have your own role, and they have theirs. I am stopping by only to put your minds at ease."

"One further note for Slither's interest, Lizzie is there with the L's and Cassiopeia because she is the only one who knows the language of the sorcery book that Cassiopeia carries with her at all times. Her role is translator so Cassiopeia can learn and teach her daughters the craft."

As the Wisp whirled around to leave Adam hollered out, "Stop!"

"Yes, Adam," the Wisp replied.

"You really want Alice to march right up to the Queen and announce that she is Alice?"

"Yes, that would be wise, Adam."

"Wise?" questioned a flustered Adam. "You are

sending us to our death."

"Hmm, an interesting consideration, but unlikely. Again, the Wisp does not know everything. I must go," and he dissipated immediately into nothingness.

For a moment, two in the party were relieved to find out people they cared about were safe. However, Adam was now frightened by the prospects of dealing once more with the Queen. He was lucky to survive his first encounter and now he and Alice were leading everyone into another more dangerous situation. It was likely someone would die.

The party again mounted into their wagons and continued toward Wonderland, this time with a huge caravan of rabbits trailing behind; hippity hopping along the bunny trail. The white rabbit remained unconscious. When they traversed a small shallow stream, Smokey dipped a bucket into the water and threw it into the white rabbit's face. The rabbit spitted and sputtered, looked around to gauge his surroundings, then held his spinning head with his two front paws. A few minutes later he was able to regain his bearings and sat up.

"Thanks, I needed that," replied the white rabbit. "I am able to travel with the other rabbits. He leaped to the ground, miscalculated the distance and face planted into the ground.

"Nope, you're not ready yet," commented Smokey, who dismounted and gathered the white rabbit up by his ears and once again tossed him into the hay covered wagon bed.

"Does rabbit meat taste good Gurgle?" asked Slither. "I never had rabbit, but that rabbit isn't going to make it if he keeps falling down. He could end up as my dinner."

Surveying the massive number of rabbits following their wagons, Gurgle smiled and replied, "Looks like if you've got a hankering' for rabbit you'll have a good supply, Slither. But have you forgotten the last time you reached for a rabbit? That almost didn't end well. I advise against going there. There are far more of them than us. Drumbolt would miss you, but he'd laugh if that was the way you went out."

Slither thought better of his inclination to dine on

rabbit. After a few more miles the spires of the castle came into view. The first of the Queen's many roadside sentries lay ahead. They dressed in beautiful white silk uniforms with large red hearts on their right shoulders. Their shields were white as white could be, and also with red hearts. Even their sword sheaths were encrusted with raised hearts

"Halt," one cried out. "Dismount and present identification."

Swords were un-sheathed and spears were at hand, when one of them spotted the Teal brothers. "Oh, sorry Smokey and Sunny. We didn't see you back there. And who is that with you?"

"We bring guests to see our mother," said Smokey.

The white rabbit regained consciousness from the wagon and peered above the wagon bed sideboard. "From the looks of assembled masses behind you, you bring many visitors to Wonderland," said one of the guards.

"No, they are going on to the valley beyond. They are all afraid of war," replied Sunny. "May I introduce you to my friends, this is Slither and Gurgle."

The sentry noted, "The Queen will not be happy to see a little person, Smokey. You must be careful and avoid angering her. She is quite happy now with her new commander but the sight of a little person may set her off."

"New commander?" questioned Smokey."

"Yes, there are posters all over town explaining that the previous commander conspired with OZ. We are lucky the new commander was operating as a spy for us and discovered the relationship between the old commander and OZ."

"Wow" said Sunny. "And let me introduce Alice and Adam," said Smokey.

"Alice! Smokey are you crazy? The Queen hates Alice's. She will have her be- headed on sight." The guard walked over to the wagon containing Alice and Adam.

"Ma'am... Hey you. Weren't you a prisoner of the Queen?" pointing to Adam.

"Go on, tell him the truth," urged Alice.

"Yes, I was held by the Queen, and I escaped."

"Yes, you did. Apparently, you escaped the Witch of OZ too because I was at the slaughter of monkeys. We would have gotten you for sure, if those damn monkeys hadn't been present."

At his disparagement of monkeys, Little Lady rose up from the hay bedding of the wagon and hovered around Alice.

"Hey, that's a flying monkey right there. I thought we killed them all." The sentry readied his sword to dispatch Little Lady out of the air.

"Stop!" screamed Sunny. "You cannot do that. These are our friends." "Yes, they are!" added Smokey. "Put down your weapons."

The sentry refused to comply. "Are you and Sunny being held captive by these people?"

"No, they are not." said Slither.

Slither lobbed a harmless smoke sparkler toward the sentries. It exploded upon contact sending out waves of sparkles. The sentries, in their attempts to escape what they perceived as an attack, stumbled and fell backwards. Slither laughed as did Sunny and Smokey.

"Get up on your feet," ordered Smokey. "You are in no danger." They quickly arose to their feet still holding their swords and spears. "Did these people attack when you were sprawled upon the ground," asked Smokey.

"No,"

"Then put your weapons away. They mean you no harm."

"Smokey, do you understand how much the Queen hates little people," anyone named Alice, and flying monkeys, not to mention Adam, the first person to escape her dungeons in I don't know how long. I'm not even sure she'd like to see the dark skinned one who threw that thing into the air into an explosion. You are bringing trouble into Wonderland."

The sentry turned to Alice once more, "Ma'am, you seem nice enough."

"She is," interrupted Sunny, "very nice."

"Yes, very nice," confirmed Smokey.

"Ma'am, as I was saying," he stopped and looked over at Smokey and Sunny, expecting them interrupt him again, "You seem nice. But the Queen does not like women

463

named Alice. It has something to do with a book written about her by some guy many, many winters ago."

"The guy was Lewis Carroll, sir," replied Alice. "I know all about the book and the Queen of Hearts. I am going to see the Queen. I have a message for her."

"She will not like it." replied the sentry

"I can assure you she will not." said Alice. "None the less, it is Alice's time in Wonderland."

"We are soon to have a war with OZ. It would be so much better to wait ma'am, may I call you Alice?"

"You may. It has been decided I am to enter Wonderland before the war." "To stop it?" inquired the sentry.

"No, to start it. Things must happen in this universe for the good of all. I cannot explain more at this time."

The sentry was thoroughly confused and stepped aside. "OK Alice, it's your head." The sentry signaled with mirrors to let them pass. It was the same for each of the next five roadside guard gates. As they approached the last two gates, they discovered a road leading to the valley beyond the castle. Arriving at the fork in the road, the alert and composed white rabbit was placed on the ground and Smokey pointed him in the direction of the valley.

"Thank you, kind sir," the rabbit replied, as he motioned the flowing mass of rabbits behind to follow him down the road to the valley.

Finally, the gates of the castle stood before them. "Well this is it Alice. Are you sure you want to do this?" asked Adam.

"Yes, it's a destiny thing. I have no idea what will come in the next few days."

She paused and leaned over toward Adam, "I love you, no matter what happens," then she kissed him tenderly.

# A Near Death Experience 19

The gate masters saw messages from the mirrors at the previous roadside gate and swung open huge doors to allow the three wagons to pass. Word passed along to the Queen that her sons have arrived with visitors in tow. The Queen looked out upon the wagons but was angry at seeing not only a little person, but a flying monkey in the entourage. If her sons had not been in their company, she would certainly have ordered her men to slaughter the visitors on sight. She brushed past her attendants to complain, "Smokey and Sunny displease me. I must deal with this immediately."

The Queen hustled down a flight of long stairs to the throne room. She was dressed in another combination of a white-on-white silk gown with a heart decorated shoulder strap. A royal attendant approached Smokey and Sunny. "The Queen requests your presence in the throne room, masters Smokey and Sunny. She is not in a good mood. "

"Sunny whispered to Smokey, "How angry do you think she will be?

"Quite angry," said Smokey defiantly. "However, we are grown men and lords of our own castle, therefore we make decisions as to the people we choose to associate with. I like these people, they are nice"

"Yes, they are," agreed Sunny. "I will stand beside you my brother."

The brothers entered the throne room, followed by Gurgle, Slither, with Little Lady hovering above the assembled group. Then Adam, and Alice followed.

"What is the meaning of this?" said the angry Queen. "You have disrespected me, Smokey and Sunny."

"We mean no disrespect mother," said Smokey. "They are our friends who stopped by our castle and we wished you to meet them."

At this point the Queen's new commander, Thomas Thorns, joined the Queen at the throne. "You know how I feel about little people, openly sneering at Gurgle."

"This is Gurgle," announced Smokey. "Although you may know him as The Lion of OZ."

"So, this is the Lion of OZ, is it?"

"Yes, I am," said Gurgle stepping forward.

"You are the father of many children I hear. You have come to impregnate our women have you?"

"No, not at all. I regret my previous behavior and have expressed that to the leaders of the little people's village."

Thomas Thorns stepped over to confide with the Queen. "We searched for him in the village; he was sought by the new king of OZ. We beat up the mayor and three of the Lion of OZ's children. However, they remained loyal to him and would not reveal his whereabouts."

"And what about the flying monkey commander?" The Queen whispered to her commander. "I thought you said they were all slaughtered."

"All the monkeys that were in pens that morning were killed. It is possible this one was not present, my Lady." replied the commander. "Give the order and my men will gladly kill this last flying monkey."

The Queen resumed her questions, "And who are you?" pointing at Slither.

"I am Slither, parallel universe traveler extraordinaire."

"And what does that mean, Slither?"

"You are far too beautiful, oh Queen, to be so angry. I must say you are without a doubt the most beautiful of any women I have seen in any universe. Your red hair, creamy white complexion and revealing gown. You are no doubt beautiful in or out of your beautiful gown, wow."

"Silence!" ordered the commander. "You will not talk to the Queen in that course manner." The Queen was intrigued by his boldness, "Let him continue commander." Smokey and Sunny exchanged glances.

Sunny whispered to Smokey, "But he's not nice."

"No, he's not, but mother isn't exactly nice either as we know." Slither looked around to Alice and Adam and arched his eyebrows.

"I am a dark warrior from another universe. There

are none like me here. I can be pleasant company. You will find me very agreeable and satisfying."

"Hmm, here I am presented with the father of many and a dark man who claims I will be pleased with him. I am not sure what to say," she replied faintly smiling. And who are you, pointing to Adam. What claims to fame will you make?"

"I am Adam, I escaped your dungeon," he replied confidently and without fear.

"So, you claim. There are many claims being made here."

"But it is so, your majesty. There are no doubts among your men. Some here remember me. One of your sentries stationed at one of your checkpoints admitted he had seen me previously."

A guard stepped forward, "My Queen, he was indeed in the dungeon and did escape, moments before he was to appear in your chess match."

"Ah, so you are that one, Adam."

"Yes I am, your majesty."

"Are you afraid to compete in my chess match?"

"No, in fact I have come back to participate in your chess match!" he announced.

His boldness confused the Queen. "So, you wish to participate in my chess match and die for me. Do I understand you correctly?"

"If that pleases you!"

"Alice pulled at his sleeve and whispered, "Aren't you taking this a little too far here. I'm not willing to die and neither are you." "You're the one who said tell the truth."

"But you're not willing to die for the Queen!"

"But I would for you. Same thing."

"And who is this woman, who cares that you live?" Alice stepped forward to announce, "I am Alice." A murmur spread through the throne room.

"You say Alice? You have the audacity to come here and tell me you are Alice."

"Yes, that is my name. However, I am not that Alice. I am a different Alice and I am certainly not the Alice of *Alice's Adventures in Wonderland.* But I am Alice, and you must deal with me as I am."

"Shall I slay them now?" whispered the commander to the Queen. "No, let me amuse myself with them first."

"So, Alice, why have you come now, at this moment to Wonderland? And what are you doing with my sons?"

"We met your sons on our way to Wonderland. They are fine young men who we have gotten to know over the past few days. You should be very proud of them. They are good and honest men."

"There are lots of good and honest people in my kingdom."

"Yes, we know," spoke up Adam. "Many of your subjects are pleasant and good. I was treated with respect and dignity by everyone from your palace guards to your staff, even the dungeon guards. I will add with regret, all but you, your majesty."

"Are you trying to anger me?"

"From what I hear you are already mad," added Slither. "Quite beautiful, and quite mad. I'm attracted to madness and instability. May I approach your highness?"

"Oh, why not," the Queen replied.

Slither walked stepped the three stairs to her throne and bowed to the Queen, while kissing her extended hand. The commander was now more than a little upset.

"You are even more beautiful up close he whispered. We should spend time together away from all these people," he suggested with raised eyebrows.

He whispered a few more words to the Queen causing her to blush and smile.

"You may sit at my feet if you wish." Slither assumed a seated position at the side of her throne opposite the scowling commander who was by this time, livid. "Alice, you are indeed not that Alice. However, it has been a tradition in Wonderland that all Alice's lose their heads here."

"Of course, I understand," said Alice. "You may have my head if you so wish."

Adam grabbed her sleeve and pulled her back

beside him. "What are you trying to do here? You just offered her your head."

She whispered back, "I did indeed. You yourself just offered to die for her. I just offered her my head. We're even."

"Is there some reconsideration going on down there between you two?"

"None from me," stated Adam.

"Nor from me either," replied Alice, who was glaring at Adam.

"Alice, this is too easy. I must ask; are you also a witch? These offers suggest some sort of sorcery. If I go to take your head will you turn into some beast and devour us all? Or perhaps you will simply disappear as the sword descends? Answer me oh witch."

"Since I am not a witch, I cannot answer your question great Queen of Hearts."

"I have offered you what you asked for, my head."

"Well commander, they seem amenable to my wishes. I accept their offers. You may do as you wish with the monkey and Gurgle. On second thought, wait. Gurgle may prove valuable."

"May I suggest you spare the flying monkey in return for my head," offered Alice.

"But I already have your head," countered the Queen.

Slither spoke up, "My Queen, it would mean a lot to us if you would spare the flying monkey."

Gurgle moved up beside Adam and Alice and whispered, "Well at least something nice is going happen to one of us, pointing in Slither's direction." The three giggled.

"Something funny?" asked the Queen.

"No, we're just ecstatically happy for the turn of events. We wish you and Slither well," said Alice.

Sunny interrupted, "I would really, really like the flying monkey to live, mother." "You would?"

"It would please my brother greatly. He cannot keep his hands off the flying monkey." Smokey implored, "Give him the monkey."

The Queen of Hearts paused momentarily, "All right, Sunny the monkey is yours, as long as it behaves."

"Yes," exclaimed a now clapping and jumping for joy Sunny. "Would you also like Alice's head too?"

"No, mother, but she's very nice and polite. She should keep her head," replied Sunny.

Alice interrupted, "Little Lady lives, so now you may take my head." Alice started up the stairs bowing her head while ascending the three steps. She then knelt on her knees and placed her hands behind her back and extended her neck.

"Make it quick and humane dear Queen, I do not wish to suffer."

Slither was sitting at the foot of the throne and reached down into one of his patches to grab an incendiary bag if necessary. The commander drew his sword and took a step toward Alice. At the same time Adam and Gurgle trained their rings upon the commander.

"Commander," called out the Queen of Hearts, "this is neither the correct time nor place. Beheadings are always done for public consumption to obtain maximum impact. Alice shall not lose her head today." The commander sheathed his sword and withdrew, then realized the visitors were well armed and this was all a charade. They had let in well-armed adversaries into the Queen's throne room and everyone was now at risk. Slither could also compete with the commander for the attentions of the Queen. Things suddenly were turned upside down. The commander was frustrated, and he promptly withdrew from the room, making an excuse that he had to prepare Wonderland for war.

"Alice," ordered the Queen, "please get up. This is not your day. It will come, but not today." Alice rose, bowed to the Queen and returned down to Adam's side. "For the moment, all of you shall have visitor's rooms and be provided the hospitality of the castle. Do not dismiss my actions this afternoon for a reprieve. Both of you will meet your fate, but until then, enjoy as many more evenings as I decide to grant. The Lion of OZ, however shall be held in the dungeon. You are a commodity of great value that I may be able to employ at an appropriate time in the coming war. As for you Slither," as the Queen approached him seated on the floor then rubbed his head,

"I have quality wine and a fresh bath available for you back in my quarters. You will be quite busy until tomorrow."

Slither gathered himself into an upright position and smiled at the others while obediently following the Queen from the throne room.

"Eww," commented Smokey, "that was unpleasant."

"You think so?" replied Sunny. "Mother looked happy to me."

Adam and Alice shared a moment with Gurgle before he was led to his quarters in the dungeon. "The food is good down in the dungeon. The guards will make sure you are comfortable. Ask for blankets. They will even sneak you wine if you ask for it." Gurgle was then led off to the dungeon.

"That plan worked well, don't you think?" said Alice.

"You came close to losing your head. The commander was prepared to ignore the Queen and take off your head in a flash."

"But he didn't, because the Queen has a hankering for something strange," laughed Alice.

"It would be stranger if she chose Gurgle for the evening," replied Adam, amused at the thought.

Sunny was just in earshot of Adam's comment, "I would have expected she'd spend time getting to know Gurgle rather than Slither."

Smokey, a bit more experienced than Sunny, replied, "Sunny, Adam's talking about, well..." He couldn't finish the statement. Sunny was not there yet and there was no point in using their mother as an opportunity for a bird's and bee's discussion.

He mumbled "Eww" under his breath and walked away shaking his head.

"Hey Alice, I get your pet monkey," exclaimed Sunny, his mother's situation now fading from his short memory cycle.

"Yes, after I'm gone," replied Alice.

Little Lady hovered above the assembled group and descended back onto Alice's shoulders. "Alice not going anywhere." She said.

"No Alice isn't going anywhere," replied Alice.

Little Lady joined Gurgle in the dungeon. While the Queen did not mind Sunny having a new pet, she had zero interest in having anything flying around her castle. For the moment all was calm within Wonderland. Adam and Alice retired to a well-appointed room with all the luxuries associated with a fine castle. "I could get used to this," said Alice.

"Sure. offering your head up for chopping and then sitting around awaiting the Queen's whims to dispatch you. That's really an idea of a good time."

"We were close to blowing apart everything back there. It would have been pure pandemonium."

"Yes, and some good people would have gotten hurt, including possibly Smokey and Sunny." replied Adam.

"Well we all have our time in the universe and then it's 'whatever' for eternity, or until we find a new purpose. Does life in this existence really matter? Is it a stepping stone to a better existence?" asked Alice

"You were close to finding out back there in the throne room."

"You know that guy Patrick I brought back from dimension two?"

"What's he got to do with this discussion?"

"He said when he died and ended up in the black void he lost all fear of death.

"Maybe that's the clue to life, not fearing death," she theorized.

"You know there are some in our dimension, Alice, who say you are not afraid of death. That story about you walking through a bunch of large predators in a field in the lizard world has been recited so many times in our universe. You are a legend. A lot of young girls want to be like you."

"I'm afraid of death. I like life far too much. I would hope those little girls hunger for more than just being Alice. Many times, it is not so great being Alice."

"Well it's so much better than being Adam. I can attest to that."

They slept well in fine down bedding until a knock on the door, followed by the entry of the Queen's commander accompanied by two guards. It was barely dawn. Alice and Adam repositioned themselves in bed with rings ready. "What is the meaning of this Commander?" said Alice "It is quite rude to bust in on the Queen's guests."

"You are not the Queen's guests! You are the Queen's prisoners. She only let you stay here as a courtesy to her sons."

The commander dismissed his guards by ordering them to stand outside the room so he could interrogate the occupants. "And just what was that over the top theatrical performance yesterday offering your head to the Queen? You had no intention to give up your head Alice."

"It was a gift to the Queen, commander. Perhaps I am tired of life and wish to escape."

"Bullshit," replied Thomas Thorns. "Each of you have your green rings, which I know to be weapons. If the Queen ordered me to take your head I would have been blown out of there. A lot of people would have died including the Queen."

"Green rings?" questioned Adam. "You mean this?" Now holding his hand up and pointing it toward the commander.

"Yes, that and the one Alice is wearing. Gurgle and Slither also are equipped with them."

"They are simple identification rings commander." laughed Alice.

"Sure, I know Lily used one on the OZ commander. If it had not been a glancing blow, he would not be commanding his forces today and I would be the King of OZ."

"You met Lily? How is she doing?" "I think she is dead by now."

Alice laughed. "My dear commander, Lily lives and is safe. She will join us soon."

The commander looked perplexed. "She is here?" "No, but she is safe."

"And what about Cassiopeia, her daughters, and Lizzie?"

"We do not know about them commander,"

interrupted Adam. "We have heard nothing and must assume the worst." Alice looked over to Adam and nodded in agreement.

"You expect me to believe that?" "Which part?" replied Alice.

"All of it," hollered a frustrated Queen's commander. "You toy with me."

"OK, let's go playground here."

And like an eight- year-old child Adam replied, "Just what are you going to do about it?" Adam was now waving his ring in the air in  defiance.

Sensing he was on this losing end of this confrontation, the commander asked Alice and Adam the only question he could think of, "Why are you two here in Wonderland?"

Alice retorted, "Respect, a nice meal with a good desert, and maybe a reward for not killing everyone yesterday."

The answer only flustered the commander more. Their firepower was not even invented here in

Wonderland so all the commander could resort to was to counter with swords, maybe some arrows, or spears.

"What do you want here?" he asked again.

Adam replied, "We are looking for other travelers, like us who may be held in the dungeons of Wonderland or OZ."

"That is all?"

"Well, maybe we could stay around long enough to watch Wonderland and OZ destroy each other." replied Alice. "What do you think about that?"

"You may search the dungeons. Gurgle, the monkey, and Slither will be happy to see you." "Slither? I thought he spent the night with the Queen."

"He did, however this morning the Queen took her bath and told her handmaidens to make sure Slither got cleaned up before breakfast. Slither managed to convince her handmaidens to join him in the Queen's bath pool and the Queen was not amused when she discovered them together. Slither was led down directly to the dungeon wearing nothing but a towel. In the process he somehow managed to immobilize two of my men who are now unable to stand on their feet, but they report feeling is slowly returning to their legs. We do not know how or what he used, but he is dangerous."

Adam interrupted, "Slither is quite dangerous. Your men are lucky, some never walk again."

"Well, we tied his hands together behind his back for the rest of the walk to the dungeon. From now on he will be clasped in rope or chains during transport. The three hand maidens sharing the bath with Slither lost their heads. Their heads are currently on display this morning at the Queen's news board along with notice of Alice's beheading in two days following the Queen's chess match. I believe all of you will be participants in one way or another." Alice let out an "Eww!" in response.

"Such instances happen in Wonderland, a lot," replied the commander. "Now we must proceed to the dungeon. Yes, I know you can blast your way out of here, but sheer numbers are likely to rule the day. Shall we go?"

Alice and Adam rose from the bed and threw yesterday's clothing on and followed the commander to the dungeons. The commander conducted a search of the dungeon occupants. Most were common local criminals, deadbeats, drunkards, swindlers and one was a bounty hunter from OZ in search of the Lion of OZ, but he wound up in the Queen's clutches. It was appropriate his next-door cellmate was the Lion of OZ. All of them were selected as pawns in the Queen's chess match. They entered Gurgle's cell, visited with Little Lady and then entered Slither's cell. He was asleep on the hay covered in nothing but a towel. "You got visitors," yelled the commander.

A groggy Slither looked up from his bedding. "Oh, hi you two."

"I guess things didn't go so well last night, uh, Slither?" inquired Adam.

"Actually, everything went OK, if strange though. This morning, when the Queen ordered her handmaidens to clean me up, I thought they were included in the evening's entertainment."

"They weren't," said Alice, "and they lost their heads because of you."

"Yeah, I was advised of that." He looked up at the commander, "Can you see that I get my clothes back?"

"No, by now the Queen has had them burnt," replied the commander.

"I doubt it. Please request them. I'm kind of partial to my clothes. I like the patches."

"Sorry, that's not my problem," said the commander. "Come!" the commander ordered Alice and Adam. Alice and Adam were shown to their individual cells. "Again, I am aware you can fight your way out of here, but I don't think that is the way you want it. Correct?"

They nodded in agreement.

A short time later Smokey and Sunny paid a visit to the dungeon, accompanied by two security guards. Alice's door opened to let Smokey and Sunny in. The guards were told to remain outside.

"Alice, we are very sorry about this." said Smokey.

"Yes, we are quite apologetic," added Sunny. "Mother was supposed to allow you to stay upstairs, but something changed."

A hedgehog entered the room as they spoke. It rolled around on the ground for a bit picking up dust and particles and left to deposit its accumulated dirt from the floors outside. It departed through a small door at the bottom of the next dungeon, where it was expected to repeat the task. This was Wonderland's version of good housekeeping. Smokey and Sunny watched the hedgehog finish cleaning before continuing the conversation. "Industrious little critter," said Sunny.

"Yes, I must agree," replied Smokey.

"Where were we?" continued Sunny. "Oh yeah, something happened. I guess mother was displeased with Slither."

A voice from a cell across the way hollered out, "She was not!" It was Slither. "Can you get me my clothes?"

The guards walked over to his cell and looked in. "You're naked," said one.

"No shit," Slither replied. "I need my clothes. See if the Teal brothers will get them from their mother."

"We will ask," replied a guard. "Would you like some hot coffee, or a blanket? It's a bit chilly down here."

"I'd like to get out."

"The Queen's orders, Slither. Otherwise we would be happy to let you out. I apologize for your discomfort," said the other guard.

Sunny heard the exchange and looked at Smokey, "The guards are nice down here in the dungeon. We need to see if mother will allow us to choose some for our castle. "

"Yes, I like these two also," replied Smokey. "We'll ask."

The Teal brothers walked over to Slither's cell and looked in. Slither was staring back at them buck naked. "He's in better shape than we are," noted Sunny.

"I say so," replied Smokey. "We need to get more exercise."

"You think?"

"Slither, we'll see about getting you some clothes" said Sunny. "Want us to have them washed?"

"No," hollered Slither, "Never, ever, wash my clothes, and don't store them near any furnace. They are flammable! Seriously guys, don't do it!"

"OK" replied Smokey. The Teal brothers checked in

on each of the other team members and went upstairs searching for Slithers clothing.

After everyone left, Alice called over to Slither. "You can get other clothes Slither. "

"No, I can't, you don't understand."

"Yeah. I know you love your patchwork clothes," replied Alice.

"No, it's my weapons, Alice. My weapons!"

"Oh, I get it."

"Thanks, I thought I was talking to the Teal brothers there for a second."

"A bit snarky this morning are we Slither. Didn't go quite so well," voiced Adam.

"It went real well for a while."

"Yeah, we heard all about it, well at least the aftermath. Still if you really impressed her, you'd still be up there and so would we."

"Don't go blaming this all on me," replied Slither.

"By the way," interrupted Alice, "The commander

knows about the rings. He said Lily used one in OZ to knock down their commander. He hasn't tried to disarm us and he hasn't told the Queen. I think he's trying to figure out what course of action is most beneficial for him. He mentioned that if Lily killed the commander he would likely be King of OZ. "

"We have a mercenary in our midst," replied Adam. "We may be able to use that to our advantage." A short while later the Teal brothers returned with Slither's clothing.

"They were in the trash," said Smokey.

"No one cared if we recovered them, so here they are," announced Sunny. Sunny had the guard open the door and threw the cloths into Slither.

"You guys are the best," said Slither "I am sorry about everything I ever said about you two."

"I am sorry," said Sunny, "mother is planning for you all to participate in her chess match. I guess most of you will not survive. Alice, she has said you will lose your head after the chess match. I guess you don't mind, because you didn't seem to mind yesterday in the throne room."

"No Sunny I want to keep my head. That was all just an act."

"You convinced me." said Sunny as he looked over toward Smokey.

"Look, during the chess match you and Smokey need to promise me you guys will watch it from far away and hide behind some columns, OK?"

"That's nice Smokey, she doesn't want us to watch the violence."

"Right," said Alice, "promise me?"

"OK,"    said Smokey, "we'll stay back from the chess match and hide our heads.

We don't really want to see any of you die."

"Hey thanks guys for my clothes. I owe you." added Slither as they were leaving.

Just beyond the dungeon door, Sunny said to Smokey, "He wasn't that nice before mother spent the night with him. She taught him manners."

"Sure Sunny," said Smokey shaking his head as he accompanied his brother out of the dungeon

# Meanwhile in OZ 20

It didn't take long for the King of OZ's guards to discover their prisoners had chosen to split. An hour after sunrise, a battalion assembled in the courtyard and were dispatched in all directions to search for the fleeing daughters of the Witch and their two accomplices, Lily and Lizzie. It was believed they escaped through a door on the main floor, so no search of the dungeon was ever conducted. The helpful guard was home free. He walked over to a small window to the outside and watched the search parties scour the castle terrain for the missing women. He stood at the window for some Now's, pleased he had helped them escape and free from blame for their disappearance. The penalty he risked and escaped from was sure death. His status as dungeon guard meant he would not be required to fight on the battlefield. So, with most troops away doing battle, he looked forward to an abundance of sun time during the next few days. Everything worked out quite well for him, which was unusual in the dungeons.

The burnt body of what was assumed to be Thomas Thorns was discovered tied to a tree. There was little reason to suspect a ruse, as the body was burnt beyond recognition. Neither the soldier killed by Lily nor Thorns had any close family in the near environs, and no one asked questions. The King vowed revenge but had to retract it later as the little people were important pawns for his battle plans. He needed to execute a roundup of the little people for the war effort.

A search of the Witch's quarters produced few clues, as did the interrogation of her staff. The staff endured beatings and torture but remained silent. Their loyalty was unquestioned. Finally, the King dispatched them to a future existence with a public display of cruelty. He ordered them slain by his archers in the town square. The King's archers and guards were aghast to be called upon to engage in such cruelty. Many broke into tears after the executions. They felt caught in an ethical no man's land. To survive they followed orders and there was a war coming. To initiate an insurrection and take OZ back from the King would have depleted the forces and  the

Queen of Hearts would have surely taken their heads for prizes. They were more fearful of the reputation of the Queen known for brutal displays of inhumanity than the developing tastes for violence displayed by their own King.

Envoys to the little people's village were dispatched, comprised of men, women, and children, all supposed volunteers to assist the little people in rebuilding their village. They arrived in wagons carrying supplies along with a variety of animals to replace those lost. The mayor met them in the courtyard. "And what is all of this," he inquired to the people in the forward wagon.

"It is new supplies and animals to replace the animals you lost," said Willis.

Willis was a senior commander whom the little people had never met. He dressed in regular clothes to avoid suspicion. Many other guard members were disguised similarly. The women were members of an elite women's guard. They had brought along their children and instructed them to never talk to the little people. Everything looked normal to the little people.

The mayor took to the balcony, "Men and women

of our wonderful village, OZ is making good on my request that they rebuild our community. They have brought wood, tools, and supplies along with animals to replace those which they destroyed. It was the Witch who ordered the destruction of our community, but she has been overthrown."

A cheer went up from the assembled audience.

"This is Willis," the mayor said introducing the emissary from OZ to the audience. "He will speak a few words."

"Men and women of the little people's village, I bring you greetings from the new King of OZ. Change has come to OZ and it is wonderful change, which means throughout the land of OZ, you will now find security and tolerance for others." Cheers arose from the crowd.

"As many of you know, there is a war brewing between Wonderland and OZ. OZ is prepared to be victorious. I invite the little people of OZ to travel to the castle in wagons we have used for resupply. You will be provided shelter behind the great walls of OZ. Many of us will remain here to rebuild your village until the time of war is upon us. You can assist the war efforts while at the castle sewing clothes, assembling supplies and some of you with blacksmithing skills will assist in supplying weapons for our guards in battle. We hope to return you to your village in a few sunrises. We expect a short and victorious war. "

Again, cheers went up. The people were tired of sleeping in the great hall at night and sifting through burnt out possessions for memories. Preparations for travel were immediately made. The ill and infirm would remain with a few caregivers. Suitcases and trunks were full, and the little people mounted into wagons. Soon, many more appeared on the horizon to assist in transportation. It was a herculean effort by OZ. Their trip was joyous, as musical Instruments were broken out and singing ensued. At checkpoints OZ provided food for the travelers as the journey was nearly a full day's travel.

Little did they know that the little people who chose to stay behind because they were unable to travel or were caregivers would be slaughtered like the flying monkeys before them. The King's plan worked brilliantly and his guard's disgust for the little people made it all efficient. Hatred was an effective tool to equip the King for genocide.

As the caravan approached the castle, the little people were joyous. The thought of clean comfortable beds, and regular food was a welcome change from their current circumstances. They approached the gate and were suddenly diverted onto a road just outside the castle that led to a series of warehouses. "Unfortunately, we do not have room for you in the castle yet, so you will reside in the warehouses. They are comfortable and divided for family privacy. In a short period, everyone disembarked from the wagons and took lodging within the warehouses. It was not the fine lodging they expected, but they received a roof over their heads, and many beds. A cooking center was set up in the rear quarters, stocked with supplies. If it was not home, at least the little people could feel like it was home.

After Willis successfully guided his battle shields to their temporary residences he reported back to the King. The return of the men, women and children who formed the ruse that encouraged little people to compliantly travel to the castle was good news. The weak and infirm little people left behind were eliminated as would be the remaining little people in the upcoming battle. The plan was going as designed.

Back in the empty village of the little people, a Wispy cloud looked down upon the bodies of the infirm and disabled little people who were slaughtered. This was an unplanned development for the Wisp. Unplanned developments and unexpected consequences are rare for the Wisp, and this event gave rise to fear that he was losing control of the events transpiring in his universe.

It remained a tranquil setting in Oz for two more days. While the little people were sequestered outside the gates, they were granted entrance to shop and dine and encouraged to watch as war preparations were organized. On the third day the little people were called to an assembly in the early morning. Willis began his announcement.

"The King needs a show of force at the front lines of the battle. We must appear to be more than what we are, as the forces of Wonderland may have a slight advantage. There is good news; our King has determined we will not need the green men who are not men for battle. They are dangerous and hard to control. They would be a hindrance more than an advantage. However, he has honored you, the little people of OZ, to contribute by forming the front lines of our battle force. You may bring weapons to appear well armed, but you are not being asked to fight. When the fighting begins you will slip behind our horsemen and return to the security of rear guard and provide supplies to our brave guards.

"The King deems you valuable to OZ and very much required to ensure our victory. The King promises you will receive an equal share of the spoils of war for your efforts." The news was not initially received well, but upon reflection, it seemed reasonable to the little people, and the promised rewards were essential and needed. The little people agreed. The mayor stepped forward, doffed his hat and in a typically political manner waved it in the air as he spoke, "The little people offer you our wholehearted manpower and assistance for the war."

They prepared to march toward Wonderland. Some would travel by foot, some by miniature horse, while women and children rode in wagons. The march to war began.

# Reunion 21

Cassiopeia arrived at the great library a day after Lily, Lizzie, and her daughters, Lemon and Lime arrived. Her carriage driver double backed multiple times, and traversed multiple streams, and even drove the carriage into stream beds to hide his tracks. In addition, the driver fixed branches to the back of the carriage to drag along the ground to obscure the carriage's tracks. The King of OZ's men found little evidence of her travel and gave up after only a day.

Lemon and Lime ran out of the castle doors to hug their mother, shedding tears of joy. "I am so happy to see you my girls," responded Cassiopeia. Lily and Lizzie looked on at the mother- daughters' reunion.

"Mom, I was afraid they discovered you and killed you." said Lime.

"You are not wearing your lemon and lime gowns and you've dyed and cut your hair!"

"Clarity told us if the guards or bounty hunters traveled near here and saw such clothes and colored hair, it would give us away." said Lemon.

"What do you think? Do you like the new short look mom?" asked Lemon.

"Yes, I love it! It looks so nice on you. I think I will change my own appearance."

"No mom, don't cut your hair. It's too pretty, but please stop wearing black," said Lime. Lily and Lizzie joined them in the courtyard when Lizzie asked, "Did they ever come close to finding you?"

"No, I never saw anyone, at least no humans. There was a strange talking tortoise out looking for spies and such. He wanted to die because his friends would all soon be dead. He was a very sad creature. I never knew tortoises could talk."

"Many animals talk over here in Wonderland," added Lizzie. "It's kind of weird, but I like it."

"So, tell us how you escaped?" asked Cassiopeia.

"Your daughters knew all the tunnels and secret rooms to help get us away," replied Lily.

"They did?"

"Yeah mom," said Lemon, "you don't know this, but we used to play hide and seek in those stairways, tunnels and secret rooms. We took everyone down the back stairs through secret passages and into the sorcerer's room."

"Sorcerer's room?" questioned Cassiopeia.

"You didn't know about it?" asked Lemon.

"No," replied her mother.

"See, I told you mom didn't know."

Lemon continued, "We emerged into the dungeon. I knew there was a door to the outside down in the dungeon and thought it was the last place they would search for us once they realized we left the room."

"Unfortunately, a dungeon guard found us, but luckily he didn't know about you abdicating the throne. We told him Lily was a powerful witch who was visiting our castle and looking for ideas for a castle she wanted to build. He took us on a tour of the dungeon. Then he helped us escape through a secret tunnel he knew about."

"Let me tell her the rest," interrupted Lemon. "Lily wanted to know if there were any people in the dungeon. The guard told us the dungeon was empty and some guy named Adam..."

"Yes Adam, the guy who gave me the slip," interrupted Cassiopeia.

"This guard told us this guy Adam came to OZ through a tunnel from a small field near the castle. We asked him to show us the tunnel and he did. Can you believe it? He even told us he was too fat to enter the tunnel with us. We told him he was no longer needed and he immediately returned to his dungeon assignment."

"Well, if the King finds out he helped you, he will be no more," said Cassiopeia.

"I hope not." said Lime "All he wanted to do was help us. He recognized us immediately down in the dungeon." Just then, a castle staff member ran up to Clarity and whispered in his ear. Clarity announced that dinner was being served, and suggested Cassiopeia should get cleaned up and choose her wardrobe from an array of dresses available for the occasion.

She looked over at Lily who was wearing pants and a long sleeve blouse and said, "I'd like something like Lily is wearing. I'm tired of wearing dresses. And I want my hair in a bun like Lizzie's." It was an entirely new look for the Witch of OZ. Cassiopeia brought her sorcery book to dinner to discuss when and where sorcery lessons would be held. "Clarity is there a private room where all four of us could study from this book?" asked Cassiopeia.

Clarity shuffled over to an empty seat next to Cassiopeia. "Ah, so this book has not been lost after all."

"Are you familiar with this book?" asked the Witch.

"I've heard of it. In the early days, your grandmother made residence in this castle for short sabbaticals to prepare for events. This was quite strange considering this is Wonderland, and she was from OZ. But at that time there were three or four great witches in OZ."

"So that part about multiple witches in Frank Baum's book, *The Wonderful Wizard of OZ* is true?" asked

Lily.

"Very much so. His book caused a great sensation back in the day. I believe there was much jealousy. Some said a failed friendship fueled the story. Frank Baum visited here and then returned with his book, *The Wonderful Wizard of Oz,* which we still have here in the great library. He wrote of water melting your grandmother, which obviously never happened. I just think they never got along very well. They were both strong personalities. She was no doubt infuriated when Mr. Baum labeled other witches as good witches. But unlike the book, no witch ever melted and to my knowledge there was never a Dorothy, or any kind of flying house landing here and killing of any witches in OZ. It was all made up stuff."

"Well there is a Toto in OZ once again," said Lemon, holding her little dog up for everyone to see. "I named her Toto after the book."

"So, I see," replied Clarity.

"But we're in Wonderland now," corrected Lime.

"True, we're not home," replied Lemon.

"Can you read this book," inquired Cassiopeia of Clarity.

"No, unfortunately, there is no one walking this universe who knows the language. Your grandmother was the last."

All three women pointed to Lizzie. "Well she does," stated Lemon.

"Oh, that is most unusual!" said Clarity. "A little person knows an ancient language from a sorcery book. Do tell us how you know this."

"It's a long story" replied Lizzie "I must save it for another day."

After dinner, Clarity took the four women up to a quiet room on the second floor. "This room has a fine table with plenty of room and no windows. I don't want to replace any windows if you screw up an incantation or whatever. I am an early to bed guy these days, so please excuse my early exit."

The witch and her disciples started reviewing the book while enjoying a variety of fine wines and after dinner drinks. Night flew by quickly and soon it was mid-day before they even thought about any food. They were ignoring periodic knocks on the door throughout the morning, but finally they answered. A staff member with a platter of sandwiches entered. They thanked her and immediately continued their study. A full day and a half rolled by before they exited the room. The four of them cleaned up and exited the castle where they found a small meadow nearby to practice their new skills.

The invisibility incantation was mastered by Lime, but difficult for the other women. Interestingly, one individual who didn't want to be a witch, Lily, mastered it the quickest. Not only did she acquire the ability to make herself disappear, she learned to make others invisible. Then, everyone practiced the flower spell Lemon had mastered. All the women learned to create fields of flowers wherever they walked. They almost literally drowned themselves in flowers.

Cassiopeia attempted her first weather spell. It was a glorious event. She mumbled the words and immediately clouds formed. The clouds grew dark and then a deep black. Lightning flared out from all directions. With a motion of her hand she determined where the lightning would strike. The others judged her to be scary good. Then, at a moment's notice, she turned a gray, cloudy day into a beautiful sunny one. "Now that is witchcraft," she yelled for everyone to hear. Lizzie, Lily, Lemon and Lime each applauded after coming out from their cover positions. Cassiopeia added, "Some of my powers still don't work, such as turning a frog into a prince. But then again that never worked in real life either."

Lizzie responded with a thoughtful response: "What woman really needs a prince anyways?"

Cassiopeia tried a forest wall incantation, which worked well. In a vacant section of a field there was nothing. In the next minute, a solid wall of wood appeared shielding the sorcerer from threats from the other side. She could make it narrow or extend to the horizon by a simple sweep of her hand. "This will be quite beneficial," she declared. More incantations were attempted; some partially worked, others not at all.

"It must be our word pronunciations that are tripping us up." said Lily.

Lily tried one more spell: frogs falling from the skies. It was like a winter snowstorm except everything falling was green and emitted croaking sounds.

"What would one do with that spell?" she asked the others.

Cassiopeia dryly replied, "There has been more than one suitor that I could have used that on to make an exit." Everyone laughed.

"Let's go have some drinks!" said Lizzie.

The 4 L's and Cassiopeia ran with heightened enthusiasm back to the castle. Things no longer seemed so bleak. Cassiopeia had new spells and hope. The women entered giggling and laughing. Some of the staff were watching from a small meadow and drew back in fear. They watched Cassiopeia change the weather and direct lighting strikes and throw a forest wall and then quickly take it back.

Clarity was also watching and admonished his staff, "Do not be afraid. They are here as guests of the Wisp."

"But it is the wicked Witch from OZ," said one.

Clarity laughed, "That was written in a book, but the book is fiction. Nothing written in that book is real, or at least most of what is written there is not real. Mr. Baum simply used OZ as a framework for his novel and proceeded to embellish the story to make it more interesting. Authors of fiction books provide us visions of things based on real places, and sometimes places that never were and never will be. They are an escape that takes us to these other places and allows us to imagine and escape our humdrum existence. In this case, there never was a wizard, never a Dorothy, there was no Tin Man, no Scarecrow or Lion in OZ. But just because it never was doesn't make it any less a wonderful story about OZ"

Another staff member spoke up, "But those people who were just here sure looked like Dorothy, the Tin Man, Scarecrow and the Lion. In fact, one of them is known as the Lion of OZ."

"Good point. But remember, they only looked like those characters. Did you know the lady's name is Alice."

"*Alice in Wonderland?*" the staff member shrieked!

"No, she is not that Alice. She is just Alice from another universe, somewhere else. She is here searching for those like her who may have been imprisoned in our universe. Remember, here in Wonderland, things are never as they seem. Trust me, the women who stand before you are good people."

Cassiopeia, inquired, "May I say a few words to the staff of the wonderful great library?"

"Of course, we wish you would."

"I am the Witch of OZ, and here are my daughters, Lemon and Lime. Honestly, I am barely a witch. My mother did not survive long enough to teach me all her spells and incantations. My daughters have limited powers. We mean no one harm in OZ or Wonderland. I fled OZ when the commander expelled me and proclaimed himself King. There is now a reward for my death. I fled here on the instructions of the Wisp. There is a great war coming between Wonderland and OZ. It is not of my making. There is much evil on both sides.

"I must tell you my existence here is a risk to all who reside here now, as the new King of OZ and Queen of Hearts are each dedicated to ending my life. If either side comes here for me I would not blame you for turning me in, but I hope you will instead protect me and my family. I have a role to play in the war. I do not know yet what that may be, but I plan to be the difference that brings peace and justice to our universe."

Lily stepped forward, "I am a member of the other group that one of you suggested looked like Dorothy from the Wizard of OZ. I am a woman of the Lion of OZ. Yes, he is a little person. He like me is not from your world. We have come to search for fellow travelers who may have been incarcerated here. Unlike the others, I possess a powerful weapon, which some of you have seen when I have disrobed."

Lily pulled back the sleeves of her blouse and revealed weapons on each of her arms. "I wear a full upper body system to protect me and which can generate a colorless laser weapon that sets targets on fire. It burns threats and melts any defensive material. This weapon system is far beyond your understanding. Swords, spears arrows, shields and castle walls are no match for my arsenal. I have not yet used this weapon and hope I will not have to, but please understand I do not hesitate to do so, should I, or these women and the other members of my party come under threat." The staff drew back in awe and fear. Lily smiled and then giggled, "I am also a budding witch, watch." She mouthed an incantation and immediately Clarity disappeared into thin air but returned a moment later.

The staff gasped.

Clarity looked around, then up and down his body. "I just had a feeling I wasn't here, but I know I was. I could see everyone, but I could not see my body. How strange."

"You were invisible Clarity."

"Well that was fun," he chuckled

"Anyone else like to experience invisibility?" "Is it safe?" one asked.

"Yes, I haven't lost anyone yet."

For the next few Now's, Lily demonstrated her invisibility skills with a variety of the staff. It was a great hit among them and reinforced their loyalty to her and the rest of her group.

After lunch, Clarity called everyone back to the incantation room. "War is near my friends. Sources tell me they are assembling in OZ and Wonderland and soon will be on the march immediately after the Queen's chess match. Unfortunately, I must tell you Lily that your friends are participants in the Queen's chess match and it has been announced Alice will lose her head after the match."

Lily gasped. "No! I must go there to save them."

"The Wisp advised me you must remain here, no matter what happens in Wonderland. You and your companions have a role to play in the war which is much bigger than anything that may happen to Alice in Wonderland."

Lily looked to Cassiopeia, "I must go!"

Cassiopeia replied placing her hand upon Lily's hand, "You will stay."

"Lily," advised Clarity, "The Wisp will be there and intervene if needed. He always does." A few moments of reflection passed, before Clarity said, "Perhaps some time practicing your witchcraft, will take your mind off the events transpiring in Wonderland and you can hone your skills." With that Clarity left and the women returned to the book of incantations.

# The Queen's Chess Match 22

It was a quiet two days in the Queen's dungeon. The dungeon guards provided for their every need and were increasingly polite, catering to every whim. They were given a choice of meals, fine wines, deserts, and snacks. Each had time to stretch and get some sun. It was the same for Adam the last time he was incarcerated in the dungeon. Except for the hay bedding, the lodging was better than they often receive traveling to other places. The evening guard even let them out to play card games till quite late.

"You can easily escape," the guard noted while sitting at a table with Adam, Gurgle and Slither. Alice chose to skip the card game and spend time instead with Little Lady.

"We could, but as I understand it," said Slither, "the castle is a beehive of activity. Our chances of passing through five or more sentry stations and getting away are nil."

"Probably so," replied the guard as he dealt out another hand. "It's a shame you are scheduled for the Queen's chess match tomorrow. None of you will survive if you are an opponent to the Queen's side. You are nice people I hate to see nice people killed in her blood sport."

"So why do you allow it?" replied Adam.

"We have no choice, the Queen is immortal, and cannot die. If someone kills her, she comes back as herself in minutes. I saw it myself, many winters ago. We are trapped in an existence where we have no escape except death. Some of her subjects have volunteered for her chess matches just to end their miserable existence in Wonderland. We bury those who choose death in her chess matches in a special cemetery to honor them. If I did not have a family I might do that myself."

Gurgle spoke up, "Why not just leave and escape this existence?" "And go where? I hear the evil witch in Oz is just as bad"

"That is not true," said Adam. "I have met her. I was once a prisoner in her dungeon. She treated me respectfully. We spent many hours discussing our lives while I was there. She is simply a lonely individual."

"The Queen has provided many postings about OZ and its witch. It is told she dines on human flesh, that her flying monkeys are men she has turned into monkeys. Of course, she also posts on other subjects. There are always the spies she executes. She promises great rewards for the completion of projects, which of course we never see no matter how hard we work. We no longer can decipher between truth and lies here in Wonderland." He paused for a moment to deal another hand.

"Our Queen is often lonely too. She entertains men in her quarters for a night or two and then sends them to their deaths. Sometimes she beheads them herself."

"This was not the same," replied Adam. "I was not a play toy for the witch's whims. We just talked."

Slither spoke up, "Well I guess I am a perfect example of what you speak of. I spent a night with the Queen and we did more than simply talk. Now here I find myself scheduled for her chess match."

"Well our Queen is quite beautiful, so it was not all bad. I am sure you enjoyed yourself."

"Sort of," replied Slither, "She has a big thing about hot dripping candle wax. It wasn't sensual, it was painful. And there were whips. I'll leave it there. I've had more fun! Then she told her handmaidens to clean me up. I made a mistake and thought she was offering them to me. She came back after a while and found us all in the hot bath together. I got the heave ho and down to the dungeon I went."

"You do realize her handmaidens lost their heads over that!" "I've been told that numerous times. I feel horrible about it."

"Don't!" said the guard. "They are just as evil as she is. It is said sometimes she ties up her lovers when she gets bored with them. She then instructs her handmaidens to torture them to death. They do it willingly and it is said they enjoy it. You will see their enthusiasm for blood tomorrow in the chess match. They are dangerous; none of you should turn your backs to them during the match. They are known for dispatching combatants from behind when the Queen is in danger of losing."

"Thanks for that advice," replied Adam.

"As I said you could easily escape and take your chances outside." "We will remember that."

The game went on long into the night. The lowly dungeon guard was a fount of information about the chess match, its lack of rules, and the Queen's tendencies. They parted as friends. Meanwhile, Alice consumed the evening by teaching Little Lady more words to increase her language skills.

The morning light peeked into the dungeon. It was an indirect light, filtered from an opening well down the hallway. However, it was enough to awaken those in the dungeon. Shortly thereafter breakfast was served. It was quite large, perhaps to suggest a last meal. It would prove heavy on the stomach and slow them down if consumed in its entirety.

"Do not gorge yourselves," Adam advised the others, "they want us sluggish and slowed by full stomachs."

They took Adam's advice and ate lightly then

pushed their plates back out the door. A few Now's later a visitor, the Queen's commander, Thomas Thorns knocked on Adam's dungeon door with the butt of his sword. "It is time." he announced entering Adam's room.

Adam asked a question, "It's been bothering me, why have you not tried to disarm us? It doesn't make sense."

"I'm playing the odds." he said. "If you should create some sort of event with your weapons and the Queen dies, well then, consider this: I become King."

"You couldn't become King in OZ, so it's on to Wonderland?"

"Something like that. I have worked all my life for leadership. It is time for my reward."

"When the Queen finds out we are armed, she will blame you, do you realize that?"

"I will tell her the dungeon guards were recruited as spies from OZ and they supplied you weapons. She is very suspicious and obsessed with the belief that OZ somehow infiltrated Wonderland and is leaking information to them."

"She will kill these poor guards who have done

nothing wrong. That doesn't bother you?"

"It saves my hide."

The commander walked by each dungeon cell and instructed everyone to get ready for the chess match. While at Slither's cell, he paused, "You have displeased the Queen have you?" he chuckled. "I am still commander because I understand the Queen is everything and the only thing. When you lie with the Queen you must show no interest in others. She is the center of your universe. Or you will not see many sunrises in Wonderland."

"You could have told me that the other day," replied Slither.

"By the way the wax and whips, they did not bother you?"

"Wax and whips? I know nothing about them. You must have brought that out in her. Or perhaps she just wanted to lightly torture you before her handmaidens finished you with the hardcore torture. Apparently, you were appealing to her handmaidens and they decided to play before offing you. Be thankful for your charms, Slither, they saved you from a certain death. Now prepare for your fate."

The four travelers and the flying monkey were led out of the dungeon to a large field behind the castle. Little Lady sat on Alice's shoulders and looked around with fear and concern. There were stands for the attendees on both sides of the chess board. However, because of the war effort they were only partially filled this morning. The Queen resided in a large chair on an elevated platform. A similar elevated platform was on the other side. It was vacant. Her opponent had not arrived yet.

On the board were a variety of players. The sides were unequal. On the Queen's side were her private guards in full uniform, many with helmets, shields, swords and spears. The knights were on horseback. A handmaiden played the role of the Queen on the chessboard. The King was played by a senior staff member. The bishops were expert swordsmen. The rooks were not human. Two large, brown grizzly type bears stood to their full height, restrained by chains in the hands of their trainers. The guard spoke of these rook pieces the previous night. Only one individual, the poor guard who the Queen eventually dispatched herself ever emerged victorious in combat with the bears. If the Queen's rook took your position you were doomed.

On the opposing side were a variety of ill equipped men. Some had simple swords, none with shields or armor. The Queen piece was represented by an effeminate male, thin and gangly, one who probably never experienced conflict. This was to be a slaughter for the Queen's entertainment.

The travelers assembled at the base of the Queen's platform. On the platform were some of the Queen's handmaidens, Thomas Thorns her commander, her sons Smokey and Sunny, a few senior guards, and staff members. It was lightly attended.

The Queen rose to greet them. She was dressed in another elegant white silk gown with the heart symbol on a shoulder strap. There were small red hearts throughout the expanse of the gown. Say what you might, but the Queen's seamstresses showed impeccable tastes.

The Queen addressed the travelers. "Good morning. It is a beautiful morning. Take a deep breath and smell all of creation, for it is the last morning you shall see, my friends. Unfortunately, because of the war effort you will not have a huge audience for your last moments. It is an intimate affair," she said with a smile. She paused for a few moments and looked down upon Slither.

"Slither, how are you this morning? Have you enjoyed my dungeon? Was it worth the moments you took with my handmaidens?" She seemed to be still dealing with anger over his slight.

"Yes, it was," replied Slither. "I found them so much more exciting and entertaining than my time with you."

The Queen flew into a rage, "Off with his head," she commanded her guards. Her guards instantly grabbed Slither by the arms.

Alice yelled, "STOP! My dear Queen! If it is to be my last day alive I wish the honor of being your opponent in the chess match. I believe the rules you set states that one may challenge you for the right to face you personally in the chess match. I also believe your rules state that should I be defeated, I will lose my head. Since I am already scheduled to lose my head I would like the honor to face you in the great chess match. If granted I will employ Slither to be a pawn for me."

The Queen's guards relaxed their grip on Slither. "And how do you know about my rules?" inquired the Queen.

"I inquired of your subjects. It was simple curiosity. It would be an exciting manner to end my days and an honor to face you."

"How do you know of chess?"

"I traveled to many places and in one they played chess. And while those games are simple games with wooden or plastic pieces, my experience gives me the skills to be a worthy opponent."

"So, it shall be Alice. I accept your challenge. Guards, release Slither so he may die upon the board. And you WILL die Slither!"

"Take flight my Little Lady and rest upon the shoulders of Sunny who is on the platform. You are his." Little Lady hugged Alice and flew up to Sunny.

"Aww," commented Sunny as Little Lady lit upon his shoulders. He was happy.

"Thank you, Alice." Sunny replied.

Alice walked among the Queen's men who were situated in their positions on the chess board, as others walked around the outside of the chess board. She strolled up to one of the bears who was on all fours.

"He is magnificent," she said to his handler.

"It's a she," the handler said. "She is with cub and is quite eager to get back to her cub. She is not happy to be here."

"Does she talk?"

"Do I talk?" replied the bear. "What a foolish question. Yes, of course I talk. I am angry to be here instead of with my cub. I am anxious to make quick work of you and return to my cub. Perhaps the Queen will allow me to return with your head as a play toy for my cub."

Alice hollered up to the Queen, "Oh great Queen, this bear requests my head after the chess match so she may give it to her cub as a play toy. I hope you will grant her this wish."

"Agreed," replied the Queen. "The bear shall have

your head."

Alice walked over to her assembled pieces. "What a motley crew you are! Have any of you ever held a sword?"

"No," a chorus arose. One raised his hand. He was the OZ bounty hunter still inebriated from an alcoholic last meal. "Well, you will do me no good." She walked over to the effeminate male Queen piece. "You are dismissed from my board. I will play Queen in my own game."

"Thank you, oh thank you," he said, and hurried off the board. He had only gotten ten feet from the edge of the board when one of the Queen's handmaidens ran him through with a sword. Alice now angry turned toward the Queen.

"I dismissed him from my team and you had him killed? This is my team and I choose who plays and who does not."

"Yes, but it is my board Alice, and I choose who can leave the board." replied the Queen.

"This will not go well for you Queen of Hearts," she threatened. The Queen laughed. The board was set with Alice as the Queen. She asked Adam to be her king. He declined and asked to play the rooks pawn on the King's side. Gurgle was made King.

Slither became the queen's knight's pawn on the opposite side of Adam. Everyone was spaced across the board. There was a strategy in place. Alice called out to the Queen. "May my men have shields? It would be much more entertaining for everyone assembled to witness competitive matches."

The Queen nodded her head yes. Alice's team was unskilled and unlikely to defend themselves properly using the shields, so it would not make much of a difference. Each of Alice's team members received a shield, though they were of dubious quality.

The Queen was playing the white pieces and moved first; Queen's rook pawn to A4. Alice responded with Queen's knight's pawn to B6, which would slow up a confrontation for Slither and release her ill-equipped bishop onto the board. It was obvious the Queen wished a confrontation with Slither first, so she could release her bear upon the board. She advanced her pawn to confront

Slither at A5. This gave a clear path for the bear. The Queen's pawn was a skilled swordsman from her private guard. He had moved from the other side of the board to assure the Queen had the best opponent to confront Slither. She anticipated a quick satisfaction for Slither's insults.

Alice declined the opportunity to engage Slither and the Queen's rook pawn, and instead moved Adam who was King's knight's pawn to E5, placing Adam into the middle of the board, just in case Slither needed support. Alice was not going to obey the strategy of chess if it meant loss of any of her men.

The Queen engaged her pawn to take Slither's space at B6. In normal chess the Queen would take Slither's pawn and it would be removed the board. However, this was not normal chess, it was Queen's rules, and they were designed for chess board battles. So, the pieces fight to the death and the winner either retains his position or if the chess player wishes they move the piece to the former position of the vanquished. With their swords drawn, the two circled each other for almost two minutes, feigning attacks then withdrawing, each of them assessing the other's skills and strategy.

After a bit of time someone in the assembled crowd yelled out, "Will someone just fight! Are we here to dance or fight?"

Slither laughed and proclaimed to the audience. "I prefer to dance. I am a much better dancer." The crowd laughed. Even some on the Queen's platform joined in. The Queen silenced them with a glare.

The Queen's pawn attacked with a direct sword plunge, but missed the mark, as Slither twisted out of the way. Slither swung his sword and struck the guard's shield, producing a loud clang resonating throughout the field. They continued circling each other, then the guard spun his shield like a Frisbee and watched as it undercut Slither's legs, sending him to the ground. It was a practiced move the guard used many times and always led to the death of his opponent.

The Guard closed in immediately for a killing strike but was met with the front of Slither's shield. The sword dented his poorly made shield but did not run through it. Slither rolled across the ground and with cat like reflexes gathered himself back to his feet. The guard took a second to retrieve his shield and then moved toward Slither. The guard was unaware that Slither had reached into one of his patches and retrieved a smoke bag. Slither tossed the smoke bag to the guard's feet which exploded into a cloud of thick smoke. The guard was momentarily lost in the smoke allowing Slither to circle and thrust his sword into the guard's back. As smoke cleared, the assembled crowd saw only Slither withdrawing his sword from the guard's back, who was now laying on the ground. Slither discarded his dented shield and quickly grabbed the guard's superior shield from his dying hands and held it on high. The crowd roared approval.

Having won his match within the Queen's rules, Slither announced he would remain in his current lane, rather than cross over into the line of the Queen's rook. Alice approved.

The Queen stood, "So we have a warlock among us. That changes everything. I will reward the one who kills this warlock with a bag of jewels." No one moved, as a warlock is a dangerous foe. Slither turned to the Queen, raising his sword and shield high into the air.

"Bring more, oh Queen. Is that the best you have?" he taunted.

One of the Queen's handmaidens stepped upon the board and withdrew a dagger from her waist band, racing toward Slither from behind.

Alice hollered out a warning, "Slither, your back!"

It was the last thing the handmaiden would ever do as Slither spun around and dispatched her with one swing of his blade.

Alice called out "Knight's pawn to B5"

Having a free path onto the board, the Queen called out "Queen's rook to Queen's rook A5," anticipating a battle with her bear.

Alice countered by moving Slither to Queen's knight B4. The Queen moved one space to Queen's knight B5. Alice responded the only way possible by moving Slither to Queen's knight B3. This put him in conflict with both the Queen's bishop's knight pawn and from the rear a Queen's rook who would move into battle. The Queen could choose to challenge with either her pawn or her rook. The Queen announced, "Rook to Queen's knight

B3."

The bear and Slither now were face to face. Slither moved toward his right and the bear mirrored that move so the bear now had her back to the Queen's pieces. The crowd was silent in anticipation of a violent tussle.

"Off with his head, bear," screamed the Queen.

The sudden scream distracted the bear's attention. By the time the female bear turned to face Slither, he had drawn a sparkle bag out from a patch. He threw it to the ground and it exploded into a black cloud with sparkles splashing out in every direction. The bear panicked and turned in fear away from the cloud and back among the Queen's pieces. It slashed and clawed its way through a startled group of the Queen's chess pieces.

Men drew swords in response, but she was too quick, like a blender, she sliced and diced her way through the chess pieces; disemboweling some, slashing others across the face, even crushing the head of one unfortunate pawn with its mouth. The bear playing the King's rook on the other side panicked and ran through the back of the line of chess pieces toward the only exit.

Being almost as large as a horse she mauled the nearby King's knight astride his horse who attempted to block the path back to her cubs. With a swift upward movement, she disemboweled the horse with a swipe of her paw. The horse fell to its knees instantly from the killing blow, and the Queen's poor knight piece tumbled into the bears clutches. One bite of the knight piece's neck released blood gushing everywhere. The bear now was drenched in blood and exploded into the bishop piece like an uncontrolled freight train flattening everything in its way. The bishop piece was frozen into inaction and watched the knight meet his fate. He could only throw up his hands in surrender. One swat of massive claws left him in ribbons. The king piece at least tried to flee, but stumbled into the queen piece and fell to the ground.

The bear's crushing foot stomps cracked the king piece's ribs like a popcorn maker. Pop, pop, pop went the ribs, some entering the king piece's lungs, and other organs. He died instantly. Finally, the bear grabbed the poor handmaiden who played the Queen piece and slammed her to the ground, crushing her skull. Standing on her hind legs and growling at everyone in all directions, the bear twirled like a toddler dancing through a fountain splash pool amidst the rivers of blood left by those that she and the other bear mauled. With no one to impede her advance she approached the edge of the Queen's platform. At full standing height, her shoulders and head stood above the platform.

A spear was thrown in her direction by one of the Queen's personal guards. She swatted it away like a pesky mosquito. A guardsman rushed at her with his sword held on high. She grabbed his leg and yanked making him fall backwards onto the platform. She then ripped him off the platform and nearly sliced him in two with one huge swing of her claw. The Queen, her handmaidens, and guards drew back expecting it to climb up over the edge of the platform. Instead it turned and returned to all fours and swiftly rushed to the exit. In the midst of this pandemonium, Smokey, Sunny and Thomas Thorns sought cover behind columns at the rear of the platform, periodically peeking out to see what new carnage was occurring.

Meanwhile, Adam faced a threat from the Queen's knight who escaped the bear's wrath and was bearing down on him on his horse with sword held high. Adam saw an abandoned spear on the ground and grabbed it. He flung it toward the horse. It failed to connect and got twisted up in the horse's legs, which tumbled the horse forward to the ground. The knight was tossed over the horse's shoulders and past Adam onto the ground. He rolled over and leapt to his feet.

His sword was flung far away, leaving him with only a dagger in his belt. He grabbed the dagger and drew his arm back to throw it into Adam. Amazingly the spear Adam used to send the horse tumbling had bounced right back at Adam's feet after tying up the horse's legs. He took it and thrust it into the guard's abdomen as the knight's piece was throwing his dagger. The knight's throw was high and to the left sending it off toward the Queen's platform. The spun through the air end over end, seemingly in slow motion until it stuck into the right side of the Queen's throat. Blood gushed down her neck and spilled onto her white silk gown turning it crimson. She collapsed onto the ground screaming and soon bled out. An unexpected hush fell upon the assembled audience.

Slither froze in place, hands at his side. His sword

lay still on the ground. He stood stunned by the carnage he had just caused. He thought this worked even better than I imagined it could. I've killed two people and led the bears to maul most of the opposing forces. This was almost too easy he thought. He stayed frozen in place watching Adam eliminate the King's knight and then finally saw the Queen die at the hand of an errant throw by the one of her own chess pieces. He stood there on Queen's knight space B3, expecting the return of the Queen.

Many of his side's chess piece players raced toward the exits of the Queen's chess field. One ran headlong into Slither. He managed to keep his feet, hardly aware of the interaction as the pawn fell to the ground. The pawn picked himself up by holding onto one of Slither's hands and then raced off to the exit. He was in his own world. One of the Queen's pawns raced toward him with sword raised but stumbled over a body on the ground and impaled himself. He lay on the chessboard screaming and writhing in pain. Slither stayed in his place and looked down upon the dying pawn. He had no idea how close he came to the end. A figure emerged from behind him carrying a sword and grabbed his arm yanking him around. It was Alice. "Wake up Slither," she screamed.

He simply replied, "I'm waiting for the Queen to reappear."

"If she does, you're dead meat along with the rest of us! Wake up and get out of here." Slither nodded in the positive and was helped along by Adam who joined them and pulled at a still stunned Slither.

"Where's Gurgle?' she questioned. Alice looked around and about 20 yards away spotted a small figure with a mop of brown hair lying face down on the ground. He wasn't moving.

"No. Gurgle!" she screamed.

Adam and Slither looked at the figure Alice was rushing to. Suddenly the mop of hair shook, and Gurgle raised his body from the ground with his forearms.

"Gurgle, are you injured?" screamed Alice from 10 yards away.

He raised a hand, "No, I just tripped over a body. I'm OK." Alice expelled a huge sigh of relief and the four exited the Queen's chess field.

Meanwhile, Little Lady took leave of her perch on Sunny's shoulder and flew off to follow the escaping travelers.

Everyone on the platform was stunned. Smokey and Sunny ran to their mother's now lifeless body. "Mother!" they cried in unison. They reached down and shook her shoulder. There was no response. They dropped to their knees in tears and hugged her body without any concern about the amount of blood smeared over their bodies.

"Mother, O' Mother," cried Sunny.

Meanwhile Thomas Thorns approached and cried out, "The Queen is dead, long live the King. I as her senior commander proclaim myself King of Wonderland!" The remaining chess pieces turned their attention to him, as did the assembled crowd. "We have a war to fight, ye people of Wonderland. Our brave Queen gave her life, we must avenge her death at the hands of these spies from OZ. Men, I command you to find the spies and return them to this place of death where we will execute them!"

A group of guards stood motionless for a few moments. The self-proclaimed King reissued his orders before they left. As he watched them leave, Thomas Thorns thought this is going well, very well. I will now rule Wonderland and take OZ too.

He jumped from the platform onto the field below, taking charge of the care and removal of the injured; assuring everyone that revenge would be theirs. Amidst all of this activity, no one noticed a figure emerging from beyond the platform stage. It was the Queen in a black as night silk gown and a brilliant, almost blinding florescent red heart upon her shoulder strap.

"My commander," she spoke. Her words sent chills down the backs of nearly everyone. "I am still Queen and it is I who rule Wonderland."

The commander looked up from the field, stumbled backwards from shock and nearly fainted. It was the Queen standing over her own body starring out at him and pointing a finger in his direction.

"You are quick to dismiss me my commander. Have you forgotten I cannot be killed?"

Thomas knelt before her amidst the gore beneath his feet. "No, my Queen, I have not forgotten." He shook with fear, "Forgive me I wanted only to insure our preparations for war with OZ continued in your absence, your Grace."

Smokey and Sunny stared up from their mother's lifeless body at the new apparition of their mother. "What form of sorcery is this?" called out Smokey. "Our mother lies here and you tell us you are the Queen."

Smokey, Sunny, I am your mother. The form before you is my former body. I am immortal. I do not die. That is why I rule Wonderland and will soon rule OZ. My immortality is the greatest weapon in our universe."

"You have died before?" asked Sunny.

"Yes, remember when I was stomped by a horse some time ago?"

"Yes, we thought you were just bruised."

"No I actually died, but you were so young I knew you would never understand.

You are older now."

"Are we immortal too?" asked Sunny.

"No, only those who are pure are immortal my sons. I will be present for your funerals, and your children's and grandchildren's funerals. I have died many times, and will die many times more. I even died in childbirth when I delivered you my sons."

"Oh mother," they said in unison and ran to embrace her. They both towered over their mother. "It is all right my dear sons." Pushing back from their embrace she moved toward the platform edge.

She looked down at Thomas, who was more afraid than ever.

"And how did Slither get these weapons my commander?"

"I do not know my Queen. They must have been hidden in his clothes. When I saw him in the dungeon he was naked. He said his clothes were in your quarters and asked me to retrieve them. I ignored his request. Someone retrieved them from your quarters for him. Perhaps a guard or a handmaiden? I do not know."

Sunny and Smokey ended the embrace of their mother while she stepped forward to interrogate her commander. They looked at one another. Sunny whispered to Smokey, "Mother would have our heads if she knew it was us."

Smokey replied, "Shush, stop talking, mother can hear us."

The Queen, turned away from her commander, then looked back at him for a second, "Clean up this mess and find those people. We have a war to fight; we must not let the spies from OZ escape."

Alice, Gurgle, Adam, and Slither ran back into the castle through a side door and down into the dungeon. It was the last place that was likely to be searched. The guard from the previous night was on duty.

He looked surprised to see them, "Did they cancel the Queen's chess match?"

"Sort of, "said Adam. "We want to take you up on your offer to help us escape. When I was here before I fled the dungeon by entering a cavern which led me to OZ. We do not want to go to OZ now, we are wanted there to, but

I understand the cavern leads to other places."

"Yes, it is said to lead to many places. Follow me and I can guide you to the cavern."

They slipped away. No one was present on that side of the castle. They heard commotion from all directions, but all was quiet in their location. The guard moved a small bolder aside which revealed a path underground. "If things work out and we are free of the Queen, please remember me. I must escape this hell."

"I will," replied Adam.

"We will return for you," assured Gurgle.

As they lined up to enter the cavern, Little Lady eased down and rested on Alice's shoulder. Once underground, the light flies surrounded them, providing more than enough light to navigate through the cavern. The cavern smelled of mold and was quite humid. As before, Adam stayed within the pieces of red cloth strung within the cavern. They walked for some distance until they came upon a fork in the path. The light flies lit up one path, the one to the right. They followed. Soon they came to a doorway, as they passed through it they were greeted as before, by Clarity in the great library.

Clarity smiled as they entered the castle, "Welcome back my friends. The Wisp informed me you were on the way. There are others here who want to see you."

They passed through a wood paneled room into a large hall. There before them stood Lily and Lizzie. Behind them were three strangers, a woman in pants and blouse with her black hair rolled into a bun and two younger women with short hair. Lily ran up to Gurgle and hugged him with all her might, "When Clarity informed us you were participating in the Queen's chess match I was sure we would never see you again."

Gurgle replied, "You can thank Slither and his sparkle bag that we all thought was useless. It created pandemonium and enabled us to get away. The rooks, which were massive bears, freaked out when he deployed it. They tore through the Queen's chess pieces, killing many. It was total insanity." Gurgle paused as he felt the hard support frame of Lily's weapon." What is this around your body and your forearms, Lily?"

"Gurgle, my love, it is a great weapon designed by Loco. A high-powered laser weapon that melts and burns almost anything. Now tell us more about what happened, we can discuss my weapon later."

Gurgle continued, "Adam here ran one of the Queen's knight pieces through with a spear as the knight launched a dagger at him. The spear caused the knight's throw to go off trajectory and his dagger sliced through the Queen's throat by mistake, killing the evil Queen instantly."

Lizzie spoke up, "But she is not dead?"

"Correct," said Gurgle. She came back to life as we snuck out. We never got a glimpse of her. We could hear everyone's gasps though. We heard her senior commander, Thomas Thorns, attempt to declare himself King just before she returned. Apparently, he did not know she cannot die. I would have loved to see the exchange between those two."

"Thomas Thorns, why he was one of my senior commanders. How did he get into Wonderland?" asked Cassiopeia. Adam suddenly realized the woman standing in the background was indeed the witch of OZ, Cassiopeia.

"Cassiopeia, I did not recognize you. You've changed."

"Yes, I am dressing like Lily for the present. These are my daughters Lemon and Lime. They don't usually look like this either. We are in hiding and trying to fit in. So, tell me more about Thorns."

Adam responded to her request, "Thomas Thorns was a spy for Wonderland while in OZ. He fashioned himself as a future ruler of OZ, but with the commander there that was never going to happen. So, he was compromised by the Queen's other spies who were working in OZ with promises of a high position in Wonderland. When we met him in Wonderland he assumed the position of the Queen's commander. Evidently he convinced the new King of OZ to follow his battle roadmap to disaster in the coming war before he left OZ."

"So, there is no honor among thieves," commented Cassiopeia.

"It's more complicated than that." replied Adam.

"Thorns knew we were armed with our rings because he saw Lily use hers in OZ. Despite that knowledge he allowed us to remain armed. He hoped we would dispatch the Queen and he could assume the title as King of Wonderland and capture OZ as well. He wants it all. Thorns is very resourceful and knowledgeable about OZ's battle plans, so we doubt the Queen dispatched him."

Alice spoke up, "Thorns is only loyal to himself and owes his allegiance to no one but himself. That is something to remember when war starts." Lizzie embraced Slither warmly, but was not overly affectionate. Slither expected more, but the opportunity for the limelight was his greater concern.

"That was so much fun," Slither announced. "I killed one of the Queen's personal guards using one of my smoke bags and a sword, and then turned my attention toward the bears and used them against the Queen with my so called useless sparkle bags. So, Alice and Lily, it was not exactly child's play toy was it? More than just pretty, huh Alice?"

Alice rolled her eyes.

"Gurgle, what feats did you perform at the chess match?" asked Lily.

"Nothing, nothing at all! I was Alice's king piece and all I did was stand there next to Alice and watch everything develop. I never had a chance to do anything! I tripped and fell face down on the grass then got up and ran out away from the chess arena on my stubby little legs. I was not the hero today, I was just a little guy trying to stay out of harm's way."

"I still love you my Gurgle. You will no doubt have more chances soon."

"I prefer just watching, it's a lot safer. Honestly, I probably would not have survived if I had to defend myself on the chess board. Those were trained assassins. With my stubby arms and short legs, I am in no way as agile as Slither, I would have surely ended up on the wrong end of a sword or spear." The truth of Gurgle's comments dampened the enthusiasm of the moment.

"Come, let's gather in my quarters and everyone can share more of what they have experienced so far here in our universe," requested Clarity. "There is much information to process." When settled down in Clarity's quarters with ample food and drink available, they talked about their experiences. Lily started by informing the other members of her experience meeting the Wisp, and the burning of the little people's community, which Gurgle was unaware of.

"Are my children OK?" asked a concerned father.

"Lizzie replied, "Two of your sons and a daughter were pretty beat up by the King's men. But they are OK now"

"Was Ray there?"

"No, Ray led the first group into the thorny forest to safety," replied Lizzie. "Most of your children were with him. He played an important role delaying the Queen's men. The mayor also suffered at her men's hands."

"I am sorry," said Gurgle.

"That first night in the little people's community Lily killed one of the guards who accosted her. They came to believe she was a powerful witch, especially after she nearly killed the commander with a blast. Lemon and Lime arrived at the village the next day."

"They healed your two sons, one of your daughters, and my father." continued Lizzie, "Lemon and Lime were a great help to us. We became friends. That friendship, plus a fear of Lily, protected us from the guards."

"When did you meet Thomas Thorns?" asked Adam.

Lily replied, "He was present when I killed one of his men by striking him with the metal portion of my forearm weapon. He also saw me blast his commander, or your commander, Cassiopeia. If I knew your commander was going to be King I would have killed him on the spot. We met Cassiopeia when we arrived at OZ."

Cassiopeia interrupted, "Can I add to this conversation?"

"Absolutely," said Alice.

"A lot of this is my fault. I was despondent and no longer cared about being the ruler of OZ. I faced daily challenges from my commander, Thaddeus, who now calls himself King. He no longer followed my commands. And who would blame him? He had come to realize I was hardly a witch. My mother passed away when I was very young, and she did not have time to teach me the craft. All I could do until recently was heal people, Hardly terrorizing skills."

"Healing is a great power," said Slither.

"Yes, but of little value for defending yourself and others, and certainly not to rule. In addition, I can make flowers appear wherever I walk. I can make it rain indoors- which creates another set of problems. And finally, I can make a person lose all will if I bite and break their skin"

"I can attest to that." Said Adam.

"Sorry I bit you, but it was easier if I did that. If I had not and you attempted to escape, my palace guards would have killed you. Once you were under my spell my guards did not consider that you could escape, and they stopped paying attention to you. Besides I was lonely and needed someone new to talk to. I really enjoyed hearing about your travels. I would love to do that one day. I forgot to bite you again. My bite wears off. I was distracted by the commander and his threats."

"Glad you didn't remember. One of your dungeon guards helped me escape."

"Yeah, I believe he helped us out of OZ too," replied Lemon.

Cassiopeia continued, "My commander announced OZ was his. I would be allowed to leave, but without my daughters, or Lily and Lizzie. They intended to kill Lily and Lizzie."

"Unlikely," added Lily. "They never disarmed me. We encouraged Cassiopeia to leave, as they said they would attempt to kill us all if she did not."

"We faked it as if we were all very ill when they came to escort my mother out of the castle," commented Lime. "Lily and I forced ourselves to puke, and others followed suit. It was real messy, but they left us alone out of fear of catching our disease. We then traveled down the back stairs and hidden rooms and chambers to the dungeon, where the guard helped us out. I hope he is still alive."

Cassiopeia continued, "The Wisp visited us before I was deposed and advised me to abdicate OZ and escape to the great library. He said we had roles to play in the great war. Cassiopeia paused for an extended moment, then spoke, "Little Lady I am afraid I have bad news, the new King slaughtered all the remaining flying monkeys. All of them. He told us this directly. I am so sorry."

Little Lady screamed, "No." She took flight, flapping around the room in frenzy. "Cannot be. I should have stayed." She collapsed again in Alice's arms with tears, and sobbed uncontrollably. "Bad, bad, bad. I will kill the King." Alice hugged her tightly and cried with her. Everyone gathered around Little Lady to console her. "I am the last," was the last she had to say, and remained silent, staring ahead into the black space of a distant wall.

"We saw the Wisp once more," commented Lily, "in the tunnel. He helped us arrive where Clarity met us. Thank you, Clarity, for everything you have done for us. We all know it is great risk for you to do so."

Clarity replied, "I am quite old. I have lived a long and wonderful life. It is not the risk younger people assume it to be. I look forward to a new form and maybe a new life, whatever death offers me. I will protect you as I do Smokey and Sunny."

"Who are Smokey and Sunny?" asked Lily.

"The Queen's sons," answered Clarity. "They are

also known as the Teal brothers, because they ate of the forbidden teal fruit and their skin turned to a teal color. It is permanent. They are good boys, despite their heritage. This is their home."

"Adam interrupted, "They are good young men, perhaps a bit unusual."

"Quite chatty too," replied Slither. "Like non-stop, never ending chatterboxes. Everything is a debate for them."

"So, you do not like them," said Cassiopeia.

"I've grown somewhat fond of them to tell the truth. They retrieved my clothes when the Queen threw me out of her chambers stark naked."

Lizzie inquired, "So you've slept with the Queen" "Yes," said Slither.

"But she didn't like it later than morning when she came back into her chambers and found three of her handmaidens sharing a bath with him," added Gurgle now chuckling. "Slither believed they were included in the bargain."

"Men!" said Lily. "Are you teaching him your tricks,

Gurgle?"

"No, really, I didn't have anything to do with that, at all. Honest!"

"One of her sons mentioned at the time that he would have preferred his mother have entertained Gurgle rather than Slither." added Adam, now laughing at the thought. "I would pay good money to see that!"

"Adam!" exclaimed Alice. Lily disapprovingly shook her head back and forth.

"Well, just putting that piece of information forward while we are sharing information."

Clarity burst out laughing. "Ah, I wish I were young again and could entertain someone, anyone," said Clarity. His comment created a jovial mood within the room.

Adam continued, "We met the Teal brothers after we traveled through the large buildings north of here."

"You went through the giant buildings?" asked Lizzie.

"Yes, I found out they are shrines for each of the Queen's lives. When she dies her subjects apparently decorate a giant house as a tribute to her. There are a lot of houses."

"She's died many times," added Clarity.

"Well, there'll be a new shrine soon because she died during the chess match."

Clarity nodded his head in agreement. "The giant buildings are shrines and an illusion to convince OZ that giants live in Wonderland. I am not sure they really believe it anymore in OZ. In my mind it is more a shrine than a wall to keep the little people and the others in OZ out of Wonderland. Walls never keep people out, at least determined people."

"Well, we now understand where Lewis Carroll got his idea about Alice shrinking and growing in his book. Those houses," added Alice.

"Anyway," Adam continued, "we met Smokey and Sunny sitting on a foot bridge over the river reading books. Guess what books they were reading?"

"I don't know," said Lily, "Alice's Adventures in Wonderland?"

"Yes, that book and The Wonderful Wizard of OZ! How strange."

"That is not strange, there are a few of those books in Wonderland," said Clarity. "The Queen forbids almost all books, except her own terrible book. I have some copies of both Alice's Adventures in Wonderland and The Wonderful Wizard of OZ here," he said with pride, "And a lot of copies of the Queen's books. Funny no one wants to read hers. People who love to read come here for the books I have, from both Wonderland and OZ. Many little people come here, nodding toward Gurgle and Lizzie."

"I've read both." said Lizzie, "a long time ago."

"I do not remember ever meeting you here," replied Clarity. "I have never been here. My father, the mayor got them."

"I know of your father Lizzie, I do not remember him having been at the great library?"

"He probably just sent some underling to retrieve them." "Umm, probably right," replied Clarity.

Adam continued once again, "When we first met Smokey and Sunny, they thought Alice was Dorothy and we were the Tin Man, the Scarecrow and the Lion."

"Well you sort of did look like the characters," said

Clarity.

"I guess so," replied Adam looking down at his silver clothing and then over to Slither and Gurgle.

"Smokey and Sunny led us to the great library where we stayed a short period before traveling to Wonderland. Before we left, Clarity told Alice to tell the truth in Wonderland. And that's exactly what she did."

"It was a suicide mission, if you ask me," said Slither. "When Alice announced her name was Alice, it sent the Queen into a fury. Ever since that book was published, Alices are not allowed in Wonderland. If they stray into Wonderland it is off with their heads. Imagine if you would, you have a woman named Alice, who the Queen hates, and those who escape your dungeons and make a mockery of your security, a little person and a flying monkey to boot, and then they all show up with your sons in your castle. Needless to say, it was not her best day. I on the other hand charmed her and received an invite into her chambers. Adam told the Queen he came back to participate in her chess match. And Alice offered her head to the Queen; right there in the throne room! She bowed down and extended her neck for the Queen. Crazy, totally crazy."

"Yeah but we were all armed and if she had not stopped Thorns from coming forward to take off Alice's head we would have killed many in her castle."

Adam chuckled, "I have to credit Slither again for creating the perfect distraction by offering his body to the Queen." Everyone laughed.

"Hey, I didn't offer my body, I just accepted her invitation"

"Alice and I were originally allowed to spend the night in the castle, while Gurgle and Little Lady were escorted to the dungeon. The next morning Thorns knocked on our door and announced Slither had been kicked out of the Queen's private residence and was now in the dungeon. We were then led into the dungeon ourselves. Thorn announced we would all participate in the Queen's chess match and Alice would lose her head at the end of the chess match.

"Strange, all of her guards were quite nice and apologetic over having to hold us in the dungeon. One even offered to help us escape and told us that her subjects were all forced against their wills to comply within her wishes, because she cannot die. He said some even have chosen to participate in her chess matches in order to die and escape her rein. They are very unhappy. Without the Queen, I do not believe they would be who they are. They have no interest in conquering OZ."

"Yes, but my former commander is interested in conquering Oz," said Cassiopeia

"Agreed," added Lily.

"Who is good and who is bad? Asked Alice. "The Wisp told us that good and bad would be difficult to differentiate."

"So, I did," announced a wispy pair of yellow eyes and a wide grin hovering above the group of people. "So, I did." The cloud of nebulous material coagulated upon a corner of a large table the individuals were seated around. "Please tell your staff Clarity, that I am not a cat. I almost had to take off someone's hand the last time I rested on a table."

"As you wish," Clarity replied.

"You all now see the difficulties you face in the coming war. Separating the good from the evil is not so simple. That is why I encourage you to experience the many facets of this universe Alice, Lily, Adam, Slither and Gurgle. I do not want you to come here blasting away with terrible weapons without knowing who is good and evil. You have discovered since you have been here that the Queen and her palace staff are most evil, yet her sons are not. Thomas Thorns is evil, yet he acted in an unusual manner choosing not to disarm you for personal reasons. He preferred you defend yourself against his own men."

"Why, I'll never figure out," said Adam.

"Adam, Thorn's unfettered ambition created one who will play both sides between good and evil. He is still choosing sides and maneuvering to achieve what he wants most of all, power. He is quite dangerous, but there is an internal battle within him between good and evil that is undecided. He may or may not be an ally in the end. I do not know."

"But don't you know everything. Are you oh Wisp not playing both sides of good and evil?" questioned Adam.

"Yes, but I want good to win." The Wisp paused for a moment. "May I continue? Where was I? Oh yeah, Cassiopeia and her daughters are good and yet, most inhabitants of OZ, except for the little people are quite evil. The majority of residents of Wonderland are good, but they are forced to act with evil intent because they fear their immortal Queen. Light and the dark are all intertwined in our universe. Sometimes those that shine the brightest in our universe are the poor wretched souls who toll away in the most disagreeable jobs, as you have found in the simple dungeon guards in both OZ and Wonderland."

"So what is our lesson today?" asked Alice

"The answer lies in Adam's statement." "Which statement?" asked Adam.

"But don't you know everything," said Alice.

Wisp said, "The answer is I do not. I assumed some of you would not survive the Queen's chess match. But you did!" He paused for a moment and turned to Lizzie. "This is going to hurt some Lizzie. The guards under Willis, a senior commander of the King of OZ, deceived the people of your village. They are now in OZ under the belief when they support the war effort they will be rewarded with the rebuilding of their village.

"They will not be rewarded. They are going to be used as the front line in the battle which begins tomorrow. The King is intent on sacrificing your people in battle. The infirm and elderly of your village remained when your people were transported to OZ. Commander Willis slaughtered those who remained."

An angry Lizzie shrieked, "Those bastards! I cannot believe the people of OZ would commit genocide. I expect that of the Queen, but not OZ." There were no tears. The Wisp's reveal was met with an angry glare.

"I am sorry, Lizzie." said Cassiopeia. "I feel it is my fault. But I have no power to alter this. Until you empowered me with the sorcery book I had no real power."

"I am not blaming you Cassiopeia."

"Kill King," said Little Lady speaking her first words in some time.

"Yes, the King must meet his demise," replied Lily.

"And so he will," replied the Wisp, "as will many more tomorrow. Cassiopeia, thanks to Lizzie's knowledge of that strange language, you have amassed great power, the power to alter events tomorrow. Combined with Lily's great weapon and her emerging sorcery powers it should be enough to turn the tide for good versus evil. But then again I would never have predicted the bears would run amok and destroy so many of the Queen's pieces."

"You are a witch now?" asked Gurgle

"Yes, my Gurgle," Lily said, laughing, "I can now turn you into a prince or a frog,"

"Not quite yet Lily," reminded Cassiopeia, "Not quite yet."

"Ok, you get a reprieve for now Gurgle."

Lizzie remained silent and thought to herself, so a King and a Queen shall die tomorrow. Cassiopeia continued, "All of us, my daughters, I, Lily and Lizzie have powers."

Lizzie nodded in agreement, but continued to gaze ahead, thinking of other things. "Tomorrow you shall see some of my many new powers, thanks to Lizzie," said Cassiopeia.

The Wisp spoke up once more, "Men are assembling in OZ, there are already faint clouds of dust in the air toward OZ. Wonderland has not marched yet, but will soon. They are preparing their own surprise for OZ."

"What surprise?' asked Lily.

"It's not important unless you are an OZ commander. It will not be pleasant, but I cannot change the course of history."

"He's not reassuring," said Gurgle.

"Cassiopeia, Lemon and Lime, you all must return in your former clothes and makeup by this evening, for one more time. You must present yourself as you are known to the forces of Wonderland and OZ."

"Aww, I was just getting used to these," said Lime. "I think I'm prettier this way." "Cassiopeia, you and your daughters have important roles tomorrow."

"Lizzie, you have the most important role for the little people. You, Lily, and Gurgle will position yourselves near the little people when the war starts. It will be dangerous."

"What about Adam and I?" asked Alice.

The Wisp ignored her question. "One final piece of knowledge, you will have unexpected visitors late tonight." The Wisp suddenly twirled around like a spinning top eyes and teeth, seemingly merging in a whirl and then he disappeared.

"Great, more riddles," said Slither.

"OK Lily what powers do you have," asked Alice. "Spill it."

"Ok." she said with a faint smile, "I can make flowers grow where I walk, I can heal, and I become invisible. With that she whirled around said a few words and was gone. She just as quickly reappeared.

"I can make you invisible too Gurgle," and with a few more words Gurgle went poof, and then back again. He was gone again, then back again. Gurgle hollered after reappearing. "Stop Lily! You're making me dizzy." The others laughed.

"Better than turning him into a frog I guess", said Slither. In a moment Slither too was invisible and made visible again.

"Another trip on merry go round Slither?" Slither raised his hand with an out stretched palm, "No, I surrender."

"Better than your tricks, huh?"

"Yeah maybe so. Can you teach me that?"

"Yes, we can, but we won't," replied Cassiopeia, "it's a girl thing."

"What else you got"?" asked Alice.

"We'll save it for tomorrow," said Cassiopeia. "For now, we beg your leave, we have to get back into OZ clothes." Cassiopeia, Lemon and Lime all headed out the door. Lizzie followed. She needed a new set of clothes herself and had become attached to the family of witches. In a few minutes Clarity invited everyone to freshen up and get ready for dinner.

He stated, "There would be visitors joining us for dinner," but he did not further explain his comment. As evening drew near the skies were ablaze with flickers of sunset dancing through the clouds, kissing one cloud, then another before shading to purple and grey, before turning dark. A wagon pulled up outside and two large figures stepped down from the seat. In the dark the figures' teal skin reflected nothing.

In a minute they had burst through the front doors.

"Home again," announced Sunny.

Clarity welcomed them back, "So the masters have returned!"

"Clarity," said Smokey, have we got a story to tell you."

"You are not going to believe it," added Sunny.

"No way!" exclaimed Smokey.

"Let me see, bears ran amok at the chess match after Slither tossed a sparkle weapon and people died. Alice escaped, and your mother died and came back to life?"

"Wow, you're clairvoyant Clarity, said Sunny. "Isn't he Smokey?"

"No Sunny, you can't guess that," he said smacking his brother across the back of his head.

"Oh," exclaimed Sunny. "Alice is here isn't she?' "

"Yes, and there are others."

"Boy I thought Alice was a goner," replied Sunny. I was afraid to look when Slither and the bear faced off. I was sure I was going to see little bits of Slither all over the place."

"Smokey, how do you suppose Slither got that sparkle stuff?"

"Probably from the clothes we returned to him in the dungeon. We are lucky mother never found out," replied Smokey.

"Oh yeah," guess mom would be really mad at us."

"More likely our severed heads would have been sitting on stakes near one of her announcement boards, Sunny."

"Think so, Smokey? I mean she loves us. She wouldn't do that to us, would she?"

"Clarity, why didn't you ever tell us our mother is immortal? That's important information to not share with us!" asked Smokey.

"Boys," Clarity was interrupted by Lemon and Lime running into the hall.

"What do you think, Clarity?" hollered a very excited Lemon.

Each wore their signature outfits; Lemon was in

yellow and Lime in lime. Lemon's shorter hair was yellow, and Lime's was now lime green."

Smokey and Sunny were stunned.

"They are so pretty," whispered Sunny to Smokey."

"Yeah, they are."

Lemon and Lime giggled. "Now that's different," whispered Lemon to Lime.

"Teal skin? I never saw that before. They are pretty, for guys."

"Yes," said an entranced Lime. "Very."

Clarity began the introductions, "Boys, this is Lemon and this is Lime Chiffon. They are guests here this evening at the great library. Lemon and Lime, the young men before you with the strange colored skin are masters Smokey and Sunny. This is their home." The pairs shook hands. Lemon blushed as she grasped Smokey's hand and held onto it a bit too long.

"She won't let go," said Smokey to Sunny.

"Oh sorry," apologized Lemon, and she withdrew

her hand.

"Smokey and Sunny ate from the forbidden Teal fruit tree. It changed their skin color. It is permanent I'm afraid." added Clarity.

"But we like it," said Sunny, looking down at his teal colored beefy arms

"Yeah, we do," said Smokey, also looking down upon his teal colored arm.

"I like it too," said Lemon, "A whole lot," she said extremely slowly

"Me too," chimed Lime. "That's cool," said Sunny
"Yeah it is," said an enamored Lime, looking dreamily at Sunny.

Hearts skipped beats, skin flushed, and the girls moved in to be closer to the boys. Choices were made. Lemon would not keep her hands off Smokey, as she gently ran her hands up and down his shoulder. Lime brushed up against Sunny and like a magnet clasped onto him.

"I need to tell you one more thing young people. It might have some effect on what's happening here. Smokey and Sunny are the Queen's sons. Lemon and Lime are the witch of OZ's daughters. Your houses are mortal enemies."

"So?" replied Lemon. "My mother is no longer the ruler of OZ, she's been deposed. She doesn't even want to rule OZ."

"Sorry you lost your castle," said Sunny. "You are welcome to stay at ours." Like two powerful magnets, the couples remained in contact.

"Girls, what's the meaning of this?' Cassiopeia's voice rang out. "Who are those boys?" Mother bear was in the house and there were questions to answer. Cassiopeia strode over to the four dressed in a black as night gown, her long black hair released from its bun and white as white skin.

"Mom it's OK! Clarity says this is their home. We are just getting acquainted."

"Clarity?" She questioned.

"I was introducing your lovely daughters to Smokey and Sunny. This is their castle."

"Smokey and Sunny are sons of the Queen," blurted out Lemon. "The Wisp said they are good. Don't you remember?"

"Hmm, they better be or I'll turn them into toads."

"She really can't do that," whispered Lemon to Smokey.

"Are you sure? I mean a toad, maybe a frog, but certainly not a toad. They got warts and stuff," replied Sunny. "These pretty girls wouldn't like us much if we were toads." worried Sunny.

"Maybe not," replied Smokey.

"Besides not only would we be teal in color, but we'd also be toads. We'd starve to death because no flies would get within 100 yards of us." Said Sunny.

Cassiopeia burst out laughing at the nonsensical exchange. "Oh boys, you are so cute."

"You're very pretty," said Sunny to Cassiopeia

"Thank you, ah, is your name Sunny?"

"Yeah Sunny, and he's Smokey. I've got the splotch of blond hair. That's how you tell us apart. Well there's one more way, Smokey's got a mole on his rear!"

"Sunny, you're not supposed to tell them that!"
"The girls giggled."

"Sunny questioned Smokey, "You probably should show them so they know, right?" The girls giggled more as Clarity interrupted them.

"Masters, there will be no showing of moles this evening!"

"Thank you." replied Cassiopeia.

The Teal brothers and Chiffon sisters made their entrance into the dining room, with Cassiopeia and Clarity close behind. Lemon intertwined her arm with Smokey's for their grand entrance.

"Well, I see the introductions went well," said Alice.

"Yes, but perhaps a little too well," replied Cassiopeia. "I fear I will have to keep an eye on my girls tonight."

Lizzie entered the dining room wearing a peasant outfit with her hair wrapped in a scarf. It might be described as romantic, Barbizon school little people fashion or pretty farm worker ready for the fields. "Trying to fit in tomorrow," she said.

"Well you definitely will not stand out," said Gurgle.

"Where's Little Lady," asked Cassiopeia.

"She wasn't hungry. She's depressed and angry about the slaughter of the remaining monkeys."

"Is she going to be OK for tomorrow?" asked Slither. "She's going to have some really important tasks she needs to do tomorrow. She's the only one who can do it, unless one of you witches can fly?"

"She's really angry, Slither," replied Alice. "She will definitely be motived tomorrow."

The dinner, and after dinner strategy sessions went long into the evening. Much wine was consumed. Since tomorrow could be everyone's last days, Cassiopeia did not question when Lemon and Lime asked for another glass of wine. Nor did she seem concerned when Lemon and Smokey strolled off to a more private area of the castle. To be followed shortly by Lime leading Sunny off in another direction. Lily noted the pairs fading off into the distance and nudged Cassiopeia. "Your girls," she whispered and pointed.

Cassiopeia sighed in response, "I don't feel like playing mother tonight. Tomorrow is going to be brutal. I was going to pair them off with a pair of old geezers back in OZ to keep them safe. This accomplishes the same thing, only with younger men. Maybe if something goes wrong tomorrow it will be better for them. I believe the Queen will be victorious tomorrow, so I gamble my daughter's lives on that conclusion and pray I am able to balance out good and evil as the Wisp so desires. What will happen tonight, will happen."

Long into the night as the party ended, Slither and Lizzie retired from the room.

"My room?" questioned Slither.

"Slither, there is much you do not know about me. Before you left for Wonderland, you were a dalliance for me. A night of fun, and we did have fun Slither. But that is all it was, nothing more. Tomorrow, I would give my life for you if needed, but we have other paths. Goodnight Slither. You are a wonderful man, just not my man."

Slither walked back to his room slightly inebriated and very confused.

# The Great War        23

Tendrils of light weaved across the morning sky as dawn announced its coming. However, for some time the forces of OZ were advancing onto the battlefield. The little people were roused from their beds in the middle of the night and herded onto the trail. Everyone was included, women, young mothers, nursing infants, no one was excluded from the march. "Why must even the mothers with newborns march off to war," asked a very confused mayor. "It is unheard of."

Willis, the King's senior commander answered, "All must assist in the effort. We may be out numbered; every person who can lift even a towel must aid the war effort."

His answer made sense to the Mayor, even though Gurgle's son Ray heard the same thing and was deeply suspicious. Nursing mothers, young children and those with disabilities were loaded into wagons. The others marched alongside the wagons. Something is not right, Ray thought. War is no place for nursing mothers.

Willis excused himself from the Mayor's presence and rode back to the King.

"All is well so far. The mayor thought bringing nursing mothers to battle front was unusual, but he accepted my reasoning."

"Good," said the King. "They will form a forward line. The Queen's horsemen will initially resist riding through the little people and their women and children. That will be their undoing. Our archers will rain arrows down upon them as they try to breech our forward line of little people."

"Few of the little people will survive the initial thrust by the Queen's men and that shower of arrows." reminded Willis.

"Those who do survive will be motivated to fight upon seeing the Queen's men riding through their midst. They may not be an effective fighting force, but they will occupy their Queen's men long enough for us to surge to an advantage."

"So it shall be," answered Willis as he rode off to

check on other troop movements.

Back at the great library, Smokey and Sunny rolled out of their beds in the early twilight of morning. Mother wanted them to join her in battle. Lemon and Lime returned to their own rooms a bit earlier. They dressed in their finest silks with hearts on their uniforms. While they were not warriors, they were titled and thus wore the family colors of the Queen of Hearts. Smokey and Sunny made their way to the dining room. Even at this early time of the night, there was Clarity. "Does he ever sleep?" questioned Smokey.

"I don't know Smokey. He's always up when we are. Gotta sleep!"

"Think so?"

"I would believe so, he's really old," replied Smokey.

"I hope I live to be that old," said Sunny.

"I just want to survive the day," said Smokey. "We are not immortal like mom." "Yeah, that's weird," said Sunny. "How can she be our mother when she keeps dying and coming back?"

"Good question Sunny. I hate leaving Lemon. She's so pretty and nice. We, uh, well, you know."

"Yeah same here," smiled Sunny. Just then Lemon and Lime burst into the room, still wearing nightgowns. "Please don't be a hero, Smokey," said Lemon running up and embracing Smokey.

Lime leaped into Sunny's arms, hugging and kissing him. "You are going to be out there today too?" asked Smokey.

"Yes," replied Lemon, "but I'll be invisible and safe."

"Remember Sunny, you are fighting OZ not us," reminded Lime.

"Of course," replied Sunny.

The girls walked with them into the courtyard where two white stallions stood draped with the Queen of Hearts silks and heart emblems. Smokey and Sunny mounted the stallions, waved and rode out of the great library toward the advancing troops of Wonderland.

"I would not say anything about Lemon and Lime

to mother, Sunny. She could get really angry."

"Let's just wave to her and then go to the back. That way we will not slip up and tell her," commented Sunny.

Smokey was surprised by Sunny's solution to their problem. He usually never comes up with a viable solution to any problem, he thought.

Sunny looked toward the sky at the glimmers of light that streaked across a light blue canopy and thought, it is going to be such a beautiful day, dry, with clear skies. I wish Lime and I were just riding for pleasure instead of fighting for survival. This is not the way it should be. A cloud of dust and debris rose from the west and the east as the advancing armies grew nearer. A blast of horns from OZ broke the stillness striking fear in Smokey and Sunny. They were near.

They rode up to a ridge and were greeted by a very unusual scene. Wonderland's troops were herding gigantic masses of animals in front of their forward guards. A sea of pink washed across the land as thousands of flamingos ebbed and flowed across grasslands. Their wings were clipped, so they could not fly. The flamingos were followed by hundreds of huge black and white ostriches. The ostriches in front were pecking at the flamingos pushing them to speed up. Neither of these bird species could speak, so communications was solely by nudge and peck. The massive herd of rabbits which accompanied Smokey, Sunny, and the travelers when they entered Wonderland followed. They passed by the crazed rabbit they had seen before who looked dazed and concentrated on simply putting one foot before the other. After the rabbits came wild boars, eager for the opportunity to gore the residents of OZ.

"We are going to have to run over these damn rabbits before we can get to our enemies." said one large boar.

"Maybe the flamingos too!" said another in reply.

As Smokey and Sunny passed by, one boar hollered in defiance, "Hey what are you two looking at? We make mincemeat out of guys like you!"

Smokey rode toward the defiant boar, drew his sword and smacked the boar's hindquarters with the flat side of his blade, sending the boar tumbling through the grasses. Smokey and Sunny although not the brightest or sharpest tools in the shed, were excellent horsemen. The other boars laughed as the mouthy boar regained his footing. "I guess he showed you who's boss," said one of the boars' sidekicks. The chastised boar remained silent.

Returning to Sunny's side, Smokey commented, "I can understand why the boars are marching, they are mean and deadly fighters, but the flamingos, ostriches and rabbits. They'll be slaughtered. This isn't right."

"I know," said a concerned Sunny. "Why is mother doing this?"

"Do we even know who she is?" replied Smokey. "But you're not sure if mother is actually our mother?"

"No," replied Sunny "I don't know who she is. She is a violent, sadistic, and cruel person. I would hate to think she's actually our mother."

"Did you talk to Lime about mother?"

"Yes. She's not familiar with mother, never heard too much about her. I told her what I knew and what I had seen; she was shocked. She didn't know what to say."

"Did you talk to Lemon about mother?"

"No, we didn't do much talking last night." Smokey smiled for some time remembering last night.

Behind the boars came bigger animals; steers and buffalo type creatures with large horns and mean dispositions, but not bears. After yesterday's chess match debacle, it was decided the bears were likely to flee if any sparkle clouds were dropped risking needed troops. Finally, mother and her commander Thomas Thorns came into view along with many, many troops.

Smokey and Sunny kept their distance and waved as they traveled toward the back lines. The Queen called out, "I may need you later, stay ready." They waved in acknowledgment and continued toward the back.

"My sons are good horsemen, but not bright. I do not want to sacrifice my guards to protect them. They were stupid enough to bring Alice and her group into Wonderland. If it had been anyone else, I would have taken their head."

"Do you want some guards to accompany them?"
"No more than two."

"It is done." With that, Thomas Thorns rode off a short way to a pair of men on horseback. They were fellow spies in OZ and loyal to Thorns.

"You are to accompany the Queen's boys to the rear and stay close by. They are not immortal as is the Queen. If the Queen goes down I will set her aflame immediately with one of these bags I stole from Slither's clothes the other night. If she's immolated immediately she likely will not be able to resurrect herself and we will be rid of her. Then, I will give you the signal to kill her sons."

"With pleasure," said one of the spies.

He returned to the Queen's side. "Done," is all he said to her.

A few more Now's and the forces of OZ and Wonderland faced off perhaps a quarter of a mile away. Each was surprised by the front lines of the others. Off to the side on the hillside where the great library stood, Alice and the others observed troop movements. They were shocked to see the front lines. To the left were masses of poor creatures being led to their slaughter. To the right every little person left in OZ. "It is time," said Cassiopeia.

"Lemon, Lime, Lily, and Lizzie, now go invisible!"

They whirled around, uttered a few ancient words and were gone. Just as commanded. "Gurgle, you too will be invisible!" And he was. Cassiopeia, was in command and advised Slither to weaponize Little Lady with a fire pack to drop over the leadership of OZ at the right time.

"Slither when you are needed down on the field I may turn you invisible."

"What if you can't because you are wounded or dead? What if you die before you can turn me back to visible?" replied Slither.

"Any of us witches can reverse the spell, including Lily."

"But she has got to see me to find me. I could walk around forever as Mr. Invisible."

"Trust me Slither, we know when someone invisible is near."

"Well I'm still not crazy about the idea. You aren't invincible."

"Slither, there are a lot of people dying today, I will not be one of them." said Cassiopeia. Slither raised his hands and shrugged.

"Slither, swing a sword at me," she commanded. "NO!"

"OK, Alice, stab me with anything?" "No of course not!"

"Adam, last chance, please swing your sword at me."

Adam said "OK," but half swung his sword flat edge toward her so as to only bruise her. It was deflected before it struck her.

"Wow, can you do that for everybody?" asked Adam.

"No, just myself."

"I have learned a spell for invincibility" she announced.

"OK, I'm ready to be invisible when you need me." said Slither. "Have we got some surprises for everyone down there."

Alice spoke, "What about Adam and me. We have no roles. Last night you talked about the things that were expected of us?"

"You are to stay here with Clarity. Protect the great library if needed." Replied Cassiopeia

"With what?" questioned Adam, "Two swords and a flying monkey?"

"Exactly as the Wisp requested this morning."

"You saw the Wisp this morning?"

"For a moment. He said you are to stay at the great library. And one more thing, he said you've found what you came for, then disappeared," responded Cassiopeia.

"Another riddle from the cloud in the sky," chuckled Slither. "Well you two can cool your heels, have a couple glasses of wine and some cheese. Relax. We'll be done by mid- day, maybe earlier," as he looked down upon the masses of harmless animals leading the Wonderland march.

Clarity remarked, "They are not drinking wine and eating cheeses while you are fighting down there! Preposterous!"

Adam, laughed, "Slither, always the joking eternal

optimist. I wish life was as easy as you always want to make it!"

"Rest assured Slither, if things go south we will join you down there." said Alice.

"We know," replied Cassiopeia. "but the Wisp wants you safe up here for some reason." Alice and Adam watched Cassiopeia descend to join the others on the battlefield. She remained visible for an extended period, then whirled and was gone.

Alice turned to Adam, "So witches are real and animals can talk?"

"Only here in OZ and Wonderland," replied Adam.

"What a strange and interesting place," answered Alice.

Down on the field below, battle lines drew closer. A horseman with a white flag advanced from Wonderland to the OZ lines.

"We wish a meeting before we go to war," he yelled out. "To surrender?" replied an officer of OZ.

"No, we need the measurements for your coffin!" replied the Wonderland representative. A member of the

OZ King's personal guard rode out to meet him.

"The Queen wishes to meet with your King."

"And why?"

"It is not for us to ask those questions."

"I will relay your request," said the King's representative.

The time spent organizing the meeting allowed Gurgle and Lizzie to get closer to the assembled Little People. Close enough that Gurgle could identify Ray and a few of his other children.

Meanwhile, Lilly and Lemon traveled to the far side of the field, while Lime remained on the other side accompanied by her mother. Everyone was in position. The thing about the invisibility spell was that those who were invisible could see not only the real world but others who were also invisible. An incalculable advantage, when the numbers are small. The Queen rode a fine stallion emblazed in white silk with numerous hearts throughout the cloth covering. She wore a silk gown with hearts throughout the fabric.

Beside her was Thomas Thorns who shielded his

596

identity by a helmet. Riding out to meet them at midfield was the self-appointed King Thaddeus and his right-hand commander Willis.

"King of OZ, my legions are massive, we have numeral superiority. We have thousands of animals who volunteered to give their lives and be sacrificed on the front lines against those disgusting little people. They will not last but a few moments before Wonderland's animals are at your troop's throats. Following them will be masses of boars eager to tear into your troops. Beyond that are large horned animals who are so large your men will not be able to stand up to their rush. Then King of OZ, my archers will dispatch those who are left, before my horseman ride into your midst and decimate the remaining OZ troops. Finally, my footmen will chase you back to your castle and slaughter your women and children before your eyes. "

"Queen of Hearts," responded the King, "Your words are like an afternoon mist, a minor inconvenience that quickly passes. You expect us to be afraid of flamingos, ostriches, and bunny rabbits?"

Willis let out a hardy laugh. "An army of flamingos

and bunny rabbits? We are so scared. Even little people with small swords will repel these creatures and send them backwards into your boars and larger animals. You can't control your front line of animals. We hear your chess match went badly yesterday and your own bears mauled your palace guards and handmaidens. The same thing will happen today."

The Queen looked troubled that he knew of the debacle.

"We hear Alice survives and may be coming for you oh great Queen." said the King. Thomas Thorns, sensing the Queen was losing some of her confidence removed his helmet. "Oh, great King, or should I just call you Thaddeus the Imposter? The Queen knows of your battle plans for I have informed her."

The King's mouth fell open. "I thought you said he was dead" said Willis. "He looks very much alive."

"He is," replied the Queen "Your days are numbered."

"We shall see about that," yelled a very angry King as he turned his horse around and rode swiftly back to his lines.

"Someone ride back to the castle and release the green men," barked the frightened King. "Now!"

"Willis was much more controlled in his exit. As he turned he simply said to Thorns, "I will eat your heart in front of my men." He then rode off to join the King.

"He has a very interesting diet," dead panned the Queen. "Commander let them make the first move. I wish to see those disgusting little people separated from their troops before we unleash the animals upon them." Thorns nodded in agreement.

"Explain to me again why the flamingos and rabbits are in our front lines my commander," requested the Queen.

"They contribute a congestion factor to their front lines, and the passive little people who are reluctant to take up arms against these poor creatures. Thousands of flamingos running at their lines, followed by much larger and more dangerous ostriches, and then finally by a thousand large, white aggressive rabbits. They will be getting underfoot, clinging to boot straps and creating a diversion that requires their little people and men of OZ to pay more attention to the ground instead of the boars and large horned creatures descending upon them," replied Thorns. "Once decimated by the larger more aggressive creatures running through the little people and into the front lines of OZ creating disruptions, fear and disorganization, I will give the order to our archers to let loose a wave of deadly arrows and then order our men to charge."

"Interesting plan," said the Queen as they arrived back to their lines. "On the surface I would think it a quite foolish plan, but now as you explain it, it sounds ingenious."

The King of OZ issued an order to advance into combat. The little people who had been told they would retreat to the rear to provide support were ordered to advance. But they remained in place.

"You told us we would retreat to the rear. We cannot fight, there are women and children here," yelled the mayor to Willis as the din of blaring horns and cheering warriors almost drowned him out.

"You will charge their position!"

"It is suicide. We have few weapons and none of us are warriors. We will be slaughtered. Please I beg of you," said the mayor as he fell to his knees with clasped hands. "Please commander, let us retreat."

"You will do as ordered. Those who survive will be heroes."

"No," the mayor cried out.

The commander turned toward his archers, "They need some encouragement."

The archers drew their bows targeting arrows in the direction of the mayor and his little people.

"The choice is yours, die a hero or die a coward!"

The little people erupted into anger. "You can't do this. We have women and children, you heartless bastards."

Threats were issued. Many shook their fists, some raised swords and advanced toward the commander. The wailing of the women increased and spread throughout the little people. Suddenly a little person made a run toward the Wonderland lines and veered to the right, attempting to flee the battle. He was cut down in a hail of arrows. Another young little woman with a newborn suffered the same fate, as she and her child took their last breaths as arrows struck them down. Some of the OZ guards cheered, some cried. The brutality of the death of the mother and child silenced the little people. Tears fell from many of the faces as they contemplated their last moments.

Lizzie and Gurgle remaining invisible observed silently from a short distance away but could do nothing lest they reveal their presence and positions.

"Now do you obey my command or must more die?" commanded Willis.

Having no options, the little people turned toward the Wonderland lines and advanced. Many openly prayed while others silently accepted their fate.

In the rear of the column of little people, two young males, brandishing crude swords whispered, "He is getting closer, another few feet, and we will turn, charge, and bring him down."

"Kill him," one called out as they turned. The over exuberant little person had given away their intentions. They were cut down by nearby archers well before they reached Willis.

Willis called out a warning to the little people, "Anyone else wish to try that?"

The little people grew silent. Accepting fate, they moved slowly forward, men and woman hugging each other and their children one last time. After the little people advanced about one hundred yards out from the front lines of OZ, an invisible Lily powered up her colorless laser and ran across the field behind the back line of the little people setting fire to the grasses. A line of fire in the grasses erupted between them and the OZ forces and raced across the battlefield.

Smoke obscured the vision of the OZ front lines. The skies behind the OZ troops which were a cloudless blue, now turned angry as puffy white clouds appeared, and turned grey, then black, sucking wind into them as they developed. The wind sucked the flames toward the men of OZ and away from the little people.

The little people, fearful of being consumed by the fire, started to scream thinking the fire was set by the forces of OZ to push them into combat. As it drew away from them, cheers were heard on the battlefield. "Their plans have backfired," yelled one little person. The King and commander Willis, looked confused.

"What manner of sorcery is this?" questioned the King. Across the field the forces of Wonderland stood quite puzzled.

"Have they set fire to the fields to force the little people to charge?" asked the Queen.

"That was not in the plans," said Thorns.

"Well, if they deviate from the plans you gave the King, then it is going badly for them."

"What is your pleasure oh Queen?"

"We will sit tight and watch. That fire is growing because of the weather behind them and it could do the job for us."

Lizzie turned Gurgle visible and then herself, just 50 feet in front of the massed little people. The sudden appearance of the Lion of OZ, excited the little people. "The Lion of OZ has come to save us!" shouted some.

Lizzie strode forward toward her father within the column of little people. "Mayor, split our people into two and have them flee to the edges of the battle field, and then mass on the flanks, now," as she pointed in each direction.

Her father ran up to Lizzie and hugged her. "I thought I'd never see you again."

"Where have you been?"

"I have been with the travelers, the Witch of OZ and her daughters. I too am now a witch father." She whirled around and said the ancient words which allowed her to disappear. Then just as quickly she returned. Ooh's and Ah's greeted her return. "Now follow my orders mayor."

The little people split up and ran in opposite directions, as the flames of the grassland fire licked ever closer to the OZ position. The Wonderland troops were frozen in place confused by the events before them and remained quiet. It seemed a strange battle plan, many thought. "What do you make of this commander?" asked the Queen. "Are they setting a flanking position using the little people?"

"It doesn't make any sense, my Queen."

The little people took positions at the sides of the great field where they huddled and looked back upon the field. The smoke from the grass fire obscured the legions of OZ troops. Those from Wonderland remained in place.

Suddenly on both sides of the field, rings of flowers encircled the little people. Some plants nearly waist high. They extended ten feet in every direction. Invisible Lemon and Lime had entered the fray amid a wall of flowers defining the positioning of the little people. The troops of OZ could still not see through the smoke from the grass fires which obscured their vision.

Wonderland troops on the ridge above the battalions of animals on slopes of the grasslands, pointed in either direction. The circular flower distracted the troops. Even the orders of commanders riding upon their horses could not maintain their military formations. "What manner of magic is this?" said a soldier. "Is there a witch at play?"

"Maybe the Wisp?" said another. They broke ranks and gathered in small groups arguing and pointing toward the positions of the little people.

"Obviously there is some sorcery involved," noted the Queen to Thorns. "Our men have dissolved into unruly gatherings, please fix it!" she commanded.

"As you command."

Thorns rode over toward the group and swatted a solder with the flat of his sword sending him tumbling. "The next time you will feel my blade. Back into your ranks!" he ordered. They followed. Once the flower walls were established, the angry boiling clouds subsided and with that the grass fires burned themselves out. A small amount of rain drenched the field as the storm subsided. The men of OZ retreated another one hundred yards during the fire and looked down upon small patches of fires before them.

Willis looked right and then left, noting the huddled masses of little people behind a wall of flowers, exclaimed, "What matter of magic is this?"

The King replied, "It is the witch's nonsense. She can make flowers grow, make it rain indoor and heal things. Not exactly the most frightening of spells."

"But what about the storm?" said Willis.

"That is not her doing, and anyway it's gone now. Look above and see the skies are blue and clear. There was a slight atmospheric disturbance, but it is now gone." replied the King. "Let's concentrate on defeating Wonderland. The little people are on the sidelines where they will consume too much of our resources and expose our men to Wonderland forces. Ignore them. We will slaughter them after the great win. Advance our troops, just approach closely enough to employ our archers. We will sow disarray among the animals and cause them to charge back into the forces of Wonderland, much like the bears did yesterday during the chess match."

The order to advance was given as was the order for the Wonderland troops. The soldiers of OZ closed in on the masses of birds and animals advancing toward them. A clash was imminent.

The animals pushed forward, amidst grumbling,

and squawking. Within minutes arrows rained down into the flock of flamingos. Many fell. The ostriches panicked at seeing some of their fellow birds dropped by the arrows, and ran in all directions. Some trampled flamingos to the front and bunny rabbits in the rear. The poor bossy rabbit was one of the first to go at the feet of an ostrich, splattered by the weight of the running bird. Rabbits ran in all directions. Some ostriches made it into the OZ lines of archers and ran them over. As the lines were breached, the boars followed.

"Where are the little people?" said one huge boar. "They told us we would get to trample and gore the little people?"

"They must have run away. Hey, let's get the archers ahead before they get us," said another boar.

Arrows flew into the air. Many harmlessly bounced off the boar's thick skin, some penetrated into the outer layer of fat, but most animals were unaffected."

"Just a flesh wound," said one, who had an arrow sticking out of its shoulder. The wounded boar sliced into the line of archers, dragging one to the ground and the goring began.

The archer's screams permeated the air, as valuable archers were sliced and diced along the front lines. Eventually the boars succumbed to the swordsmanship and spears of the mounted men who attached from behind the line of archers. The few boars who survived retreated. The grassland was now awash in pinks, blacks, whites, and multicolored hues of brown and the greens of OZ fighting colors. Red streams of blood flowed throughout the grassy canvas. It looked like a gory abstract painting. The ribbons of these colors of death were visible from the Wonderland position.

Action ceased as combatants took time to assess loses. For Wonderland, only animals succumbed to the forces of OZ. For OZ, they lost many valuable archers to the boars. Some lay writhing in pain along the front lines. They were transported to the rear lines. The scene was crimson gore. There were few places that anyone advancing would not step into either blood or an animal's tissue.

Back on the Wonderland side, the flamingos were all but completely wiped out. The weary, stunned birds that remained were allowed to pass through the lines back toward Wonderland as were the seven ostriches which survived. They were in foul moods and took the opportunity to peck at soldiers as they passed through the lines.

"I'm so sorry," many soldiers said as the birds passed through their ranks. "This is terrible"

"I hate the Queen!" said another soldier.

Some stroked the birds as they passed through the ranks or rubbed blood off their feathers with handkerchiefs. Instead of cheers and excitement over the success of the charge, the gory scene of bird and boar bodies piled high and the squawking of injured birds and grunts of wounded boars demoralized the troops of Wonderland.

The larger buffalo creatures moved up for a second charge. They saw the carnage before them and were left agitated and frightened. They remained in place despite orders to charge. A bull pawed the ground with its feet and spoke out, "We will not charge. We do not wish to be slaughtered."

Thorns took matters into his own hands and rode to the front to drive his sword into the shoulders of the large bull. He watched it fall to the ground and did not move.

"Charge, we said. Charge, or we will kill you all."

The animals turned to face the troops of OZ and began a slow march toward certain death. "OK, enough of this," said Cassiopeia as she emerged on the near side to the great library.

"No more poor animals shall die!"

Using various incantations and with raised hands to the skies she brought forth the angriest of boiling black clouds. These did not develop slowly as before, but grew rapidly into massive thunderheads, so high one could not see their tops. Lightning exploded over the troops of OZ.

"First Wonderland, then OZ," announced Cassiopeia at the top of her voice.

She threw her hands downward and pointed. Wherever she pointed a lightning bolt struck. The first few struck in the open grasslands between the forces of Wonderland and OZ. Then closer to the buffalo like creatures.

The lighting caused the large horned animals of Wonderland to bolt back through the ranks of Wonderland. "Get out of my way," said one bull charging toward the front lines of Wonderland.

Carnage ensued. A wave of silk and red heart-uniformed men flowed without resistance to each side of the battle field to avoid the charge, which allowed the charging animals direct access to senior commanders. The animals plowed through the senior commanders upon their horses.

A bull gored one commander's horse bringing the commander down. He was promptly trampled by the next charging animal. Some commanders had time to draw swords and take down some of the animals with well-placed thrusts. One had sunk his sword into a charging horned animal only to find himself lifted from his steed and flung to the ground. With sword still impaled in its shoulder the animal ground the commander into paste upon the grassland.

The animal was taken down by one of the Queen's archers. Two of the seven senior commanders lay dead upon the field. Two more suffered varying degrees of injury but remained on the battle field. Many junior officers were strewn across the battlefield. Thorns and the Queen sought safety within a stand of trees and could only watch in horror.

"No more animals," shouted the Queen. "They are unreliable."

Smokey and Sunny remained far removed from the field of battle and shadowed by Thorn's spies who were waiting orders to kill them.

Cassiopeia turned her attention to the forces of OZ. Lightning strike after strike hit the troops of OZ. A thousand and more now lay stunned, burnt, or dead upon the grass land. The strikes continued for an untold duration. Suddenly the clouds dissipated, and skies filled with birds, insects and a single flying monkey. The battle field grew still. Only squawking from a few birds above was heard. Willis survived along with a few senior commanders who took cover under a few trees at the rear. He lay prone upon the ground during the barrage of lightning strikes in order to avoid them. The King sat nearby, dazed by the great conflagration.

"Where did that storm come from?" he exclaimed toward Willis.

Willis along with many senior commanders, walked out from beneath the canopy of trees. "My King," Those were the last words he would ever say as Little lady tossed a well-placed fire bag down upon the assembled senior leaders. It was a direct hit upon Willis, who burst into flames, screaming and writhing upon the ground, until he was silenced. The intense fire from a phosphorous-based weapon consumed Willis and injured others in varying degrees.

When the phosphorous landed on the men it was impossible to put out. Their clothing continued burning, then burst into flames. Soon all were smoldering black masses. Another bag was dropped intended for the King. It missed the mark. With only one more available, Little Lady dove down toward the King to deliver the bag personally. An injured archer interrupted her dive with a well-placed arrow and she spiraled to the ground and was consumed by the fire bag.

Alice watched from afar, screaming as she saw Little Lady hit the ground into a ball of fire. She started to run toward the battle field, but was caught by Adam, who pulled her back.

"Nothing you can do Alice, she's gone."

"I can kill the King," replied Alice

Adam pointed in the direction the King, "I think Cassiopeia will beat you there."

Cassiopeia noted the demise of Little Lady and strode in a visible form through the lines of OZ. Her black gown glistened in the bright sunlight almost blinding the nearby soldiers. Her progress was noted by Thorns who watched from the safety of the Wonderland side.

"My Queen, we may not have need to expend our forces against OZ. The Witch and the King of OZ may well do themselves in."

"Gather up those commanders fit to fight, promote two of our worthy men to commander to replace those we lost, and move the troops forward," ordered the Queen. "We have many to kill. Send some to the flanks and exterminate the little people while we march to engage what is left of OZ."

Commander Thomas Thorns rode amidst the Wonderland men, "You and you," he pointed, "are now commanders." Two mid-level officers saluted in acknowledgment. After the command was given, those at the Wonderland front complied, but in a slow deliberate manner, as the senior leaders now reorganized in the rear and joined their forces.

The remaining troops of OZ looked upon Cassiopeia in awe. One rose and attempted to attack her with a dagger, but it bounced harmlessly to the ground. She glanced at the soldier then moved her gaze toward the King. An archer near the King drew his bow and fired at Cassiopeia, it struck directly in the middle of her chest, but failed to penetrate, dropping harmlessly on the ground. She picked it up, broke it in half and tossed it back on the ground. A few ancient words were said whereupon flowers grew wherever she stepped. Soon paths of flowers grew at the outer edges of the forces of OZ, the works of still invisible Lemon and Line. A third line of flowers followed slightly to the left of Cassiopeia. Lily was on the march. Soon the forces of OZ were enveloped by flowers. Many put down their weapons.

The forces of Wonderland paused in amazement at the sight of the ever growing mass of flowers. Something strange was in the air. They were frightened.

"Well King, it is time," announced Cassiopeia as she approached him. He cowered as he witnessed her deflect two weapons.

"I thought you had no powers." he stuttered.

"I understood you were going to kill my daughters and sent men out to kill me, oh King of OZ."

"That is not true at all," he said in a hurried response, now looking around for a means of escape.

"You killed off my flying monkeys, I understand you slaughtered the weak and infirm little people in their village. I personally watched you kill two fleeing little people and two more who sought to stop the slaughter of their people. Are those charges not true?"

The King looked to the ground and back toward OZ. "Thaddeus, this is your last day, announced Cassiopeia." Just crossing over a ridge were six large green colored men who were not men, being driven by two of the King's horsemen. They were late, but offered an escape. He attempted to distract Cassiopeia by pointing in the direction of Wonderland.

"Wonderland is almost upon us," he said, then broke toward the men who are not men.

"You have chosen your path," yelled out Cassiopeia. She allowed him to reach the rescue group and then with a few more words a huge wall of wood surrounded the men who are not men, the two horsemen and The King. All were silent for a moment within the barricade set by Cassiopeia. Then the sound of men hollering and barking orders was heard accompanied by growls, screams. Frightening sounds of death and dismemberment filtered out to those nearby from the enclosure Cassiopeia had erected. The end came for the King. She was now for perhaps the first time truly in charge of OZ.

Lemon, Lime, and Lily became visible once more. Lemon and Lime ran up and hugged their mother. Turning to a now visible Lily, Cassiopeia said, "OZ is now yours if you wish. I have my own plans."

"I am not from here," she replied.

"But you belong here Lily. You do not have to decide now, but it is my wish."

"Mother, where shall we go?" asked Lemon.

"I think that decision was made by you girls last night."

"Oh," she replied and smiled.

"I know," said their mother, now stroking each of the heads and then releasing them.

"Now on to Wonderland. We have business there," pointing toward the amassed troops of Wonderland who were frozen into place. "Girls you are to return to the great library and await the others. Your role is done here on the battle field." They hugged their mother and then retreated from the battlefield. They turned on their flower powers and a path of flowers followed them to the ridge where the great library stood.

Cassiopeia addressed the remaining men of OZ. "It is time to go home to your families and assist the little people in the rebuilding of their community. You will have my protection if you are of good of heart and deed. If not, I will handle those issues, as I have handled these today. Cassiopeia and Lily passed by the charred remains of Little Lady and paid their respects.

"She was the last of my flying monkeys. How horrible. I so liked them. She was the brightest and my favorite."

Lily replied, "She was the last, Cassiopeia, it would have been lonely for her with any of her kind. I hope Alice is OK."

They looked toward the great library and saw two figures standing on the ridge looking down upon them. They raised their hands to wave. Cassiopeia and Lily waved back.

"Come we have a Queen to depose." Said Cassiopeia.

"But how? She cannot die?"

"We will figure a way, somehow," as Cassiopeia gazed off toward the troops of Wonderland. In a short period of time they were joined by Slither who came down from the great library and remained visible. Gurgle and Lizzie remained with their respective little people gatherings.

"Too bad about Little Lady," said Slither.

"How's Alice?" asked Lily.

"She's upset, but OK. Adam has kept her from joining the battle. So, what's the plan you two?"

"We don't know." said Cassiopeia. "How do you kill someone who cannot die? If we decimate her forces, she will still remain."

"Problem is," reminded Lily, "Most of her people are good. They follow her out of fear. The Wisp would not want us to slaughter them for the sake of slaughtering them."

As they walked toward the lines of Wonderland, something interesting happened. The men of Wonderland were laying their weapons down as Cassiopeia, Lily and Slither approached. Seeing this,

Lizzie and Gurgle left the confines of their respective walls of flowers and ran to join the group walking towards the front lines of Wonderland.

As the advancing group reached front lines, soldiers of Wonderland, resplendent in their finest silks and uniforms, parted to the sides, like curtains being drawn aside. A few dropped to their knees and bowed heads. Of the five remaining commanders, three retreated to the side of the Queen and two rode off to the sides, dismounted and bowed to Cassiopeia's as she passed. Unseen from the ridge of the great library, Lemon and Lime made their way down to the field circling around from the back. Their teal men were easily spotted at the rear of the forces. They both said a few words, twirled and became invisible.

The Queen stood upon ground that was left with Thorns and three commanders all on horses, five archers and a few loyal handmaidens and palace guards, no more than 20 at most. As they approached the Queen, she ordered the archers to fire at the approaching group of people. "Kill them all," she cried.

Arrows rained down upon Cassiopeia, but harmlessly bounced off an invisible shield created by a spell. A few arrows aimed at Lily reached their marks, but were all aimed at her chest area and glanced off her protective weapon system. Slither had veered out to the right of the group, so no arrows came his way. Finally, Lizzie stood in front of Gurgle and intercepted an arrow that tore into her blouse sleeve and grazed her arm. She grasped her upper arm and held it tight to stop the bleeding. She was lucky it was only a flesh wound.

Gurgle asked, "Are you OK,"

"Flesh wound," she replied and reached down to pick up the arrow which struck her. She secured it in her belt for safe keeping. The cut was not deep and no longer needed compression. Remnants of her blood dried on the edge of the arrow point. Gurgle thought, I guess she wants a battlefield souvenir.

Lily responded by firing up her laser weapon. Aiming her right arm toward the ground at the feet of the archers she lit up the grasses, causing them to jump back. The archers reloaded and aimed but were hit with a blast from Slither's ring which sent them to the ground. Stunned, a few reached for their bows.

"No, No, No," he yelled to the archers. "This is a terrible way to die!"

A handmaiden pulled a dagger from her belt and threw it in Slither's direction. It connected and buried in his thigh muscle. Slither spun to the ground. On his way down, he hit the handmaiden with a direct ring hit. Blood, guts and body parts flew in all directions. She was no more. The archers now covered in the handmaiden's gook, thought better of their intentions. They dropped their bows and lay back upon the grass with their hands raised high. Soon others joined them to lay prone on the ground with their hands raised in the air.

Three senior commanders charged the group on horseback, creating a diversion which allowed the Queen and Thorns to retreat. Slither fired his ring weapon, but it had no charge left as they bore down upon Lizzie and Gurgle. Before Cassiopeia could create a spell to protect them with a wooden wall, Lily fired a blast of her laser sweeping the commanders and their horses. The red-hot heat from the powerful laser broiled them in an instant, leaving them steaming upon the ground. Body fluids steamed, popped and sizzled. Lily concluded they were well done.

Thorns sensed the flow of power ebbing from his Queen and pulled out the fire pack and threw it onto the Queen. It exploded in a white-hot flame consuming her. All watched as she twisted about in the flame, and finally crumbled to the ground, much of her burnt beyond recognition.

"You stole that from me," yelled out Slither as he lay upon the ground.

"Indeed I did," said Thorns. "The Queen is dead! You owe me your gratitude and safe passage from this battle field for slaying the Queen."

The group gathered around the smoking remains of the formerly beautiful Queen. They gazed down upon her charcoaled body in wonderment. No one saw Thomas signal his henchmen to kill the Teal brothers. They moved closer to the brothers.

"Well, she was smoking hot," commented Gurgle.

The group laughed. A few moments passed when a voice from a few yards away called to them.

"My dear commander Thorns, you have no loyalty,"

It was the resurrected Queen once more clothed in a bright white silk gown this time lacking a heart emblem. Thorns stumbled back to the ground. Off in the distance he saw his men had the Teal brothers at sword's end. He played his final card.

"My Queen, look behind you. My men have your sons at sword point and will run them through if any harm comes to me." The Queen looked back to her sons and then down to the sprawled commander, ignoring those around her.

She cackled, "My foolish commander, those two boys mean nothing to me. I can have more. I have had many children over the winters. I will have more! My children, grandchildren and great grandchildren always die. I have buried so many. It matters little to me if they die of old age, accident, or at the hands of your men."

Looking around at those now surrounding her, she

627

made an observation, "I am outnumbered amongst you, but as you see I cannot be killed. I will just continue to come back again and again. You may slay me, but eventually I will slay you and you will be no more. I cannot lose no matter how many of you there are. Now commander Thorns, it is I who will order my son's deaths. Kill them!" she called out to the commander's henchmen.

As the Queen issued her order she pulled a shrouded dagger from her belt and threw it at pointblank range at Thorns. It buried into his neck and severed his carotid artery. Thorns with eyes now wide open reached for his throat and emitted gurgling sounds. He never expected the Queen's move. Thorns twisted about as blood flowed down his white silk uniform and onto the ground. Thorns reclined back upon the ground and grew still. There would be no more acts of treason from Thomas Thorns.

Smokey and Sunny could see some sort of a tussle was underway at their mother's location. Thorn's henchmen stood ready for the order, and had their short swords drawn upon Thorns command. One henchman chose Smokey and had him at swords point, ordering him to carefully drop his sword from its belt. The henchman who chose Sunny crept up behind him and held a sword to his throat, ordering him to drop his sword from its belt. Both complied. Sunny looked over toward Smokey with a frightened, wide eyed look. "We screwed up," said Sunny.

Then Smokey and Sunny heard their mother issue the order, "Kill them." Smokey replied, "Mother actually ordered us killed."

"This is how it ends?" observed Sunny. From out of nowhere Smokey's sword which was laying on the ground rose up and sliced through the henchman who had his blade pointed at Smokey's throat. The henchman dropped to the ground as his internal organs made an escape from his ribcage. Smokey now free of the henchman tackled his brother and grabbed hold of the henchman who was holding Sunny.

The effort worked, but the henchman's blade sliced into Smokey's shoulder. The tackle caught the tall scrawny henchman by surprise and when he hit the ground under the weight of both Sunny and Smokey his breath was knocked out of him. Sunny rolled away and Smokey grabbed the henchman by the throat with his one good hand and squeezed hard while holding the forearm containing the short sword against the ground with his injured arm. He outweighed the henchman by more than a hundred pounds. Sunny gathered up the dead henchman's sword that the invisible Lemon had dispatched to another existence. From his knees, Sunny brought the sword down upon the henchman's hand holding the short sword and sliced it off at his wrist. The henchman screamed and was no more as Smokey rolled off him while Sunny impaled the henchman with the sword he had recovered.

Lemon twirled and became visible. "You are hurt," she cried as she rushed to Smokey. Lime did the same running to Sunny's side. Everyone's attention was drawn to the wound suffered by Smokey which was gushing blood.

Lemon stood over Smokey and looked back toward the Queen, raising her hands summoning the powers of healing. She knelt down to Smokey and placed her hands upon Smokey's shoulder. The bleeding slowed and then stopped. A short time later the wound miraculously healed. Except for the torn bloody cloth covering Smokey no one could ever know he had been injured. Interestingly the wound healed into a flesh tone rather than the Teal color of his surrounding skin.

"I think you will always be that color where the wound healed, remarked Lemon.

Looking down upon his slash of flesh colored skin he remarked, "Hey I got a stripe!"

"Yes, it looks cool," said Sunny.

"You were very brave trying to save me, Smokey."

"You are my brother Sunny. I would risk my life for you anytime."

Sunny looked at the Queen and others standing 50 yards from their position.

"Mother ordered them to kill us. Did you hear that Smokey?"

"Yes, I did. She is no longer our mother Sunny. She may have been at one time, but no mother orders their children's death."

"I know."

"Thank you, Lemon, I guess that was you who killed the man holding the sword at my throat. That was very brave of you."

Lemon just smiled and tightly hugged Smokey. Lime likewise held Sunny close to her.

Meanwhile, the Queen watched helplessly as the henchmen were dispatched by Smokey, Sunny, a woman in a bright yellow gown with short yellow hair and another woman in a bright green gown and green hair.

"You have now met my daughters Lemon and Lime, oh Queen."

The Queen turned toward Cassiopeia, "I will have the pleasure of watching you and your precious daughters Lemon and Lime die very soon. All of you will die before my eyes," she sneered.

Lizzie was holding a bow and standing only fifteen feet away. The arrow that pierced her upper arm was loaded in the bow and pointed toward the Queen. She stood silently staring at the Queen.

"Go ahead you foolish little person. I will come back once again and take great pleasure in killing you and all your kind. You people are evil. You are lazy, You are criminals who bring drugs into Wonderland, You…"

Lizzie's arrow interrupted the Queen's tirade and lodged at the center of her chest. Her eyes grew wide. For the first time she felt real intense pain. She gasped and stumbled trying to keep her feet.

Lizzie removed her scarf which was tied about her head to reveal her beautiful red hair. "You will not be coming back this time, my sister."

Cassiopeia gasped and held her hand to her mouth. Gurgle was stunned into inaction as was Slither. The Queen stumbled into Lily, who pushed her away. Blood gurgled up from her throat and cascaded down upon her white as white gown. She reached out toward Lizzie as she stumbled toward her.

Lizzie just smiled, "Die my evil sister, die."

With a final gasp, she collapsed to the grass below, and was silent.

Lizzie announced, "Yes I am the Queen's sister. And like her, I cannot die. Now that she is gone only I can take my own life." "Why didn't you tell us?" asked Lily.

"My sister would have killed me if she knew of my whereabouts. We were separated when we were young children. She had no idea I was a little person because we were both small when we separated. I have been leading a life of obscurity for so long. I hid under an alias for generations amongst the little people. It has been a long-kept secret amongst the little people."

Smokey, Sunny, Lemon, and Lime joined the others at the scene of the Queen's death.

"I am sorry Smokey and Sunny that I had to kill your mother," said Lizzie. "I am your aunt and the only one who could extinguish her evil flame."

Smokey replied looking down on what had been the woman claiming to be his mother, yet had just ordered his death. "She was not our mother Lizzie, at least not in this reincarnation. She ordered us killed. No mother does that."

"I am still sorry," replied Lizzie. They stood together contemplating everything they had witnessed and experienced.

"So much destruction and death and for what?"

said Lily.

After a few more moments Cassiopeia spoke, "Smokey and Sonny you must come with me to address the men of Wonderland. Wonderland is now yours."

"Can Lemon and Lime come along?" "Yes of course." she replied.

Cassiopeia stood among the gathered masses of Wonderland men. "The Queen is dead. She was killed by her sister, Lizzie," as she pointed toward the direction of the little person standing off in the distance, still with bow in hand.

The crowd exploded with cheers and smiles, and relieved the Queen was dead and they would not have to fight and risk their own deaths.

"The Queen's sons, Smokey and Sunny are good men. They will serve you well as your new leaders."

Cheers again erupted as Smokey and Sunny were well liked among all in Wonderland.

At their sides are my daughters Lemon and Lime. I anticipate that there will perhaps be a merging of the families of OZ and Wonderland and an end to hostilities between our people. I Cassiopeia, Witch of OZ, will step down from my rule over OZ. I have asked another to rule in my place. However, I will always be nearby, and you will live under my protection until I am no more."

Cheers again filled the air.

Smokey stepped forward. "Wonderland," looking over the thousands assembled, "There will be no more cruelty. No more chess games. You will not have to live in fear, and peace will reign over our land. It is time to return to your families and our wonderful Wonderland." He looked over to the sides of the battlefield toward the little people who left their flower barriers and moved down toward Wonderland's position.

Pointing toward the two groups, Smokey spoke to his subjects, "I ask one favor of you. The little people need help returning to their community. They are traveling with women and children. They have been through a lot. Please empty your supply wagons and gather these fine people up to help return them to their homes. In the future they should be welcomed and revered for it is one of them,

Lizzie, the Queen's sister, who rescued Wonderland from the Queen."

The men chanted "Lizzie, Lizzie, Lizzie," in her honor.

Wonderland responded and shortly the women and children were helped into the wagons. Food and drink were provided for the trip home.

Cassiopeia, Lily, Lemon, Lime, Lizzie, Smokey, Sunny, and Gurgle started their trek back up the ridge to the great library. In the background, a voice called out, "Hey did you forget about me? I'm injured! Hey, guys you can't leave me here I'll bleed out." It was Slither.

Cassiopeia turned to the voice in the distance, and then commented to Lizzie,

"He gets awful whiney when he's not the center of attention." The group chuckled.

Lily spoke up, "You know if we bring him back he'll be insufferable, describing how his magic tricks turned the tide of battle."

Cassiopeia, yelled back to Slither who lay upon the

ground with the dagger still sticking from his leg. "We're debating if you're worth bringing back." She paused for a moment. "It's a close vote. If I promise everyone that you won't hog the limelight regarding how well your tricks worked I think they'll vote to allow you to return."

"Oh, come on," yelled back Slither. "I'm maybe dying here and you're making a joke?"

"You're not dying Slither. Wait a moment and I'll be there."

Cassiopeia strode over to Slither, followed by others. He would have an audience.

"My poor man," commented Cassiopeia. "Does that little dagger hurt?"

"Hell yes!" replied Slither "Can I get some help here."

Cassiopeia knelt down to Slither, "This is going to hurt." She grabbed the dagger and quickly pulled it from his thigh. Blood gushed out. "Not really bad. I've seen worse."

"It's bad!" countered Slither, now in more pain.

"Aww, poor baby," replied Cassiopeia

"She knelt down and tore open the pants leg to open the thigh up to her hands. Placing her hands on his leg and saying a few ancient words, the blood subsided then stopped. With a few more incantations the skin drew around the wound. Soon only the pink skin of a newly healed wound was visible. After the healing, Cassiopeia returned to her feet.

Sunny said, "Hey' he's got a stripe like you do Smokey.

"Yes, he does, sort of pink against his nice black color." replied Smokey. "But I like my stripe better."

Smokey and Sunny debated which colors they would prefer, as Lemon and Lime looked on. They thought it was quite funny and endearing; but then again, they were in love.

Slither called out, "Will you two stop debating everything and someone get over here and help me up"

"He's back to being not so nice," said Smokey.

"Yes, he is," agreed Sunny.

"He can get up on his own." said Smokey. Smokey and Lemon turned back toward the great library, followed by most of the group.

"Hey," cried out Slither as the group walked away. Gurgle shook his head and returned with Lily to help Slither to his feet.

"No showboating," reminded Lily.

"Yeah, no showboating, I'll be a good boy." replied Slither.

It was a quick jovial march to the great library. Alice, Adam, and Clarity awaited the victorious team. Hugs, backslaps, and embraces were the reward for all. Alice looked toward the battlefield where Little Lady had gone down. The forces of both OZ and Wonderland moved about the field tending to the wounded. Whose side they were on no longer mattered to the men of OZ and Wonderland. They only concerned themselves with the wounded who needed help.

Tears welled up in Alice's eyes. "I'm going to really miss her," she softly cried as she and Cassiopeia embraced.

"Me too, I will send someone down there Alice to

gather up her remains and transport them back to  her home in OZ."

"Thank you. The thought of her lying out there exposed to everything. I didn't want that."

"I know, neither do I. She will have a place of honor in OZ."

After a little time, the group entered the great library.

"I can't wait to get out of this gown," said Cassiopeia. "I am never wearing a gown again! From now on its only Lily and Alice fashions.

Lemon and Lime followed suit, "No more." said Lemon. "But I might wear a lot of yellow pants and blouses."

"Lime for me," said Lime.

Everyone retired to their rooms for hot baths and some alone moments. As the Now's passed, each one of the group came out of their rooms in fresh clothing. Lemon emerged in bright yellow pants and a blouse. Lime was in a matching green set. Only Lizzie wore a dress.

She shrugged as she made her appearance, "No small people's pants, unless I want to wear Gurgle's clothes."

Lily laughed. "Lizzie, I am sure that is the last dress you may have to wear in the future. Everyone will be thrilled to dress the one who vanquished the Queen."

They all assembled in the great hall except for Slither. Finally, he entered. No more patches, just nice brown slacks and a beige shirt.

"Whoa," said Adam, "new duds Slither."

"Call me Samuel," he said. "After this battlefield soiree, I've decided to retire the name Slither and retire from parallel universe travel. Until this day, I never was injured in any of my travels. I should have been, but I never was. I have a feeling my time's up if I continue. My old buddy, Drumbolt, asked me to become his monitor replacement before I left. He is tired and wants nothing more than to relax and enjoy his final years. My travel home will be my last trip to another universe."

"I'll believe it when I see it," mumbled Adam to Alice.

The group surrounded Slither, who was now to be referred to simply as Samuel, and they congratulated him. As the group dispersed to seats within the room, a small cloud swirled above their heads and soon yellow eyes and a familiar row of teeth were visible. The Wisp descended from above into a large comfortable chair.

"Well, that went well my friends." he announced.

"Hi Wisp," said Alice "and why do we have the honor of your presence?"

"Why to congratulate you! You accomplished so much more than I expected."

The Wisp smiled widely and whirled around and then returned to the sitting position upon the chair. A staff member was unaware the Wisp was paying a visit and walked over to the Wisp.

"Shoo cat, you're not supposed to be in the chair," as she flicked a towel in the Wisp's direction.

"I am not a cat dear lady," he replied.

The staff member jumped back as she did not expect a cat to speak. Cats are rare in this world and they do not speak. Everyone laughed.

"Dear Clarity," the Wisp spoke, "will your staff ever give me any respect?"

Clarity laughed, "You have to come and visit us more often. Otherwise they will simply know you as a cat."

The Wisp turned to Alice, "I am sorry for your loss Alice. I very much liked Little Lady. She was smart and good."

"Thank you, Wisp."

"Now Lizzie, you were quite a surprise. I knew of your existence, but was unsure whether you still lived. I did not expect you to be a little person. Nor did I expect that you would keep your existence hidden for so long. You are older than I, and yet no one knew you existed."

"The little people have always known I existed. However, they did not know I was the Queen's sister. When I did not die, nor aged beyond middle age, they knew I was special. Some thought I was a witch. Some thought I was some sort of spirit. None the less, I was one of them. Neither OZ nor Wonderland had much use for us little people, so they left us alone. The secret was easy to keep because the outside never communicated with the little people."

"You always knew you were the Queen's sister?" asked Alice.

"Yes, but all I could do was watch from a distance. I was not welcome there and sometimes word of her atrocities filtered down to our village. To try and intervene would have been a fool's errand. My appearance in Wonderland would raise suspicions and I would have been treated poorly as a little person. I would have ended up in one of her chess matches and when killed, I would have regenerated, and my secret would have been revealed. My sister would have immediately killed me, ending all hope that we could be rid of her."

Smokey spoke up, "Lizzie you are always welcome in Wonderland."

"Or OZ," said Lily. "I am accepting your offer Cassiopeia, if it is still available."

"Then OZ shall have a new witch to lead it!" announced Cassiopeia.

"Huh," said Gurgle.

"Yes, my love, I am staying here. I love it here. I look forward to learning more about my witchcraft skills. And you my Gurgle have many children and some grandchildren to raise and be a part of their lives here in this world."

"I would like that," said Gurgle.

Everyone issued congratulations and many hugs were exchanged

"And so it shall be," said the Wisp. "Oz will have a new leader and Gurgle will become a part of this world. I am thrilled."

The Wisp spun around, lifted into the air and came to rest upon a table corner top. "Alice and Adam, without you this could not have happened."

"But Wisp we did nothing at the end. We just stood on the ridge and watched," said Alice

"As it was meant to be," replied the Wisp.

"Huh?" said Adam.

"Adam, there never were any travelers held here in OZ or Wonderland. I played some games with your mind while you were here."

"What?" replied Adam. "This was all just a wild goose chase? I, we could have been killed."

"But you were not. You were from somewhere else, had powers and knowledge we did not possess here in this world. You were necessary in order to balance good and evil. I needed your help along with Alice's, who I did not know at the time."

The Wisp paused for a moment and then continued. "You two showed great courage. Alice, you challenged the Queen and won the chess match, something no one had ever done before. That brought hope to many. As did you as well, Adam. You volunteered to participate in the Queen's chess match and exhibited valor in your chess match battle. Adam, during your first visit here, you met all of the groups here in my world. You gained knowledge and provided inspiration to many who met you."

"I was running for my life!"

"You were in control and no one sensed you were afraid."

Cassiopeia added, "Adam, unlike others you were

calm even when faced with the dungeon and an unknown future. Those hours we spent together talking gave me hope for something else as I feared for my life and my girls' futures."

The Wisp continued, "Alice and Adam, you found what you came here for."

Alice spoke, "That's what Cassiopeia said you told her. But we found no one."

"You found each other," said the Wisp.

The room grew silent for a moment as Samuel came over and draped his arms around Adam and Alice.

"He's right you two. That thing, the Wisp, is smarter than all of us." "Slither, or perhaps I should address you as Samuel," the Wisp added. "Yes please." He replied.

"You were amazing out there. Your weapons turned the chess match into a fiasco for the Queen. The fire bags took out much of the evil leadership of OZ. I did not expect that. You saved many lives, perhaps many of your own team's lives."

The group braced for Slither's famous showboating but all they got was… "Thank you, Wisp."

Sunny spoke to the group, "Uh, I'm not the smartest here or the bravest here, but I would like to invite Lizzie to come and make her home at the great library. You are my aunt. Smokey and my family, or at least I would like you nearby."

"I would as well," said Smokey.

"But no dying, OK." replied Sunny. "I'm scared of that."

"Me too," said Lizzie. "I have never died." "You haven't?" asked Sunny.

"Nope, perhaps that is why I stayed good. I value life. My sister obviously considered life cheap and perhaps that shaded the way she looked at others." "Perhaps you are right," said the Wisp.

Clarity spoke up, "Lizzie you will live forever, it would make sense if you became the permanent librarian in the great library since you are going to live here."

"I would like that Clarity. It would bring purpose to my life."

Lily added, "the great library is only a day's travel

from OZ. Perhaps it is the fitting place for Cassiopeia's sorcery book to be kept. It would give me reason to come here often to study with you Lizzie."

Lizzie hugged Lily, "I would like that very much. You have become a sister to me during our journey. Well, a good sister, not like that other sister."

Everyone laughed.

"Gurgle," said Lily, still arm and arm with Lizzie, "You must inform the little people that they are welcome in Wonderland and OZ. There is no reason they should live off by themselves now."

"Agreed," replied Lizzie. "It is time we little people become one with OZ and Wonderland."

Smokey and Sunny huddled together for a moment. "We have an announcement," said Smokey. Sunny shall remain at the great library as King. I shall be King of Wonderland. If Lemon will consent to be my Queen."

Sunny interrupted, "And Lime mine. We shall rule our kingdoms as one."

Lemon and Lime each hugged their men and said "Yes."

"Then we shall have two weddings" said Cassiopeia.

"Three, suggested Gurgle, "If Lily will be my bride?"

Lily bent down a bit and hugged Gurgle, "Of course."

"Well this has ended very well," said the Wisp. "My job is done here." "But will you be at the wedding?" questioned Smokey.

"Of course, I would not miss it." Then he disappeared into nothing.

The festivities of the victory party went on into the late night. Samuel tried his best to gain company for the remainder of the night.

Lizzie reminded him, "You were a simple dalliance my Samuel. I will live forever and shall never fall in love because I will bury everyone I love. So, the answer is no, but thank you for the wonderful night we shared.

Slither tried his hand with a very exuberant and somewhat inebriated Cassiopeia.

"Really Samuel, you do realize I might be able to turn you into a frog or toad. A frog or toad might have difficulty monitoring whatever you guys monitor in your world." It was a polite no.

Samuel sighed and then announced to all, "I've apparently have now lost my touch and shall now retire to bed." A goodnight was wished by all.

# Farewell                    24

The immediate Now in this dimension was spent cleaning up, reorganizing and getting back to the normal lives in the lands of OZ, Wonderland, and the community of the little people. When given the choice many little people choose to seek residences in OZ and Wonderland and were warmly received. However, some preferred to rebuild their community and live apart. The past injustices would fade over the many future winters as the presence of Gurgle and his offspring in OZ, as well as Lizzie in Wonderland would change perceptions among the inhabitants of both OZ and Wonderland.

The nearby Now's lead to a quickly planned triple wedding of Smokey and Lemon, Sunny and Lime, and Gurgle and Lily. It is held in the largest hall in the universe, the grand hall of the Wonderland castle. The wedding was well attended by residents of every community. Adam served as best man for Smokey and Sunny, while Samuel did the honor for Gurgle. Lizzie filled in the role as mother of the grooms. Cassiopeia was not only the mother of the brides, but also functioned as Lily's maid of honor. Alice did the same for Lemon and Lime. The wedding reception was legendary and went on for two days. On the morning of the second day, Alice and Cassiopeia sat down for a private brunch, leaving the others to their own devices.

"So, what are you going to do with yourself now that you have renounced your position in OZ and your daughters are now married off to the new Kings?" asked Alice.

"One thing I do not want to be is the meddling mother in law." "How will you spend your time, where will you go?"

"I haven't a clue. It's just time for me to do something else. The only thing I have to do is deal with the issue of the men who are not men," observed Cassiopeia.

"Where are they now?" asked Alice.

"They are caged in the cavern below the dungeon. They are big hairy beasts, with surly moods. They are creatures who tend to be overaggressive and quite dangerous. Their green color is actually from some form of algae that grows on their hair. They smell horribly too.

"So you've spent time down in the cavern?" asked Alice.

"Even worse, remember when I walled in the King of OZ in with the creatures that had just arrived at the battlefield?" "Yes."

"Well I couldn't leave them in the enclosures to die after they slaughtered the King and his horsemen, so I took some of their best soldiers to the field and removed the spell and the wall. The King, his men, and horses were all dead and decaying. It was quite gross. The men who are not men were well surrounded and did not attempt to fight or flee, until the men started roping them and tying them down on the ground. That was pretty brutal and some of the soldiers were injured. I healed many that day, including some of the creatures. Anyway, once they were secured I inspected them and had a small spot on their arms shaved so I could bite them and put them under my spell. They smelled awful because they do not bathe."

"Gross" said Alice.

"They were compliant however, and I had no problem leading them back to their cavern home. My concern is that the cavern is not a humane home for them. I cannot free them to live in this universe as they are too dangerous. But there is no way I will allow them to be slaughtered. They may not be the best of creatures, but they do have a right to live. Any ideas, Alice?"

"Perhaps. There is a lizard world, another dimension where huge lizards, some call them dinosaurs, live. It is a hard world. There are other creatures, some similar to these creatures, who live in that world."

"How would we get them there?"

"Basically, the same way you got them back to their cavern. Maybe four or five at a time. How many are there?"

"About 40, some are females with children and young creatures who are not fully grown. From what I can tell the dominant male mates with all the females, the other males do nothing except fight with each other because they are trapped in the cavern."

"Oh, that's terrible."

"Yes, I believe if they were released to the wild, they would form better family units and perhaps multiple villages."

"Would you and Adam be able to organize and take them there?"

"Only if you joined us. You're the one who possesses the magic to keep them in line."

"I love that idea Alice. I have no role here and need something else."

"You'll face resistance from Drumbolt and the other elders when you get back. We have a policy not to import others into our universe. Although I violated that with another visitor just before we came here, and Adam brought the very nasty Little Lady back with him when he escaped here. I usually get my way, however."

"Little Lady nasty?"

"Well nasty as a flying monkey with dull teeth and small claws can be." she replied chuckling. "Oh how I do miss her. She warmed right up to me immediately and we became buddies."

"I'm sorry Alice."

"What's done is done. It was her choice to dive

bomb the king. I almost think it was a suicide dive." Alice paused for a moment or two, "Anyway, you'll need a good deal of training and instructions, but you'll fit in, if you want it."

Adam looked in on the private brunch, "How are you two doing." "We're just discussing our next parallel universe adventure." "Our next adventure?" replied Adam.

"Well Cassiopeia and I will have another parallel universe adventure. You can come along if you wish."

"She's coming back with us?"

"Yes," they said together with smiles.

"Well I guess Cassiopeia you're returning with us. Welcome to the world of parallel universe travel. And what is our next adventure?"

"Transporting the men who are not men to the lizard universe." "That could be dangerous Alice."

"Isn't everything?" she replied. "Once Cassiopeia bites them they'll be a passive as newborn babies until we get them to the lizard universe."

"Well it worked well on me," said Adam. "Let's be honest Alice, you just like the idea of getting back to one of your favorite universes."

"I do!" said Alice. "Now go back out and mingle while we girls talk." A Now or two later plans were made and goodbyes said as the travelers prepared to leave.

Cassiopeia informed her daughters of her new life. They were apprehensive, but thrilled for her.

Samuel went first. His job was to break the news to Drumbolt that not everyone was coming back and to inform him of the new dimension traveler. Samuel hooked up his visualization belt at the site of the flying monkey slaughter, located the entrance, and was gone.

Drumbolt was on duty in the monitoring room sitting alongside Yeager and Loco.

They were discussing sending Yaeger and Loco to the dimension to check up on their fellow travelers. The monitoring boards lit up giving notice of the entry of another traveler.

They eagerly watched the entry room to determine who it might me. In walked Samuel, who was no longer clothed in his patchwork clothing.

"Slither! Welcome home!" called out Drumbolt over the speakers as Slither appeared in the entry room. "We were starting to worry about you. I've got Yaeger and Loco with me."

"Be there in just a Now or two," Slither replied to the screen above.

Slither undressed and then entered the cleansing tubes, progressed through the other tests and was quickly released into the room with Drumbolt. He chose a non-patchwork clothing style. "No patches, Slither?' asked a now smiling Drumbolt, who was thrilled to see his old friend back.

"Nope! No patches. And no nicknames. I have chosen to be known by my given name, Samuel." Drumbolt, Yaeger, and Loco looked at one another.

"Not only that, but I am retiring from dimension travel. I'm going to take you up on that offer to be a monitor."

"Wow!" said Yaeger. That'll get some getting used to."

"Oh good!" said Loco. "A vacancy in the traveler ranks."

"Where are the others?" asked Drumbolt.

"They are coming soon," replied Samuel. "However, I've got something to tell you. I brought back two other travel belts with me. They are in the entry room."

"People are not coming back?" asked Drumbolt as he paused and held his breath for Samuel's answer

"Who?" asked Drumbolt, now growing nervous about his Alice.

"Alice is safe and should be back next. It is Gurgle and Lily who are not coming back."

"They are gone? Gurgle? Lily?"

"Yes, they are never coming back."

"No!" exclaimed Yaeger.

"Relax," said Samuel, "Just messing with you. Gurgle and Lily are not coming back, that part is true. But they are just fine." Drumbolt sighed in relief.

"It's a long story," said Samuel.

"Just give me the abbreviated version for now, please," he said, puffing on his pipe. "You can be long winded another time my old friend." said Drumbolt.

"OK. They're married. Gurgle's met his children. I think he's got about 12 children and two or three grandchildren. Man, he was busy. They call him the Lion of OZ."

"That's cute!" said Drumbolt.

"Lily is a witch," continued Samuel.

"A witch?"

"Yeah a witch. Not like a pain in the ass girlfriend, but a real witch. Or perhaps a witch in training would be a better description. She can do some stuff, just not the heavy duty stuff. She's also now the ruler of OZ."

"The ruler of OZ?" repeated Drumbolt.

"Long story Drumbolt, you just asked for the abbreviated story." Just then the monitoring screen lit up.

"Must be Alice," said Samuel.

In walked Cassiopeia in form fitting white pants and wearing a long sleeve golden stripped blouse with a blue background. She had long black hair and creamy white as white skin. "Now that's a real witch," said Samuel.

"Beautiful," was all Loco could say.

Drumbolt huffed for a second, "Now... you know the policy, Samuel!"

"Alice's idea." The monitor screen lit up again and in walked Alice.

Cassiopeia looked around at her new surroundings and then back at Alice. "What now?"

"We get to strip," Alice informed her. "Everyone does it. We need to go through the wash cycle to remove contaminants and then into the biohazard section to search for critters that are unwanted in this universe."

"Alice!" Drumbolt exclaimed. "Policy!"

"Yeah, yeah. This is Cassiopeia she's joining us for the next adventure. We are moving some very dangerous creatures from OZ to the lizard universe." "That's not authorized yet," said Drumbolt.

"Never mind him Cassiopeia, he's harmless."

Alice waved at the screen above and called out, "Love you Drumbolt!"

Drumbolt looked over to Jaeger, "I'm getting too old for this. I'm losing control here."

"You never had any control over Alice," replied a now smiling Yaeger.

Drumbolt sighed, "I guess you're right."

Cassiopeia and Alice quickly stripped and entered the cleansing tubes then on to the biohazard section. With the exception of a small parasite Alice brought back with her they were clean. They quickly dressed and joined the others in the monitoring room.

"So, you're a witch?" asked Yaeger

"Yes, shall I prove it?"

"I'd like to see that," said Drumbolt.

Cassiopeia said a few words, whirled around and poof she was gone. Alice did likewise and poof she was gone."

"Alice?" called out Drumbolt, a bit worried.

Alice and Cassiopeia whirled back into view. "I'm sort of a budding witch myself. But it's about the only thing I'm good at as of now," said Alice.

"That could come in handy," replied Yaeger.

Loco spoke up, "Man what a great weapon for our travelers, invisibility!"

"Sorry to tell you, but I think you have to start your training in OZ to learn that trick," replied Alice Suddenly the monitor screen lit up once more and in strolled Adam.

"Hi everyone," he called out from the entry room. After stripping and cleansing procedures, he joined everyone in the monitoring room, giving Alice a big kiss upon entry.

Alice turned to Drumbolt, who now had tears in his eyes seeing Adam and Alice together once more. "Things happened there. It's quite a magical place, if you let the magic happen." noted Alice

"We'll be getting married soon too!" announced Adam.

Drumbolt turned into a blubbering old man, "I am so, so very happy for you. Maybe now there'll be a little Alice while I still walk this universe."

"Where's Little Lady?" questioned Yaeger. "I

expect she'll be here soon or did she stay?"

"Yaeger, she did not make it. She died in the battle between OZ and Wonderland." said Alice

"So sorry to hear that." replied Drumbolt. "I know how much she meant to you."

"It was her choice. She was the last of her kind. The others were slaughtered by a cruel king in OZ. She was our hero. She killed many of their senior commanders. The war between OZ and Wonderland was a war between Cassiopeia here and the evil of both OZ and Wonderland. The two sides barely interacted. Cassiopeia brought in the forces of nature, and some very interesting incantations which subdued and eliminated the evil in both lands. The rest of us played minor roles. The Wisp seemed to have planned much of it."

"Wisp?" replied Drumbolt. "What's a Wisp?" "That's a long story for another time." replied Alice

"Well it sounds like Cassiopeia will be a very valuable addition to our dimension travel program," said Drumbolt, as he dabbed away the remaining tears from his cheeks with a handkerchief.

Alice, walked over to Drumbolt to hug him and kiss him on the cheek, and then the returning team left the monitoring room behind to begin Cassiopeia's adaption to life in dimension one.

Gurgle and Lily never left the universe of OZ and Wonderland. Fate was good to them and they lived very long lives, enjoying peace and happiness in their adopted land of OZ. Gurgle fathered four children with Lily, two like him and two of normal height. They in turn gave Gurgle and Lily many, many grandchildren. Many of his little people children and grandchildren settled in OZ to stay close to Gurgle. Somehow, he found time to be a great father to all.

The dungeon guard who helped Lily, Lemon, and Lime escape OZ was well rewarded. Lily removed him from the cold dark dungeon duty and made him her special ambassador where he could enjoy the sun as much as he wanted. It was a title with little duties and no requirements to be in attendance for the Queen. Despite the lack of duties and requirements the guard known as Herman showed up at dawn and left only upon being discharged by Lily at the end of the day until his dying days. He was not the dimwitted guard people had supposed. He just never had a chance to be more. He became one of Queen Lily's most trusted advisors and the member of the palace staff who connected the best with the everyday people of OZ. It is recorded in the great book of knowledge that he loved escorting Gurgle and Lily's children on long walks in the sun. His funeral some Now's later was attended by every resident of OZ.

Smokey and Sunny in the two years after marrying Lemon and Lime developed a short-term wanderlust for parallel universe travel and joined Samuel on two short but quite legendary parallel universe adventures. Having scratched the itch for dimension travel, Smokey and Sunny returned to their kingdoms forever; wiser and better educated.

Smokey and Lemon, were never seen apart during the remainder of their marriage, which probably explains their eight children. Wonderland became a place where almost everything was possible. Animals talked, white magic was practiced by many and life was calm and fruitful for all within Wonderland. Their reign was long and they passed just moments apart from each other. It was said they could not bear to be separated in life or death.

Sunny and Lime remained close with their siblings and oversaw operations for the great library and its staff. It was a comfortable existence for them and they often welcomed those from OZ and Wonderland who traveled to their kingdom for education and learning. Under their guidance the great library became a cultural center for all within the universe. They lived their final days in comfort and shared the love of their four children and many grandchildren.

The Wonderland dungeon guard who assisted Adam, Alice, Gurgle and Samuel in their escape was rewarded with a ceremonial job as captain of the front gate guards. It had little responsibility, except for scheduling. However, Philip as he was known, went on to multiple leadership roles within the palace guard. He also ran a very mean card room down in the dungeon, which was converted to Philip's Emporium, since there never was a need again in Wonderland for a dungeon.

Clarity survived only a few more Now's. He said he looked forward to a new beginning and was rewarded with a quiet and comfortable passing into a new life in the great beyond. Before he left he taught Lizzie everything he knew, and shared the contents of the secret library that he kept hidden from the mad Queen of Hearts. He also supported Lizzie's efforts in sorcery as the keeper of the great book.

Cassiopeia, Alice, Adam's, and Samuel's stories are for now left unfinished, to be continued at another time.

Lizzie of course is immortal, and so lives on to this day. She has guided and tended to the needs of the children, grandchildren, great grandchildren of her closest friends: Lily, Gurgle, Smokey, Lemon, Sunny, and Lime. She managed to be alongside each at the time of their passing to another existence. She continues to wear dresses and gowns to this day, and has let her beautiful red hair grow to waist length.

She hasn't aged a day, nor taken a spouse or had children. However, her life has been full and complete watching over the many generations of her friend's offspring and tending to her many responsibilities as librarian in the great library. As librarian for the great library she encouraged reading and writing skills which has fostered many an author and filled with library with a variety of treasures.

Over the many Now's her friendship with Cassiopeia resulted in some dimension travel to Alice's universe where she met and encouraged scientists and other learned individuals to come to the great library and assist in bringing OZ and Wonderland into the modern world. The worlds of OZ and Wonderland are no longer the medieval lands from the Now of Alice, although the animals continue to talk, and wonderful magic fills the air. Lizzie can still be periodically seen walking the fields of the great battle spreading flowers across its width as a gift to the spirits of her friends now long gone.

And the Wisp who guided everyone and brought much good to this universe? Why he died a happy Wisp many Now's later, to be resurrected as a younger Wisp with many hopes and dreams in the wonderful worlds of OZ and Wonderland.